**"I know the treasures you hide. I've seen them."**

He rasped the words against her damp skin, and she trembled. . . . He'd begun loosening her hair, and she wanted him to.

With each kiss, Annalía wanted to show this brutal Highlander more of her, to bare her breasts and let her hair down so he could run his fingers through it. But when it fell about her, he didn't touch her so gently. He wrapped the ends around his fist as his lips returned insistent to her neck. His tongue flicked her skin, and her eyes flashed open then slowly slid closed.

But he tensed and drew back, releasing her.

*"Què li passa?"* she murmured in Catalan. As if coming out of a daze, she opened her eyes and repeated in English, "What is it?"

She heard it then—the coming of riders into the manor's courtyard.

"Stay here," he ordered, his face more menacing than she'd ever seen it. "Lock the door behind me and doona come out for any reason. Do you ken?"

In the space of a heartbeat, the fierce look of intent had vanished, replaced by one of barely controlled fury. Her lips parted in surprise.

When she didn't answer, he cupped the back of her neck. *"Anna, do you understand?"*

"Yes," she began, but the deep voices of several men sounded, just before a pounding on the front door.

They were Scottish.

"We're lookin' for Courtland MacCarrick," a man shouted.

MacCarrick relaxed and put his forehead against hers. "They're no' known for their timing."

## Acclaim for *THE PRICE OF PLEASURE*

"A splendid read! The sexual tension grips you from beginning to end."

—*New York Times* bestselling author Virginia Henley

"Sexy and original! Sensual island heat that is not to be missed."

—*New York Times* bestselling author Heather Graham

"Savor this marvelous, unforgettable, highly romantic novel by a fresh voice in the genre."

—*Romantic Times* magazine (Top Pick)

"It is hard to believe that *The Price of Pleasure* is only Ms. Cole's second romance. I think it safe to assume she has a long, successful future ahead of her. I strongly urge readers to become familiar with this talented new author; read *The Price of Pleasure* today."

—*Romance Reviews Today*

# If You Dare

## KRESLEY COLE

POCKET BOOKS

New York    London    Toronto    Sydney

This book is a work of fiction. Names, characters, places and incidents are products of the author's imagination or are used fictitiously. Any resemblance to actual events or locales or persons, living or dead, is entirely coincidental.

An *Original* Publication of POCKET BOOKS

POCKET BOOKS, a division of Simon & Schuster, Inc.
1230 Avenue of the Americas, New York, NY 10020

ISBN -13: 978-1-4165-0359-0
ISBN -10:    1-4165-0359-5

First Pocket Books printing May 2005

10   9   8

POCKET and colophon are registered trademarks of Simon & Schuster, Inc.

Cover illustration by Craig White
Handlettering by David Gatti

Manufactured in the United States of America

For information regarding special discounts for bulk purchases, please contact Simon & Schuster Special Sales at 1-800-456-6798 or business@simonandschuster.com

*For Ginny,*
*the sister I never had, because we've been best friends since*
*preschool. And because I'm on the phone with you*
*as I'm writing this and wish you were here.*

# Acknowledgments

I would like to acknowledge the wonderful people at the Catalan House of the University of Florida for their gracious gifts of time and knowledge, with special thanks to Mireia Vilamala for her help with translation and to Juan Torras-Costa for his assistance with Andorran geography.

Many, many thanks to Dr. Domhnall Uilleam Stiubhart in the Celtic and Scottish Studies Department at Edinburgh University for his help with Gaelic translation and Scottish history.

And I think I will make a tradition of acknowledging all the incredible support Sally Fairchild has given me with this book and the two previous ones. Just when I think I know how fantastic she is, she still amazes.

*No reason under heaven excuses bad manners.*
—Lady Annalía Elisabet Catherina Tristán Llorente

*Might makes right.*
—Courtland Eadd MacCarrick

# Prologue

*Carrickliffe, Scotland, 1838*

Read from the *Leabhar nan Sùil-radharc,* the Book of Fates:

<u>To the tenth Carrick:</u>
Your lady fair shall bear you three dark sons.
Joy they bring you until they read this tome.
Words before their eyes cut your life's line young.
You die dread knowing cursed men they become,
Shadowed to walk with death or walk alone.

Not to marry, know love, or bind, their fate;
Your line to die for never seed shall take.
Death and torment to those caught in their wake,

Blood obscured the last two lines.

# *One*

*The Principality of Andorra, 1856*

*Y*es, yes, very well then. Take out his heart."

For the first time since his beating began, Courtland Mac-Carrick's split, bloody sneer faltered. The general's impatient command seemed unreal to him, the words sounding hollow and indistinct, probably because Court could see nothing, blinded by blood dripping from a gash on his forehead and by his swollen lids.

The henchmen restraining him whaled two punches into his stomach, unable to contain their excitement at the prospect of killing off a mercenary, and a rival at that. Court could do little to defend himself in his condition and with his wrists bound.

"If you kill me," he bit out as he labored for a breath, "you know my men will avenge my death. You would no' risk that over simply payin' us what's owed?" His voice was thick with brogue, as it hadn't been since he'd left the Highlands years before.

"No one will avenge you, MacCarrick, because they'll all be dead as well," General Reynaldo Pascal said in a casual tone. Though he couldn't see, Court knew the man had a thoughtful expression on his face. The Spanish deserter had never looked like a power-crazed zealot—more like a benevolent statesman.

"My kin will keep comin' until they've stamped you out."

The general sighed. "In any case . . ." Court could imagine him giving an impatient hand wave, signaling the end of the subject. ". . . do make it painful and prolonged."

"You will no' do it yourself?"

He chuckled softly. "You of all people should know I hire men to do my dirty work."

As the two yanked him away, Court said over his shoulder, "Aye, but do the fools holdin' me know that you doona pay them for it?"

They jostled him, heaving him from the room, then strained to pull him down the stairs and outside onto the rough slate street.

As soon as he felt the sun on his face, he heard a woman gasp; an older man said, "*Mare de Déu,*" but Court knew better than to expect anything from the people here other than a sharp turning of their heads and the ushering of children inside. Their fear of Pascal was ingrained. Court could be butchered in the town square and no one would lift a finger. Actually, that was a close estimation to what he knew was about to happen.

Yet he didn't feel as though that was the direction they were moving in. He heard the din of rushing water, realized they were traveling to the river beside the village, and futilely turned his head toward the sound. "No execution in the town center?" he rasped. "Careful that I doona feel slighted."

"We are being more circumspect with our . . . activities," said the one on his left.

"Too late. Pascal's already angered Spain." He bit out the words with conviction, but in truth it was little more than a hope.

"And we will be ready," the other replied, just before they slammed him up against what had to be a bridge railing. And Court couldn't fight because he couldn't see.

The water was directly below them, pounding furiously over a drop-off. The Riu Valira was always an angry torrent after rains to the north. He struggled to remember how high this bridge was. Would the Valira be deep enough? . . .

He heard a knife being unsheathed. What choice did he have?

"If you do this now," Court said in a low, deadly tone, "my men and my kin will descend on you. They live for killing." *And kill for a living.*

Court knew he couldn't talk them out of planting that knife. These weren't merely two among the general's army— these were assassins, part of the Orden de los Rechazados, Order of the Disavowed. Court just wanted time to get his bearings. A second stalled was *possibility* . . .

If he jumped, they wouldn't chase him down the river. They'd consider his battered condition, with his hands bound and with the impact of the powerful falls, and reason that he would drown for certain.

Unfortunately, they'd probably be right. . . .

The knifepoint pricked his chest as though poised there— almost comforting because at least he knew where it was. Then . . . gone. Drawn back for the blow—

He shoved himself back, the force pitching him over the railing, tossing his feet over his head before he landed in the icy water.

The impact stunned him, his body taking the hit as though crashing into a wall. He sank down so far pain stabbed his ears from the depth, then struggled upward with bound hands.

Though it went against every instinct, he forced himself to reach the surface facedown as though dead. He sensed the pull of the water and realized that facedown in this case meant being swept from the falls' pool headfirst.

The Rechazados shot just as the rushing water began propelling him over the rim of the elevated basin. The bullets ripped through the water so close to him he could feel their percussion, but he didn't flinch even when he was forced to dive from above, then ride another series of falls into the main current.

The river boiled with rapids and swiftly carried him away. Just when he could stand it no longer, he raised his face for breath, but inhaled mostly foam.

The churning force drove him into rocks, the larger ones knocking him above the surface for lungfuls of air, but his weight quickly wrenched him down to the river bottom lined with jagged slate. The fractures snagged his clothes until they were in tatters, and then his unprotected skin. Each hit took him closer to oblivion.

Yet he continued to fight and managed to turn himself feet first. The water had washed away the worst of the blood, and the icy temperature had lessened the swelling, allowing him to see from the slit of one eye.

A high jutting rock approached; he lunged for it, looping his bound arms around it. The current swept on relentlessly until the wracking pressure on the ropes snapped his wrist. He didn't care—he gulped air. After only moments of rest, the bindings sliced away, leaving him to the mercy of the river once more.

He'd been in and out of consciousness for what felt like days when the current finally calmed. In the lull, he perceived that the freezing temperature had muted the worst pain of his injuries. In fact, he felt nothing but the subtle warming of the water as he drifted into a static pool by the bank.

Succumbing to the blackness was an overwhelming temptation now, nearly stronger than his will, but he forced himself to crawl to the stony shore on one hand and his knees. Free of the river, he collapsed onto his back and cradled his broken wrist.

The sun warmed him, taking away the worst of the chill, and for how long he lay there he didn't know. He only noticed when a shadow passed before it. He squinted to bring a thin line of vision to his one good eye.

He must've sucked in a breath—his bashed ribs screamed that he did—because a woman with shining hair knelt beside him, peering down with widened green eyes. Her lips were parted in surprise, and an unusual stone glinted light from a choker around the pale column of her neck. When she tilted her head at him, a breeze blew a dark curl across her cheek.

Breathtaking. "*Aingeal . . . ,*" he murmured as he resisted the blackness once more.

"*Perfect,*" she answered with utter sarcasm as she rose and put her hands on her hips. "Simply perfect. This animal's alive."

Tea.

Annalía Elisabet Catherina Tristán, daughter of the family Llorente, had ridden out for flowers to brighten the afternoon tea. Where did the marsh marigolds grow best? By the river. By the cursed river, where apparently the cursed mercenaries wash to shore.

She hadn't known what to think when she'd spied the body from afar. Perhaps a shepherd had fallen in the Valira during a storm to the north? Yet as she approached she'd recognized that this giant was no shepherd, and she hadn't missed the nationality. Around his waist he had a thick, wide belt, the style of which was foreign. Attached to the belt had been a swatch of plaid left from some larger cloth.

Plaid meant Scot. Scot meant killer.

She bemoaned the situation yet again and tugged on the reins looped over her shoulder, trudging forward, pulling along Iambe, her hunter, who had two hundred plus pounds of Scottish deadweight attached to her. Neither she nor Iambe was used to such labor. Annalía sighed wearily—they were both thoroughbreds born for a different purpose altogether.

She was ill equipped for a rescue—or truly anything more involved than *gathering flowers*—so the conveyance she'd fashioned consisted of a rope tightened around his chest, pinning his arms to his sides, then another rope pulled under both his arms and tied to the saddle.

But why was she dragging him up the steep mountain incline to her home? Scots were hated in Andorra, and yet she was taking one straight through the narrow rock entrance—the only entrance—to the three higher plateaus separating the river from the manor. Her ancestors had gated the passage, and for five hundred years it had kept the horses on their ranch in—and strangers out.

Surely he was one of the Highland mercenaries brought here by Pascal. Their tiny, almost hidden country so high in the Pyrenees wasn't exactly overrun with Highlanders. But what if he was the singular Scot who came here for other reasons? And she let him die? She thought he'd called her an angel and he'd looked so relieved to see her, as if he had every confidence she would save him.

If he was one of Pascal's men, she'd simply have to heal him, then kill him herself.

After plodding past the crystal lake Casa del Llac derived its name from, she and her baggage arrived in the manor's central courtyard. "Vitale!" Annalía called for her steward but received no answer. Where was he?

Smoking, no doubt. Over dice. "Vitale!" This whole place

was going to ruin without her brother. "I know you're smoking behind the stable, and I don't care just now!"

Vitale leVieux peeked his craggy face around the side of the stable. "Yes, mademoiselle—" he began before he gasped at the injured man, smoke wafting from his open mouth. His crinkly gray hair bounced as he rushed to her side. "What have you done?" he exclaimed, his French accent sharp. "He's Scottish—look at the plaid."

"I saw the plaid," she said in disgust. Spotting Vitale's ancient dice partners lining up to see the spectacle, she said in a hushed voice, "We shall discuss this inside."

Undeterred, he cried, "He must be one of the blood-drinking Highlanders the general hired!"

One of Vitale's friends mumbled, "Highlander, you say?" When Vitale nodded emphatically, his compadres called goodbyes and shuffled off with their canes for hills unknown.

Apparently everyone had heard the tales of their brutality.

"Why would you save him?" Vitale demanded when they were alone.

"What if he isn't one of the mercenaries?"

"Oh, of course, he must be here for the . . ." He trailed off, scratching his head as though stumped, then flashed an expression of realization. "I have just recalled—there's nothing here to see!"

And everyone wondered where she'd gotten her sarcasm.

She gave him a lowering look. "Are you going to help me? I need you to get the doctor."

"The doctor went north to join your brother's men." Vitale looked the man over, all nine feet of him, it seemed. "Besides, we bring the injured to you."

"You bring injured animals and children to me, not beaten-senseless giants bleeding from every limb," she corrected. When Annalía was younger, her Andorran nanny had taught her to treat some injuries—broken bones, burns, cuts, and the like, but then she'd probably never envisioned a patient like this one. "It's not proper for me to attend him."

He gave her a patronizing smile. "Perhaps mademoiselle should have thought of that before dragging the enemy into our home? Hmmm?"

Lips thinned, she replied, "Perhaps mademoiselle is displaying the same compassion she showed when she hired Vitale the Old." Though they both knew her taking him in from the streets of Paris to her home in Andorra hadn't been simply because of kindness. Gratitude had compelled her.

He sighed. "What do you wish me to do?"

"Help me put him in the room off the stable."

"We can't lock that room! He could slit our throats while we sleep."

"Then where?" He opened his mouth to answer, but she cut him off, "And don't you dare say back to the riverside."

He closed his mouth abruptly. They both looked down at the man as though searching for the answer.

Vitale finally said, "We should put him in the manor house so we can lock him in a bedroom."

"Where *I* sleep?"

"Mademoiselle has demonstrated compassion"—he smiled too serenely—"which is but a slippery stone away from hospitality."

She ignored his expression. "The only room downstairs that locks is the study and that's private. I don't want him to know our business affairs."

He gave the man a rousing kick in the hip. When no response came, he cackled.

"Vitale!"

He turned to her with an impassive face. "So mademoiselle suggests upstairs?"

"We simply can't do it. My *horse* had problems pulling his weight."

Some of the ranch hands' children ran by then, eyes wide, reminding Annalía of the state of the man's clothing. Most of it had ripped away. A tear spread up his thigh, close to his . . . She straddled his legs, sweeping her skirt over him for cover. "Run along." Her voice was strident.

They looked to Vitale, and though he rolled his eyes, he told them, "Untie the ropes and go take care of poor Iambe." Facing her, he said, "If you're insisting it must be upstairs, we can attempt it. Besides, do we really care if we drop him?"

So by dint of strategizing, straining, and yes, using the children she'd pleaded with to return, they managed to get him to the nearest guest bedroom and transferred onto the bed. Though she was exhausted, with her palm jammed into her lower back like a washerwoman closing the day, she knew she still had to tend to him.

While Vitale shooed the curious children from the room, Annalía assessed her patient, noting the broken wrist and the possibility of a couple of broken ribs. She removed her riding gloves, then ran her hands through his thick, damp hair past his temple and along the side of his head. She discovered a nasty knot, and the same inspection on the other side revealed a second head injury. His eyes were so swollen she doubted he could open them when awake. To cap it all, ragged cuts covered his skin, no doubt inflicted by the river bottom.

"Vitale, I need some shears. And some bandages. Bring two big wooden spoons and some hot water as well."

He exhaled as though very put out. "Forthwith." He added something in a mumble. Even his mumble could convey a heavy Gallic sarcasm.

When he returned with all the supplies, she scarcely noticed him. "Thank you," she murmured.

He said nothing, just bowed, turned on his heel, and abandoned her.

"Fine! Go," she called. "I have no need of you anyway. . . ."

And then she was alone. With the big, terrifying Scot.

She really should be having tea right now.

She billowed a sheet over him, then blindly endeavored to cut away his ruined trousers underneath it. Frowning in concentration, she placed the shears only to yank her hand back. She was fairly certain she'd stabbed his waist.

Focusing on the opposite wall, she tried again, but pushed the sharp tips into his skin once more. This time he moaned and she jumped back. She'd bet her Limoges porcelain that any red-blooded male would rather die than have an exhausted, unseeing woman cutting near his groin.

So she tugged the sheet down to his waist to shear away the remains of his shirt. His boots they'd discarded as unnecessary weight on the stairs. Which again left . . . his trousers.

Biting her lip, she unfastened and pulled free his sodden belt, noticing that his torso was flat, the ridges of muscle pronounced, with a thin trail of black hair leading down.

He was so heavy and yet he hadn't an inch of spare flesh on him. A strong body—he would heal fast if she helped him. But she'd never seen a grown man wholly nude before. No one here swam unclothed. There simply wasn't the laissez-faire attitude about nudity here as in neighboring Spain and France. And he was about to be completely unclothed, where she could see if she chose.

She would *not* choose! *Disregard these thoughts,* she commanded herself. Putting her shoulders back, she assumed a brisk attitude. She was a nurse today, and a lady always.

She opened the front of his trousers, ignoring the foreign, remarkable textures, the fascinating shape she brushed. With the fastening undone she was able to pull and cut around until they were off, always striving to keep the sheet between him and her eyes. And mostly succeeding.

Wiping perspiration from her brow, she began on his wrist, splinting it with the spoons and tight linen strips until she could cast it with flour in the morning. When she finished, she lay his arm back above his head and spread the other arm out to the side to wrap his ribs. Again and again, she pulled the cloth around him, tightened it, then forced the material under his back. His chest was deep, and bandaging it meant reaching over him, grazing him.

When she was done, she was oddly irritable and fidgety.

Though she wanted nothing more than a bath and her bed, her gaze kept returning to his good hand. Finally she gave in to temptation and leaned beside him in the bed to lift it. The fingers and back of it were as scarred as the rest of his body and the palm was abrasive. Her brows drew together as she placed the palm flat against her own.

She marveled at the size of his hand, at how it could swallow her own, and pressed each finger against his matching one. If he was a mercenary, and he must be, judging by all the battle scars, she wondered how many guns and knives and swords he had wielded with it. Had he ever used it to strangle the life from someone?

Had she been completely crazed to bring a man like this into her home?

For the last two days Annalía had wondered if he'd ever wake up. She'd browbeaten Vitale into washing the man each day—there were just some things she *refused* to do—and into helping her set his wrist with a cast. Afterward she'd settled into a daily routine where she would check the Scot's ribs and wrist and grapple to pour broth and water down his throat.

Each day some of the swelling around his eyes and jaws receded, but she suspected that even uninjured he still would look like a ruffian.

This morning had already heated the casa miserably. The wind was absent, and even the usually cool mountain nights had been balmy this summer. Though she'd already checked on him, she should probably return and make certain that Vitale had locked up after he tended to the man earlier.

Who was she fooling? Vitale was still convinced the Highlander would murder them all in their sleep without the proper precautions.

She would go because she was restless and watching the even rise and fall of his chest was . . . agreeable.

As was touching him. Every day she would trace the starburst scar just below his temple, along with each mark across his broad chest and down his muscular arms. She'd memorized them all and had imagined a scenario for each.

Though he was surely her enemy, his presence broke up the monotony and loneliness in the house. Since war was on the horizon, many of her people had fled to mountains even more remote than this one, and she could only get cooks and maids from the valley to come by a few times a month. With her older brother away fighting Pascal and her parents dead, Annalía had been living alone in the main house. She'd invited the ranch hands' wives and their children to stay, but they were ill at ease in the luxurious home. Even Vitale declined.

Before the Scot, she'd been alone in the echoing house, and she'd hated it.

When she unlocked the door, she saw he tossed in bed, with sweat beading his forehead. After a check of his bandages and cast, she felt his skin but found no real fever. He was probably just hot from the stuffy room. The window was open but offered no relief. She nibbled her bottom lip wondering if she should cool him, try to make him more comfortable.

Decided, she poured water into the bowl at the dresser, then soaked a cloth. Returning to the bed, she ran it over his forehead, neck, and chest above his rib bandages.

After guiltily looking around her, she pinched the edge of

the sheet on each side of his hips and tugged it down, placing it, arranging it perfectly so his privates were just covered. Her hands shook as she lifted the cloth to the strip of skin below his bandages. She ran it across his hard stomach, and frowned when the muscles rippled and dove in reaction.

When she inadvertently dripped water on the sheet over his groin she could see his manhood outlined beneath it. Could see it even more than she'd been able to on the previous days because it was larger, harder.

She tilted her head, wondering what it would feel like—

"Tell me, lass," the man's voice rumbled, "do you like what you see?"

# Two

$\mathcal{T}$he woman gasped in surprise, dropping her cloth, the cloth that had started on his body clinically and purposefully, as he'd awakened, but had soon skimmed over him in sinuous movements.

Her heels clicked on the polished wooden floor when she retreated. Court watched as she smoothed her already crisp dress, then the perfect knot of hair at her nape, then the choker at her throat with slender hands. At each of these tasks, her chin rose higher.

"I-I was merely caring for you," she answered in accented English.

Instead of coming to in a haze of pain, he'd woken to her breasts glancing over the hair on his chest as she reached across him, and to one of her soft, pale hands gripping his hip while the other rubbed over his skin. As he'd felt fat drops of water hitting the sheet, he'd caught the scent of her hair, making even his beaten body stir. "Then consider me still in need of your care."

Her cheeks turned pink.

He tried to sit higher in the bed, then grimaced in pain. As if in answer, all his other wounds finally sounded the call. He glanced down at his wrist to find a cast. "Who are you?" he ground out. "And where am I?"

"My name is Annalía Elisabet Catherina Tristán. I am mistress of Casa del Llac, where you abide now, and daughter of the family Llorente." Her accent told him English wasn't her first language, though she spoke it perfectly and without hesitation, the words rolling from her tongue in a manner that was pleasing to the ear. She'd said the name Llorente proudly, as though he'd recognize it. He did feel as if he'd heard it before but couldn't place it.

"Where did you find me? And how far are we from the village?"

"Straight down this mountain on the banks of the Valira, four mountain passes to the south."

Four passes away? He wondered if his men thought him dead. He needed to send a message—

"I would ask the name of my . . . guest." She indicated him with a nod.

He studied her face, noting the high cheekbones and bright hazel-green eyes that matched the green-gold stone at her neck. She looked familiar to him—though he didn't see how he could ever have met then forgotten her—and he had a vague impression that she didn't like him. So why was she "caring" for him? "I'm Courtland MacCarrick."

"You are a Scot."

"Aye." At his answer, he could have sworn there was a flash of sadness in her eyes.

"And you are in Andorra because . . ." She trailed off.

The truth whispered in his mind: *Because I was hired to tyrannize the people here.* "I was just passing through."

The sadness he'd sensed disappeared, and she said in a

haughty voice, "You chose to *pass through* a tiny country in the Pyrenees known for some of the highest mountain passes in Europe? For future reference, most simply go around."

Her condescending tone annoyed him, and his body was rapidly becoming a mass of pain. "I'm a Highlander. I like *high lands*."

She glared at him, then turned to leave, as if she couldn't wait to be away from him, but he needed information.

"Was I out for an entire day?" he hastily asked.

She looked longingly at the door, but then faced him. "This is your third day here."

Christ, three days? And from the feel of his ribs, he'd be another week healing before he could even sit a horse. "How did I come to be here?"

She hesitated before saying, "I found you on the shore and dragged you up here."

She looked like a stiff wind could blow her away. "You?"

"My horse and I."

His brows drew together. "There was no man who could do it?"

He was nearly six and a half feet tall and weighed more than seventeen stone. He could imagine how difficult it had been to haul him back even with the horse—especially if she lived high on the mountainside.

"We managed fine."

Court owed her a debt of gratitude; he despised being indebted in any way. He grated, "Then you saved my life."

She peered at the ceiling, appearing embarrassed.

Forcing the foreign words, he said, "You have my thanks."

She nodded and turned to go, but he didn't want the lass to leave yet. "Annalía," he said, unable to remember anything else from her catalog of names.

She whirled around, eyes wide, no doubt at the use of

her given name. In a flash, he remembered her. Her beautiful countenance and curious expression had waned into sharp and glaring by the riverside. He rubbed his forehead with his good hand. In fact, she'd lamented the fact that he lived.

"That is Lady Llorente to someone such as you! You would do well to remember that."

His eyes narrowed. He'd been right. "Why did you call me an animal? Because I was so beaten?"

"Of course not," she said with an incredulous look. "I could tell you were Scottish."

Court wrestled with his temper. "Scottish?" Many people held prejudices against Scots, and some hated them sight unseen, but no context on earth gave an *Andorran* the right to look down on one. "Then why would you save 'someone such as me'?"

She shrugged her slim shoulders. "I would spare a mangy, rabid wolf suffering—"

"So now you think me a mangy, rabid wolf?" His head had begun pounding on both sides of his skull.

She stretched out one hand and studied her nails, a perfect picture of disdain. "If you'd let *a lady* finish her thoughts, I would have added that I lowered my standards to accommodate you."

He'd be damned if he'd allow this prig-arsed Andorran to look down her pert little nose at him. "A lady?" He snorted and glanced around the room. "Alone with me. No chaperone." He lifted the sheet to glance down before giving her a smirk. "And you got quite a gander. If you're such a lady, then why were you two seconds away from takin' me into your hand?"

She looked as though she fought for breath. "I . . . I was—"

"Granted, you doona seem like you're used to entertaining men in their rooms." He looked her up and down, not bothering to hide his blatant perusal. "But I'd wager you'd be a natural at it."

She stumbled back as though hit, her lips parting.

When she rushed out of the room, with her shoulders, which had been jammed back, now slumped, his brows drew together. He was puzzled as much by her behavior as by the unfamiliar seed of guilt that lodged in his chest. As he tested to see if he could rise from the bed, he wondered why a cold-hearted bastard like himself would regret his treatment of a woman who thought him no more than—no, worse than—a beast.

He was determined to find the reasons for both reactions.

Annalía had feared she was one of *those* women ever since she'd known of their existence.

She'd feared that she could be one among those who lusted and acted on their passions even to their own ruin. Her discovery that the Highlander's brawny chest could fascinate her for hours had been dismaying. Realizing that each glimpse of his private place, outlined beneath the thin linen sheet, made her heart race had been devastating.

Now, worse than her own fear, a thick-skulled, barbaric Scot had looked her over and concluded she was a "natural."

Just as her Castilian mother had been.

Denying her true nature had been easy before. If she heard whispers about her "hot blood" in the village, she ignored them. She kept herself busy with the estate and with the people here. But after the Scot had come, each night became a struggle.

Just last night, she'd lain in bed thinking about his body—all of his body, which she'd studied and touched—until she'd slowly unbuttoned her nightdress and bared her breasts. The meager breeze fluttering past the curtains had grazed over her heated skin, making her shudder, making her . . . *long.*

She'd never known what to call the urges she'd felt in the night—not lust, because they never had been focused on any one man. So she'd thought of them as longing, but not last night. She'd truly felt lust, and it had been so strong she'd finally run her fingers over her own breast and down her belly.

A noise had startled her—just the house settling—but she'd jerked her hand away, ashamed.

Not only was she one of those women, she was alone in the house with a man who knew it. . . .

When she'd finally guided the shaking key into the lock of his door, she'd fled outside, hurrying in the direction of the meadow in front of her home.

Vitale met her on the path. "What has happened? You're white as a sheet."

"It's nothing. The Scot woke."

"He's a mercenary?"

"I'm almost positive, though I am convinced he's an obnoxious man." At least he'd be gone soon. She was sure that he'd be eager to return to indiscriminate killing and sharpening knives and practicing pistols and whatever else mercenaries did.

"Did he frighten you or threaten you?"

"N-Not exactly . . ."

"You never listen to me!" Vitale cried with a volley of Gallic hand gestures. "You've been too sheltered—can't comprehend that there are bad people in the world that shouldn't be saved! You're too . . . *soft!*" He said the word with disgust.

"I am not soft!"

"When I saved you from that footpad, you were too stunned to give him your choker and you quaked like a little girl."

"I *was* a little girl and I wasn't quaking." Nor had she been too stunned. The choker had been her mother's, and she'd already known how much she needed it.

He eyed her. "The Scot will still be weak enough that we can throw him back like a bad catch."

"Vitale!" Unconsciously, she drew her hand over her neck. Frowning, she glanced back at the house, puzzled at her uncanny feeling that she was being watched. There was no way he could have risen. No, not with those injuries.

The sun was directly in her eyes, and she could see nothing. After a last squint, she said, "Vitale, he'll be out of our lives soon enough. One day we probably will find him—and our silver—gone." With that, she walked on.

Once in the meadow, she sank into the carpet of narcissus cladding the entire shelf of land. She'd always been able to lose herself in the scents and daydream as she gazed out over the lake and farther beyond to the twining river.

On the next plateau down, their champion horses played and jumped, their copper coats gleaming in the sun. On the lowest plateau skirting the river, rose of Canolich swathed the ground in yellow. But here, a cloud of white blooms. She plucked a flower, brought it to her nose, and inhaled, closing her eyes with pleasure. . . .

He'd said she was a natural! Her eyes flashed open. What was it about her that made people continually come to this conclusion? She'd saved his life, and he made disparaging comments? When one is nursing a man, contact is made and . . . parts are seen.

Especially when they were drawing attention to themselves. She shivered.

She would simply forget the scene, banishing it from her thoughts. She might be one of *those* women, but she'd been trained to be a lady. Burying uncomfortable thoughts was one thing at which ladies excelled. She looked down to find the flower crushed in her hands.

Soon he'd be gone, and life would return to normal. Unfortunately, even then her existence would be anxious and cheerless. She continued to await some news from her brother Aleixandre, the only family she had left. She had heard nothing for more than a week, and worry preyed on her.

A strong breeze blew for the first time in days, it seemed, flattening the grass in waves and teasing a lock of hair loose from her tight braid. Out here, the compulsion to rake it back into place wasn't so pressing, but still won over. She smoothed her hair and picked another flower.

Even when her brother routed Pascal and returned, she still would be in a vulnerable position. This fight had only postponed Alcix's desire that she wed. When their father died two years ago, she'd been brought home from school so that a marriage could be contracted for her. Just as Alcix had begun narrowing the choices, Pascal had arrived.

Before he'd shown his true nature, Pascal had surprised them by asking Aleix for her hand, though they'd never met. Aleix had refused, incurring the general's anger, but her brother had never trusted the man even before his vile army of mercenaries and deserters had taken over the area.

Aleix repeatedly lamented the fact that he hadn't forced her to marry earlier. At twenty-one, she was more than old enough, and she'd been born and raised for it, but she'd never met a man she wanted. She never could imagine doing the perplexing things the girls at school had whispered about, those painful, aggressive things done in the dark—no matter how much she *longed*. Whenever she'd envisioned those acts with any of the men she'd been introduced to, she'd cringed.

Besides, she'd been so content to help care for Aleix and Mariette's baby that no man tempted her.

Yet now there was no baby, no Mariette, and all the happiness that had been in Aleix had died with them.

Annalía turned sharply toward the house. The feeling was back. When a cloud passed the sun, she held her hand to her forehead and scanned the windows.

The curtains in the Highlander's room swayed—to the side—then settled back into place.

# Three

*W*hy the hell hadn't she returned? Court thought as irritation sniped at him.

Vitale, the sometimes mute, sometimes caustic old Frenchman, had been by to warily bring food in and clean the room, but *she* couldn't be bothered to come again.

Court's body had at least ceased weakening, and he was becoming restless. He was finally able to dress himself, in clothes borrowed from Annalía's brother, or the "master," as Vitale called him. He'd scoffed when Vitale had said the garments would fit. The woman might be five and a half feet and had a tiny frame, and he couldn't see a sibling of hers even broaching six feet, but apparently this "master" was a big bastard.

Forays to the window marked Court's only exertion, but they no longer made his eyes swarm with black dots. He was never one to sit still, yet he'd done just that since he'd awakened four days ago. The only thing that broke up the monotony was watching her from the window. With not a thing else to do, he'd watched her a lot.

He could admit he enjoyed seeing her playing with the children in the courtyard, chasing the laughing bairn. No matter how tired Annalía appeared, each child received the same amount of attention, even when she looked like she wanted nothing more than to put her feet up.

Then there was spotting her returning from her morning ride, breathless, with her perfect hair finally fighting its bonds. He never failed to shake his head at the proud—no, the *cocky*—way she sat a horse. Welcome sights, when he could forget her disdain. For others she always had a smile, even when her eyes showed distraction. He often wondered if he was the reason her brow was drawn when she thought no one could see her. . . .

When the unseen clock downstairs tolled eight, Court's body tensed like a dog that'd been trained, and he rose to drag on the pair of borrowed trousers. As he did every day at that toll, he scuffed to the window, because within five minutes the front door would groan open.

Right on time, she glided out the door, her slim hips swaying beneath her bright blue skirts. She always wore bright colored dresses. Not garish or overblown, but a world away from the subdued colors favored by the women of his clan. She wore them, he would wager, not to attract attention, but because she was so ridiculously feminine that she found them *pretty*.

Morning sun shone down, glinting off her hair, making it appear golden in places. As usual, it was braided up in an elaborate style, as intricate as any Celtic knot.

Next she would meet Vitale, who would have her hat that she continually forgot, and then they would speak for a few moments. He was impertinent to her and she allowed it, even sometimes cocking a hip out and looking up at the sky with clear frustration. They had an unusual rapport, but they obviously cared for each other.

Like clockwork, the old man met her on the path just downstairs. They didn't talk for long before she was off to the stable for her ride. Damn it, he wanted to look at her for longer. She always wore the choker, but something was different today. Was she wearing new jewelry? Earrings that dropped down?

*Enough of this.* He wanted more information, and he was getting strong enough to where he could begin demanding it. When she left, Court knocked on the glass and motioned for Vitale—who'd bemoaned Court's recovery and had placed his food on the ground "as was fitting for an animal"—to come up.

The old man gave him a lewd hand gesture, but the front door did sound soon after.

"Tell me about her," he asked when Vitale had unlocked and entered the room.

He cast Court a sour expression. "And why would I do that?"

"Because if you do I'll no' be so disposed to beating you down when I recover fully," Court informed him as he leaned against the windowsill.

Vitale swallowed hard.

"I ken what you're thinking, old man. You're wondering what harm could come of it. None could. I harbor no ill will toward the woman who saved my life."

"What do you want to know?" he asked hesitantly.

"Where's her family?"

"Her parents are dead and her brother is away." He added, "On business."

A vague answer, but Court didn't press. "No husband? No other family she could stay with?"

"She and her brother are estranged from their relatives. And she was about to be married when Pascal came to power. Now escaping his notice is our top priority. Since you are his hired killer, I suppose we should have escaped your notice as well."

Court ignored the last comment. "And why is this place so deserted?"

"Many fled Pascal. Some have gone to fight him. But you would know all about that, wouldn't you?" He shook his head. "I told her to take you back to the river and let you rot, but she never listens—"

"Pascal ordered this done to me," he interrupted. "How much loyalty do you think I have to the man who sought to kill me? I barely escaped into the river."

Vitale eyed him, clearly trying to determine if he spoke the truth, then asked, "Who beat you?"

Court admitted, "Two Rechazados."

His eyes went wide, scanning the room wildly. "My God, you'll bring them down on this house. Every day you're here already weighs on her terribly. If you are in league with Pascal, she fears you'll lead his men here. Now when I tell her what you've told me, she'll know that Pascal's assassins will be searching for you to finish the job."

Pascal would be searching, but there weren't enough of his prized assassins to spare. "He will no' waste any Rechazado for a task like me." Their order never numbered more than forty-nine based on a twisted reading of the seven letters of the Apocalypse, and if they lost men they still only inducted new ones twice a year. "Besides, they'll have thought I died."

Vitale marched to the second window to peer out though he couldn't have expected to see Annalía. Court knew she'd be well out of sight by now. "Why should I trust what you say?"

"You probably should no'." He unsuccessfully crossed his arms, too late remembering the bloody cast she'd forced on him. "I want to talk to her, but she will no' come back. Get her to."

"The mademoiselle? Attend you now that you're awake?" He snorted.

"If she will no' come to me, then I'll have to stumble out to find her." His expression turned cold. "You ought to warn her that I might feel . . . put out when I catch her."

He stepped back. "I will see that she comes tomorrow."

"After her ride?"

Vitale scowled at that. "If she knew you spied on her, she'd be very uneasy. She's an extremely private person. But yes, after her ride."

Court nodded. "I need to get a message to my men. If I give you directions, can you see that it is done?"

"Again, why would I do that?"

"The sooner I contact them, the sooner I can leave."

"I'll return directly with pen and ink."

Court debated how to handle Annalía when she came for their meeting, and had to admit he was at a loss with a woman like her. She seemed complicated and mysterious, which meant she wasn't like straightforward Highland women at all.

And as much as he was unused to a woman like Annalía, she was surely accustomed to gentlemen, to polite behavior and nonthreatening men. So he decided to stay in bed and act as though he couldn't rise easily, to appear less intimidating, but the gentlemanly behavior was proving elusive. Court didn't exchange pleasantries because he wasn't a pleasant person. He was brusque and direct. She would not respond well to brusque and direct.

When she glided in hours after her ride, smelling of the flowers she'd been tarrying among earlier, he bit out, "Good afternoon." He couldn't remember the last time he'd said that phrase, when in fact it hadn't been a better-than-average afternoon.

"To you as well." She appeared surprised by his gruff words, then suspicious. "Vitale said you desired to speak with me. What do you require?"

Her words rolled from her tongue in that foreign way, and he found he liked listening to her, even as her obvious reluctance to be near him grated. A woman whom he found beautiful and who was kind to others was disgusted with him. He felt like a caged animal she was wary of—and all because he was Scottish?

And perhaps he'd found the exact chink in her armor and had hurt her that first day, a voice in the back of his mind reasoned.

"I'd like to ask you a few more questions." *Pleasant enough.* She gave one tight nod.

"How have you escaped Pascal's notice this far?" Court had never heard of this place and wondered why Pascal hadn't looted it.

She didn't hesitate to say, "Probably by not dragging his mercenaries into my home."

"I answer to him no longer."

"His ex-mercenary, then," she said with a flick of her hand as if the difference was trifling. "Vitale told me as much."

At his irritated look, she added, "I don't know why we've been spared." She was clearly lying, but he let it go.

"I have another question."

She remained there, though she didn't deign to meet his eyes, and he found the question he'd meant to ask forgotten, replaced by, "Why do you hate Scots?"

She blushed to the tips of her small ears, her skin pinkening against her crisp white blouse and her ever-present choker. "If you please, I would rather not discuss my dislike of Scots *with* a Scot."

"You can tell me. I will no' bite."

She gave him a wide-eyed look that said she wasn't sure on that count at all and hadn't thought about the possibility until he'd brought it up. Finally she said, "I've heard very unfavorable things about them—about you. Worse than any of the other outsiders Pascal has lured here."

Court exhaled, reckoning it might be time to admit that his crew's Highlander tales had worked too well.

Whenever they arrived in a new area, his men spread rumors to the people underlining the Highlanders' brutality, their lust for blood, and their enjoyment of torture. Then, when the thirty-five Scots in their company, some painted, some in kilts, all nearing or exceeding six feet tall, gave a savage battle yell and charged with the requisite crazed look in their eyes, the combatants ran. They almost always ran.

The farmers and ranch hands in Andorra had fled so fast that even his quick cousin Niall could barely swat the last one on the arse with his sword.

Only one leader and his men had stood their ground....

Court's eyes followed her slim hand when she smoothed an already immaculate crease in her skirt—today a bright red one. "And what did you think of Scots before we came here?"

She frowned, appearing genuinely confused. "I didn't think of Scots."

He scowled at that. "And now?"

"Now that you've come, you've shown yourself to be the epitome of all I've heard."

He waved her on with his cast.

She crossed her arms over her chest and took a breath.

"Violence surrounds you, as shown by your beating, but also by the gashes on your fingers. I'd wondered how you could receive such a peculiar injury, then concluded you'd cut them on someone's teeth when you hit him in the face."

Court nodded, extremely impressed. That was exactly what had happened. He nearly smiled remembering the satisfaction of splitting the Spaniard's lips, of the blood he'd spat for at least an hour afterward. . . .

"You have a history of it as demonstrated by the scars covering you. I'd heard that your people live in bands—"

"Clans," he grated. "They're called clans."

She shrugged. "And that these *clans* fight with each other constantly because you are a bloodthirsty people more concerned with warring than with culture or refinement." He noticed she'd begun pressing one finger after another against her crossed arms as she ticked off points. "You are mannerless. Your halfhearted gratitude to me for saving your life bespeaks a sense of entitlement—"

"It bespeaks lack of practice in being beholden."

She raised her eyebrows in an expression that said if he continued to talk, she would cease. "You look like a blackguard. Except when you are angry. Then you look like a brute that could readily kill me. Your insulting me that first day was hurtful and uncalled for. I've heard it's that way with your people—a complete lack of delicacy. There's little thought behind your eyes. . . ."

"I've heard enough," he snapped when she appeared to be just gathering steam. Many held these misimpressions, and he and his men played on them with the stories they spread, but to hear them voiced back to him by an Andorran? . . . Scots were a thousand times prouder and more accomplished than these medieval crag-of-a-country people cut off from the changing world.

She blinked as if taken aback by his seething tone, then

turned to walk out, tossing over her shoulder, "Indeed, your vocation may be the least of your failings."

*Damn it, I wasn't finished talking to you. . . .*

Though the movement pained him, he reached out and grabbed her wrist. She gave a startled cry, snatching her hand from his. It flew to her mouth, but he still heard her hiss in Catalan, *"Bèstia,"* before she dashed out the doorway.

Court knew Catalan fairly well, and he definitely knew the word for beast; he'd been called it the first day his cadre had arrived and had heard it in whispers daily thereafter.

She had to try the key several times before getting it into the lock. He'd shaken her. Unfortunately, Court knew he *looked* like a beast. He'd studied his reflection this morning, imagining how this woman might see him.

And winced.

The vessels in both eyes had exploded, so the whites were red. The right side of his face was still mottled black and blue, and his normally squared jaw looked even more so with the swelling and with a week's worth of beard highlighting it. She was highborn to her toes—she'd probably never seen a man in this condition before.

Just now, when she'd peered at him as she might at something on the bottom of her boot, he'd *felt* like a barbarian, like the animal she'd called him. He was beginning to despise her condescending tone and her sharp looks of disgust, even as he struggled to comprehend why he could possibly mind enough to be bothered by either.

Today had been the first time Annalía had faced the Scot with the definite knowledge that he was a mercenary.

Before Vitale had confirmed her fears, she'd hoped Mac-Carrick wasn't a killer for hire because she'd felt some small, minute—piddling, really—spark of curiosity about the intractable man. But no longer.

During their meeting this afternoon, she had focused on the injuries still marring his face, reminding herself that it didn't matter if he and Pascal had had a falling-out—the evidence of their history was glaring. MacCarrick's every day here was a risk and it was one she refused to take to help a boorish, pawing mercenary like him. As soon as he was able, she'd demand he leave her home. . . .

"Mademoiselle," Vitale called from the doorway behind her, interrupting her thoughts.

How long had she been ambling mindlessly through the house? She turned, dismayed to see the sun setting behind him.

When Vitale met her, he was crushing his hat in his hands. "The boy from the village has brought a letter for you."

"Is it from Aleix?" she asked, heart in her throat.

"It is not. But it might contain information about Master Llorente."

As he pulled it from his vest pocket, she murmured absently, "Please get the boy a nice dinner and a soft bed." No reason under heaven excused bad manners.

"I've already seen to it." He handed over the letter, his face drawn.

She nodded and turned for the study, walking with a stiff spine and unhurried steps, but once Vitale was out of sight, she sprinted down the hallway, sliding on the rugs. Tripping inside the room, heart thudding, she nearly ripped open the paper before she got there.

Impertinent Vitale followed her in, which meant he'd heard her running, but she couldn't be bothered with that now. Her brother hadn't written in weeks, and waiting for word had been unbearable. He was the only family left to her since her father's death, and Aleix had been more of a father than Llorente had ever been prepared to be.

She didn't care what men said—waiting for someone to

return from battle *had* to be much, much worse than the battle itself.

Her nerves were taut.

At the old oak desk, she shoved back the leather chair and lit a candle, chasing away the growing darkness. Then, letter opener in hand, she flipped over the missive.

The room spun. She stared blankly at the sender's name—General Reynaldo Pascal.

Instead of tearing it open, she now cut it slowly. She had to scan parts of it several times because her hands shook so wildly—and because she could scarcely believe the content.

"What does it say?" Vitale asked anxiously.

By the time she reached Pascal's arrogant signature, bile had risen in her throat. Her hands went limp, and the letter fluttered to the top of the desk, nearly catching the candle flame. In a daze, she sank into the chair.

Vitale snatched up the letter as if to read, even though he'd refused to learn how to. "Tell me what it says!"

She hardly recognized her own deadened voice when she related, "Pascal defeated Aleix's men more than a week ago, capturing them all. Aleix is imprisoned, his life in the general's hands. There is only one thing that can convince Pascal to spare him."

Vitale sat back into the oversized chair opposite her, looking very small and weary. "He wanted to wed you before. Is he demanding to now?"

She nodded. "I just don't understand how he found out who I am." When Pascal had asked for her hand, she'd feared he'd discovered she was the last female descendant of the House of Castile, but Aleix had assured her the general had probably become infatuated after he'd seen her at a village festival. Now, looking back, she realized Aleix had always known and had tried to spare her worry. In the back of her mind she wondered what else he had spared her. . . .

"Maybe some of the villagers remember when your mother came here, and they told Pascal."

She nodded, lost in thought. Her mother, Elisabet Tristán, had been banished from Castile, Spain, to the mountain cage of Andorra, married sight unseen to Llorente, the wealthiest count there. Elisabet, the daughter of a princess, had been given to the much older man and exiled into a land that might as well have been an island, so isolated was it. Because she'd let passion guide her.

It ultimately destroyed her as well.

"Mademoiselle?"

She glanced up. "Of course, that must be it, the villagers. I'd just believed we'd been so circumspect, remaining here, avoiding that connection." She and Aleix had never drawn attention to themselves and had forgone any of the benefits their positions might afford, partly because they shunned that kind of life. Yet Annalía's isolation wasn't only to avoid notice. Fearing she would be like her mother, Llorente had kept her secluded as much as possible—in fact, only Aleix had persuaded Llorente to send her to school instead of a convent.

"The rumors that Pascal plans to take Spain must be true." Vitale shook his head slowly. "The damned fools have allowed an army to build up right on their border because no one cares about tiny Andorra."

"I thought he wanted to take control over Queen Isabella like the other generals who have, but that's not it. Think about it—if he wants me, then he doesn't want to simply control the queen."

"You think he wants to replace her?"

She nodded. "He probably plans to use me to control Aleix, setting him up as a figurehead of some sort."

Vitale frowned. "But you've told me your house has no claim to that throne."

"Well, no real one. At least not in the last hundred years. But Isabella's hated. *Mare de Déu,* if she thinks we are exerting . . ." She put her hand to her neck, for once not to check her choker.

She stood to pace. Ever since she could remember, she'd always paced when upset. Her prickly Andorran nanny had complained of her wearing thin a rug when she was only five. She recalled that a few years after her father had caught her. He'd been so angry, so . . . *disappointed* in her. "People pace because they have no control," he'd said, his voice laced with iron. "Will you be one of them? Or will you be a Llorente?"

The memory made her drop down into the chair as though pushed, but without the soothing rhythm—the pacing forth and then the always dependable back—despair set in. Fighting tears, she stared at the paper and the broad, scratching strokes of ink within. She couldn't think of all this now. All she wanted to know was if Aleix was hurt. Was her courageous big brother fearful at all?

"Vitale," she murmured. She was about to cry, and it would pain her for him to see it.

He knew her so well, he didn't ask, just reached forward to squeeze her hand over the desk. "We will talk tomorrow. Ring the bell up here if you need anything."

She waited until she could be sure he wouldn't come back and then when she finally blinked her eyes, two fat tears spilled over, followed by more. After several minutes of struggling, she gave in and put her head in her hands.

"What's in that letter, lass?"

Annalía raised her face, astonished to see her patient up and *roaming freely.* She frantically dashed at her eyes, mortified that he'd seen her like this. *No one* saw Annalía Llorente crying. This was far too personal. How had he escaped?

"Tell me what makes you cry so."

He sounded angry that she cried. Not disappointed or disgusted but angry. She frowned. *How puzzling.* His eyes were focused on the letter as though he would kill it. Focused on the letter. . . . She caught it on the candle flame and tossed the burning page into the empty fireplace.

He gave her one tight nod at the action as though she'd impressed him. "That's the only thing that could prevent me from reading it."

"Obviously manners and respect for privacy hold no sway over you." She was still drying tears, trying not to shudder with embarrassment. "How did you get out?"

"Picked the lock. Now what did it say?"

"It's none of your business," she said tartly. Her face was finally dry, but now felt tight. "Please leave me alone."

His expression hadn't changed. He had the same expectant look as if he'd just asked the question again and she *would* answer.

"It doesn't concern you," she felt constrained to say again. And it didn't concern him. Not for certain, at least. But what if the Highlanders were the ones who had defeated her brother's men? What if this one was responsible in some way?

And she'd saved him.

She had to get away. Shooting to her feet, she grabbed her skirt and swished around the desk. When he saw her approaching and didn't step aside, she decided she must forgo manners as well and barrel right past him.

He blocked her exit, putting a stiff arm in front of her.

Fury snapped hot within her. "Stop this, this instant, and let me pass!"

He looked unmoved, his watchful gaze flickering over her face, studying her as if learning her reaction. "What's upset you?"

"Let me go or I will scream."

He bent his arm and leaned into it, looming closer to her. "And who'll come to your rescue? Vitale? I've noticed there are no other men about who are younger than he is."

She'd feared he would come to this conclusion, and he was absolutely right. All of the ranch hands had followed Aleix. *And were now captured or dead.* Her hand rose to her lips as the thought arose.

Studying, watching her. She cast it down.

"I asked nicely," he grated. "My patience wears thin."

*His* patience? "As does your welcome!"

"I want you to tell me."

"Why would you even care?" For the life of her, she couldn't imagine.

"Maybe I doona like to see a pretty lady cry."

Utter frustration robbed her energy. "And what would you do about it?" she asked in a deadened voice. "Solve my problems? Slay my dragons?"

His brows drew together as if he'd just realized he shouldn't, in fact, care.

She gave him a disgusted look in return. "What you should be concerned about is leaving my home and removing the threat you pose to everyone here." She feinted left and ducked under his right arm.

As she hastened away, he called, "You're bonny when you're angry, Anna."

At his mocking use of her given name, she stumbled, shocked to the core.

Back in her room, after locking her door, she stood thrumming with indignation. She would have thought that this heinous encounter, coupled with the crushing news, would have made her weep beyond measure.

Strangely, the anger invigorated her. The Highlander

might have seen her cry, but she'd never again give him the satisfaction of seeing her weakness—no eyes swollen from tears or face wan from pacing until the moon set.

When she cast him from her home tomorrow like the morning rubbish, she'd look like the princesses her foremothers were.

# Four

Court lay in bed staring at the ceiling, more restless than he could ever remember being. Now that he'd sent word to his crew, he was stuck waiting, a task hard for a patient man and impossible to tolerate for Court. Worse, he waited with an old man he'd like to toss from the window and with a mysterious woman he wanted to tie up so she couldn't flee until he'd actually finished questioning her.

What in the hell had been in that letter and why had she been crying?

Court didn't like mysteries. To him, they had a taunting aspect, as if their mere existence accused him of not working hard enough to solve them.

He was used to doing as he pleased, and right now what would please him would be learning more about the secretive Annalía. She'd most likely be asleep, but her room could tell him much.

Rising from bed, he dressed, then ran his hand under his mattress to grab the ivory knitting needle he'd found in a drawer. His own lock hadn't withstood it, and hers shouldn't prove any different.

He strode down the landing, checking doors until he found one locked. When he stuck the needle point into the keyhole and pressed to the side, the corner of his lips curled at the click. Creaking open the door, he entered the room and approached her bed. The night had just a hint of breeze, with a growing moon shedding light inside.

He found her lying on her front with a thin sheet stretched across her back and her hair spilling across her pillow. Stunning. Thick, glossy curls shone in the moonlight, fascinating him, as did the feeling that arose when he realized, when he knew in his gut, he was the only man to have seen it loose and free. He had the urge to touch it, to smell it, but he forced himself to turn from her and investigate the room.

All of her belongings were stored with an obsessive neatness, and the ornamentations, like everything about her, were incredibly feminine. Lace predominated, but her bookshelf was like a man's: mathematics, botany, astronomy, and studies in four different languages. He spied another text beside her bed, this one on the Greek language.

An ornate display cabinet, polished until it reflected like a mirror, was the center point of the room and housed a porcelain collection arranged on glass shelves. He could see why Annalía might be unconsciously attracted to the pieces. They were bright and striking but fragile, which was exactly how she appeared. They were also unmistakably expensive.

An unfamiliar and wearisome feeling crept over him when he realized her *hobby* was worth more than he made in a year working tirelessly and risking his life.

His mood improved when he silently opened a drawer—not that he cared overmuch if he woke her, because what could she do?—and discovered a cache of steamy gothic novels in every imaginable language. He grinned. Lady Annalía's dirty little secret.

Beside the books was a thick bundle of letters. He drew it out, then crossed to the moonlit window to scan them. They were all from girls at a place called The Vines, which was apparently a school. The recognizable surnames were like a partial compilation of the world's wealthiest and highest-ranked families. He had to wonder even for Annalía's beauty and wealth, how she'd gotten in. He would return to the letters tomorrow during her ride and read them all by daylight—

She kicked off her sheet in the heat of the room, and his brows rose at what was revealed. Her nightdress was silk—he wouldn't have expected anything less from her—and rode up her creamy thighs, high. The lace edge brushed just below her backside, which was lush and full—that he hadn't expected. He hissed in a breath when she bent one knee and drew it up beside her so that her legs were parted, with only shadow concealing her.

His hands itched to run up the backs of her thighs to palm her curves . . . until she raised her hips to him with need and spread her knees . . . He fought to bite back a guttural sound and failed.

Though she didn't wake, she sighed something in Catalan and turned on her back, one slender arm stretching out to the side, her other hand resting on her chest. Perfect, generous breasts strained against the tight bodice, and he groaned, clenching his fists and crushing the letters. She'd hidden more than her hair from the world.

She was exquisite, sensuous, and when he left this place behind he knew he would never forget this image of her. Then from nowhere, a single word whispered in the back of his mind. *More.*

He froze, every muscle in his body rigid. *No.*

He'd been attracted to her—mightily so—but before when he'd imagined taking her, he'd envisioned pinning her arms over her head and driving into her hard until she cried out in pleasure and surrendered to him, until he could make her look up at him with something other than disdain.

Yet now he imagined seducing her into letting him lick every inch of her golden skin and the hours he could take tasting her sex. He wanted to seduce her into letting him spend deep within her, knowing he could never get her pregnant.

He roughly ran his hand over the front of his trousers. Apparently he wanted her furiously. But a woman that fine wouldn't desire him, and he would never force a woman.

Court was a bastard in anyone's book. He did things that made other men unable to live with themselves, and he did them without a heartbeat's hesitation. But even he wasn't so far gone that he would remain alone in a house with an exquisite virgin, when right now waking her with his tongue against her sex seemed a brilliant idea.

If he stayed, he would try to bed her at every opportunity even as he knew he shouldn't. He was sick of waiting anyway. The best course would be to leave this place and go find his men.

Though it took will to do so, he turned from her. He was a disciplined man, and damn it, he could do it. He tossed her letters back in her drawer, then kicked it closed, daring her to wake, but she slept on. The entire way out of her room, he opened and clenched the shaking hands that had been so ready to fondle her.

With long strides he made it outside to the stable. The horses recoiled in their stalls as if they sensed the violent turmoil within him.

He didn't want to take her horse, not the one that he'd seen her touch foreheads with while she murmured to it. He couldn't see very well, so he went for a larger horse. After much coaxing, he led out a stallion, vaguely noting it felt superior, and found a saddle for him, using his good hand and the inside of his other arm to carry it. The black dots blurring his vision when he hefted the saddle and tightened it should have warned him that he was pushing too fast, but he continued as though chased.

He glanced back at the house, saw the curtains flickering in and out of her window as though beckoning. *Remember how you felt when you saw her crying,* he told himself. Gritting his teeth, Court put a boot in the stirrup and stepped up.

The black dots returned and exploded.

Chiron, the ranch's primary stud, was missing. After several hours and to Annalía's horror, they'd found the horse, still saddled, merrily impregnating a mare that had not been in the ranch's schedule.

Now, armed with the knowledge of an attempted horse theft—of a stallion worth his weight in gold—she followed a thick trail of hardened mud directly up to the Highlander's room. Her outrage escalated with each step.

Of course, the door was unlocked. She marched in, fury making a door slamming seem a worthy gesture.

At the sound, he cracked open bloodshot eyes. "What?" he grumbled as he turned on his back.

Mud everywhere. The lace coverlet ruined. "Rolling in the mud, MacCarrick? What a fitting recreation."

He put his good hand behind his head, insolently leaning up on the pillow and peering at her with a too-sly expression, a far too . . . *familiar* expression. As if he knew a secret she didn't. *Was he staring at her breasts?* "You were just going to steal away in the night? And I do mean 'steal,' since we can add horse thievery to your extensive list of shortcomings."

He waved her statement away with his cast, which was also streaked with mud. "I was going to send it back."

"Is that why, of all the horses in the stable, our ranch's stud was found saddled and with a-a . . . he was saddled and wandering?"

"No, I took him because—" He broke off. "Just forget it."

"I want to know why!" Why that and why he would just leave. Without a word of thanks. And why should that nettle her so much? She wanted him gone.

"And I said"—he leveled a forbidding glare at her—"to forget it."

Obstinate man! "I want you out of my house today."

"And how should I accomplish that, since I could no' sit a horse last night and barely got back inside?"

"I don't care if you have to roll down the mountain. Pascal's men will come for you, and when they do, we will all pay for your selfishness."

"Unlike you people, I canna run up and down sheer mountains all day—like bloody mountain goats—when I am strong. Much less with bashed ribs and a stone of muscle lost."

"If you could make it outside last night, you're well enough to leave a place that holds no welcome for you."

He crossed his arms, his eyes growing darker.

"So, MacCarrick, if you have no other objections—"

"No."

"Good."

"No. I meant no, I'm no' leaving."

*Remain calm! Ignore the increasingly familiar urge to close in on his face and screech at him.* "You will, because this is my home."

"Who's going to throw me out? The old man? The bairn? No' a single man in sight who can do it."

*Mare de Déu,* she wished he'd stop saying that. Because he

was right. He could stay for as long as he pleased. Wrestling with her temper, she forced herself to say in a soft voice, "I saved your life, and I'm asking you to leave my home. If you are a gentleman that must count for something."

"If I honor your wishes, you'd have saved my life in vain. So it's bloody convenient that I'm no' a gentleman."

# Five

*I*f Pascal's first letter had been the judgment, his second had been the sentence. Annalía stood dazed at the oak desk, the paper in her hand crumpled and damp from her palm.

She'd waited for his instructions, more nervous than she'd ever been. The last four days had been more nerve-wracking even than when a coach-and-six unexpectedly crunched into the white gravel drive of her school. If a carriage came, no one raised an eyebrow. A carriage meant a day trip. But a coach-and-six struck fear into the hearts of the girls, and they would all tear across the schoolroom to look out from the balcony, praying their family's crest wouldn't be emblazoned on the door.

A surprise coach-and-six meant some girl's life was about to drastically change.

As drastically as Annalía's was.

Pascal had called for her. The hours had dragged by as she'd awaited his summons, hours made more miserable by hearing the Highlander restlessly stomping all over her home.

He'd been like a loosed bull in the manor, which necessitated her behaving like a frightened hare to avoid him. Their game would end tomorrow. The general expected her to join him then and marry him by the week's end.

She wasn't even near Pascal, and yet already his hand stretched far to control her.

She burned the letter in the study's fireplace then paced until her legs ached and the sun had set, uncaring as to what her father would have thought. Apparently, she couldn't help it. She remembered another time when she'd been home briefly from school and he'd caught her at it. She'd been sixteen. That time his hard, weathered face had looked grave, his eyes full of pain. "Elisabet used to do that."

Of course, she would have. Everyone always said Annalía was just like her mother.

When Annalía had first arrived at The Vines, one of the older girls had whispered, "Watch out for that one with the gardener. She's *Castilian*." They'd regarded her and determined things about her that she hadn't recognized at that young age, and they hadn't even known that Annalía's mother had been caught making love to her family's former stable master. Before *and after* her marriage to Llorente.

She ran her fingertips over the choker at her neck. The stone attached was a reminder she was never without—

"Why are you pacing?" The Highlander. His voice was a rumble she *felt*.

She exhaled in irritation, then faced him. Her first impulse was to leave the room, but she'd tired of running in her own home, tired of him taking over everything that was hers, and instead she sat behind the desk. She ignored his question and asked, "Why are you here?"

"I want whisky. Occurred to me that even you people might have some."

She closed her eyes to get her temper under control. When

she opened them, he was at the liquor cabinet, noisily opening the crystal decanters, smelling their aromas, then setting them down. The silver tags on each decanter clacked against the glass.

"You can read the labels rather than smelling each one. That is, *if* you can read."

"Canna read them in this light."

He was right. She'd bought them in Paris for Aleix, delighted with the flourishing engravings, but soon realized they were difficult to decipher even in daylight. *Pretty but serving little use.* No wonder she'd bought them. She almost laughed.

"By all the saints . . ." he said, finally finding one that kept his interest. He poured a generous draught into a crystal glass. And placed it directly in front of her. She stared at it as if he'd just positioned some dead thing there, something foul like what the barn cats insisted on gifting her doorstep, and vaguely heard him pouring one for himself.

Drink in hand, he sank into the spacious chair across from the desk. Llorente had always wanted whoever was on the other side to feel small and insignificant. She rolled her eyes. Of course, the deep chair fit the Highlander perfectly, and he leaned back, seeming surprised that it suited him so well.

*Wait.* He'd shaved. How had he . . . ? He'd pilfered her brother's belongings! And his cast was gone? She'd probably find the remains of it chewed off beside his bed. Brainless man. . . .

Yet after Pascal's letter, she just didn't have the energy to vent her annoyance. Instead, she stared while he swirled the whisky as if with reverence. His hands were large and callused, but he held the glass gently, his dark gaze fixed on its flickering colors by the candle's light. When he finally took a drink, he exhaled with pleasure.

The scene was like watching someone relish a meringue. Soon all you could think about was eating meringue. She

looked on in horror as her hand shook its way to her glass.
Brows drawn, she lifted it. She glanced at him; he smirked at
her—the horse-thieving Scot—expecting her to back out.

Why not drink it? It was imperative to wipe that look from
his face.

She'd never touched spirits, never overimbibed rare tastes
of table wine. She'd never done *anything* she shouldn't have.
And look where her life was culminating.

As Pascal's bride.

The glass shot up to meet her lips, her hand and head tilting far back. Fire rushed down her throat in a long continu-
ous stream. Propriety demanded that she stop. Alas, she and
propriety were losing touch. She continued until the glass was
drained.

Refusing to gasp, she stared at him defiantly through watering eyes, then choked back a cough until she could reduce
it to a gentle clearing of her throat behind her hand.

"A woman who likes her whisky," he said while refilling her
glass. "Careful that you doona steal my heart, Annalía."

"It figures that the one requirement you'd have for your
woman is 'whisky drinker.'"

"Aye, but that's only after 'walks upright.'"

He'd said the words in his customary low and threatening
voice, making it sound cutting, but she felt warm, and her lips
slowly tugged into a smile.

He stared at her lips, at her smile, and strangely his jaw
tensed, bulging at the sides. He had such a squared jaw. *Far*
too masculine.

"Opposable thumbs rate high as well," he said, shooting
her a significant glance, but she didn't know why. *Opposable
thumbs?* She wasn't familiar with the phrase in English. Her
English was flawless, as was her French, Catalan, and Spanish,
her vocabulary in each language stellar. For this brute to
know something she didn't rankled.

He probably made it up.

Still, the way his gaze moved over her, lingering, with an expectant look, made her blush all the same. She felt it heat her face and creep to her neck.

Immediately, he asked, "What's the stone you wear at your neck?"

She brushed her finger over it. "Peridot. It's called peridot."

"I've never seen the green-gold color. It matches your eyes."

Embarrassed, she quickly murmured, "It was my mother's. It's said to have been Cleopatra's favorite gem."

"You have something in common with the lusty Cleopatra?"

"I didn't say *I* liked the stone," she bit out.

He raised his eyebrows at her tone, as if noting her reaction, then changed the subject. "So whose whisky am I enjoying? Your father's . . . ?"

"No. My father is deceased."

He inclined his head to her slightly. In a moment of insight, she thought that's how a gruff Highlander might say, "I'm sorry to hear that."

"Your brother's, then? The big bastard whose clothes I wear?"

"He's no bastard!"

Studying. "It's a figure of speech. No' literally."

Her face colored again, and she brought the glass to her lips. "Oh. Yes, it's his."

"And where is he, leaving you alone like this?"

She set the glass down. Had it wobbled? "He's away on business, but is expected to return this week."

"Is he, then? This very week?" he asked, plainly disbelieving her.

"Is that not what I just said?" She sounded exasperated.

"How is it you speak English as well as a native? Spanish and French, I understand, but no' the queen's English."

She frowned at the abrupt change in topic. Polite conversation followed rules. Topics were sequential, orderly, and flowed from one to the next like a gentle current when all those conversing were skilled. Why deliberately disrupt it? She sighed in a put-out way, then replied, "I went to school abroad and learned it there. English, you might not have heard, is the worldwide language of the nobility."

The truth was she'd had to learn it to communicate with many of her schoolmates. The Brits and Yanks couldn't seem to string together a foreign phrase to save their lives, though everyone else was at least trilingual. Worse, the Yanks polluted the language with irregular phrasings and slang that were difficult to keep pace with. As difficult as they were secretly amusing.

"Which school?"

"It's very exclusive. I'm sure *you* wouldn't have heard of it." She absently tapped her nails against her crystal glass. Apparently, he took that as a sign to refill it. Since it was empty.

"Try me."

"It's called Les Vignes."

"Aye, The Vines. Just outside of Paris in Fontainebleau."

She just stopped herself from dropping her jaw. How had *he* heard of it?

He smirked. "Aristocrats and heiresses."

"Indeed," she said in a pained tone. His gloating look rattled her, but also simply thinking about the school made her yearn for her time there. Life had been simple then. She'd loved it there, loved acquiring knowledge, but most important, Annalía had attained her coveted aura of worldliness.

Unfortunately, this worldliness was, as yet, a façade. She'd never been farther north than Paris or farther south than just past the border with Spain. She had never even seen the sea. The Highlander, just by virtue of his traveling from Scotland to Andorra, was worldlier than she.

But MacCarrick would never know it because she could put on a grand show. She'd learned contemporary American sass and slang from a princess of railroad royalty, fashionable disdain from a pouty French inheritrix of some medical patent, and British loftiness from a "fifteenth from the throne" duke's daughter.

"It's very exclusive," she repeated absently. In fact, she'd scarcely been received. Annalía wasn't so closely related to a throne, unless you followed Pascal's insane despot logic, of course. However, she was distantly related to *eight* of them.

"Yet you were born and raised in archaic Andorra."

Her expression felt brittle. She should have known he would cut through the façade and go straight to the heart of her insecurities. When she didn't answer, he continued, "I've always said there are just no' enough Andorrans in the world."

"And what makes you so sure I was raised here?"

"I've heard you speak Catalan to the people here. You've never spoken it to anyone outside of Andorra, have you?"

She'd yearned to visit other Catalan-speaking countries, but Llorente had forbidden it. "Why do you ask that?"

"This country hasn't changed much since medieval times and neither has its language."

"Are you saying I speak with a medieval dialect?" She couldn't.

He leaned back and nodded with obvious enjoyment.

"And with you being a Highlander, I'm sure you recognize medieval when you come across it." *Ha!*

His lips curled at the side. Not quite a smile. "So the Scot and the Andorran. We're no' so different."

She was decidedly different from *everything* that he was. "I'm *Castilian*," she snapped, surprising herself. That information rarely came out sounding like a declaration. Next to a Scot she could be proud of anything, she supposed.

"A hot-blooded Castilian, then? Collared with Cleopatra's

jewel." Never taking his eyes from hers, he lifted his glass and growled over the rim, "Fascinatin'."

She barely prevented her lips from parting in disbelief. *Straight to the heart.* How did he manage to brush so closely to her secrets? He didn't *know* her. He knew nothing. He was merely provoking for reaction. . . .

The next several minutes were odd. If she tilted her head, his eyes narrowed. If she touched her hair, he scrubbed his good hand across the back of his neck. When she drank more, he stilled, as if awaiting something. That was one thing she realized about him—he was always scrutinizing, always weighing, and deciding. She wondered what he'd decided about her.

Here she sat drinking with her worst enemy—well, worst after Pascal—but not because she wanted to be near the man. Certainly not that. And not because she'd forgotten what he was. He was a Highlander, and it was because of people like him and his miserable kinsmen—those cursed killers for hire—that the general had enough power to force her to his will. He was her enemy and she didn't care.

She'd heard that liquor made one brash, but now Annalía knew it also made one uncaring. Underhanded, even.

Because she would use him.

What if *she* could hire him and his men to help her? What if she could tempt him to *want* to help her? If she was one of *those* women—if the whispers about her were true—then surely she could have some effect on a man.

What did she have to lose by trying?

Before her courage failed her, she stood, then walked around the desk toward him. When he quickly stood as well, she stopped and reached back for her glass—just one more little sip for courage. . . . She turned back and he was directly in front of her, looking at her face in his intense, watchful manner.

He took a gentle, shuffling step closer, as though he didn't want to frighten her away. She backed up to the desk, but he kept drawing nearer, surrounding her with his body, with his appealing scent. And some common, base part deep inside her reveled in his size, reveled in the heat she could feel from his skin.

His gaze caught hers, as if he couldn't stop looking at her. Up so close, she could see how much his eyes had cleared, could see how remarkably dark they were, the irises black like obsidian. And the *way* he looked at her . . . as though he was hungry for her. As though he *lusted,* and understood like no man had before how incredibly much she did, too. She felt like she'd caught fire.

She set her palms against the edge of the desk, wrapping her fingers around it, then nervously licked her lips, unsure of what to do. He must have realized she wasn't leaving, wasn't moving from this spot, because he appeared baffled, his brows drawn. It was as though she could hear him thinking. She knew he was suspicious of her behavior. She also knew he would decide to enjoy now and figure it out later. As if on cue, his expression changed to one of intent.

As she'd seen women do on bridges across Paris at sunset, she brushed her hands up over his chest and then rested them on the back of his neck. When her fingers twined behind him, his breaths hastened. "MacCarrick," she murmured. "Do you . . . like me?"

His gaze was flickering over her face, sometimes resting on her lips, but now meeting her eyes. "Right now I like you very much."

She threaded her fingers in his hair. "After tonight, do you want to be my . . . friend?"

His voice was deep and husky when he said, "Among other things."

"Can I trust you?"

He nodded slowly. "With this? Aye, I'll no' tell a soul."

She frowned at his comment, but went forward with what she had to do. "If I asked you for something, would you want to give it to me?"

He seemed to stiffen at her question, and a muscle in his cheek twitched. Then she had the impression that he was forcing himself to relax. "Anna, I will give you something that you want."

Though he'd turned her words around, she still murmured, "MacCarrick . . ." He bent lower to hear her better, and she whispered against his ear, *"Kiss me, MacCarrick."*

He shuddered.

Her breath against his ear made this mercenary react so strongly? She wondered what her touch might do. If she was the type of woman people accused her of being, then maybe she was also the type of woman who could "bring a man to his knees." She rather liked the thought.

He put his palm on the back of her head, drawing her in. She thought he would kiss her, but he hesitated, as if to let her body grow accustomed to his, as if savoring that he was *about* to kiss her as he had savored the whisky.

The second he placed his lips on hers and slanted his mouth, heat shot through her body. When he kissed down the side of her neck, she sucked in a breath, staggered by the feelings. His hands found her backside and he yanked her into him—hard—until she could feel his erection, huge against her belly. *This is wrong*— His lips were warm and firm and quelled the thought.

He molded her backside with insistent fingers, squeezing her into him, then grasping her around the waist to—oh, *Mare de Déu*—move her pelvis against him. *Wrong!* her mind cried.

Just as she would pull away, he gathered her closer to kiss her earlobe, and she wondered, mystified, why she'd deemed this so terrible. They weren't doing more than pressing bodies together. Of course, he wouldn't make love to her.

Before she had any comprehension of what he was doing, he'd unfastened the top few buttons of her shirt and would've done more if she hadn't seized the next button in her fist. He made some noise as if her action amused him, but he didn't continue. He spread what he'd opened, uncovering her upper chest to her chemise, then placed his hands on her back to arch her to him. To her bewilderment, he groaned deeply and rubbed the side of his face against the tops of her breasts. She *felt* the low guttural sound, and it frightened her, but not more than it exhilarated her.

Her brows drew together as she watched him—he kissed her skin as if he'd lost himself. That's what had happened to her—she'd lost herself. Her mind was separate, as if looking on, noting her body's response as he set her atop the desk to stand between her legs. Her breasts were growing heavy and sensitive, and her own panting breaths sounded loud.

She was embarrassed that he heard her like this, and that he was the cause. Embarrassed that he saw her with her skirts hiked up her legs nearly to her garters and her blouse partially unbuttoned.

"Let me see your hair." He rasped the words against her damp skin, and she trembled. "I know the treasures you hide. I've seen them."

Hazily, she wondered when, but then he kissed at the line of her chemise, and she couldn't bite back a soft moan, the pleasure was so intense. He raised his face to brush his lips over her ear, and she could feel his warm breath there. He'd begun loosening her hair, and she wanted him to.

With each kiss, Annalía wanted to show this brutal Highlander more of her, to bare her breasts and let her hair down so he could run his fingers through it. But when it fell about her, he didn't touch her so gently. He wrapped the ends around his fist as his lips returned insistent against her neck. His tongue flicked her skin, and her eyes flashed open, then slowly slid closed.

But he tensed and drew back, releasing her.

"*Què li passa?*" she murmured. As if coming out of a daze, she opened her eyes and repeated in English, "What is it?"

She heard it then—the coming of riders into the manor's courtyard.

"Stay here," he ordered, his face more menacing than she had ever seen it. "Lock the door behind me and doona come out for any reason. Do you ken?"

In the space of a heartbeat, the fierce look of intent had vanished, replaced by one of barely controlled fury.

When she didn't answer, he grabbed her shoulders. "*Anna, do you understand?*"

"Yes," she began, but the voices of several men sounded, just before a pounding on the front door.

They were Scottish.

"We're looking for Courtland MacCarrick," a man shouted.

MacCarrick relaxed and put his forehead against hers. His hand rested on her face and his thumb stroked her bottom lip. "They're no' known for their timing."

More of them? The thought of additional Highlanders traipsing across her property made her insides roil. She prayed Vitale wouldn't wake.

Now that the fire in her blood had cooled, shame set in. With fumbling hands she pulled her blouse together and turned her face away. He drew back from her and seemed angered by her reaction.

"More Highlanders?"

"Aye. We'll stay until I can ride."

"*Stay?*" She choked out the word. "They don't have permission to be on this mountain. You *will* tell them to leave."

"Always imperious. One day you'll learn that I doona take orders. You might also ken that men like me doona appreciate it when lasses like you try to play with them."

She'd been buttoning her blouse and slowed at his last comment. She knew she'd made a mistake, but still cried, "But they're not welcome here!"

"You said I was no' welcome as well," he grated in an impatient tone. "Yet you were moments away from gladly taking me into more than your home."

She gasped. "I was not! A kiss is a far cry from lying with a man."

"No' just with 'a man,'" he bit out. "With *me*." He pushed forward once more, forcefully wedging himself between her closed knees. His body was hot against her even through her clothes.

"Then I *certainly* was not going to!"

His lips curved into a cruel smile. He put his hand against her backside again, trapping her closer, and growled the words, "I was about to enjoy you on this desk. Rip aside your skirts and take you here like the animal you called me."

"A-Against my will?" she responded unevenly, almost rendered speechless by his words. She tried to inch back on the desk. "Because that's the only way it would happen."

He leaned in to say at her ear, "No' against your will. You'd be begging for me inside you." He lingered there, as if to make sure she heard him, then lightly touched his face down her neck.

She gasped again, her shame deepening because even his words stirred her, made her want his lips against her breasts again, his breath hot against them.

When he drew back from her, his expression was cold. "If you ever try to use your wiles on me again, expect that I'll use you back a thousand times—"

"Court? Are you in there?" one of them called from out side. "Is anybody home?"

He exhaled a long breath, then eased her legs closed to brush down her skirt with great familiarity, as if he *knew* her, as if they'd done this a hundred times. Strangely, that gesture was more confusing to her than anything he'd done before.

"Listen to me. We will no' be long here. Just a couple of days." He turned to walk away.

"And I should take your word for it?" she whispered, but he heard her and strode back once more, his hand shooting out to palm the back of her neck and force her to look up to him.

"Know this, Annalía. You should *never* take my word. When you trust me, you *will* regret it."

"I don't want them here," she said in a low voice. "Any more than I want you."

His expression darkened ominously. "The only thing we respond to is force." He raked his gaze over her. "And you doona have any."

# Six

$\mathcal{A}$s Court made his way through the house, he tried to get a grasp of what had just happened. Staring at her eyes, at her plump lips, he'd had a hard time concentrating, but he'd known that she didn't want him—at least not at first. Her actions had been calculated. She'd had an agenda, and it had been a blow.

He'd finally gotten to kiss her, and he'd been left . . . empty. That she'd seemed to catch on fire like a wick soothed his pride somewhat. Christ, he'd spoken the truth—he'd had a real chance of taking her on the table. And he wouldn't have hesitated.

But now the emptiness turned to ire. He'd truly wanted her while she only wanted something from him—to what end he was sure he'd find out soon enough.

At the front entrance he paused, putting a hand against the wall beside the door, shaking off her effect on him. He curled his fingers against the plaster, willing his body under control, then finally opened the door wide to five of his crew.

"Court!" exclaimed Gavin MacKriel, the oldest of their band. "By God, it's good to see you."

When the man took his shoulders, Court frowned and slapped him on the back with his better hand, then again until Gavin released him and moved on.

MacTiernay, the one-eyed giant, looked him up and down, then punched him in the upper chest in greeting before walking past.

Court stared after him. That was more emotion than Mac-Tiernay had ever demonstrated. Then Niall, his cousin, slapped him on the back, and Liam, the youngest, was about to as well until Court gave him a look of warning. The last inside, Fergus, who'd earned the nickname The Sleeping Scot, actually looked awake and glad to see him.

He showed them in and then on into the parlor. As if he owned the place. "Where are the rest?"

Liam had already nabbed a pear from a fruit-laden bowl in the foyer. At nineteen he was still growing and could eat double his weight in food every day. He took a bite and said between chews, "They *have* been searching for a body for your kin to bury."

"I appreciate the sentiment." Court took a seat at the main table, feeling weak from their greetings. Nothing like Highlanders striking you to get your mind off a woman. "You were that sure I was dead?"

"We followed your pair of Rechazados," Fergus answered as he eased himself into a seat, "then persuaded them to partake in one last conversation. They told us they'd killed you."

"That was the plan. You took out two? We're at forty-seven, then?"

"Forty-seven and counting," Gavin said. "I hope you told them we were coming to kill them."

"Aye, I did. It dinna have the effect I was hoping for, but satisfies now."

Niall stood to survey a wine sideboard. "After we got your message, I sent the rest of the crew to the smuggler's lodge to wait for us."

Niall was to take over their band if anything happened to him, and Court nodded his approval at Niall's decision. They'd stumbled upon the isolated lodge while exploring the back passes along the border with France. It was filled with long-abandoned luxuries, dust-covered crates packed with silver, porcelain, and crystal that some smuggler had never made it back for.

"And I brought your gear," Niall added. "You doona look like you're hurting for clothes, but I bet you miss your weapons."

"You've no idea." When he'd heard riders coming, he hadn't known if he'd finally brought Pascal's men down upon this place. He hadn't known how he'd protect her from them.

"So whose home is this?" Niall asked.

"An Andorran lass's." Court wondered if they could see he was thrown. No battle, no violence had ever made him off balance like this.

Niall gave him a razor-sharp look. "She's bonny?" Yes, Niall could see.

"Aye," he admitted. Moments ago, that beautiful woman had sunk her fingers into his muscles to get closer to him. He'd thought her reaction was real and reveled in it, but if she was willing to manipulate him . . . He caught them regarding him quizzically. "She found me half dead by the river and dragged me back here. No men around, so I've just been lingering on."

"Dragged you? So she's a *big,* bonny Andorran?"

"She and *her horse* dragged me. No, she's just a wee thing. You should see her—a good gust would send her reeling." Court noticed Niall studying him and changed the subject. "Have you heard any news?"

Niall removed a bottle of wine and whistled at the label before saying, "We heard word that Spain might come for its deserters any day now. And if they doona, France will."

"It's about bloody time." Court had been continually disgusted with the lack of action against the invasion. Yes, Andorra was small, but its location was critical, as Pascal well knew. "Where'd you hear this?"

Gavin scratched his neck. "From Otto."

"Otto, huh?" Court's eyes narrowed. "Now why would he be contacting us?"

Gavin hesitated, then said, "He's . . . overextended again."

"He usually is." Which was why Court had broken from the Prussian's company years ago and formed his own. "What's it this time? Sixty against five hundred?" Otto kept his band winnowed down and repeatedly contracted for huge jobs. Great way to make a lot of coin. Sure way to get killed.

"Could be that many," Niall said absently as he returned the bottle and selected another. By the look on his face, this one was even more valuable. Not that Niall was such the wine expert, but he had an uncanny sense for money and could perceive value like a dog could scent a trail.

"And he's coming to us hat in hand?" Court didn't like where this was going. Some of his men didn't mind playing the odds, no matter how bad they were.

Gavin nodded. "We might be able to recoup some of the pay we lost here."

Court shook his head firmly. "We have no' lost it yet."

"No shame in cutting bait," Niall said. "Another crew, those Tyrolean sharpshooters, left without pay."

Gavin added, "The region's unstable and everybody's tails are twitching. No one wants to go head to head with Pascal, especially no' after what he did to you."

Niall removed his gaze from the wine to study Court. "They banged you up good?"

So much that Court was still astonished that he'd lived. "Them and the river. I had to jump blind into the falls, then ride them headfirst."

"And your wrist?" Niall asked. Court had never met a more sharp-eyed person than his cousin. "Looks odd and you're favoring one hand."

His wrist should look odd, since it was very stiff and sorer than usual, due solely to the fact that ten minutes ago he'd had both hands splayed on Annalía's lush bottom. "Broke it. Had a cast on it. I think another week till I'm right."

"A cast?" Niall asked with disbelief. "What's wrong with leather between the teeth until it stops paining you? Casts are for bairn and lasses when they fall off their ponies."

Only Liam and Gavin laughed. The impassive MacTiernay had never indicated he was capable of it, and Fergus had already crossed his arms over his chest and was slumped back asleep.

"I dinna have any say on the cast." Court gingerly flexed his fingers. "The Andorran did it when I was knocked out." He frowned at Niall, who was returning to the table with the bottle uncorked and a clutch of wine glasses. Perhaps they ought not be drinking this bottle if it was dearer than the one that Niall had whistled over.

"So how long were you out?" Niall asked as he poured a round.

"Two days." Though Court wasn't normally a wine drinker, he accepted a glass, curious to see what it'd taste like. His drink of choice was whisky because it rendered him as jovial as he'd ever get. Wine? Not so much. "I'm just surprised Pascal dinna find me in all this time."

"He's searching the countryside, but not as he might in the past because he's been busy. Hark this—he's taking a bride," Niall said. "She's some Spanish aristocrat, supposed to have royal blood or some such. Marrying her will give him more claim to Spain than any of the generals before him."

Gavin drank and gave Niall an impressed look as if he'd grown the grapes, then added, "Rumor is that she's happy about the nuptials."

Court leaned back, disgusted. "Then they deserve each other."

Liam drank his glass in one gulp. "So where's this cast-making lass?"

"She'll be in her room." He surveyed his men, trying to imagine what she'd think of them, and added, "Most likely for the night."

Liam got a sly look on his face. "You tire her out so much that she canna leave her bed?"

He scrubbed a hand over his mouth and couldn't help saying, "I wish."

Niall raised his eyebrows. "A lass Court MacCarrick canna have? That breed does no' exist."

He exhaled loudly. "It does in the Andorran mountains."

They'd simply taken over the house, ransacking the wine cellar, flipping through books, pilfering a stash of tobacco, and Court suspected they'd already cleaned out the larder. Two hours and over a dozen bottles of wine between them later, Court was discovering that the stone of weight he'd lost ensured he was drunker than usual.

He'd just pushed aside his last glass when he heard the front door groan open. "I'll be back," he said, his words just shy of slurred as he dashed out of his chair.

He caught up with Annalía on the path and took her shoulder. "Where do you think you're going?"

"To sleep *elsewhere*." She flung her shoulder back to break his grip.

"No, I doona believe you will," he drawled, finally releasing her.

"You think to order me in my own home?"

He said easily, "Aye."

She smoothed her hair. She'd put it up again, but it was looser. He suspected she still might be drunk.

"It's one thing to remain in a house with an incapacitated patient," she said, with her accent thicker than he'd ever heard it. "It's quite another to be an unmarried young woman staying with a gang of mercenaries."

"Ah, Annalía, you have no' even met them." Suddenly, he wanted them to see her, to understand what he'd been tempted with. He took her arm.

"What are you doing? MacCarrick?"

He hated that he liked hearing her say his name. She'd whispered it in his ear while testing her wiles on him—wiles that infuriated him because he knew if she'd had any experience . . .

He swung her inside and into the parlor, announcing, "And this would be the lady of the house. Lady Annalía Llorente."

The men rose and her eyes widened at their size even as their eyes narrowed at her. When Court moved to sit and watch, they advanced on her until she backed to the wall.

" 'Bonny' was a bit of an understatement, then?" Niall said over his shoulder.

Court shrugged and retrieved his glass.

As Gavin introduced himself, he took her hand and kissed it. Court could see he was rubbing her skin with his thumb, and he wondered why that raised his hackles and why he now regretted showing her off. Gavin told the others in Gaelic that they had to feel her hands.

They did so, one at a time, introducing themselves, with Liam exclaiming, "You have yourself some wee, soft hands."

Niall alone didn't touch her. Probably because he'd determined exactly what Court was thinking.

Their petting seemed to put her in a panic, but her reaction to the men didn't surprise him. They were all huge and scarred. Fergus was missing fingers and MacTiernay was taller than all of them and had only one eye. She'd been intimidated by Court, too, but she'd still initiated a kiss. Whatever she wanted of him, she wanted it very badly indeed.

"Lady Annalía, thank you for allowing us to stay here," Niall said.

"She didn't," Court informed them. "She wants all of us gone."

She put her chin up. "Mr. MacCarrick, my first priority is to the people of this place. Even if you are not allied with Pascal any longer, your presence still jeopardizes everyone here."

Court gave a harsh laugh. "Now that sounds very noble, but why do you no' tell them what you told me at the door? You want us gone to preserve appearances."

She didn't back down. "That is important as well. If my reputation is tarnished, I will not be able to make the match that is expected of me."

Niall muttered, "Court, she's right—"

He interrupted, "You were planning to ask me for something tonight, were you no'? Do it now."

She opened her mouth to speak, then closed it and turned her face away.

"Perhaps in the morning you'll be inclined to make your request. Perhaps we'll be inclined to hear it—if we stay here."

She faced him again. "Very well, stay. We can speak when I return—"

"You stay here, too."

She straightened her choker, appearing so miserable he almost relented. He could feel his men watching him and her, knew they were confounded by his behavior.

She swallowed and then said in a pained tone, "Yes, of course. I extend my welcome to your men and look forward to our meeting."

"Go to bed, Annalía. You'll need your rest after the night we've had." She looked like she'd been struck, gasping a breath before sweeping from the room.

Niall didn't wait until she was even out of earshot. "What the hell is wrong with you?"

"Doona start on me. She's no' as helpless as she appears and she's been insulting me regularly for a week." When Niall looked unconvinced, Court added, "She's calculating and she's spoiled, and tonight she sought to manipulate me, cutting her teeth and testing her wiles." He ran a hand over the back of his neck, uneasy because he knew if she'd had any experience . . . she could've worked him like dough. "It was no' right."

Niall shook his head. "I doona believe I've ever seen you treat a lass this poorly."

"That's because you've no' met a woman like her. I'm telling you, you've never known such an arrogant female in your life. Tomorrow you'll see."

# Seven

*A*nnalía had awakened before dawn to wretched memories of her deeds the night before.

She'd known several unsavory things about her character. She'd realized flaws in her morality apparently inherent flaws. Now she knew another fact: In the presence of whisky, the simple application of a man's lips to her own, and then to her chest, induced her to lose her mind.

And this morning she would have to ask that Philistine for his help in front of his hulking . . . associates. She would force herself to do it, even though she knew that *if* he did decide to help her, he would first make her . . . grovel.

But by no means did she count on his assistance. Before the sun had risen, she'd dragged Vitale from bed and instructed him to have Iambe ready. She was due at Pascal's today, and if she couldn't persuade the Highlander to help her, then she was gone. She'd left her travel bags in the stable, confident that if she needed to leave in a hurry, she could.

Yet Vitale had quarreled with her over her plan because he didn't want her to leave under any circumstances, whether she could sway the mercenaries or not.

Even lusty old Vitale feared what a monster like Pascal would do to her on their wedding night. She wasn't as nervous as she had been, though. She quite liked kissing, and that had been with a ruffian she *loathed*. The rumors had it that Pascal was very meticulous about his dress and cleanliness, so truly, how much worse could it be?

She'd returned to her room before the Highlanders had risen and had taken extra care with her hair and dress. Now that she heard them milling about, she descended.

When she approached the parlor, she had to bite her tongue to keep from screeching at their boots on the table, at the smell of tobacco cloying inside the room, at the food they'd already rooted through.

*Mare de Déu!* There were empty bottles of wine everywhere. She glanced around, eyes wide. Had more Highlanders come in the night? No, just the six of them had run through the abundant supply in the sideboard and raided their collection in the cellar.

They saw her then, and she forced a smile to her face. "Good morning, gentlemen," she said, pleasantly enough. When they stood and seemed as if they might approach her, no doubt to touch her hands again, she backed to the doorway and pressed her palms against the molding behind her. "I trust you slept well."

"Aye. Thank you for your hospitality." She thought that one was Niall. They'd introduced themselves last night, but all their names had sounded the same, alike in their oddness and unfamiliarity. More ridiculous, every surname began with *Mac*.

"Should we no' cut through the chatter and get to what you wanted to ask me?" MacCarrick muttered. He appeared exhausted, his eyes bloodshot again, and when she'd walked in he'd been rubbing his forehead.

A brittle smile. "Of course, Mr. MacCarrick. Your directness is always . . . refreshing."

He raised his eyebrows. "Refreshing, is it now? How did you put it before? Aye, I remember. You said my people lacked delicacy."

She could feel herself blushing. These mercenaries looked embarrassed *for* her. She hated this man. *Hated* him. But she would do whatever it took to help Aleix. *Remember that, Annalía.* "I would like to hire you to help me and my family."

He smirked, clearly relishing her discomfiture. "And just what would you have us do?"

She was a private and mistrustful person by nature, and above all else she was proud, but she would have to overcome these traits for they didn't serve her now. "M-My brother, Aleixandre Llorente, has been captured by Pascal."

She scanned the room to see their reactions. The youngest one was about to say something, but then there was a sound under the table, as if he'd been kicked. He shut his mouth. What had he been about to tell her? Did he know something?

MacCarrick insolently waved her on, and with effort she continued, "He is the only family I have left, and he is in Pascal's jail. I would pay to have him freed. I would pay more than Pascal."

MacCarrick asked, "Why would you think he's still alive?"

She felt the blood leaving her face at the thought of Aleix dead, and to her shame her eyes watered. She found herself twining her fingers in front of her, then forced her hands to her sides.

The older man hissed something to MacCarrick in a foreign language.

MacCarrick shot him a look and snapped, "It's a valid question."

She didn't know how to handle these people. She'd been taught a perfect stitch and elegant table manners, but no one had instructed her on how to negotiate with ruthless men. Her idea of trying to manipulate MacCarrick with a kiss last night had been laughably far off the mark, but if she was as everyone thought, then why hadn't it worked? "He will be alive because he has value to Pascal. The people here love him and would do anything for him. The general will use that as leverage over them."

"Why does he need leverage over them, when he's already terrorized them into submission?" MacCarrick asked as he leaned back in his seat. He sounded gloating about the fact.

"He terrorized them? Or his *lackeys* terrorized them?" She regretted her words the second she said them.

He glanced around to the men with his eyebrows raised as if she'd just proven some theory, then his lips curled into a mean, mocking smirk. "Run along, Annalía. We'll be here for only a few days more."

This cretin was ordering her in her own home, and yet she pleaded, "But I will pay you!"

"Do you have coin on the property?"

"No, but I have jewelry. Priceless jewelry."

He gave her a patronizing expression. "And where could we sell that around here?"

"Then my fortune. If you free Aleix, he can get it for you. I'll give it freely."

"Canna imagine your 'fortune' would be the kind of money we usually command."

"That's because your imagination is limited!" When the man called Niall and two others chuckled, she again commanded herself to bite her tongue. "Take anything you like in this house, anything! I'm sure you could find your pay here."

"Anything, then?" he asked with a strange expression. Niall

shook his hung head, then rose to leave. The four followed him out.

Still she nodded eagerly. "Just name your price, Mr. Mac-Carrick. I will gladly pay it."

"Then it's settled." He looked her over shamelessly. "I want you."

"P-Pardon?"

"You heard me. I can sense desperation and you're there. You were willing to kiss me last night to sway me to your cause, and I'll bet you're willing to do more than that. Why no' do it with me?"

Her eyes went wide. *Hate you!*

"I will free him, but before I do, I'll get to enjoy you," he said, his tone smug. "Those are my terms."

She bit out each word when she said, "There is material wealth here that could satisfy even you."

"You mean 'someone such as me.' Forget it, then." He unfolded a dated newspaper, shook it out to read, then kicked his boots up on the table. "I'll no' work for you for anything less than you," he said behind the paper.

Her brows drew together in bewilderment. Those were Aleix's boots, stolen. And they were carelessly propped on her table. Hers and Aleix's table. She and her brother, who was more like a father to her, had breakfast there each morning and talked about the ranch. Aleix was gone. No one would help her and she didn't understand why.

The other men returned and sat. She dimly noted that they appeared angry.

The realization struck her that for the first time in her life she truly needed help and had asked for it, and no one would give it to her. For the first time in her life she'd been . . . vilely propositioned.

As he continued reading, ignoring her, MacCarrick

crossed his ankles, and a bottle by his feet drew her attention. She recognized that particular wine because it had been bottled the year of Aleix's marriage to his beloved Mariette and had been stored with great care. They had saved it to toast the birth of their first baby. The wine never, never should have been drunk.

Yet it sat on the table, opened and nearly full, forgotten among the refuse they'd scattered.

She began to move, and frowned because she had little idea of what she was doing. She watched her feet advancing her toward MacCarrick, and perceived her hand closing hard around the bottleneck just before she raised it high and poured the wine on his head. The growling noise in his throat was getting louder and louder, and still, when the bottle was empty, she dropped it, hitting his thick skull. She thought he bellowed, thought someone might be restraining him. She said in Catalan to no one in particular that the wine had had meaning for her and that they could all go to hell.

The grandfather clock struck eight. She plucked up her skirt and waltzed from the room. She grabbed her gloves at the table by the door, then strolled to meet Vitale in the stable.

It was time to go riding.

MacTiernay and Niall wouldn't release him until they saw through the window that she was riding away. Court had been so shocked, he'd hardly comprehended what she was doing. Then, when he'd lunged for her, MacTiernay snagged him as Niall caught his other arm.

He shrugged them loose and whipped his drenched head around to find Niall glowering at him.

"Again. What the hell is wrong with you, Court?"

"With *me*? Did you no' just see the most arrogant woman ever to live pour a bottle over me?"

"You deserved it, every drop of it. Talking to her that way after she asked us for help."

Gavin added, "And turning her down? Granted, we doona go about doin' good deeds, but there's wealth here like I've never seen. She could pay us just as well as anyone else."

Court wiped his sleeve over his face. "In case you dinna realize this, she *never asked* for anything, and in case you dinna understand, she just told us all to go to hell." He shook his hair out and wine splattered everywhere. "Still, I was going to help her. Niall, you ken that I would. I would have before this. I only wanted to bait her a bit. Just for a day."

Niall's expression was incredulous. "I've seen you happily snap necks and slit throats, but I've never seen you be callous to someone who is weaker than you and in such a vulnerable position. Her only family is in that bastard's cell, and you would use that over her? To *bait* her?"

Court ran his hand over the new knot on his head. "God damn it, I said I'd get him out."

"Aye. Because you're the one who put him there."

# Eight

When Annalía arrived in the village of Ordino, she heard dogs barking to each other from unseen vantages, yet nothing else stirred. Although it was early evening, the streets were eerily quiet.

She and Iambe clacked along the slate drive to the largest building, a sizable home built of ancient stone. She'd seen it before on visits here and wondered what had happened to the people who actually owned it.

She'd just reached the front entrance when a man strode from the inside. Her eyes widened. He was one of the Rechazados—she could tell by the cross tattoo on his bare arm. She'd heard of these legendary assassins, had heard they were every bit as evil as the Highlanders, but colder. Without warning he wrenched her down from the saddle, dropping her to her feet.

While he seized her bags, an unkempt deserter in a ragged Spanish military uniform arrived to take Iambe. She wanted to make sure he cared for her horse properly, but the Rechazado snapped his fingers for her to draw closer. She called on every ounce of bravery she had to walk toward him, toward what her whole being knew was a *threat*.

The women in the valley had said you never saw emotion, never could detect when they would strike. Another had admitted softly that the first hint her sister had that they were about to violate her had been when she hit the ground.

He snatched her arm to drag her up the steps to the front doors, then inside the dimly lit house. She reasoned with herself that the Rechazados were known to follow their orders to the letter. To the point of death they would fulfill their command, and surely Pascal would have commanded them not to touch her.

They climbed a sprawling staircase that led to an even darker landing. The room he shoved her into was the last, in the farthest corner of the house. Inside, he emptied her bags on the bed and rifled through her clothes. With a malevolent look, he exited, but he didn't lock her in. Of course there was no reason to expect her escape.

She exhaled a wavering breath, then surveyed her surroundings, surprised to find the room was large and looked comfortable enough with plenty of rugs and candles and a clean bed. The window was raised and overlooked a lantern-lit courtyard. Had she been expecting a cell? Yes, because she'd thought of herself as condemned.

She washed off the travel grime as best as she could with the water at the dresser, then changed from her mud-coated habit behind the door. After rinsing and repinning her hair, she folded her garments back into her bag, hung her dresses, which were *severely* wrinkled, then she did the only thing left to do—she sat on the edge of the bed and waited, having no idea what to expect.

An hour had passed—during which she relived her confrontation of the morning, envisioning scenarios where she could shock MacCarrick right back and leave *him* gaping—when the door opened. A pretty young woman about her age sauntered in, and Annalía's heart leapt. Was she coerced into being here as well? They could be allies!

"So you're to be my stepmother," the woman said with a dismissive smirk.

Pretty until she opened her mouth, that is.

Annalía hadn't foreseen this, but it made sense that the much older Pascal would have children. "If you're Pascal's daughter, then I suppose I am. What's your name?"

"Olivia."

"And exactly how many more stepchildren am I to have?"

"All but me have been disowned or have fled him." She tilted her head at Annalía. "You look so distressed. Aren't you excited about the nuptials?" Olivia was taunting her.

"Would you be happy in my situation?"

She shrugged impudently, ignoring Annalía to walk to the window and scan the courtyard.

"Olivia, do you know if my brother is safe?"

For long moments, she waited, then turned, as if to size up Annalía and determine if it was worth it to spare a kindness to her. "Llorente lives."

"If he were dead, would you lie to me?"

"Yes," she answered without hesitation. "Now come with me. Your new lord awaits."

Annalía followed, but only because she was ready to get this meeting concluded. She couldn't imagine what the general would look like. He'd probably have a cruel face, with harsh angles as MacCarrick did. Perhaps that would be wishful thinking for him to have at least the Highlander's looks.

"He's in there." Olivia jerked her chin toward a door. When

Annalía's feet wouldn't move of their own volition, it seemed, Olivia snapped, "Go on!"

Annalía pushed open the door, making her manner brisk. And was dumbfounded when Pascal turned to her.

Annalía had never seen a more beautiful man in her life.

Court stared into his just-poured glass, sinking back and propping his boots on a low table, attempting to relax after a day that had started out . . . *wrong* and had only gotten worse. At a table nearby, Liam, Niall, and Fergus played cards, though Fergus yawned repeatedly, while Gavin smoked a pipe full of expensive tobacco. MacTiernay rocked with his eyes—or rather his eye—closed, probably reliving old battles.

When Court had finally gotten control of his temper after the wine incident and had shaken his dogged hangover, Niall had suggested he put himself in Annalía's shoes. After all, they'd hit her property in a manner a plague of locusts would aspire to, and Court had spoken to her in a way that clearly no man had ever dared. Court also suspected that being fondled by his crew had made her . . . skittish. Creatures that got skittish always came out biting if backed into a corner, and she had.

So he'd taken Niall's advice and left her alone for the day. Though he'd wanted to see her later, Vitale had told him that the people here would "give" them until sundown to leave, and that the mademoiselle was so upset by "MacCarrick's vile proposition" that she was staying on the other side of the mountain for the night.

He could swear the chit was put on the earth just to make him feel guilty. Or try to. Luckily, he wasn't one to wrestle with guilt.

Usually on a night like this when they weren't working, Court would sit and dream about Beinn a'Chaorainn, his run-down estate in Scotland. He would picture the possibilities that no one else could seem to see, and he would count the days until he'd paid for it completely and all those hills, trees, fields, and the ancient stone keep would be *his*.

For a man cursed to have little else, Beinn a'Chaorainn kept him living. Yet now thoughts of Annalía somehow overrode dreams of his land. Damn it, so he'd treated her poorly. He was most likely going to get her brother for her tomorrow night, if Llorente was still alive. . . .

A violent pounding on the front door interrupted his brooding. "Liam, go answer the bloody door."

Liam laid down his cards, then tromped from the room. Minutes later, he called out in a bored tone, "Court, there's a pitchfork rebellion here to see you."

"*What?*"

"A collection of doddering old men, torches, and farm tools. I fear for our safety and advise fleeing posthaste."

With a weary exhalation, Court kicked his feet down to stand. When Gavin raised his eyebrows, and MacTiernay and Niall laid hands on their pistols, he shook his head. "I'll take care of this."

At the front door, he found Vitale with a half-dozen men standing behind him, spread out like a rickety fan. Their faces blanched at their first glimpse of Court's expression, and he thought he heard their knees knocking.

"We've had enough of your ill-treating the mademoiselle and stealing the master's belongings and we want you gone," Vitale declared in a moderately even voice. "You've no right to stay on here."

He almost answered, "Might makes right," and slammed the door. Instead, he asked, "Does she know you're doing this? Did she put you up to it?"

"Of course not! She warned everyone to stay clear of you, fearing what you would do."

Did she think he would hurt the people here? Did *she* fear him? Is that why she'd avoided him when they were alone in the house? He'd kind of thought of the last few days as a game they played. "Vitale, if you leave now, we'll no' hurt you. You know you canna fight us."

"We might not be able to, but we'll gather more and then you'll be sorry."

Liam piped in over Court's shoulder, "We're all aquiver."

Court gave him a look that made him skulk from the foyer. When Vitale opened his mouth to say more, Court's patience wore thin. "Vitale, doona make me kill you." Seeing the old man's eyes fill with dread, he felt like the bully he was. For the first time in many years, the feeling grated.

As he was shutting the door, Vitale cursed him in a diatribe of French. Court narrowed his eyes. His French was not as strong as it could be, but he thought Vitale had said . . . *le mariage.*

The wedding?

"Lady Annalía," Pascal said in a deep voice. "Welcome to my home." The room's lantern light reflected off his shining medals and his thick, dark hair.

He walked toward her with his perfectly manicured hands outstretched to grasp hers. He was so debonair, his heart-stopping smile so engaging, she raised them to him, until she remembered this man was a murderer and abruptly dropped them.

He took them anyway, though she turned her face away, recoiling.

"My dear, Annalía." He rudely called her by her first name as though their engagement had lasted more than one week and wasn't born of coercion.

"Pascal." Her tone was scathing.

He drew back, releasing her hands to scrutinize her.

"I didn't think you could be as lovely as they've said, but you are."

She stared at the ceiling and he tsk-tsked. "Won't say thank you? Now where are your famed manners?"

"Famed?"

"Quite. All the Andorrans love to whisper about the royal concealed in their midst. How else do you think I found out about you?"

She gave him a blasé look.

"They say other things about your simmering Castilian blood," he murmured, drawing closer. "I can hardly wait to get to the bottom of the rumors."

"My manners?" she hastily asked. "Is that why you chose me?"

He moved to a polite distance, but gave her a look that let her know he was patronizing her. "No, I will wed you because marrying the daughter of the oldest family in the land is strategic."

"Why all this trouble for tiny Andorra? I can understand why someone like you would set your sights so low, but why not Monaco?" She tapped her cheek. "Isn't the Vatican a country?"

He chuckled. She hadn't meant to entertain him—she'd meant to make a point.

Taking a seat behind his desk, he motioned for her to sit as well. She didn't. He motioned more sharply, and something unsettling flashed in his eyes.

Gritting her teeth, she sat. "You want Spain, don't you? Those are the rumors."

"Yes. After I've solidified my place here."

She gave a sharp scoffing sound. "How original. What would you be? The sixth general *du jour* to try in the last two decades?"

He laughed again, seemingly delighted with her, and the smoothness of the sound grated on her nerves. "I'd be the sixth general to *succeed* in the last fifteen years. But unlike my predecessors, I will have something that the others didn't." He stood to approach once again, then touched her face, and she knew every fear she'd had about him was true.

The queen and her general weren't good rulers, but they had to be better than Pascal. If she could get a message to Aleix, he could warn the outside. "You said in your letter that you would free my brother and his men as soon as we marry. How can I trust you to keep your word?"

"Because my first priority will be your happiness," he said so suavely.

She raised her hand to stop him. "I've agreed to this charade, but I refuse to pretend when it's only you and I."

He inclined his head. "Very well. Llorente will be my supporter. He's descended from kings—he'll be a worthy enticement in the eyes of the people."

"Never."

"Just as you would never agree to marry me?" He smiled down at her. "I've found that all it takes is the right incentive to make anyone do as I wish." When he touched her lip with a too-soft finger, she cringed. "Now there's a dress laid out for you in your room. Go upstairs and get ready for a dinner tonight. We are having guests."

Ordered. *Another* cretin was ordering her. She rose and regarded him with all the arrogance bred into her, then turned to leave.

"And Annalía?" She froze, shoulders tensing. "Any servant found helping you communicate with your brother will be publicly eviscerated."

She turned back to him, lips parted, aghast. His seemingly genuine smile was still in place, his expression earnest. His broad shoulders filled out his uniform and his medals were colorful and proud. Her future husband was perfect.

A perfect monster.

•    •    •

Well into the night, Aleixandre Mateo Llorente pounded on his cell door, yelling until his throat—and the bottoms of his fists—were raw. Today Pascal had notified him that they would be brothers.

Annalía was going to wed a killer thinking to save him, but Aleix knew he would never leave this windowless, dank room alive.

He also knew nothing would prevent her from going through with it, and that conviction ate at his gut. The marriage would only damn them both. How he wished for one minute with her—to convince her that she was no martyr, especially for such a lost cause, to shake some sense into her. "*God damn you all*," he bellowed. "Open this door."

And then someone . . . did, but the shock of light blinded him after so many days of darkness. When his eyes painfully adjusted, he found a young woman there with her hair free and clad in nothing but a gauzy nightgown. His breath whistled in. She was beautiful, even with her eyes heavy lidded as if she were still half asleep. And even with the gun she had trained on him.

"If you don't shut your mouth," she snapped. "I'll kill you myself."

This he never expected. "I apologize if my wish for freedom—and my wish not to *die*—have disturbed your sleep."

She shrugged. "I reside directly above you. You must cease knocking on the door."

"Who are you?"

She frowned. "What purpose would it serve to tell you?"

"A dying man's last wish?"

She shrugged again. "I am Olivia."

She couldn't be his daughter. "Olivia Pascal?" he asked in a low tone.

Her chin went up either proudly or defensively. "*Sí.*"

"I should take your threat more seriously then. If your blood is any indication, you are capable of any atrocity."

Her smile was a cruel curve of her lips. "Very capable. I'm also capable of whistling for the guards to beat you again just on a whim."

In a heartbeat he started for her. She took one step back, but coolly cocked the hammer, her hand steady. "Don't be a fool." Her voice was hard, her face like marble. "I'll do it just so I sleep better."

Assured she would, he moved to lean against the wall, arms crossed. "I've never heard of that. Someone who sleeps better at night *because* they killed someone."

"Who said *killed?* I only have permission to maim you until your sister is wed." She began closing the door. "But I promise to wish them well for you."

Court's hand shot out to wrench Vitale through the doorway. "What did you say?" he demanded as he slammed the door behind him.

The others raised their eyebrows when Court dragged Vitale to the parlor, then tossed him into a chair.

"I said you are a pig, an ingrate. My mistress saved your life—"

"You said something about a marriage."

He refused to answer so Court jostled him until he said, "That's where she's gone!" He gestured heatedly. "To save her brother. The general was holding him to force her."

"She's gone to marry him?"

When Vitale nodded, Niall said, "Aye, Court, a real spoiled, calculating woman. Marrying Pascal to save her brother's life. She's chilling."

"This canna be right. The rumors were that he was marrying some Spanish royal. Not Andorran nobility. How do you account for that?" Court recalled her snapping to him, *I'm Castilian,* but royal?

Vitale hesitated. "Why should I tell you?"

"Because if you do, I might just decide to go get her back."

His eyes widened and he blurted, "She and her brother are the last direct descendants of the ancient House of Castile. They hold the last titles."

"That's impossible. Her father was no' Castilian."

"The titles passed through the mother."

When Court still looked unconvinced, Niall added, "Some houses can pass down matrilineally."

"This is insane. That would make her. . . . That would mean she's . . ." Court could barely believe what he was hearing, even while thinking that this would handily explain her arrogance. "Why did she no' plead for her family's help?"

"She did. As I told you before, she and her brother are estranged from the family and shun that life, but she swallowed her pride and attempted to contact them. We think the message never made it out of Andorra."

Niall whistled and said, "Pascal's a clever bastard. He's going after Isabella's crown."

"But that would mean Annalía's useless to him while her brother's still alive. The minute he has her, Llorente's dead."

"No, he won't be," Vitale declared emphatically. "Pascal will try to use Master Llorente as a figurehead."

"Wrong." Court shook his head, giving Vitale the same expression he knew his five men were giving him as well. "Your master's going to be killed if he is no' already."

"And you just ensured she'd go," Niall muttered from behind him. "Good on you, Court."

He shoved a hand through his hair. "Damn it! Why did she no' ask again or explain everything?"

Vitale cast him a black look. "She told me just before she

rode for Pascal that she would rather be a murderer's wife and possibly have access to free Llorente than be a mercenary's whore and have to trust a fiend like you with her brother's life. She said six or half a dozen—either way was unbearable."

When Court pictured her alone and afraid in Pascal's always darkened home, he had an off feeling in his chest, like a painful shifting. "Oh, bloody hell, Vitale. You might've mentioned this earlier."

"Six or half a dozen?" Niall swore under his breath. "Court, you really are cursed."

# Nine

Last night for the dinner welcoming several odious supporters of the general, Annalía had been given a demure yet luxurious gown. Tonight Pascal had sent her a wholly red, ridiculously low-cut farce to wear. While everyone else enjoyed the village festival, she and Pascal were to have a *private* dinner. Just the two of them. With a dress like this, Annalía could guess why.

She was endeavoring to work it higher over her breasts with hopping and yanking when Olivia entered without knocking. The witch strolled straight to the wardrobe to survey Annalía's clothes with an acquisitive gleam in her eyes. This morning her jewelry had suffered the same indignity.

"What do you want?"

"Tell me," Olivia said casually as she took out, appraised, and returned a gown, "why he is unmarried."

In an instant, Annalía had her whirled around and her hands clenched around Olivia's arms. "You've seen Aleix?" She could tell she'd surprised her. "Have you?"

Olivia shoved her arms loose. "Why isn't he married?" she stubbornly asked again.

Did her curiosity mean she was attracted to Aleix? All the women in the village thought he was handsome with his tall build and his somber, golden-colored eyes. *Mare de Déu*, could this spawn of Pascal have feelings for him? And how could she use that to their advantage?

"He's a widower," she admitted, though she felt as if she dangled a bare foot to a viper. "His wife died in childbirth."

Olivia's face was a blank slate. Annalía couldn't read her. "He has a child?"

"No, his daughter died as well."

Olivia shrugged. So that Annalía wouldn't slap her, she forced herself to imagine that Olivia hiked her shoulders every time something particularly upsetting was said.

"Why are you interested?"

She ran her finger across the coverlet on her way to the window. "I was merely curious about my father's prisoner."

"Let me tell you more," Annalía said as she perched on the edge of the bed. Olivia turned to stare out the window, but she didn't say no.

"Aleix is a good man, a strong man. He lives in a beautiful manor overlooking pastures filled with his champion horses. Each day he watches them run, and though he says nothing, I know how pleased he is with them."

Had her shoulders relaxed somewhat? "He's very intelligent and well read. He went to school overseas at Cambridge. He's somber now, but he wasn't always." Annalía decided then to divulge something she considered private. "He's just very lonely up on his mountain."

Olivia shrugged again. "I can't abide this prattle any longer." She crossed the room to the door.

"He's here, isn't he?" Annalía asked. "I'm in the far end of this house because he's in the other."

Olivia turned, with her gaze flickering over her, and Annalía could tell she was calculating her answer, knew she would never say anything unless it somehow served her. "Pascal wants you downstairs in five minutes. Do not displease him. Both of you will suffer for it."

She hadn't denied that Aleix was here! Though she hadn't said anything to confirm it either, Annalía was convinced. "Thank you for the advice. I'll give you some in return. You're about to be married, Olivia. And to one of those loathsome men last night."

"Hold your tongue. How would you know that?"

"In cruelty and killings, I'll gladly defer to you, but I know marriages. Pascal's in a tenuous position and he just happens to convene a meeting with his supporters? How convenient that each one is socially and politically well connected in Spain—and unwed."

*Coach-and-six.* A father would pay a surprise visit to his daughter at school, and when she walked into the drawing room, he'd introduce her to her new, rich, politically connected fiancé. The man's looks and temperament would be incidental and would rarely match his prospects, but the commerce of marriage would've been decided before the girl ever had any idea she was leaving. With a handshake, her life was snatched from her.

Annalía didn't know that she could wish one of those men even on Olivia.

Olivia glared at her. "You won't manipulate me into dissension. I'll simply ask Pascal." She turned for the door.

"And I'm confident he'll tell you the truth," she called after Olivia before hurriedly tussling with the bodice one last time. Finding no success there, she made sure her choker—or her "collar" as the hateful Scot had called it—was in perfect place. With luck, her formal jewelry, which Pascal had insisted she wear, would be glittery enough to draw his gaze away from her breasts.

Though she dreaded being seen like this, she would never be late and anger the general. Her brother's treatment was to be commensurate with her behavior.

Annalía knew Aleix was in this house, and she planned to persuade Olivia to help them. Though Pascal had said he would kill any servant who helped them, surely he wouldn't hurt his own daughter if she were caught.

Annalía's brows drew together when she recalled how Pascal had smiled at her last night in a way she might describe as lovingly. She'd determined that how strong and proud and good he appeared was directly proportional to how evil he was. Remembering his charisma and startlingly handsome visage in the candlelight, she concluded that yes, he would harm his own daughter.

But then, Annalía thought as she rushed out of her room to meet him, she was ready to take that risk.

After the ordeal of dinner was over, and Pascal had escorted her from the table, Annalía asked for permission to go to her room to rest for an hour. He assured her that she would need her rest *for he had much to teach her* at week's end, then leaned in to kiss her.

When she dared to give him her cheek, patting his chest before turning toward the doorway, he chuckled behind her. "Ah, Annalía," he sighed as she strolled from his sight.

Once alone, she sprinted up the stairs to her room, then wedged a chair against the doorknob. She scrubbed her face with water before sitting at the mirrored vanity, staring blankly. She would become a shell of her old self under Pascal's "tutelage."

She'd said six or half a dozen, but now that she knew Pascal, if she had to relinquish her innocence to one or the other, it would definitely be to MacCarrick. At least she wasn't personally aware of his atrocities.

The general was more handsome than the Scot—more handsome than any man she'd ever imagined—but it didn't matter. Next to Pascal's engaging smile, soft hands, and murderous impulses, the Highlander's scarred face, blunt speech, and aggression were practically seductive.

And still the hours until her wedding kept creeping by. *My wedding.*

People had wondered how she could be around Aleix and Mariette, so completely in love and devoted to each other and not crave her own marriage. It was *because* of their love that she couldn't. She'd seen what God in heaven had had in mind for a man and a woman, had seen their fidelity to each other, and never would she have knowingly slighted herself with a loveless marriage.

*Especially not to the degree that I'm about to* . . . She couldn't think like that! She was able to help Aleix now. She had a value with which to bargain—

Guns went off, their shots popping, making her jump. The lowbrow revelry of the deserters consisted of drunken yells and shooting pistols in the air. Adding insult to injury, her hair was curling, escaping its pins. She reached for her brush. She liked the clacking sound her bracelet made as she raised her arm, and the strokes across her hair were soothing.

Her mind drifted again to thoughts of the Highlander. "I'll no' work for you for anything less than you," he'd said in that rumbling, gruff voice. Despicable man. She prayed Vitale would heed the last command she'd given before riding away—that he stay clear of him. She wished she had. . . . She froze, the brush halting in midstroke.

On that night in the study, had MacCarrick said he'd seen her hair? He had! Her hair and the *other treasures* she'd hidden.

She slammed down the brush. The only place she wore it loose was in the bedroom. MacCarrick had spied on her while she slept! Why would she expect anything different from an ill-mannered ogre like him? He would always do what he wanted regardless of other people's desires and without respect for their feelings.

Annalía was sick and tired of men running roughshod over her. What about her wants? She hated having no control. She confined her hair more tightly than usual, then adjusted her choker, tightening it, still furious—

Something scraped outside near her window. The music trilled on, punctuated by shots, but she thought she heard a noise coming from just below the sash. Maybe the breeze had stirred a lantern.

A huge boot slipped in through the window, followed by a man unfolding to his full height. She scrambled to her feet. "I know you! You were with MacCarrick." He was the oldest one. "Tell me why you're here or I'll scream!"

Another followed him into the room. Oh, not the whelp!

"We're here to take you to safety, lass," the first said as he advanced on her. "And you ken they canna hear you scream."

"To hell with you both!" Mercenaries! Bloody, cursed mercenaries. Taking her to safety, her foot! When the young one captured her wrist she screeched, "Why can't you all just leave me alone?" then lashed out, her nails and teeth bared.

"Ach, Gavin!" he exclaimed, releasing her. "She bit me. I say we tie the little witch!"

"No, no, son, let me handle— Bloody hell! She got me, too! And he forced this task on us to avoid the fighting?" Gavin muttered angrily as he reached for her again. "Lass, we will no' hurt you, you ken? We're saving you."

"If I leave here, you're condemning my brother!" She kicked at his legs, but her skirts got in the way. "So I'm not leaving!" When he seized her wrists she struck wildly, yet it was only a matter of time. To her fury, he bound her hands.

"Listen—MacCarrick is checking the jail for him right now. If he's there you'll both be freed and we'll take you to a safe place."

Her stomach roiled. "But he's not *in* the jail!"

Gavin frowned at that. "Truly?" he asked as he forced a gag on her. "Well, we'll, uh, we'll let Court figure this one out."

She shouted against the gag and swung her bound hands at him, but he deflected the blow.

"Liam!"—he jerked his chin at her traveling bags—"Grab those and stow some clothes."

Liam set to work punching ball gowns and lace and stockings without a care.

She shook her head forcefully and spoke against the cloth. Idiot! Pascal would kill him!

"Ach, wee one, we will no' treat you poorly. Everything will work out as it should," Gavin assured her, as he tossed her over his shoulder.

She dug her nails into his back with every ounce of frustration she felt. When he tensed but continued on, she screamed in fury yet only heard a pitiful, muffled sound.

# Ten

$S$tealing Annalía was proving disappointingly easy. A bribe for information, a bout of sequestered fighting with Spanish deserters drunk from the festival, and a twenty-minute decoy were all that had separated Court's men from her.

From a distance, Court spotted Liam giving him a salute. Farther ahead rode Gavin with Annalía. Court frowned to see her kicking within his arms before Gavin spurred his horse to ride for the lodge.

Court had decided not to take the time to meet the rest of his crew, and since he thought she'd go eagerly once they'd told her their plan, he'd sent his oldest and youngest to retrieve her.

At the same time, Court, Fergus, Niall, and MacTiernay had fought deserters and checked the jail, opening every cell just for the hell of it, but Llorente wasn't there. Annalía might be unwilling now, but once she recovered from the news of her brother, she'd be glad they'd saved her.

He raised his rifle, resting the warm barrel against his

shoulder, then signaled the others to ride out in the opposite direction. They took a false route away from town, then doubled back toward the northeast corner of Andorra, heading for the lodge. From there they followed a hidden smuggler's route, speeding through the winding ravines that continued ever upward in elevation.

When the trail tapered and the terrain made them slow their pace, Niall rode up alongside him. "I've been thinking."

"What about?" he mumbled.

"About the way you've been treating the bonny Andorran. And about why you slept in her room last night."

Court turned back to see if the others could hear. Fergus was nodding off and MacTiernay was too far back. "More comfortable bed, Niall. Now drop it."

"We've established that your behavior is off."

"No—"

"What we need to know is why," Niall interrupted.

"I'll be damned before I let you study me. It's my business."

"I'm your cousin. MacCarrick is my clan, too. What you do does concern me."

"How could this—"

"The curse."

"Bloody hell, doona start on that." They closed in on the lodge, the lodge where they would drop this conversation. From their vantage, he could already see it down the mountain. His brows drew together. Why the hell was the place bright with light this late?

"You canna ignore it any longer." Lowering his voice, Niall said, "You reacted as you never have before." His horse, sensing a barn and rest, tried for a trot, but Niall reined him in. "I'd thought that part of you was simply dead, and was glad of it, but it's no'."

Court hiked his shoulders. "This will be done soon. I'll get her to safety, and then it's finished." They'd planned to free her and her brother and get them to the lodge, but if Llorente was dead, Court had promised Niall he'd see the girl to a safe house near Toulouse.

"You will leave her behind in France?" he asked as they rode into the rickety stable.

"Yes," Court said firmly, but damn it all, he'd hesitated a slight second and Niall knew it. Something *was* off with him, his reaction to her unique. He was as confounded about it as Niall was.

"Damn it, Court, if you hurt her, you'll never be right. Look at Ethan—that's as wrong as a man can get."

Court's eldest brother, Ethan, was a fearsome man in both looks and deed, and his fiancée's mysterious death had only fueled the rumors surrounding—

Shrieks interrupted his thoughts. From inside sounded Annalía's screams, punctuated by loud crashes and all the men cheering.

They heard it just as they were dismounting. He and Niall shared a look, then ran into the house. They found Liam standing outside a room, egged on by thirty raucous Highlanders, as he raised his arms over his head and advanced under a barrage of vases, candleholders, shoes, and boxes. An outraged screech sounded with each hurled object.

Court elbowed through the men, who now cheered him and slapped his back to see him alive, until he reached Liam. Court tapped him on the shoulder and cocked his eyebrows, and Liam happily backed away. The men grew quiet.

Court almost felt sorry for her as he assumed his most threatening expression and readied to enter. He put himself in the line of fire, barely dodging a crystal vase filled with packing straw, but he never slowed his ominous stride toward her.

He caught her eyes, saw her in a clinging fire-red dress, with her hair curling and free and her breasts nearly spilling out, and his jaw dropped. In a thunderstruck tone, he said, "Anna?" just as she brained him with a candleholder.

Aleix woke late in the night to the sound of many footsteps descending the stairs. He rubbed his eyes, frowning into the darkness.

The guards never came this late. Comprehension stabbed at him, and he knew why they would this night.

He was about to be executed.

"Papa." Olivia's voice? She sounded as though she were on the stairs as well. "Perhaps you shouldn't act hastily with Llorente."

"What do you mean?" Pascal asked.

"I believe this is a very delicate time. The prisoner is beloved by these people." Her voice was laced with disgust. "His execution could be the catalyst they need to rebel again."

Aleix shook himself. She was right. It would enrage them.

"And this could be the last straw for Spain." The footsteps halted outside his room. "You know they are on the verge of retrieving their deserters. If they decide to become involved . . ."

*Damn it,* Aleix thought, *that's what I've wanted for months.*

"What do you suggest?"

"We must not act rashly. I know it was infuriating that she was taken, but instead of killing her, I suggest you retrieve her and carry out your plan to marry, solidifying your claim. Afterward you can dispose of Llorente, supplanting him in the people's affections."

*Retrieve? Taken?* Perhaps they had some ally who'd prevented the nuptials. His heart leapt at the thought. The first hope he'd felt in days.

"But she's tainted," Pascal said. *Tainted?*

Olivia asked, "Do you think the Highlanders will use her?" *Those animals took Annalía?*

"It doesn't matter if they do or don't—she'll be ruined in everyone's eyes. Our guests will see to that."

Aleix struggled not to yell, struggled not to ram his head against the walls in rage. Why would the Highlanders do that when they worked for Pascal? When they'd defeated Alcix and his men not two weeks ago for the bastard.

"The benefits of marrying her will still outweigh the detriments. Think of Spain, Papa. And if she does carry a child, she can have an . . . accident and you can marry again."

A pause. Alex could picture the general's thoughtful expression. Finally, he said, "I suspect it's too late, but I will try."

"I think that's a wise decision."

"You always were my most cunning child, Olivia. Cold, just like me."

"Yes, Papa. Just like you."

*That bitch.*

Annalía could see MacCarrick's expression turn menacing, his body tensing as he rubbed his temple. She snatched a pitcher from the straw-lined crate and readied it to throw.

"Doona think of it," he warned in a rasp, scowling at her weapon.

She reared back her arm, just about to hurl it.

"I said"—he seized one wrist, then the other in one hand, then set the pitcher down—"*no.*"

"And I've told you," she bit out as she kicked his knee, "to go to hell, *bèstia!*"

Still holding her wrists in a manacle-like grip, he set her away so she couldn't reach him with her pointy slippers and doubtless so he could gape further at her dress—the Pascal special she'd been trapped in. When the two ruffians had carried her inside this hovel and had set her on her feet with her hands bound, displaying her like a prize, she'd been forced to watch in horror as her breasts had nearly spilled out in front of all these men.

MacCarrick began to speak, then closed his mouth, never taking his eyes from her chest.

"You are despicable!" she cried. "Is that why you kidnapped me? Because you wanted me? Because of one miserable kiss?"

At the last, she thought she heard murmuring just outside the door. MacCarrick turned to glower, but everyone had disappeared from view. "Doona flatter yourself," he grated over his shoulder before facing her again, this time actually looking at her *face*.

"Then why?"

"I have my reasons. Chief among them is revenge against Pascal."

"But why me?" she demanded. "When will you return me?"

"We will no'."

"But you must! You don't understand!"

"Doona understand that he was holding your brother's life over you to get you to marry him? Doona understand what you are?"

She labored for breath. "Y-You know that the only thing keeping my brother alive is my marrying Pascal? Why in God's name would you take me?"

"Your brother's gone, lass."

"No, MacCarrick. He is not."

"Why do you say that?"

"I have it on good authority that as of tonight he still lived."

He shook his head. "We checked the jail for him. He was gone."

She sneered the words. "That's because Pascal is keeping him at the main house."

"And who told you that?"

She put her chin up. "A reliable source." She knew he

would scoff that she believed Olivia. And truthfully, Olivia had never *said* he was there. But Annalía *knew*.

"Tell me."

When she didn't answer, he said, "Then I'll assume you're lying and will no' listen to you anymore."

"Fine. Pascal's daughter told me."

"Very reliable source you've gotten yourself."

"You won't believe me, but know this, I won't believe you. He isn't dead, yet he might be after your efforts today if I don't get back there!" She marched past him, but he caught her around the waist, spinning her back into the room. "You can't keep me here!"

"Aye, I can. I'll no' let you risk your life when there's nothing to gain."

"It's my risk to take!"

"No' anymore," he said so easily.

"And just what do you intend to do with me?"

"We'll wait here for a couple of days, then I'm taking you to a posting house in Toulouse. It's safe there. You can contact your family."

Her hands balled into fists. "And I should just trust that your intention is to get me to safety? Out of the kindness of your heart? I seem to recall you saying 'Never trust me, Annalía.'" She lowered her voice and mocked his Scottish accent. "'I'm bluidy bad and ye wilnah liv tae regret it, Annha-leha.'"

Outright laughter from the next room. He turned with a scowl, then faced her again. "I never said I was *bad*."

"I took license!" She fought to dampen her temper. "I am . . . sorry. I just want to come to some terms." When he appeared unmoved, she resorted to begging. Clasping her hands together, she said, "I will agree to what you . . . to what you said before, but please—please—let me return to Pascal." Instead of this softening him, he appeared to grow even angrier.

"Forget it. The plan goes ahead."

"But I saved your life!"

"And I canna tell you how much I appreciate that."

*Loathe you.* So she wouldn't reach out her hands to strangle him, she crossed her arms over her chest. His gaze flickered over her breasts again as if he couldn't stop himself from leering.

And as easily as that, his mind was again on bedding her. "You are a rutting Scottish animal just as everyone said."

He met her eyes, his expression deadly. "Calling me that? When you were there to *rut* with the general."

She sucked in a breath. "I was there to marry him!"

"*Even worse,*" he roared. "Why no' tell me the truth?"

"Why should I have?" she asked, truly bewildered. "Because of our friendship? Because of the kindness you showed me? You're worse than you think he is, which is precisely why I chose him over you!"

"I dinna harm you. I dinna steal your jewels or silver—"

"You say these things as if they're noteworthy!"

"For a mercenary, they are!" He raked his fingers through his hair.

"You're no *mercenary,*" she spat the word. "Mercenaries kill and then receive money for it. From what I heard at Pascal's you haven't managed the last."

"You know nothing."

"Couldn't get the gold from him? So for revenge you kidnap an innocent girl before her wedding?"

"Innocent?" He laughed, a mean, mocking sound. "You were no' so innocent on the desk. *Milady.*"

Over her gasp, she again heard noise at the doorway. While MacCarrick strode to the door and slammed it shut, grating, "Mind your own damned business," she tried to will the blood from her face.

*Oh, my Lord.* Her skin burned, her eyes watering from humiliation that her shameful secret was known to these strange men. As long as she lived she'd never give in to passion again. MacCarrick was cruel, *taunting* her first taste of it, deriding what she'd found pleasant. *Not so innocent on the desk.* She turned from him, futilely tearing at her bodice.

"I wonder what Pascal would think about your kissing me right before the wedding."

She replied over her shoulder, "I have never lamented anything more in my entire life." A statement that was absolutely true.

He clutched her arm hard and turned her. "I've done you a favor. I saved you to repay my debt. I could have ransomed you to get back my money."

"Yes!" she cried. "Please ransom me! Send a note, and then he'll know I didn't leave willingly—he'll know I was taken."

"You've met him, you know he's a butcher, and you still trust him to have kept your brother alive? You trust him to free a man who's his biggest liability?"

"Yet you worked for him? Try to reason this out with your dull Scottish brain—if you're hired to do the dirty work of a 'butcher,' then guess what that makes you?" She yanked her arm free. "You might want to think twice about calling Pascal one in front of me."

"The opposite holds true as well, then. If we're as bad as you think, then know the fiancé you're keen to get back to was directing us," he grated. "But you think to take his word?"

"Over yours?" she asked in disbelief. "Of course I would!"

He strode to the doorway, but turned back to say, "Understand, I've locked the shutters outside—the thick, heavy shutters. And we'll all be out in the next room. There's no way to escape." He slammed the door so hard the walls quaked.

"I wish I'd let you rot by the river!" she screamed, then took stock of her situation. She would get back to Pascal or she would die trying. She *would* marry him.

The irony wasn't lost on her. She'd dreaded marrying Pascal. Down to her very bones she'd rebelled against the idea. Now she was being forced to forgo being forced to marry. This was all MacCarrick's fault, and she simply could not allow him to hurt her anymore.

Tonight it had felt *good* to fight, to lash out against those who would control her.

She balled her hands into fists and recalled when she'd once asked Vitale how he'd managed to survive on the streets of Paris. "If I hit someone," he'd answered, "I made sure they didn't see it coming." She'd shaken her head, scarcely comprehending that kind of existence, but he'd told her that she could have survived as well—that *she* could be as cunning and fierce and dangerous as the situation demanded.

Cunning? Yes. Fierce? Probably. Why not use MacCarrick to find out if she could be *dangerous?*

He wouldn't see it coming.

Court stormed from the room and found the others sitting around the table or lounging on chairs, waiting anxiously, yet attempting nonchalance.

"So she will no' believe you?" Gavin asked.

"No' at all."

Niall scratched his chin. "Let me go talk to her, then."

Court exhaled a long breath. "Pascal told her her brother lives, and his daughter did as well. Why would Annalía believe you or me when she hates us? She thinks we're savage foreigners—she will no' believe us over accomplished liars from her own culture."

"Still . . ."

"Niall, if you want to be the one to persuade her that her

brother's dead, go try." He lowered his voice to say, "And while you're at it, you can be the one to tell her that if her brother was no' dead before we took her, he sure as hell will be now." Broken glass snapped beneath his boot and he scowled. "What I want to know is why she was able to cast every object from that room. Why was she no' tied?"

"She promised us she would behave," Gavin hastily said. "She told us she'd be better than before."

"Was she worse than this?" Court asked in amazement as he sank heavily onto a wooden bench.

"Aye," both he and Liam answered at once.

"I know you said doona muck this up," Gavin said. "But she's a sly one."

Liam was nodding. "A clever lass. She looks up to you with those big green eyes . . ."

*They aren't green,* Court thought. *They're gold.*

" . . . and then promises no' to fight or bite again."

"She *bit* you?"

A few men chuckled.

"She bit, she clawed, and she kicked."

"Aye, and she's got some really strong legs for a lass. Must be from the mountains."

Shuddering, Liam said, "Those little white teeth of hers sank deep."

He could hardly fathom it. Prim and proper Annalía *bit* Gavin and Liam? So the wine bottle incident wasn't just a fluke. She really was a fighter, as fiery as they came.

And Pascal would've been bedding her, slowly killing that spirit, if they hadn't stolen her. Maybe even starting tonight, the way he'd dressed her. . . . The thought made him gnash his teeth, clenching his jaw. His filthy hands on her body—

"Court, are you all right?" Niall asked. He was staring at Court's whitened fists.

They were interrupted by a knock on the door from *inside* the room.

Court swung his head around, eyes narrowed as he rose. He strode through glass to snatch the door open and found her defiant, chin jutted in the air.

"I want to leave the room. I don't like being shut in like this."

Not a request—a statement of want. He was tired of her treating him like a lackey, tired of her looking down her little nose at him. "I'll let you out. But only to clean the mess you made."

She made a scoffing noise and began to shut the door. On *him*. Again laughter.

He wrapped his fingers around the edge, stopping her. "You're going to clean it regardless."

"Absolutely not, MacCarrick. I refuse," she said with a sniff. "You deserved it—*they* deserved it—for kidnapping me."

"You want out, you clean."

Her face took on an even haughtier look, and she parted her lips to speak what he knew would be a cutting retort. Instead, her head tilted and she bit her lip. "Very well," she mumbled.

This he never expected. "Why the sudden reversal?"

"I hate being locked up. And I'm hungry."

He knew she was up to something, but he couldn't find a reason not to let her clean up the things she'd used as weapons. "Good, then. I'll have Liam help you sweep."

She nodded, then sauntered, swishing her skirts, to the worst pile of debris. When she eased down, he tried not to stare at her ineffectual bodice.

Someone breathed, "*Christ almighty.*" Fergus? He was awake just for this?

Court noticed the others weren't any more successful in

prying their gazes from her breasts as her chest rose and fell with her short breaths.

With clenched fists and a glower at all of them, he stood directly in front of her to block their view. She looked at his boots, then slowly up his body, raising her head until her eyes caught his.

*Damn that dress.* And it *was* the dress. Not the way she regarded him with her head tilted so her hair flowed to the side. Not because he'd touched his tongue to that golden skin and knew her addictive taste.

She returned her attention to cleaning and picked up several silver accessories, a wooden jewelry box that somehow had managed not to break, and then a silver hairbrush and hand mirror—a broken mirror.

"You'll have bad luck for that," Liam said warily.

She addressed Court when she answered, "As opposed to before the breaking?"

He ground his teeth. "Liam will finish. When you've stowed those things, come eat."

She hesitated a moment, then, though she was on her knees before him, she nodded to him like a queen deigning a favor. When she returned, her hair was up and her chest was red, no doubt from where she had been tugging at the dress. She might have accomplished a quarter inch.

He sat her beside him and tossed bread, cheese, and an apple in front of her. She'd said she was hungry, but she ate nothing. And still that fire-red dress attracted every eye until *he* was uncomfortable. Under his breath, he said, "Do you no' have something less . . . garish?"

"No, I do no*t*," she answered with stress on the *t* he rarely could manage with the word. "Your young henchman—Liam, I believe is his name—packed low-cut ball gowns."

Court removed his jacket. "Take this." When she stared at it as though it would bite, he said more forcefully, "Take it."

She stood to slip it on. The jacket fell past her knees and a foot below her hands.

"Roll up the sleeves, sit down, and eat. I know it's no' food like you're used to, but you'll have to make do." When she remained standing, Court snared the jacket and pulled her into the seat.

Two seconds later: "I am uncomfortable and would like to leave."

Without eating. "Are our table manners lacking?"

She feigned considering the question, then said, "Hmmm. That's not it . . . I believe it's your abduction etiquette that's questionable. I've never been kidnapped. So rudely."

Strange, but he almost grinned. She had a well-timed wit, he would give her that. When she stood to go to her room, he did as well. She grabbed the apple, looked Court up and down, raised her nose, then turned on her heel. He let her go alone the short distance, but his gaze followed her until she reached the door.

"Looks like you've got a real soft touch there," Gavin said with a chuckle.

Court turned to them. "She adores me. Gettin' embarrasin'."

His wadded-up jacket collided with his head.

# Eleven

To clear his mind, Court had ridden alone for most of the next morning, hunting and exploring the area, but he hadn't been able to shake his thoughts of Annalía. When he found a lake, he stripped, then plunged into the icy water, remaining until his skin was numbed and his desire for her cooled. At least to a manageable degree. Only then did he allow himself to dress and return.

Straight away, he knew something was off. The men were acting strangely, glancing at the sky when Court looked at them, most setting off at once to go fish or ride. He strode to the lodge, half expecting her to be gone, but he found her still in her room as he'd ordered.

She was pacing furiously, cheeks pinkened, and for some reason this morning, it just seemed cruel to confine her in such a small room when she was like this. Chit would get dizzy. "You can come outside if you want," he muttered. Once she swept from her room, he sat, forcing himself to read a dated newspaper and to ignore flashes of scarlet as she paced by.

When she stopped to stand just before him, he lowered the paper and found her glaring at him. "I desire a bath."

He wondered how he would react if she managed to ask him for something.

Court knew she was planning some little coup. Everyone on earth, save perhaps Liam and Gavin, would know she was. "There's a stream nearby." He folded the paper and tossed it away. "You can avail yourself." With almost all his men out hunting, and the ones who stayed caring for the horses, she would have privacy.

"You're not afraid I'll escape?"

"We're miles and mountains away from any village, and if you doona have a horse—or shoes—you will no' get far." *And if I go with you and see you bathe . . .*

"No shoes—?"

She didn't get the question out before he'd risen, taken her by the waist, and plopped her in his seat. He set to her slippers, pulling them off for her. "Clear? No shoes."

"But my feet!"

She had good cause to worry. Like her hands, they were as soft as baby's skin. "The walk down to the stream is fine. It's only once you leave the trail that your feet will get sliced." He lifted her by the waist, then set her on her feet toward the door. "So doona leave the trail," he ordered as he swatted her backside.

She pivoted around, sputtering at the indignity. "You are no gentleman!"

"Established."

She cursed him in Catalan, then, in a flurry of red, swished out of the room. She still hadn't returned when he'd finished attempting the paper and two very poor cups of coffee.

Mouthing a harsh oath, he stormed from the house to the stream and swung his head around. No sign of her. Christ, she chapped him. Any other woman would've stayed. The slate in the area was sharp and murderous on a horse's hooves, much less a lady's feet, and she damn well knew they were much too far into the mountains for her to make it out with no horse. She damn well knew he'd easily catch up with her.

Court sprinted back up the hill to the stable, his ribs paining him, bellowing for Liam to saddle his horse. He rode out to follow the stream, scanning the shoreline both ways, and spotted red some distance ahead well off the beaten trail. He prodded his horse, then dropped down just behind her.

When he put a hand on her shoulder and turned her, he found her eyes were watering, her bottom lip trembling—a sight that did odd things to his chest. Was she injured? "What's wrong with you, woman?" he barked.

"MacCarrick," she said softly. "I've hurt my feet."

He looked down. They were cut, bloodied, briars still embedded.

Without thought he dropped down on one knee. "Look what you've done, you daft little—"

Her knee shot up to his chin, snapping his jaw shut. He fell forward to both his knees, and saw from the corner of his eye her skirt swinging toward his face. Strange, the material was hard as rock as it crushed into his temple.

"*Christ, witch!*" By the time his eyes focused again, she'd abandoned the rock hidden in her skirt, run to the horse, and was in the saddle, trying to calm its rearing. Court loped forward, fell for the reins, and snatched them just as the horse was tensing to run. She *had known* she needed a horse.

He grabbed her by the waist, dragging her down in a froth of silk, petticoats, and flailing arms and legs. After he caught his breath and the world righted itself, he growled, "Ye wanted a bath?"

Her eyes grew wide. While she thrashed, he stalked to the closest pool, then dumped her into the frigid water. She sputtered, rose, and slipped back in repeatedly, soaking herself.

"You'll pay for this, MacCarrick!" She scraped her thick hair from her face. "Sleep with your eyes open, you bast—"

He plucked her out of the water to swing her over his shoulder. He walked like this, leading the horse, water flooding down on him from her skirts, as she screamed and writhed the entire way back to the lodge.

After he gave the reins to a perplexed Liam, Court adjusted her on his shoulder and ignored her blows to his back. Gavin, sitting back in a chair, smoking his pipe, nodded his approval. "Really the only way to travel with that lass."

In her room he set her down, more gently on her feet than she deserved. She didn't wince or cry out. He grabbed her under the arms and pulled up one foot behind her at a time as he would a horse. A single small cut on her foot. She must've smeared the blood around to make it look worse. What a calculating—

She sucked in a breath between her teeth. She'd begun shivering, her teeth chattering.

"Get out of the dress," he ordered as he set her away. When she didn't move he said, "Be changed by the time I come back," and slammed out of the room. Five minutes later, he barged in to find her shivering more forcefully, lips pale, yet still in that wet dress. "Damn it, lass, I'll strip you down if you will no' take it off yourself."

At that she reached forward to pummel his shoulder. "C-Can't! You ignorant brute!"

He whirled her around. The ties in the back were tight and intricate. She'd been stuck in this thing. With a frustrated growl, he set to work, but gained no headway. The laces were swollen from the water, and his hands were fumbling, clumsy against her slim back.

"Stay here," he barked, then stomped outside to his saddle bag for his hunting knife. When he returned with it, her eyes went wide, though she had to know what his intentions were. Was she truly afraid of him? Was the sight of him with a knife—albeit a very large knife—so frightening? When he again turned her, she resisted. "Stay still." She didn't. "If you doona I may end up cutting you." More struggling. *"What is it?"* he bellowed.

"I-I don't want you to s-see."

In the midst of all this, she now chose to be the prim little lady again. Where was that lady when she kneed his chin? "You're no' in a position to get what you want. You forfeited any say you had when your rock met my temple. Understand?"

"I-I can manage!"

In a low, menacing voice beside her ear, he said, "In five seconds, I'm taking this thing off even if I have to put you face down on the cot, your wrists in my hand and my knee on your arse."

She went perfectly still but for her shaking. Carefully, he rent the dress. It sagged, but she caught it up to her front. Another cut and her petticoats plunked heavily to the floor. "Step out of them."

She shook her head.

*"You prefer on the bed, Annalía?"*

She stepped out of the material. He peeled the sodden dress from her, leaving her in her corset, pantalettes, and shift.

All of which were wet, two to the point of transparency.

It was as though she'd hit him again. Her body was slight but strong, and she was rounded, perfectly rounded, in all the right places. Her nipples were hard and pink, pressing against the clinging fabric. His mouth watered thinking of how he longed to lick them, now when they were wet, and he scrubbed a hand over his mouth as he took a step toward her.

She crossed her arms over her chest, hands on opposite shoulders in an *X*, and cried, "Not again!"

Her expression was one of complete disgust. His desire for her brought out disgust, yet she was ready to bed Pascal. Had chosen Pascal over him. He hid his anger and gave her a bored look. "I'm a man—you're a woman I want to tup. Get used to it."

When MacCarrick stormed from the room, Annalía dove for her clothes. Undressed like this! Here, with no lock on the door! She yanked one bag to the bed, casting away the bunch of bound wildflowers she'd hastily hidden behind it. One of the mercenaries had given them to her this morning, and she hadn't wanted MacCarrick to know his men had let her outside.

But MacCarrick returned not a minute later with a towel. He tossed it to her, and as she'd known he would, he glanced past her, scowling at the flowers on the floor. "You were outside with them?"

"How deductive you are!" she exclaimed, wrapping the towel around her.

"Who gave those to you?"

"I don't know." Some younger, fairly handsome redhead had. "Someone called Mac-something."

*"They're all called Mac-something."*

"Which is precisely why it is so difficult to differentiate, and hardly of any account anyway"—she skewered him with a look—"since you are *all the same.*"

He looked like he'd throttle her. "Is that so?"

"Aye," she said with a sneer, hating him so much it burned inside. She'd had *enough.*

Before MacCarrick had returned to toss her into an icy

stream and strip her by knife, his men had freed her, apparently for their entertainment. They'd towered over her, and on Liam's suggestion, they'd wanted to touch her "wee, soft hands," fondling her like the clan's new bizarre pet.

They'd wanted to hear her speak Catalan and French. A few asked to smell her hair, like animals, and the rest thought that a fine idea, but she'd peered up to the one-eyed giant helplessly, and he'd drawn the line. Literally. Over his throat to tell the others without words to behave. *Enough.*

"Who?" MacCarrick's huge fists were clenched, his sleeves rolled up so she could see bulging ridges in his arms.

She had to wonder if her better prospect might be letting the horde smell her hair.

"I don't know who." As the giant had shown her around, the entire scarred lot of them had come up to her and introduced themselves, and of course all the names had sounded the same. She exhaled wearily. "Mac-something."

"An entire morning with the crew?" His tone was deceptively calm and all the more terrifying for it. "They're no' a modest lot. Far from it. I bet you saw sights you'd never seen before."

She felt her face flush, which seemed to make him even angrier. It wasn't as if she'd sought to watch brawny Highlanders without their shirts, sweating and fighting in the sun. But yes, she'd continued watching, even when one tripped another to the ground and she'd discovered that at least one Scot wore nothing beneath his kilt.

She'd watched not only out of dazed curiosity—she'd also been noting *where and how* they hit each other. "I will concede that I saw . . . things a proper young lady should not."

"A proper young lady, then?" he asked as he closed in on her. "You've decided that I'm nothing but a lowly Scot and a brute, but I'm no' quite convinced what you are." He grabbed her by the waist, making her cry out in surprise, then carried her to the table in the corner. When he dropped her on the edge, the wood snagged the material of the bath linen. "Tell me, would a proper young lady kiss the first lowly Scot to come into her home?" He grasped her chin in between his thumb and forefinger. "Would she clutch his shoulders so the brute would no' stop tasting her skin?" He put his lips directly by her ear. "I doona believe she'd moan when he shoved himself between her legs and took her mouth."

She turned away, humiliated, but he laid his coarse hands on her cheeks and forced her to look up at him. At length, she said, "You are correct."

His eyes narrowed. He had the devil's own eyes. And when his face was drawn like this, the deep starburst scar below his temple whitened. When he'd first come to her home, she'd run her fingers over it. Tenderly. She was not being treated tenderly in kind.

"I'm *not* the lady I strive to be. Clearly I'm flawed. I might even be so *im*proper that I would welcome one of these men into my bed, though I was meant for better." She pulled from his hands but still met his eyes. "But it would *never* be you, MacCarrick. *Mai en la meva vida!*"

"Never in your life? But it would be Pascal? Did you let him kiss you?"

She shut her eyes to that.

"Did you? *Did he touch you?*"

"No, but he will! And I'd let him before you any day!"

"You've just sealed your fate." His jaw tensed and his hands landed on her hips, his fingers biting into her flesh. "Because he will no' before I do."

He leaned forward against her pushing hands, and slanted his lips over hers. The kiss was punishing, forceful, the stubble on his chin scraping her skin until her eyes watered. "No!" she said against his lips as she struck him with her balled hands.

When he drew back, heeding her, as somehow she'd known he would, she wiped her lips. He watched her, brows drawn, then slowly raised his hand as if to brush her stinging face. She flinched.

Then he was gone, leaving her trembling and confused and burdened with more hatred that she'd ever grappled with in her entire life.

# Twelve

*I*'ve heard you've been going to Llorente's room each night. What is this about?" Pascal demanded.

Olivia answered easily. "When I can't sleep, I enjoy plaguing him." Her face was cold.

He scrutinized her for a moment, then gave her a smile of relief. "I'd worried. Some women might find him handsome."

"He is weak. I could never see past that," she said in a steady tone. She'd learned to be like this when her relatives first sent her to live with Pascal. She'd been ten and had just lost her mother, Ysobel Olivia, who had been her entire world.

Her relatives thought her an abomination, and treated her as one, frightening and confusing her because her gentle mother had adored her and showed her how much every day. Compared to them, Pascal hadn't seemed so bad once she learned that he wanted her to be like him.

She'd excelled, fooled everyone, fooled herself, until that one night last spring just before they were to leave for Andorra when she'd overheard the servants whispering about her mother. They'd talked of Pascal and his three favored soldiers riding into her mother's village, smelling of "blood and evil." Pascal had been instantly besotted with the beautiful widow Ysobel.

As ever, he'd taken what he desired. . . .

"Perhaps you will refrain?" he asked Olivia, though they both knew it was an order.

She looked him in the eye, making her face like marble, her expression blank. He liked that about her. He'd never know the secrets her mind held. Like how she knew that the night he took her mother, he'd been feeling generous.

"Of course, *Papa*," she said, though there was only a twenty-five percent chance that he was.

After a dinner where he ate little and drank nothing, Court joined Niall outside on the porch, sinking onto a rough-hewn bench. The night was cool and the moon cast light as if it were day. Shadows framed every corner and tree, making it impossible to relax.

"How's the lass?" Niall asked. "Specifically, what state have you put her in?"

Court shrugged. She wouldn't even look at him when he brought her food, just sat on that unwieldy cot with her knees drawn up to her chest, body tense, and eyes glittering with fury. Her chin was scraped from his kiss.

She should be furious at him; he'd behaved like the beast she thought him and had no explanation for himself, much less for her. He'd never lost control like that.

She'd said Pascal hadn't touched her and he believed her, but had he kissed her? Had Pascal shown more restraint than Court had? Likely. And she'd chosen him over Court. She probably found the man attractive. He scowled at the thought, knowing every woman would find him so.

"Do you think she's planning something?" Niall asked.

"Count on it, after her stunt at the riverside."

"You'd have done the same thing in her position."

"Aye, but that does no' help me now. She'll keep trying. Do I go in there and force her to believe her brother is dead? I'm a bastard, but I doona know if I can shake that into her. Besides, Pascal and his daughter have her fooled."

"Hell, Pascal fooled us."

Court couldn't argue with that.

"Listen, your brothers'll flay me if I let anything happen to you."

"No' again," he snapped as he stood to lean against a splintery pillar.

"The curse, Court," he said simply.

*Walk with death or walk alone.* They'd all heard it.

"You know you can never have a woman of your own. And still, sometimes you look at the lass as if you'd like nothing more than to keep her."

"I doona plan to."

"Things have a way of happening outside of our plans."

"No' to me, they doona. Never in fact. And I've got a book to prove it."

"Aye, the book. 'Death and torment to those caught in your wake,'" he quoted. "Do you think the lass truly will be safe when we leave her in France?"

"Does no' matter, does it? I broke it and I'll fix it, then it's done. I dinna sign on to be her lifelong guardian."

"The idea of leaving her behind is no' sitting well with the men. Both MacMungan brothers said they'd take her to wed right now, and more are on their way. Even Liam said he'd take her if we're just going to throw her away."

Court's answer was a cruel laugh. Annalía, being so unusual and vivid, would wither like fruit on the vine among the dour MacMungan clan. Liam could never control her.

"The only reason they'd be infatuated is because they've never encountered anything like her before." He couldn't fault them for freeing her for a morning even as his ire grew just thinking about it. He was responsible for this—he'd brought a delicate foreign beauty among a band of coarse Highlanders. "I wonder if they ever considered her unbounded hatred of Scots?"

"Aye, she mistrusts us, and finds our ways strange, but her prejudice amuses the men. They know she's no' a spiteful lass, she just does no' know better. Hell, when they asked to touch her hand, she even shyly allowed it."

That made him gnash his teeth. "And how'd you find it, Niall?"

He hesitated. "Softer than I could conceive," he finally said. "But that's no' what's important. You ken she's never been treated like this, and if you'd be a wee bit more gentle in your dealings with her, she might no' be so quick to believe the things she's heard."

"Gentle? She was no' gentle when she bashed my head yesterday."

"She was afraid," he said, waving it away. "A woman like that needs to be cosseted, which she's no' been. I saw her face."

Court exhaled, then reluctantly admitted, "I doona want to be so with her." But everything about her made him crazed. Her feminine mannerisms, her accent, even the way she blushed all combined to drive him mad. In a low tone, he said, "I want to be different with her, but . . . I canna seem to."

"Then why do you no' just ride ahead to Toulouse? We can meet you at the posting house."

That thought infuriated him. "No."

"Why, Court?"

"Because I'm no' ready to be done with her yet."

"Christ, you can be a selfish bloody bastard. Sometimes I feel I doona even know you anymore."

"Of course, I can be. I'm still a mercenary and a killer. Hell, I'd sell my own sister. Is that no' what they say in the clan?"

"They say that because you will no' return—"

"I'll return when I've paid off my land—which I canna do now short of riding for Otto." At Niall's raised eyebrows, Court added, "Everyone needs that pay. *I* need that pay."

Niall gave him a disappointed look. "Life is not all about money. I thought you realized that when we broke from him."

"What is it about, Niall?" he snapped. Inside, two men glanced up from arm wrestling. Court lowered his voice. "If I canna have a woman and family of my own, and if I lose the land I've worked bloody hard for, then what exactly is my life about?"

"I doona know. You'll have to figure that out for yourself. But I do know it's no' about staying near a young woman until you destroy her life."

"You're that sure I'd destroy it?"

"Ethan did with his woman."

Years ago, Ethan had gotten engaged to Sarah, a girl he hardly knew from the neighboring MacKinnon clan. Her family had been eager, even after hearing of the curse, and Ethan's title demanded an heir, so he'd agreed. Sarah died at the age of nineteen, she died the night before the wedding, and no one knew how. "I'm no' Ethan, and I doona intend to get *engaged* to the chit!"

"And what about your da?"

Court swung around to face Niall, brows drawn, feeling as though he'd been punched. "I . . . We dinna mean . . ." He trailed off. What to say? That he and his brothers *hadn't* been responsible for their father's death? "You would remind me of that?"

"I'm sorry I needed to, Court." Niall put a hand on his shoulder before turning for the door. "You've much to consider."

To *consider?* Court would no more want to purposely revisit the morning his father had died than he would desire to truly contemplate his future. But hadn't he been doing both in the last few days? Since he'd met Annalía, he'd thought more about what he was missing than he had in the previous decade.

He started for her room, not knowing what he would say to her, not caring if she insulted him, but just wanting . . . *something.* He unlocked the door, then eased it open.

The air escaped his lungs, and he leaned his head on his forearm against the doorway. *"Bloody hell."*

# Thirteen

The hand mirror. The one he'd forced her to clean up.

She'd taken the heavy silver-plated frame and hammered it against the equally heavy hairbrush handle to chisel away the bottom pins of the shutters. Yes, they were locked. Yes, they were thick.

But now they opened from the bottom.

He stormed from the room bellowing, *"Liam, saddle up my horse."*

Just then, Liam lurched inside from the stable, eyes unfocused, hand on his head. "She's—"

"Aye, I know," Court snapped, shoving his pistol in his trouser waist. As he rushed to saddle his mount, he thought about the scene in her room. He'd never forget it for all his days. She'd propped up her battered tools, carefully arranging them, to let him know the extent of her trickery. Gloating . . .

Since there was only one route back to Pascal's, Court knew how to follow. But she must've ridden like hell was at her heels, because he didn't catch up with her for nearly half an hour. Just as he got his first glimpse of her, she disappeared. Once he rode to the spot where he'd last seen her, he understood why and didn't even have time to tense before he and his horse went charging down a steep drop-off covered in slate. She'd taken it without even pausing.

Even now, toward the bottom, she hadn't slowed her breakneck pace. Daft woman! His own horse was having difficulty flying down the terrain. He could hear the hooves fracturing the stone.

After this, the land twisted into canyons and wider coulees, and soon he was able to pull alongside her, yet every time he neared she veered away. Her riding was impressive, but in the end it was only a matter of time. His hand shot out to snag her reins, and in seconds he had them stopped and her swooped from her horse.

"Let—me—go!" She slapped at him, sounding like she was on the verge of real violence. Which she'd proved she didn't mind using.

"Riding like this at night?" He set her down but took her shoulders. "On slate? You're lucky you dinna break your neck."

"You rode like that, too. Yet I'm the one who's supposed to be considered fortunate?"

His hands tightened on her. "Why will you no' listen to reason, lass? Your brother's gone and you'd sacrifice yourself for nothing. If you'd cooperate with me, I'll get you to safety. You ken we will no' hurt you."

She narrowed her eyes accusingly. In the stark moonlight he could clearly see the abraded skin on her chin.

"That will no' happen again," he said, but she still fought to break his grip.

She kicked out, connecting with his leg, too high and too close for comfort. "Annalía, do you want a graphic lesson on exactly why it is you should no' kick a man like that?" Bloody hell if she didn't do it again and closer. "One more time and I swear tae you I'll snatch up your skirts and turn you over—" He went silent, and drew her to him, her back to his chest, covering her mouth with his hand. A sound nearby put him on edge.

Her teeth found his skin, of course, sinking deep, and he clenched his jaw. Something rustled in the bushes, getting closer. "Who's out there?" he called, as he pulled his pistol free.

After several tense moments, they heard, *"We're here to return Annalía Llorente to Pascal."*

"My arse," he muttered, cocking his gun. Had to be the Rechazados. No one else could have found them here. "Listen to me, Anna. These men are no' here to *collect* you—they're the Rechazados. Have you heard of them?"

She nodded, releasing her teeth.

"So you know they're assassins, no' escorts. Now will you cooperate with me?"

She said a muffled, *"Yes."*

He eased his hand away, shaking it to regain some feeling in the skin she'd chewed. "Now we need to get—"

"Help me!" she screamed, lunging forward when he caught her waist. "I've been captured!"

One shot rang out, the sound blasting through the arroyo like a cannon, then more rained down, pitting the earth all around them. Court shoved her behind him, keeping his grip on her wrist as he fired twice.

Too many of them. Too close. He clasped her in his arms and dove behind a hill.

The horses shrieked and reared, galloping away. *Bloody hell.* His ammunition was in his saddlebag.

"Help me!" she screamed again, struggling against his grip.

"Shut your mouth, woman. They're shooting at us, and you want to give them a bead?"

"They aren't shooting at me—they're shooting at *you!*"

"Those are Pascal's killers, and they are no' very discriminating." She still resisted, though he'd brought her hard against him, her back to his chest. "Now they'll hear the shots back at the lodge and ride out, but we've got to be smart until then. Understand?" he demanded. "If you want to live, you'll do what I say or I swear to you, you'll have a bullet in your brain within a quarter hour."

She sounded like she'd started crying.

His brows drew together. "Are you . . . are you afraid?" he asked, half baffled, having no idea what to do with this. He felt her nodding shakily against his chest and realized the lass was probably scared to death. *Bullet in the brain. Great one, Court.* But he had to be certain. "You ken they'll kill both of us?"

She whispered, "Y-You will get us to safety?"

"Aye," he said in a milder tone. Gentle. "If you do as I say."

When she nodded again, he loosened his grip on her. At once, she drove her elbow into his throat and flew to her feet. Choking out his breath, he lunged for her and stretched to catch her dress just as he fell. The fabric brushed his fingertips.

He'd missed.

She tore off into the clearing, screaming, "*Help me!* I want to return! I want away from him!"

More shots rang out. He scrambled to his feet, returning fire and was sprinting after her when he saw a smoking bullet tear through the billow of her skirt. She froze with a terrified gasp, staring into the darkness. "M-Mind your bullets!"

A split second later, her shoulder was wrenched back just before he snagged her around the waist and dove behind a boulder. He felt wetness against his hand, saw his white shirt stained dark. "Lass," he said as he dropped the empty pistol to probe her shoulders. "Is that mine or yours?"

He answered his own question when he felt her shuddering. *"It'll be all right,"* he grated, though fury overwhelmed him. They'd shot her. A defenseless woman. He ripped off her sleeve and just stopped himself from hissing in a breath.

In the moonlight he could see the bullet had torn open her arm. He prayed it had missed the bone. Taking the material from her sleeve, he tied it tight over the wound.

He hadn't been able to prevent this. He wanted to yell, to ask her why she hadn't listened to him. She was too small to take a bullet. What kind of animal would shoot a woman?

She jerked upright and looked at him as though she'd just realized something, and had just forgotten the bullet hole in her arm. "This is all your fault! *I loathe you.* Detest you!"

He exhaled. "I've heard it before."

"Do you know what this means, you bastard?" she cried.

Yes, he knew exactly what it meant. Pascal was making a statement to anyone who dared to take what was his. And she might now believe him about her brother.

*"Do you, you disgusting brute?"* she demanded again, seemingly uncaring of the shots all around them.

He narrowed his eyes. "Groom got cold feet?"

She screamed, springing forward, fingers in claw position to scratch down his face just before he caught her wrists. Still she fought him.

"Damn it! Will you stop?" He lifted her injured arm in front of her face. "Look, wench! Look at all the blood everywhere. Now faint. Should you no' be fainting by now?"

She sank back against the boulder, solemnly regarding her wound, and he could see shock settling over her. "I do appear to have been shot." Her tone was dazed, and he sorely regretted his taunt.

She was too small and too delicate. Niall was right. Women

like her needed to be cosseted, protected. Two nights under his protection and she'd been *shot*.

*Death to those caught in his wake.*

"We've got to get you someplace safe."

She blinked up at him.

With effort, he tore his gaze from hers to scan the area. He spotted her horse, frantic, caught by the reins tangled in a bush. Court tensed to run, but said to her, "Stay here! This is more serious than you know."

In a small voice, she said, "It hurts as though it's serious."

Annalía Llorente was docile, a sure sign she was in shock.

He sprinted after the horse, his ribs singing as he dodged bullets. Just when he'd finally secured the confused animal, which carried her bloody saddlebags full of dresses while his had had ammunition, he heard his men sounding the call. Soon after, he heard the guns he recognized by sound firing back at the assassins, but they were separated from him.

"Niall!" he yelled in Gaelic. "How many are there?"

"Seems like the whole order! They're everywhere."

"Bypass the lodge. We'll meet up at the posting house."

"Aye."

"Can you cover me?"

"Aye, be careful with yourself and the girl."

He rode back under the shield of Niall's covering shots. When he slid down from the horse to bend down beside her, he found her leaning against the rock, sitting very still, eyes closed, cradling her arm. Closer, he could see blood streaming in a line down her bent elbow, pooling into the dust. Her other hand was limp, palm up, and his makeshift tourniquet lay on it. Panic made his vision swim. He took it and retied it, knowing she'd only intended to look at the wound, to check how badly she'd been hurt.

"Anna!" He lifted her up. "Annalía . . ." She cracked open her eyes. "Ye need tae hold on tae my neck with yer good arm." His brogue was so thick, he wondered if she could even understand him. "I'm goin' tae get ye and me on a horse."

He had turned and was surveying the horse, figuring out how best to mount up, when he heard her say in a frail voice, "You need rescuing as much as I do."

He turned back, brows drawn. "*What?*"

She struggled against him, weak as a kitten. "I'm better off on my own."

Though he sensed she was gravely sincere, and more than a bit in shock, he clucked her under the chin. "Yer hurtin' my male pride, and will be payin' for that one."

His light response worked. She exhaled and looped her thin arm around his neck. She weighed no more than a feather as he lifted her, but he teased her, saying, "You weigh more than you look."

"You are weaker than you look," she immediately whispered.

He stared down at her in his arms and gathered her even closer. She met his gaze, looking very brave, but he could feel the tension leaving her body as she drifted into unconsciousness. Her eyes slowly closed, and her lips parted.

That's when reason left him.

# Fourteen

$\mathcal{Y}$ou're rich, I've heard."

"Did your father tell you that?" Aleix asked. Though it went against everything he was, he sat in his prison, on the wrong end of a gun, conversing with Olivia Pascal. Why would he speak with the woman who'd advocated a more advantageous and strategic timing of his execution?

In the beginning he'd hoped she would give him information about Annalía, but he'd soon realized she was too intelligent to let anything slip. So why did he continue tarrying with her? Because he was about to die? Because he wanted to talk to someone? Anyone?

And he'd done this for two nights. This room was obviously making him crazed.

"No, not Pascal. Your sister described your home. Even here it must cost something to own a mountain with herds of horses covering it."

"My family has been fortunate in that regard."

She tapped her finger against her chin. "I want to be fortunate as well."

He frowned. "Your father has as much money as I do."

"But *I* don't." Collecting her pistol, she rose to her knees. "You have something I want, and I have something you desperately, desperately need."

He grew still. "You're talking about freeing me?"

"I'm talking about striking a deal, which would necessitate my freeing you."

He was so staggered he lapsed into politeness with her. "Pardon?"

"Since your freedom has such an extraordinary value, then the price must be dear as well."

Trying not to show her how anxious he was to escape—he thought she would see that as weakness—he said slowly, "Whatever it is, I can pay it."

"Are you sure?" she asked, her gaze steady. "It will be very, very steep."

"Steeper than giving up my life?"

She glanced down and traced a finger over the carvings in the wooden handle of her pistol. "Depends on how you look at it. . . ."

*"I'll no' leave."*

MacCarrick was speaking to someone, but who? Why did their voices sound as if they'd been bathed in syrup? She wanted to open her eyes, but they felt impossibly heavy. *Best just to lie here. Yes. Rest and listen.*

"But, sir, I will have to examine her," a man said. His voice sounded young. "In my practice . . . with a lady like this . . . uh, husbands do not usually remain with their wives."

"This one does."

The gall. Had he no shame? Annalía tried to protest, tried to cry out that he wasn't her husband, but at that same moment MacCarrick had started to unlace her dress, and it sounded like a moan.

"I suppose her wedding band was stolen when you were set upon," the man said in an off-hand tone.

"Aye." *Wedding band?*

"And they left the other jewelry?"

*Clever physician*, Annalía thought hazily. *Back the liar into a corner.*

Of course MacCarrick came out fighting. In a menacing voice, he said, "Listen to me, boy. You doona need to be worryin' about that. You need to be concerned with fixin' her arm. Nothing else. Ken?"

"Uh, yes, monsieur. I will leave you to undress her and get supplies." A door clicked shut.

To her shame, MacCarrick removed her dress, skirts, and shoes. He unlaced her corset, too, she supposed when she took a full, welcome breath. Just when she comprehended his actions would leave her only in her shift, pantalettes, and hose, she felt his abrasive hand above her knee. "No, MacCarrick!" she said, but she couldn't even hear herself.

He leaned in. "What is it, Anna?"

"Stop," she whispered.

"Stop?"

She strove to nod, but her body felt boneless.

"I canna do that. You might have caught ricochet. He needs to examine you."

"Leave . . ."

"I *will no'* do that," he said as he untied the tight garters at her thighs and unrolled her hose.

She wanted to scream, but she just couldn't summon the energy.

"I'll put a blanket on you, so I doona see anything, if that's what you want. Anna? Can you hear me?"

When she chose not to answer, he rasped out a string of

harsh-sounding foreign words just as something pounded the wall hard.

She might have slept afterward, because when she woke she was under a blanket, and she heard jumbles of sound, more than one voice, all speaking soft French. Except for MacCarrick, who argued with the doctor in English, his accent thicker than she'd ever heard it.

"What are you doin'?" he snapped. She wished she could see what was happening. Her lids felt affixed together.

"Irrigating with salt water," the doctor said.

"*What?* Puttin' salt in the wound?" To someone else he said, "You brought me a bloody quack?"

"I assure you I'm no quack. I studied at Heidelberg in Germany and graduated with full honors."

"When? Saturday?"

"It's important to do," he insisted.

"No' going tae happen. Too painful." For once she agreed with him. Even if the man was a doctor, she didn't want this. Not salt. . . . She tried to speak but failed again.

"More painful than cutting away putrefied flesh?" the doctor asked.

She shivered. MacCarrick went quiet. Did he say something? Did he give the doctor a look?

"You'll have to hold her."

*No, no, no.* They'd agreed without her. *Coach-and-six.*

She felt herself falling back as a weight bowed the bed. He was behind her? Did he have her shoulders in his lap?

"Once," MacCarrick said. "Do it right, once."

"There may be powder inside—"

"*Once.*" His voice was like a snarl.

Her hair was being brushed from her forehead. Surely that wasn't MacCarrick. Her arm caught fire. She stiffened and screamed.

Again someone brushed her hair back. "*There's a brave*

*lass.*" MacCarrick's voice was close to her ear, and so low and rumbling, how could anyone hear him? "*That part's over—*"

Another pour like a hot poker. "No!" she cried as he held her down.

"*God damn it, man,*" MacCarrick bellowed. "Do you *want* me to kill you?"

"There was powder. If you care about her, you will let me do what must be done."

"Do that again, and I'll hit you so hard you will no' wake till you're old enough tae practice medicine."

Fading. But she wanted to stay awake. Wanted to know what was about to happen and be on her guard. She didn't trust MacCarrick. Couldn't remember why she wanted away from him even more desperately than before or why she hated him more than she always did. She wasn't capable of escape now, knew it as darkness fell over her, but if she could only manage to wake in the night, she'd leave him where he slept.

"You want me to marry you?" Aleix choked out.

"Yes, in exchange for your freedom."

He shot to his feet. "Why not money? I could set up—"

"Why would I not want to marry you?" she interrupted as she rose as well. "You're handsome, you're rich, and you're titled." Truthfully, these traits were mere bonuses. Listing them was simpler than explaining that she wanted a new name, and she wanted it to be his because he could hide nothing with his eyes. She would never trust a man, so she might as well find one she could read. If she was confident that she would know every time he lied, then that was like a twisted sort of trust in a way, wasn't it?

He shoved his fingers through his hair. "Olivia, I was married."

"I know your story."

"Do you know I vowed never to marry again?"

She dropped her pistol in her skirt pocket. "No, your sister neglected to mention that. But is your vow not to wed greater than your fear for her in the hands of a gang of Highlanders?" No need for Llorente to know quite yet that those men wouldn't hurt her.

"Of course not. What will you have me do?"

"Give me your word while you look me in the eyes."

He took her elbow and said, "I feel I have to remind you that Pascal will send the Rechazados after you. You are risking your life."

Of course he felt that way. Everything above board. Hell, Llorente needed her just to make sure other vultures didn't get hold of him first. "Then you'd better make the risk worth it."

"Why are you doing this?"

Because Pascal had taught her cruelty and malice, never knowing she would turn those very traits back on him. And freeing Llorente was just the beginning. "I have my motives. Besides, you need me as much as I can use you."

He scowled at that, then caught her gaze. "If you free me, I will wed you."

She stared long after. She'd known he would agree, had planned for it, and yet she still felt relief. "Then let's not waste another minute." She turned for the door. "I have two horses outside—one I have hereby appropriated from your sister." She pointed at him over her shoulder. "Make a note of that."

"Do you know where they've taken Annalía?"

"The last Rechazados' report said they were riding north into France."

As they started up the stairs, he said, "And the guards?"

"Have been taken care of."

He caught up with her and grabbed her hand to stop her. "Did you kill them?"

With her other hand, she patted his face. "No, I'm wearing my new riding habit and I'm ever the messy killer." She exhaled. "I *drugged* them. Listen to me, Llorente, I promise from now on I'll never kill or maim anyone." She jerked free of him and walked on, but turned back to eye him. "Unless they have it coming."

Four o'clock in the morning and the *doctor* that they'd roused from bed didn't even have a shadow beard. Perhaps Court was just an ignorant Scot, but he preferred two things in his surgeons: that they be sober, and that they have lived long enough to have practiced on others before getting to him.

Court had ridden straight down the base of the Pyrenees into France with Anna in his arms—a crazed trip he had little memory of—and stopped at an ancient spa town. He had the vague notion that there'd be more physicians centered around medicinal waters than in any mountain foot village. He'd been right.

There were many doctors, who unfortunately catered to rich, bored ladies with imagined maladies. Annalía had a gunshot wound—a tisane of chamomile wasn't going to do the trick here.

He'd stopped at the first boardinghouse he found, but balked when he'd seen the boy the people in the house recommended. Yet *Dr.* Molyneux, for all his youth, had been thorough in his examination.

Court looked down at her arm. The bullet had passed over the side and had burned the wound's edges, but the bone was untouched. Lass was lucky that plug hadn't shattered it. A hair closer and Court still would've been arguing with the doctor, but not over something so minor as how to clean the wound.

While Molyneux directed the boardinghouse matron for clean linen to be cut into bandages, Court brushed her hair behind her ear and watched her eyes move behind her lids.

He'd ridden as far as he'd dared, and only hoped his men could prevent the Rechazados from getting through that pass. Regardless, they needed to get on the road as soon as possible. "When will she regain consciousness?"

"Right now she's just sleeping."

He gave Molyneux an irritated look.

"I could wake her right now if I wanted to. But I don't want to."

Court's brows drew together when Molyneux put some tincture on her arm and began to roll the bandage around. "Do you no' need to suture it?"

"No, it looked deeper than it actually is because of all the blood."

"You need to suture it. You should always sew these things."

"Mr. MacCarrick, the wound simply wasn't that grievous. It bled profusely, and I'm sure it gave you quite a scare, but the actual damage to the skin wasn't enough to warrant stitches. I understand that you are worried about your . . . your Mrs. MacCarrick, but this is the best course."

Court set Annalía aside, then stood. "Gunshot wounds get sewn."

The doctor craned his neck to look up at Court, steadfastly meeting him in the eyes, though he swallowed hard. "Aside from this, your wife is the picture of health. It would be injudicious of me to put thread in her skin. Thread that can swell and break, and get dirty."

"My *wife*," he said without the slightest hesitation, "may be the picture of health, but she's small and of a delicate constitution. I'll no' have her walking around with an open gash in her arm."

"How long have you known her?"

"A while," he answered evasively.

"I don't know how *well* you know her, but your wife is not

of a delicate constitution, I assure you. I'll bet she's told you she rarely gets ill."

"She might have mentioned it," he answered, though they'd never had more than one civil conversation.

"We'll keep the wound together with linen bandages. I'll show you how to put this tincture on and how to wrap it. Just make sure she doesn't reinjure it. And of course," he added with a disapproving look, "that she isn't shot again."

Court was shaking his head. "She'll get fever."

"Yes."

"And then what should I do?"

"Let it burn." That was his maddening answer. "Just don't let it spike. You can run a cool cloth over her if it rises too high, which I doubt it will, and summon me again, but otherwise let her handle this. She's strong." And then with a last fond look at Annalía that almost got young Molyneux killed, he left Court alone with her.

# Fifteen

Apparently, Annalía finally believed her brother was dead. And blamed Court for it.

*"How can you want to be near me knowing how much I despise you?"* That had been her deadened response when he'd told her he was taking her on to Toulouse. After she'd called him a brute, a filthy barbarian, and a lowly Scot, and told him with a steady gaze that she hated him as she'd never known she was capable of hating anything.

She hadn't wanted to leave with him and would've told everyone that she was a prisoner had he not convinced her that if she stayed she'd be getting the people there killed as well as herself.

Now Court glanced back to see her lagging behind again, her expression lost. The horse he'd been able to find for her was not what she was used to, and though he'd dropped her saddlebags at the house matron's feet and said, "Fix these dresses so she can ride more comfortably in them," Annalía hadn't seemed to notice the changes. It seemed she noticed nothing.

The journey to Toulouse normally would have taken Court only a full day of fast riding. The land grew flatter as they followed the Ariège River away from the Pyrenees until it became a table plain dotted only with small hills. An easy jaunt, but he'd been keeping a much slower pace for her, and one day had turned into three.

For those last three days, she hadn't spoken, had hardly eaten, and had not uttered a word but for her only response to Court's every question, *"Fot el camp."* Go to hell.

She obviously couldn't wait to be rid of Court, and he would oblige her. When he met up with his crew, he'd ride and never look back, but until then he'd taken his responsibility seriously. Each night he had found them a place to stay, some room where he could rebandage her arm as Molyneux had shown him.

The first night when he'd removed her blouse—not her shift, just the blouse—she'd fought him as if he were stripping her, risking a reinjury. "I can do you the way I threatened with the dress," he'd told her. "Or you can let me tend to your arm." Though she was stiff and stared straight ahead, she cooperated. Each night it looked better.

Afterward, while she took the bed, he'd sink into a chair in the room, thinking about their situation, wondering why it pained him more than anything ever had to see her balled up under the covers, shuddering when she silently cried.

Simply taking care of her was so far beyond his realm of experience, it was staggering. Much less that he was caring for a woman who blamed him for her brother's death.

In less than three days under his protection, she'd been marked for death by a fanatical order of assassins and shot. He'd known he was shadowed in life, could bring ruin to those he cared for, but this was ridiculous. Still, a selfish part of him thought, *Better than married to Pascal.*

Today as they rode, closing in on the posting house, he reasoned that this was not the curse raining down on him. He'd made a decision that affected her badly. Nothing metaphysical or mystical about it. Besides, he didn't *care* for her—he *took* care of her, and only temporarily. Just to get her to safety.

He stopped to wait until she caught up with him. She sat very still in the saddle, staring blankly ahead, looking small in her bright dress and wrapper. This couldn't go on any longer. She needed to stay close to him because they weren't out of danger by any means. He reined his horse around to tell her she needed to buck up—

He turned, saw movement from the corner of his eye, and spotted a cross tattoo.

A Rechazado attacked her from the brush.

"You can't just leave me here," Olivia snapped, her face red with fury, her full lips thinned.

She'd demanded he stop at an inn for food—Aleix hadn't been hungry, wouldn't be until he found his sister and got her away from the Scot. Things became clear.

He knew better than to try to reason with her, but still said, "I will return for you, but right now finding Annalía is my primary concern."

She leaned forward over the table they'd taken, planting her elbows between plates. "Dealing with Annalía will take longer. Best to complete the bargain with me."

He leaned forward as well, catching her gaze. "Not a chance. That's not the order."

"So you won't honor our deal until you find her?"

"Correct."

"Then obviously I must expedite the search."

He gave her a short, harsh laugh. "I'm going on alone. We're already at least a week behind them."

She crossed her arms and leaned back in her chair. "You need me. This MacCarrick is a villain. *I* am a villain. I know how he'll think."

He had to hear this. "Please, share your wisdom."

"Our leads indicate he's alone with Annalía. Highlanders are clannish people. He'll be quick to meet up with his men."

"Very good. Any notion of where that will be?"

"They'll have a predetermined meeting place. Somewhere rural where a group like them won't attract so much attention, but close to a large city where they can find ammunition."

His eyes narrowed. "Toulouse?"

"Is the first possibility."

Aleix had suspected she had more information about the Highlanders than she was presenting, and now his suspicion grew. She was cunning, and knowing her, she would deal it out piecemeal, using it as leverage.

Damn it, he'd have to keep her with him. But only until she no longer proved useful. "We've got to ride faster."

She stood and gave him a bored look. "I'm waiting on you."

The assassin dragged Annalía down with little effort. Court spurred his mount—she wasn't fighting. Why the hell—

His horse's head was wrenched to the side. Court took his eyes from Annalía to find another Rechazado had snatched the harness and trained a pistol on him. Court stared down at the hollow black barrel, a chilling sight he'd hoped never to see this close again. If it hadn't been a foot away, he would've chanced it—the other was pulling Annalía into the bushes.

He'd never forget what happened next. She screamed. She screamed, and he didn't care if he got shot. *To hell with it.*

Court kicked out, catching the Rechazado's arm just as the sound distracted him. Luck was with him, and the gun flew to the side. Court dove from the saddle at him.

As they wrestled, the man drew a smaller pistol. They grappled for control.

Before his injuries, Court would've been stronger, but now . . . now the man could win. And if he did . . . Court yelled with rage—suddenly felt as strong as he'd been before. A shot rang out.

The man stared up, eyes growing blank, blood steeping his shirt in an even circle from his heart.

Court snagged the other pistol, sprinted for Annalía, then forced himself to slow, to surprise the one who had her. He looked past the bushes and found a scene he'd never expected—Annalía standing with the Rechazado unconscious at her feet and a bloody rock by his head.

Most likely one she'd been saving for Court. That's why she hadn't fought. She hadn't wanted to drop it.

Stunned, he watched her kick the man in the gut, then scan the woods, no doubt deciding where to run from Court.

"Annalía, stay," he ordered, though he was scarcely able to keep the disbelief out of his voice. She turned to him and rolled her eyes, but she didn't run.

When he reached her, he clasped her good arm, "Are you unhurt? Is your arm all right?"

She shrugged.

"Did the shot frighten you?"

"No. I saw him tussling with you over the pistol."

He dropped her arm abruptly. "I'm glad you dinna wait around to see if I would live." In truth, he *was* glad she'd planned to get away, no matter how riled he sounded.

She squinted at him as if she didn't recognize him. "Tell me again why I should care about that outcome?"

He scowled until she asked, "Is he one of Pascal's men?"

"Aye."

"Did I kill him?"

Court saw his chest rise and shook his head. When she bent to pick up her rock again, he strode over and took it from her hands. "You doona want to kill him." Court would do that. Retribution for touching her.

"I really do."

"No, Anna." When she continued reaching for it, he added, "It'll do things to you. No' worth it."

She informed him crisply, "I—need—that—*anyway.*"

He held it high from her. "For me?"

She nodded without shame.

Clever, brave woman. His brows drew together as he remembered the way he'd reacted to the thought of her being hurt. The way he'd decided a bullet between his eyes was *incidental* to the need to save her.

He swore under his breath.

"What was that?"

"Nothing. Why don't we wake up this son of a bitch and find out how many more are coming?" Her eyes widened, and he could tell she hadn't thought about that prospect. She looked alive for the first time in days. He heaved the rock away, then bent down to slap the man, but whipped his head back around. "Annalía, doona think of hitting me again."

"Two with one stone," she said waspishly.

"Be smart. They'll keep coming. You must prefer me over them?"

"I prefer none of you."

"They will no' kill you at first."

Her face paled, and she finally said, "Very well."

He recognized the man before him. He was called Ruiz the Scarred. Court only remembered him because the moniker fit so well. When the assassin roused, he spit blood.

Court had always been heartless in battle, emotionless

with the enemy. Now he felt rage building once more, making him hide his clenched fists from Annalía. This was a man who wanted to murder a defenseless woman. Once he let go of that fury, she'd never look at him the same. "Anna, go see if you can find the horses."

"No, I want to stay. I must ask him about Aleix."

"I promise you this is no' anything you want to see." She hesitated. *"Go now."* His tone was lethal. "And if you try to leave, I swear to God you will regret it."

She regarded him with a marked fear that he hated seeing, then hurried away. He faced Ruiz. "How many more?"

"Infinite numbers until you are both dead. The way of the Rechazados."

"Did you come from the group at the border?"

He said nothing, so Court raised the pistol and hammered the handle down on the man's skull. He choked back a sound of pain. "W-We came through the main pass to France. We know nothing of the others."

"Why her? She's only tried to return to him."

"A moment of anger. He's since tried to turn us from her. . . ."

"But your order never has." Court had heard that one had better think through an assassination command with them because once set on a path, no force could move them from it.

"Never." He sneered. "I wonder if she knows you're the reason Pascal had her brother?"

Court put all his weight into it when he punched the side of his head.

He needed to focus. When a Rechazado got talkative, he doubtless was stalling until he could find a way to kill you. His giving you information meant nothing if he made sure you'd never live to use it.

But Annalía had to suspect him of it—if the fool hadn't attacked . . . "Wait, you said '*had* her brother.'"

"He escaped." Ruiz smiled and flashed bloody teeth. "He knows you have his sister. He's coming to kill you if we don't get you first. *Mark your days.*"

Court was almost so wrapped up in what he'd learned that he forgot that the more talking this one did, the closer he was to dying. Almost.

When Ruiz's fingers eased down his leg to the knife strapped to his calf, and he drew, Court shot him.

The report brought Annalía running. She glanced from the body to him, her face drawn.

What he wouldn't have given to know her thoughts just then. "Did the horses bolt?"

"Yes, but I've coaxed mine back and tethered her," she answered absently. "Yours is down the hill by the stream."

He nodded. "We need to get these two farther off the road."

Strangely calm considering the circumstances, she stood watch until he'd dragged the two deeper into the woods. Afterward, he collected her horse, then started toward the stream for his. She followed him, and even sank down on her calves just beside him while he took advantage of the cool water to wash off.

"Would you believe me if I told you news of your brother?" He stood and and helped her up. "Would you trust what I said?"

"Y-You said not to trust you." A tear slid down her cheek. Damn it, why did his chest hurt all the time?

"I'll tell you the truth."

She took a wavering breath, then finally said, "MacCarrick, does he still have my brother?"

Of its own accord his hand went to her cheek and brushed the tear there. "No, no' anymore."

# Sixteen

"Why . . . how . . . explain!" she cried.

With an impatient look, he dropped his hands to his sides. She knew he resented her ordering him about, but she couldn't help it. She had to know. "K-Killed?"

"No, no. Your brother escaped."

She grabbed his shirt with both hands. "You tell the truth?"

"Aye."

She shook his collar until he raised his eyebrows. "That monster doesn't have him anymore?"

"No, Aleixandre Llorente escaped Pascal. In fact, you're in much more danger than he is."

She released him. "I must find him! Let him know I'm unhurt."

"How do you plan to do that? We just confirmed that you're a Rechazado target. That's what they're notorious for—never missing a target. They'll trail you for as long as it takes."

She held her forehead between her thumb and forefinger. "I don't know! I can't think." She began pacing.

"The posting house is up the road no' more than a few miles. You can eat, rest, and digest what's happened. And then you can plan."

He was right. They'd just been dragging bodies off the side of the road—a cup of tea wasn't an unreasonable thing to desire! She could feel herself shivering, could feel her bandage beginning to dampen.

When she nodded, he helped her onto her horse, then mounted his own.

*Aleix is alive!* her mind repeated like a mantra. *And free!* She felt lighter, she felt . . . hopeful. She would find her brother, and then they'd figure out a way to defeat Pascal.

For three days, she'd feared he'd been killed, but every second that had passed, she'd plotted to get away from MacCarrick in case he hadn't been. Now to learn her brother was alive *and* free . . .

But what if MacCarrick was the one who'd fought him? Biting her lip, she watched the Highlander ahead of her as he looked to the sky, no doubt determining from the thunderheads that they were about to get drenched.

If MacCarrick and Aleix had been enemies, who knew what this man's agenda was? For all she knew, he might be planning to recoup his money by ransoming her to her rich brother. Clucking her horse on, she trotted up beside him. "I have a question for you."

He swept a glance at her, but said nothing.

"I want to know if you attacked my brother and his men."

He didn't hesitate. "I never attacked your brother."

"You swear it?" she asked, looking up at him.

He met her gaze directly. "Aye."

"Why are you helping me now? Why not just ride on and leave me behind?"

"I plan to do that just as soon as I get you to this inn."

At least he was honest about that. If someone like him had gone on about duty or helping her from a sense of gratitude, she would've ridden away from him as fast as she could.

At his reply, she smiled up at him, and his brows drew together. "Still canna wait to get rid of me?"

*Well, that depends on how you answer my questions . . .* "MacCarrick, how did you come to contract with Pascal?" She knew why Pascal had hired his men—she'd learned much at the smuggler's lodge. The band had been together and successful for nearly a decade, their reputation notorious. They were to train the deserters and fight against Spain. She could clearly see their appeal, but why would MacCarrick sign on with a despot?

"He was hiring. We were between jobs."

"Would you have continued with Pascal if he'd paid you?"

"I canna say."

"The men told me that I had it backwards. That you quit first and then Pascal refused to pay you for the work you'd done—not the other way around."

"Did they now?" he asked without interest. But he didn't deny it.

They had, though she'd never quite believed them until now. "So why Pascal?" she asked. "Many thought his ideals were sound at first. Did you as well?"

He ignored her.

She wouldn't be dissuaded. She was about to make a decision and she needed facts. "Pascal had you beaten because you defied him. Because you thought what he was doing was wrong. Isn't that what happened?"

He shrugged. Again no denial.

*Mare de Déu,* everything she'd heard from his men had been true. "Why won't you admit that to me? Why did you let me believe that you and your men were out stealing and killing?" She put her chin up. "You know what I suspect? That you're not nearly as brutal as people think."

He reined his horse in, cutting hers off, and stared her down, looking very brutal indeed. She swallowed and caught herself leaning back in the saddle away from him.

"You've been clever in our dealings, I'll give you that, but your first major mistake would be attributin' traits to me that are no' there. I am that brutal. I'm just selective in who enjoys it."

With that, he rode ahead, but not far away. He'd given her another warning, but this time she took his words the opposite of how he intended them. Perhaps she should stop attributing malice and studied murder to him, and see that he wasn't a fiend like Pascal.

She hadn't been completely mistaken about MacCarrick. He had killed easily and could be terrifying. The look on his face when he'd been about to question that one today . . . She shivered. She'd never seen anything so frightening—it was as though borrowed from a nightmare. No, she would never underestimate the seething power she'd sensed in him, a power that he'd proved he could unleash in the beat of a heart. But it was what was *in addition* to these traits that puzzled her.

Every one of the preceding nights, he'd seen to her wound, forcing her to remove her blouse, to undress in front of him. During these times, she'd been so full of hatred and grief that she'd thought his actions were just another indignity, a chance to see her in only her chemise. Now, thinking back, she saw other things. She recalled how he'd gone to one knee in front of her and how if she winced or hissed in pain, he grated, "Doona want to hurt you."

The night she'd been shot, she dimly remembered that he had talked to her on the jostling ride to France, sometimes in rough Gaelic, most times making no sense even in English, but it was as if he'd known she hadn't wanted to hear silence.

She remembered that afterward someone had stroked her hair—someone with very callused hands. . . .

She sighed, realizing that she was both free of any real grounds to hate him—and in need of his help in this perilous time. Lost in thought, her mind a whir of ideas, she scarcely noticed the first drop of rain. Or another splatting directly afterward.

When a full torrent swept down and she lagged behind, he rode back for her. "We need to stop under the next bridge."

"MacCarrick!" She blinked against the rain. She was freezing in her light jacket and only one thought was getting her through this ride. "I want a hot bath and I want to drink tea when I'm in it!"

He raised his eyebrows at her tone, then seemed to study her and the situation as if he didn't quite know what his next step should be. She could swear he was struggling to make a decision. The second she thought he might have, he plucked her from her saddle.

"*What are you doing?*"

He placed her sideways on his lap with her back against his arm, pulling her close so he could wrap the edges of his jacket around her. After he grabbed her horse's reins, he gently used his whole hand to turn her face into his chest.

"Hold on tae me," he murmured, "and mind your arm."

She was still protesting when he spurred the horse and they flew down the road, until she was forced to put her arms around him. His body was so incredibly warm in his jacket that soon she was, too. The rain no longer stung her face.

Out of the blue, she remembered one of her nanny's sayings. *A bear is only a bear till you rub his belly. A wolf will eat from your hand if the treat is sweet enough. . . .*

# *Seventeen*

*A*fter four miles riding through blindingly dense rain, they reached the inn, and Court dropped down with Annalía to race inside. The interior was bright and cooking smoke wafted from the kitchen. The innkeeper was up and looked harried, but still acted as though he didn't recognize Court.

"We need a room," Court said.

"Rooms," Annalía corrected, shimmying out of his arms. "We need two rooms."

The innkeeper, John Groot, peered at her hard. "Nobility," he muttered under his breath. "Don't have two. Just have the one," he informed them in an English accent. "Nice one, though, once we get it cleaned up. The rain, you see. Made sure we had a full house."

Two women, one older and the other obviously her daughter, marched out of a back kitchen. "Another couple, John!" the woman exclaimed with a thick French accent. "Well, get the poor girl a seat by the fire and something to drink while we fix their room." She called to someone unseen to tend the horses.

Court led Annalía to a fireside bench, peeled her little wrapper from her, and pulled her down to sit beside him. He put his fingers under her chin and lifted her face to him. She was pale, her pupils dilated.

When Groot asked, "What will you have to drink?" Court answered for her, "Whisky."

She glared at him, but said to Groot, "No, thank you. I'm fine. I don't drink spirits."

The innkeeper shrugged and poured a generous draught, which Court retrieved and took to Annalía. Under his breath, he said, "You bloody well did before, now drink it or I'll pour it down your throat."

Her back went even more rigid. She gave a polite smile to Groot and took the glass between two fingers, as if it were distasteful, but she did drink.

Court returned to the innkeeper for a glass for himself. The liquid burned going down. As soon as he emptied it and put it back on the bar, Groot filled it again.

The bartop was freshly polished, and the place was cleaner and more organized than before. "New wife?" Court asked under his breath, as he motioned for another refill, then set to drinking it. He'd been here six months ago, and Groot had been alone.

"That she'd be," he answered in a proud voice. He should be proud. Groot, a gangly Englishman with ruddy skin and no visible chin, had somehow married that bonny French matron. Why did that seem encouraging to Court?

He had Groot pour another for Annalía, then traded her the full glass for her empty one.

The mother descended then, regarding Annalía and talking in French. Court's French was not as strong as it could be. When he'd kicked in the door to the boardinghouse with

Annalía limp in his arms demanding help, he could just as likely have been asking where they could do a spot of ice fishing.

"Is she your lady wife?" the mother finally asked him in English.

"What?" He took his eyes from Annalía once he made sure she'd gotten enough into her belly. He didn't like how pale she was. "Uh, aye, she's my wife." The liquor was beginning to hit him. He'd forgotten he'd lost a stone of weight.

She squinted at him. "You had to think about it?"

"Newly married," he bit out, looking over the woman's head at Annalía. Her wet hair hung heavy, her wee ears peeking out from the thick mass.

"In any case, you have treated her poorly," the woman informed him. "She's too delicate for treatment like this."

He raised his finger and corrected her. "She *appears* delicate."

"Certainly too slight to cover the miles you have tonight." She said over her shoulder to her daughter, who was just descending, "They are newly married."

"For shame, monsieur, riding with a new bride in such weather! That's not the way to have a babe settle within her."

He made his face impassive. There'd be no chance of that even if he'd taken her once for every time he'd imagined bedding her. He would never have a chance.

"My word!" the mother exclaimed as she drew Annalía to her feet to go upstairs. "She's bandaged under her blouse. And bleeding!"

"It's a scratch," Annalía mumbled. Both women cast him stern looks.

"No, really," she insisted in a bleary voice, the liquor working on her as well. "It's not as if *he* shot me," she muttered.

"*Shot?*" they screeched in unison just before they descended on her, clucking and cooing. He wanted to reiterate that her wound wasn't his fault. But it *was* his fault. He'd driven her out into the night. Driven her to chisel her way out of a room and run into gunfire.

To free her brother. Who'd been alive.

He drained his glass and slammed it down, feeling restless and uneasy.

"We're taking her up for a bath, monsieur," the mother said. Court didn't like the way the two women were proprietary about Annalía. *He* should be the one taking care of her since he'd done it for the last three days. Well, maybe not helping her when she'd bathed, though he'd wanted to . . .

He saw Annalía stumble. She was hurt and drunk and, damn it, she *was* delicate. He reluctantly nodded to the women.

Once they'd left, Groot said, "Fine lady you got there, Mac-Carrick. Rich-looking."

"No' mine. Just looking out for her for a bit."

"Were you looking out for her before or after she got shot?"

Court's jaw clenched, and he saw Groot warily note it. "And your crew?" he asked, in a higher voice.

"Meeting me here in the next few days. The lass is staying longer."

He raised his eyebrows.

"I'll need you to keep an eye on her." Groot wasn't merely the owner of their meeting point. Court's brothers had introduced him to this place that they used for their work. For all his clumsy appearance and shifty ways, Groot was a retired sharpshooter and weapons expert, with a sealed shed in the back filled with everything from pistols to howitzers. More important, his brother Hugh trusted him. His brother Ethan didn't, but then Ethan trusted no one. "She's been marked by the Rechazados."

Groot whistled. "I'll have to bring in some extra hands,

then—some who don't mind the added risk." When Court nodded, he said, "Hugh left some clothes here last time around. You interested?"

"Aye." Finally, something not bloodstained. He'd hated that whenever Annalía looked at him, her gaze always seemed to fall on either the bloodstains or the scar at his temple.

"Also got two letters from your brothers. You want them now?"

"Might as well," Court said with obvious reluctance. When Groot returned with them, Court kicked off his boots and put them by the fire, then tore open the first one, from Ethan.

> *Courtland,*
>     *Cut your contract with Pascal immediately. I told you one day you'd pick the wrong goddamned side.*
>     *Ethan*

Yes, Ethan had said that, and Court had told him to mind his own goddamned business. Then from Hugh:

> *Court,*
>     *Had an investment opportunity for you and accessed your accounts. Couldn't wait for your permission, so I used my signing card and told them you were dead. Fight hard down there, but remember, a sucking chest wound is nature's way of telling you to slow down.*
>     *H*

Furious, Court crumpled the letters and threw them in the fire. Hugh had a signing card only because Court liked to keep his affairs in order. Just in case. Yet here he was still alive and Hugh had ransacked his accounts to bet on an investment. Hugh had plenty of money to play with; Ethan had infinite amounts, it seemed. Hell, if Court had known it was so profitable to kill for the Crown, he'd have signed on when they did instead of stubbornly going in a different direction, as he'd always done. Maybe then he'd have enough money to pay off his land.

Court had one brother ordering him and the other doing whatever he bloody wanted, neither caring what he thought. Neither ever sought permission. He watched the last corner fold and burn. These were his ways as well.

He needed to sober up. He looked to Groot and simply said, "Food."

The passing of another half hour, a change of clothes, and a hearty meal had a negligible effect on Court's sobriety. He stomped up the stairs, passing the French women as they descended, ignoring their glares.

He'd made sure Annalía had had some food and her bags taken up to her. And of course some whisky-spiked tea. Now that the women had left her room, he expected her to be passed out asleep after such a day.

Damn, he would like to have seen her in the bath. Probably a good thing he didn't. If he ever witnessed her wet, soapy body. . . . He stifled a groan and eased open the door.

He found her on her knees, rooting through her bag, clad in nothing but a new bandage and a bath sheet wrapped around her torso. She hopped to her feet when he entered.

She had smooth, golden shoulders, and the candlelight showed them slightly damp. He felt a muscle in his cheek twitch.

"I-I need privacy!"

"You've had an hour."

"But I can't find anything to wear."

"Your bags were waxed. Your belongings will be dry." When she didn't answer, he said, "You could wear one of your silky, lacy nightdresses."

"How do you—? Oh, never mind! I refuse to wear that if you will be in this room with me. Now leave!"

"Ordering me?" He raised his eyebrows. "Of course. You must want to ensure that I will no' budge from this room."

"No, that's not—"

"I will turn my back and be glad of that," he said, his voice hoarse. Even Annalía fully covered in a bath sheet made him crazed.

"I need to get dressed and then under the covers."

"Your wish, lass. . . ."

When she finally nodded, he made a big show of turning around with a huff. The second he heard the towel fall, he turned back around. And had to run his hand over his face to keep from whistling in awe.

She was . . . unimaginably beautiful.

She had her back to him, so he was treated to a view of her full, lush bottom, tight strong legs, slim back and tiny waist. Her hair was damp and curled down to her hips.

"*Mercy,*" he breathed.

"Oh! You wouldn't!" She raced to slip the nightdress over her head, but she couldn't manage it swiftly enough with her thick bandage and injured arm. He thought about helping, was sure he would've helped—had he been capable of more than staring, jaw slackened. She finally swept it to the ground, then stepped into it, drawing it on.

She whirled around, catching him dumbstruck. "You promised! You said you would turn!" She reached forward to swipe a blanket from the bed, flashing him a thigh and breasts before she could hold it before her like a shield.

He was just drunk enough to grin. "I did turn. I simply turned back too soon, which was the most inspired idea I've had all day." Besides taking her into his lap in the saddle and having her put her arms around him. Today he'd begun to understand that all those clever bastards out there practicing chivalry weren't doing it only for the ladies' benefit.

"You are no gentleman! You are the opposite. You are a rogue and a cad and a blackguard." Her voice was a bit slurred. She wrapped the blanket around her torso over her gown and began pacing.

He plopped on the bed, leaned back, and raked his gaze her over shamelessly. "Ask me," he suddenly began. "Ask me to help you find your brother." Where was this coming from? He'd had one thought—get her to the posting house, to relative safety, because he'd jeopardized her. Break it, you fix it. Now he was adding another responsibility? Why?

Because when she'd finally relaxed against his chest earlier, it had been keenly satisfying to him.

Damn it, whisky never made a good decision.

"I could reunite you two and keep you safe from the Rechazados until then."

She halted at the window. "Why would I ask you?"

"Because you need me." He narrowed his eyes. "You've realized that by now, haven't you?"

"I've realized many, *many* things about you." She leaned her hip against the windowsill.

*"Away from the window,"* he barked.

She glared at him but did move. "And I can just imagine what you would demand in return."

"Maybe, but maybe no'. The only way to find that out is to try me. I know this is hard. I'd wager you've never really had to ask for anything in your life."

"That is correct."

He put his better hand behind his head. "Well, this is a fine place to start."

Her head tilted sharply to the side as she sucked in a breath. He knew she would ask him, and once she did, he *would* help her. He also knew she was making a mental note to make him pay for this.

"I would . . . request your"—another intake of breath—"help."

He leaned on his side. His ribs were tender after today's fight, but he wasn't about to move from his mocking position. "Given that you're new at this, I'll instruct you—"

"As if *you've* ever asked for anything."

"Would you like me to instruct you?"

Her chin went up. "*Yes.*"

"Very well. Since you still didn't *ask,* you're going to need to say 'please.' It should be very moving and heartrending if you're sincere. And clasping your hands together over your chest would no' hurt."

She swallowed. Her body was tight with tension. "*Please.*"

He nodded in a deigning gesture. "And why should I help you?"

Her voice was tight. "Because you are the one who's hurt me."

"Because of the kidnapping? I thought we established it was a good thing no' to be married to Pascal. And your brother's free. Turned out pretty damned well."

Except for the fact that she was an assassin's target and they'd already struck twice.

"Regardless."

"Well, because you've asked so nicely . . ."

"That's it? That's all you wanted?"

"'Course no'. That just got you into negotiations. I'm a mercenary and this will be hazardous business. I'll need payments along the way."

Her shoulders slumped. "I don't have money with me." Then her eyes brightened. "But we're close to a town now. I can sell my jewelry."

"Canna sell it. They'll be expecting you to do just that. Besides, you've got something much more valuable than that." His gaze landed on her chest.

She sputtered, working up a retort, but he spoke over her. "Whenever I ask for it, I want you to let me kiss you. Just a kiss. And I want you to be as fiery as you were in the study."

"I don't think . . . I can't just . . . I'd been drinking . . ." She paced again.

He nodded as if in understanding. "Of course, you can always tell me to leave."

When she glared as she passed him, he suspected she was about to do just that.

"Can you never stand still, lass?"

Anger flashed in her eyes. "Does it *bother* you? My pacing?"

"No, no' at all. Just thinkin' if you agree, we're goin' to need a bigger room in the future. Else you'll get dizzy."

Whatever he said was a winner of a response. She stilled, and her gaze softened so sweetly on him—she had *never* looked at him like that—and damned if he knew why. But he found he liked it. A lot.

"Just a kiss?" she murmured shyly.

"Wherever and whenever I feel like it."

She resumed her glare at that, but mumbled, "Very well."

Court was amazed she'd agreed. All he had to do was risk his life to keep her safe from the most vicious assassin order in Europe? And he got to kiss her, at his pleasure? He definitely had struck the better bargain. "Then we have a deal." He rose and made a sweeping gesture. "You can have the bed."

She eyed him warily before she unwrapped the blanket from her torso then hastened under the cover. The moment she lay on her side, he eased down alongside her.

She gasped. "You said I could have the—" She stopped herself. "I do have the bed, don't I? But you didn't say to myself."

"You learn too quickly, lass. I'll have no more tricks in my bag."

She stiffened, and right when she would scramble away, he threw his arm over her, careful of her bandage. "Anna, stay. I will no' take my payment now. We are both hurt, exhausted, and drunk. Nothing could stir me. Even the sight of your lovely bottom dinna stir me," he said, lying so much he thought he'd be struck down. She relaxed somewhat. "But if you took away any one of the three, then I'd kiss you."

She was silent for a moment, then asked, "Why?"

"Because you're the type of woman who needs to be kissed. Hourly, softly. Fiercely." He skimmed his hand down over her hip and murmured near her ear, "Thoroughly."

She shivered, then eased over on her back and faced him. Her breasts pressed against her nightdress, her nipples hard, and just below them she ran her finger back and forth across the cover in long, languorous movements. "That sounds like a lot of work, MacCarrick," she purred with that accent. "Will you be the man to do all that to me?"

He groaned and leaned forward, thanking God for whisky. *"Anna, you have no idea."*

She put one finger against his chest and pushed. As she turned away, dismissing him, she said, "Stirred?"

# Eighteen

*W*hat imp had caused her to taunt him like this? She didn't feel like she was rubbing a bear's belly, she felt like she was jabbing it with arrows when the beast was in bed with her. And she knew better.

It was just that the ride here against his chest had been so surprising, and then seeing him grin had been confusing. Here was the man who'd just spied on her and seen her naked, but the look on his face afterward had been . . . *rewarding?*

Or she was simply drunk. Yet again.

"I like that," he said. His voice, so husky and rumbling, always pleased her. Even when she'd despised him and the words—and accent—his deep voice conveyed, she'd enjoyed the sound. But tonight she could no longer despise him. Tonight it made her tremble.

"You like what?" she asked, too curious to refrain.

"No' that you tease me."

"Then what?"

"That you think you can tease me and actually keep *my* hands off *your* body with a finger."

She did think that. For some reason she'd always known he would never force himself on her, even when he'd kissed her at the lodge. "But I have." She needed to bite her tongue. Was she trying to provoke him? She'd already agreed to let him kiss her whenever he pleased!

"Tonight you have," he agreed, then pulled her to her back to face him. "But if you look at me like that again and speak to me in that voice, you will no' fare so well in the future." His tone was low, his eyes watchful. She realized she found his eyes as pleasing as his voice. They were dark, but now she noticed lighter flecks. She wished she knew what color those were. . . .

Oh, Lord, she feared she was looking at him like that just this second. She tore her gaze from his and studied his lips. She remembered how good kissing him had felt and absently asked, "Then what would happen?"

"Then I would kiss your lips." He rubbed his thumb over her bottom lip, and the whisky insisted that she allow it. "And your neck." He caressed his fingers down her neck. The feeling was so pleasurable, she fought to keep her eyes open and lost. Then no touch at all. Just when she was opening her eyes to his, she felt the first contact to her breast. "And then your breasts."

Never breaking her gaze from his she sucked in a breath and tensed. Because she would pull away. Now she would. In one second . . . He continued watching her, making it impossible to look away, while lower, his fingers were slow and hot on her hardened nipple.

"You mustn't do—"

He pinched lightly, and her eyes slid closed again. She vaguely perceived him levering his body above her, but she felt his lips on her neck like fire. She moaned and soon his hands covered her breasts, his thumbs sinuously rubbing her nipples. Nothing could possibly feel this good. . . .

Was he working his hand inside her nightdress? The jolt of his hot skin directly against her breast roused her, made her remember who this was and what they were doing. When she swatted his hand, he grasped her wholly. She tried to wriggle from him, and he groaned.

"MacCarrick, let go of me!"

"*Let me touch you.*" He growled the words.

"No!" She broke from him, turning away, her breathing heavy. Her breasts were sensitive as if protesting the lack of his touch. She ached between her legs more strongly than she ever had alone in her bed, and to her shame she'd grown wet there.

She felt him roll on his back and heard him exhale a pent-up breath. "You'll be the death of me, Anna."

When dawn neared and he heard her finally sleeping, he rose, still hard as iron, miserable as only a man denied could be. He'd never felt skin so soft. Never *dreamed* of skin so soft. And he'd had his hands on her, teasing her to need again. Only his coarse touch had stopped him from uncovering more.

He glared at his scarred hands. They weren't changing.

He supposed he would have to get used to nights filled with heavy, aching erections and no relief in sight. Because apparently, he'd just signed on for many more.

She affected him, and for some reason, around her, he either became like a lowly animal or strove to be noble. Both were asinine in his mind. Noble? Him? He'd had difficulty keeping his hands off her when she was violent toward him. And in the nights before, when he'd removed her shirt to change her bandage, his fingers had itched to sweep across her chest, to slip beneath her chemise and grasp her breasts and cup her. How noble was that? She most likely still hated him, but now she was teasing him? He was a dead man.

As he washed his face with cold water, he looked in the mirror, scowling at his harsh reflection, seeing nothing there that would make her *want* his touch.

He dried off, then sat for some time watching her sleep, listening to her whisper occasionally in Catalan, wondering why he'd decided to leave his crew and the possibility of any income behind. Why had he promised to get her to safety when all he'd wanted was to pay off Beinn a'Chaorainn?

Court was the only man in his family in memory to have a note on his land, and it shamed him. The only thing that lessened the feeling was knowing it was a *lot* of land. Knowing he'd purchased it for less than half its value helped as well.

To make way for sheep, a foppish English baron had cleared the lands of Beinn a'Chaorainn of tenants, forcing them to the coast to eke out a living there. Then the baron left the administration to factors, who knew little about the land, and without good management the farm couldn't compete with the wool churning out of Australia. Debts from a high life in London forced him to sell at a loss akin to robbery.

Court smiled a mean smile. The violent removal of Highlanders from the land and sometimes even their forced emigration had been happening for years. In fact, many of them had been driven to Australia.

And now they owned those wildly profitable sheep stations that dominated the world wool market and bankrupted shortsighted English barons.

*We will always win in the end,* Court thought.

Before they'd been cleared, the tenants had been prosperous, and their rents, when fair, were still substantial—not grossly so, not able to support a high life in London, but comfortable. Court liked comfortable.

He'd planned to ask them back. But he couldn't—not until he owned his home completely and could never lose it. So why the hell had he decided to put his plans on hold? Why had he chosen to help her?

At that moment Anna turned on her back in sleep. Her brows drawn, she softly murmured, "*Wolf.*"

He bolted from the room, then stomped down the stairs, uncaring of guests sleeping beneath them. Groot was already up.

"Need a coach," Court said as he sat at the common table. "And I'll pay extra for a driver worth his salt and horses that doona spook so easily."

"I can send the boy to Toulouse. Guess you're taking the lady?"

"Aye. I'll need some coin."

"Should I put the debt on Ethan's or Hugh's tab?"

It would serve them right. "Split it equally."

Groot chuckled. "And your crew?"

They would not be pleased. "I'll leave a message for them. They should be here soon." He might have wondered why they hadn't arrived yet, since he and Annalía had made such poor time, but he knew a standoff like that could take days, even weeks, to end, especially since both sides were in such defensible locations. It could take even longer if both doggedly refused to give ground. That was one thing he hated about the job—the bloody downtime.

He would write to Niall and tell him to ride for Otto. If Niall thought the odds good, he should sign them on.

When the coach arrived, he inspected the horses and quizzed the driver—a man called originally enough "Coachy." Finding both acceptable, he went to wake Annalía. Through the front window of the inn, he spied her rushing down the stairs, smoothing her hair, and looking none the worse for wear for their drinking. His head had been pounding since he'd sobered. When she strode outside, he asked, "How do you feel?"

She appeared surprised that he was still there, but covered it with a shrug. "I feel fine. Why?"

Because she'd been riding through a downpour last night, recently shot, and then got drunk, he almost answered. He was learning that the black plague personified could kiss her and she'd be fine. "No reason."

She glanced down and ran the toe of her shoe over some tufted grass by the walk. "I didn't know if you'd still be here."

Did she think that badly of him? He'd given her his word—when he was soused and under duress from needing to tup her—but still his word. "I made a deal with you, and I plan to keep my side of it."

She gave him a disbelieving expression. "Don't become testy, MacCarrick. It isn't as if you've presented yourself as the most trustworthy man."

He moved closer to her, to a point she would deem *impolite*. "If you will no' believe I'll keep my end because I'm a man of my word, then believe I will just so you'll keep yours."

She blushed and observed the grass again.

"So that means I'll be getting you somewhere I know you'll be safe."

She frowned when she faced him again. "You told me the posting house was safe. This was where you were going to leave me."

"Changed my mind after the attack yesterday, and I know a place in London."

"I'm not traveling to England!" She crossed her arms over her chest. He noticed she put her hands lower because of her injury. "You said you'd help me find Aleix, not take me farther away from him!"

"Your brother's coming for you. The Rechazado said he

was on our trail to save you from the brutal Highlanders and then murder me for revenge. He'll go where we go. And he'll thank me later for taking you to safety in London."

"Why didn't you tell me this information sooner?"

"When should I have done that? During the downpour or when I was drunkenly trying to get you out of your gown?"

She gasped, eyes wide, but then she narrowed them. "You're attempting to distract me. To keep me from saying yet again that *I am not going to England*."

"Lass, we're leaving. Now. The subject's ended."

"I can't leave without sending him a message!"

"To where? Your home? He's doubtless already in France."

She paced and he wondered how many soles she went through in a year. Didn't matter—he would *always* encourage it. "Do you have relatives in France?"

Shaking her head, she said, "No, my mother's family is in Spain, in Castile."

"Any friends or connections?"

Her brows were drawn. "There are only two places in France that I have connections to and both are near Paris."

"Which are?"

She answered absently, "My mother's grave and my old school."

*Wait.* . . . "Your mother does no' rest on your family's land?" He tried to read her expression, but she appeared deep in thought. Why the hell wouldn't she? And if not there, then at least in Spain?

"We could send a message to The Vines!" she continued as if she hadn't heard him. "He'll check for information there."

"We'll see."

"I'm not going anywhere until you promise."

"Fine, promised," he grated. "Now go get in the coach."

"Coach? But the Rechazados will catch up."

"I doona want you riding anymore. And if it rains, we'd have to stop then anyway."

"I will *not* slow us down."

"Anna," he began in a warning tone, "the coach, or I'll take my kiss and I'll take it back in the bed."

She must have believed him, because she glowered at him, but only while sashaying to stand beside the coach.

When Groot brought out their things, Court tossed the bags to the coachman, then set about loading the weapons that Hugh and Ethan had unknowingly paid for this morning. He couldn't resist running a hand over his new rifle, near lovingly. A repeating rifle, five shots in one loading—he'd heard tales of them coming in the future, tales in the same vein as those of the beast of Loch Ness, but he'd never seen one. This rifle meant dead Rechazados.

Once they were set and Groot had returned inside, she mumbled, "I still say we should ride."

"Anna, you're no' as strong as you think."

"No, I'm not," she said, her chin at a stubborn angle. "Every time I conclude how strong I am, I surprise myself. I continue to exceed my conclusions, so I must be *stronger* than I think."

She surprised him, too. Constantly. Like now, when after her rousing statement about her growing strength, the prim little lady stood outside the coach's door, directly beside the folding step, waiting for him to assist her in. She didn't even realize she should be making a show of helping herself inside, making a gesture of independence.

His eyes narrowed. Or perhaps she did realize it and wanted all things her way.

As he strode toward her—and how could he not when she put her arms out to him?—he thought about the paradox. All

Court knew was that a woman who peered at her nails infinite times in a day should not know how to hide a rock in her skirt to pummel the unwitting Scot.

Her incongruent actions went against all that was right and governable in the laws of nature.

He shook his head hard, then handed her in, growling under his breath, *"Fascinatin' woman."*

# *Nineteen*

*I*sn't the countryside lovely?" Annalía asked as she gazed out over a valley in Burgundy. The land was bedecked with patchwork fields of sunflowers and vineyards, and she smelled damp earth. When the sun came out from behind white clouds, a breeze blew, but swayed only the squares of towering blooms. And she couldn't stop smiling.

"Lovely," he agreed though he'd never looked away from her. He'd been watching her closely ever since her . . . indiscretion four nights ago, though Annalía wished he wouldn't read too much into her actions. She'd simply been reacting to the traumatic events of the day, and there'd been imbibing once more, but he acted as though something had changed between them other than the fact that she no longer detested him.

To be honest, she didn't even think she could manage to dislike him anymore. She'd seemed to grow used to him, becoming more comfortable around his size, becoming more aware when his sharp words were like teasing.

And she suspected that the impulses to be good to her and even possibly gentler with her were within him. Unfortunately, she also suspected that he didn't know quite what to do with those impulses.

She could nearly think of them as uneasy allies, except for the fact that his help would come at a price. Her knight slayed no dragons without a payment, one that he hadn't yet demanded.

As they rode through the first town in the valley, the bright colors of the homes struck her, and she thought she heard music. When she tried to work her coach window open, he quickly reached across her to shove it down with ridiculous ease. It was a gesture a Castilian gentleman might make. Except for the total destruction of the window rails.

With the breeze blowing in, she could hear the music carried along, could hear it even over the horses' hooves clacking on cobblestone. "I want to stay here tonight."

"There are hours until dark. We need to get farther on."

Each night he would take a room for her, just long enough for her to rest and change her bandage or get a bath and for Coachy to sleep on his bench. Making up for time lost to daily morning storms, MacCarrick pushed them well into the night and then had them setting out before dawn, though she never saw him sleeping.

She thought the only reason he'd stopped at all was because he didn't want her to get too exhausted. So she sighed wearily. "I just felt . . . faint," she lied. "From the arduous pace you've been keeping."

He gave her an irritated look. "You doona feel faint or I'd know it. Do you want to stay here so badly that you'd lie to me?"

She scrunched her lips. "Well, yes."

He scowled. A minute later, he called out new directions.

She gave him her most winning smile, which made him

scowl deeper, but she didn't care. She felt the sun on her face and realized she was . . . happy, genuinely happy, and it startled her.

Her brother was not only alive, but he was free as well, which was a gift beyond measure. The man with her, whom she'd suspected of awful things, hadn't done them and was actually behaving for the most part like a gentleman instead of a Scot.

Was life perfect? No, she still didn't know what to do with the Highlander during those times when he did *not* act the gentleman, and she still feared the Rechazados. On the outside, she'd acted unconcerned about the attacks, but in reality they'd terrified her. That fear was part of why she wanted to revel today.

They passed a group of giggling young women strolling along the street with their baskets swinging and their pied skirts swaying, and a thought struck her. "I want clothes."

"What?"

"I need clothes," she amended. "Mine are all gowns, except for my one decent dress, but even though it's been repaired it still reminds me of when I was shot."

Did he wince at that word? "How do you plan to pay for them?"

"You must buy them for me." They would be simple in a village like this, but she didn't care.

"And I would do that because . . ."

"You said you'd keep me safe. That was our bargain. Well, look at the clothing here. See those girls. Their garments move—*I'd* be able to move more easily."

"You're trying to convince me that new clothes equate to safety?" He looked at her as if he'd never understand her.

"Yes. How am I doing?"

"No' too well. But the way your mind works is intriguing."

•          •          •

Court was nonchalant with her, concealing the fact that nothing chapped him as much as Annalía giving him orders. She did it because she believed herself above him. He found it intolerable that she still looked down her little nose at him, that she still perceived him as a *lowly Scot.*

He wondered if there was ever a worse situation than desiring a woman who didn't even consider you a man. Because she was *meant for better.* Wasn't that what she'd said?

If she would simply *ask* him for something . . . Even as he considered it, the possibility made him distinctly uneasy. He'd discovered in the last couple of days that he wanted to be able to provide her with things she needed or desired. If she figured out how badly he wanted that, and that the only thing stopping him was her inability to ask, she would be merciless.

Once they'd arrived at the town's inn and he was securing a room, she said, "Perhaps we should have two rooms. I'm sure they have more than one and I'm recovered enough that—"

"No."

She raised her eyebrows at his tone.

"This place isn't protected." Everything about the inn that he saw as a liability she loved. The windows in their room were big and opened wide to a balcony. He didn't like balconies, especially not when thick, cloaking vines grew all along them.

But the desk in their room he could use. He called down for paper and ink.

"Are we going to write my brother?" She knelt atop the chair giving him an excited smile. "And send it to The Vines?"

The chit had a smile that made poor misbegotten bastards like him want to see it again. He shook himself. "Aye. I'm going to write directions in Gaelic, and I want you to copy them in your own handwriting."

"Why?"

"They'll probably have a dictionary at the school, and if no' they'll be able to lay hands on one. Any Rechazado who might intercept this will no'. It must be in your handwriting, so he'll trust it." After the maid brought writing supplies, he scratched out a missive, then watched as she nibbled her lip, struggling to decipher his handwriting and copy it. "This is the oddest language I've ever seen."

He gave her an incredulous look. "You were bloody studying Greek."

"Oh, that's right, you were in my room. Did you enjoy my things?"

"Aye," he answered shamelessly. "I did when I slept in your soft bed."

She glanced down, blushing, then quickly said, "Did you see all my *clothes?*"

He almost grinned at her segue. "Forget it."

"I don't understand why you are being so difficult."

"You doona need to be out on the streets."

"But you will keep me safe," she answered, as though he'd uttered something foolish.

He strode for the door. "No, you need to rest. I'll have a bath sent up and wait outside till you're done."

Just as he had his hand on the door handle, she said, "Mac-Carrick, would you please buy me just a few new garments?"

He froze. Christ, she'd actually done it. This was the beginning of the end.

She stood and lightly touched his elbow, an unnecessarily cruel and unfair tactic. "I can repay you."

He closed his eyes. He'd just have to deny her. Or put a price on them she wouldn't want to pay. He turned with a lecherous look. "Lass, you ken they will no' come cheaply."

No angry words, no scathing retorts. "I also now know you won't take advantage of a girl under your protection with no money and no family here to care for her."

He bit out a harsh curse under his breath. "Do you no' need to rest?"

"Dresses, MacCarrick," she reminded him gently.

Once the seamstress had finished up a quick hem on her new skirt and the vivacious shopkeeper had packed her purchases, Annalía crossed to the front of the store, where MacCarrick prowled outside, pacing back and forth, and called him inside to pay.

When he entered, he went no further than the tight doorway, standing there with her as he surveyed her simple blouse and skirt. He stared at her face and her breasts and all the way down and up again, unhurriedly. This wasn't the first time he'd examined her so rudely, but this time his lingering gaze didn't infuriate her. This time, it felt like a touch.

The shopkeeper murmured, "I envy you the night you're going to have."

MacCarrick must have heard her because he turned away from Annalía with a cough into his fist. But what kind of night did his look promise? Why would the pretty woman envy her that?

Both the shopkeeper and the seamstress had told Annalía she was *lucky* to have such a "handsome Scot." The seamstress had added, "Scottish men are such lusty devils!" as if this were a good trait.

When MacCarrick went to the counter to pay, the shopkeeper bent forward to present the bill—and her cleavage—to him. If Annalía hadn't been here with him, would he have kissed the eager woman? Taken her into what would've been solely his room and bedded her? What an unusual, infuriating thought. She sauntered up to him, then took his arm, giving the woman a glare. She winked at Annalía.

The French!

On their way back to the inn, she was acutely aware of

every woman who sneaked a glance at him. She'd never seen him around women like this and didn't like it, even though he seemed oblivious.

When in Paris, she'd seen gloriously handsome men walking by, and though she didn't sigh out loud like her girlfriends, she'd noted them appreciatively, but the looks these women gave MacCarrick were more sensual, more lascivious.

More . . . knowledgeable? They knew something about him that she didn't, which was maddening. So she kept his arm, and he didn't seem to mind. When she pointed out something and accidentally brushed him with her breasts, he hissed in a breath. His reaction to such a small touch was surprising and thrilling. She would make sure she did it often.

Now she gazed up at him, studying him as they walked along. He was exceedingly tall and broad shouldered. Of course, she'd known he dwarfed most men, but she'd always found his size intimidating, not attractive as other women seemed to see it. Though to be honest, there were things she *did* find attractive about him, now that she could look at him without . . . blinding hatred.

He had incredible eyes. Black like jet, but now she noticed they were flecked with silver. His face was hard, with rough features, but when these were put together, it was attractive, if one liked brooding and scarred. His hair was black as his eyes, and thick. She liked that, too.

She found herself asking, "MacCarrick, why did you become a mercenary?"

He scowled at her question. "What does it matter?"

"I'm curious about you," she said. When he didn't answer, she added, "I will answer any question you have, if you answer this one." No response.

She squeezed his arm, and he finally said, "Highland regiments were returning from far-off places talking about the money to be made abroad. After their service, some of the soldiers signed on with a foreign crew, and I joined them."

"It didn't bother you? Killing for money?"

He tensed and grated, "That's a second question."

"Then ask yours."

He pulled her into a shaded area and put his fingers under her chin. "Do you think about the night I kissed you in the study?"

She could feel her face heating.

"Do you?" he asked again.

"I might from time to time," she said, striving for an airy tone. "It *was* my first kiss."

"And when I touched you at the posting house? Do you think about that when you stare out the coach window?"

Her lips parted. How did he see so much? "MacCarrick," she began in a steady voice, though she felt anything but, "that's a second question."

"So it is." He shocked her by brushing the backs of his fingers across her cheek before taking her arm again. "But I have my answer now."

# Twenty

*T*he moment she opened the door to let him in after her bath that night, Court knew he had a problem, and was actually thinking to himself, *Court, we have a very serious problem.*

Anna, breathless and smiling, with her hair down and curling about her bare shoulders was bad enough. That and Anna in a blouse with damn little underneath it to conceal her full breasts and clad in skirts that begged to be snatched to her hips as he turned her to a wall? . . .

"Why are you dressed to go out?" he demanded.

"The maid who brought my bath up told me there's going to be dancing tonight. I love to dance."

"You ken you canna go tonight. Too risky."

"I thought you'd say that, but I am asking you to *please* let me go." She took his hand between hers and clasped them to her chest, exactly as Court had instructed at the posting house. "I know you'll keep me safe."

"Have you forgotten the danger you're in? You just opened the door without asking—"

"If the knock is really high and hard that means you. And I haven't forgotten—that's why it's so important to go tonight. MacCarrick, it was made very clear to me when I was shot how short life can be, and if you knew how much I have to make up for, you'd let me go!"

She looked so young, so eager, and damn it, there was a hint of desperation in her eyes. He'd wondered how she could lightly brush off the attacks, and now understood she hadn't at all.

"Will you let me pretend for one night that I don't have this hanging over me?"

He finally said, "You'll have your night, then. But you canna go out like that."

"Why not?" She glanced down at her blouse and skirt, then frowned at him.

He scrubbed a hand over his mouth and muttered, "Your hair's down."

She smiled coyly and confided, "I *know* it is," as if she'd pulled off a bold coup to have it free.

"Only the young women wear it so."

She put her hand on her hip. "I *am* a young woman."

"You're a *lady*, as you like to remind me incessantly. So you should dress as one."

"You're right, of course." She twisted her hair around behind her, tying it into a knot, just like that.

He exhaled as though put out, then offered his arm to escort her down. Once on the street, he braced for the torture of her breasts grazing him, fearing she'd discovered today to do that on purpose.

Still he walked proud to have a lady like her by his side. Even as he wanted to kill the men who ogled her, and envied him. . . .

Some children ran by, laughing, and she smiled after them.

"Thank you for taking me out, MacCarrick," she said with a sigh, resting her head against him.

Her voice was so pleasing and the gesture so welcome that he almost regretted one of his reasons for agreeing to do so tonight—he planned to give her something more to think about when she stared out the window.

Annalía was determined to enjoy herself tonight and as she and MacCarrick walked to the center of the village, the music, the laughter, and the excitement around them helped relax her. As did the glasses of wine MacCarrick had gotten for her, though he didn't touch a drop. She felt warm and reckless and dimly noted that she couldn't seem to stop touching him. "MacCarrick, do you think I look pretty?" Where had that question come from? Did she care about the answer? Yes. Yes, she did.

"You know very well how you look," he said, but ran his gaze over her appreciatively.

With a laugh, she asked, "Am I the type of woman who could bring you to your knees?"

He caught her gaze. "Depends," he began in a low, husky tone, "on the context."

The look in his eyes made her shiver, though she didn't understand what he was implying. "Context? Then right now, right here."

"Right now, right here, you're the type of woman that drives a man to drink."

She gave him a mock scowl to match his. "Take me to dance, MacCarrick."

"No."

Her face fell. "Why not?"

"Canna keep watch."

"Oh." Of course, he wouldn't be able to. She thought about

returning to the inn, but just then a daring young man marched up and asked her to dance. She glanced back at Mac-Carrick, but he appeared as though he couldn't care less, which vexed her, so she accepted. As she'd known it would, her hair fell loose with the first turn.

After that, she danced with man after man. The whole experience was heady, though she had the regrettable habit of comparing each partner to the Highlander. As if he were the template others should aspire to? His manner was gruff, and she'd certainly seen more handsome, genteel men. Still, she wished he would look at her as these men did. As if they were besotted. As if they were on the verge of spontaneous poetry. MacCarrick always seemed to be studying her, yet never letting her know what he had decided.

But life was short and she was young. Another man swept her into a dance and she laughed—not a practiced ladylike laugh but a full-hearted one. And why not? Wasn't she already ruined? She'd been kidnapped by a gang of mercenaries. In fact, barring pirates, she couldn't call up a scenario where one could possibly be more ruined than that.

Young and ruined—there was a lot of freedom in that. *Salut* to young and ruined! She laughed again at her thoughts, and the man leaned in to whisper in her ear that she was lovely beyond words and that he wanted her.

*Why, how adorable—*

She was wrenched from him, leaving the man stumbling. MacCarrick had a viselike grip on her good arm and was hauling her away. The men she'd danced with actually booed him until he turned back. She didn't see the look he gave them, but whatever it was made them quiet.

She frowned. Quiet and a good deal paler than before.

"Where are you taking me?" Anna asked with a hint of slurring in her voice. "I was enjoying myself."

Court bet she was. Tonight he'd recognized that while she was with him he would kill any other man who touched her. "What did he tell you?" he asked as he cut through the park, pulling her along to their inn.

She frowned. "Pardon?"

Court stopped and faced her. "The man dancing with you."

"Oh, him," she said with a grin. "He told me I was lovely and that he wanted me."

He hid his clenched hands behind him, fought to control his tone. "A fine idea. I'll take my payment now."

She blinked at him. "Your payment?"

"My kiss. I want it. Now."

"Here?"

"Here."

"Oh. Well, you are due, I suppose," she said, shocking him. He'd expected her to beg out of it.

"Then put your arms around my neck." Damn, if she didn't do just that. "And bring your lips to mine." She stood on her toes to reach him. He'd wanted to go slow, to teach her—*not* frighten her as he had at the lodge.

Yet he found his lips on hers, hard and intent, and when he flicked his tongue against her lips, she gasped. At once he touched his tongue to hers, tasting the sweet wine she'd been liberally drinking.

She pushed at his chest and broke away, breathless. "You can't do that! That's not right."

"It's a French kiss. We're in France." It was then that he noticed her choker was not on her neck. This was the first time she'd left it behind, and it signified something, he knew it, but then when she mouthed "Ohhh," he set right back, saying against her lips, "Kiss me back."

She hesitantly did, with the tiniest stroke of her tongue. Then she broke away again, a look of wonderment on her face. "That felt *nice.*"

His voice was harsh. "Then let's do it instead of talking about it."

"Oh, of course." She closed her eyes again and offered her lips up to him. He took them, kissing her, savoring her. When she lapped at his tongue, pleasure shot through him, making him squeeze her hips and grind her against him.

A last haze of sense returned to him. They were in the center of the park. No privacy. By the time they reached the inn, she would realize what she was doing. He knew her. He knew that tonight nothing would cool her ardor like the sight of a bed.

He scanned the area and saw a stone grotto only a few yards away. He took her elbow and led her inside, wondering if she would break away now, if she would come to her senses, but he didn't wonder for long. She reached up and kissed *him*, as she grasped his arms and squeezed the muscles there. He laid his hands on her face as he deepened the kiss, then slipped them down, glancing past the tips of her breasts.

She moaned against him and her hand flitted low on his torso. Without thought and greedy for her touch after her torture today, he took it and placed it against the ridge in his trousers. She froze and broke the kiss.

"I shouldn't do that," she whispered.

"No' curious? You doona have to do more. Just feel me."

She bit her lip, appearing to weigh his request, then she leaned up to kiss his chest in the V of his shirt. While he tried not to groan, she adjusted her hand on him—because she hadn't removed it.

He took her lips again as he dipped beneath the hem of her skirt and worked his hands up the sides of her thighs. He continued up, hungry to put his fingers inside her for the first time, to watch her come, but she stiffened and locked her legs together.

"No, MacCarrick."

"Open your legs for me."

"No, I-I can't."

She was an innocent, he reminded himself, but he'd still hoped he could seduce her into giving him anything he wanted. "If you let me, I'll make you feel even better than the kiss did."

She removed her hand from him and put her forehead against his chest, shaking her head, as if she regretted that she couldn't.

Growling his frustration, he rasped against her neck, "Then tell me I can kiss your breasts."

She gasped.

"I think it will please you."

"You've thought about this?"

"Every night since I met you." He was kissing lower and lower until he reached the line of her bodice. "Anna?"

When she finally whispered "Yes," he tugged the cloth down.

With the first mere brush of his lips against her nipple, her head fell back and she moaned. He'd known how much she would love this, had suspected he could make her come just from pinning her arms over her head and slowly tonguing her. And he'd hated the impossibility that a man like him would ever witness it. Now he suckled hard, savoring her flesh.

"Oh, my God," she cried, and his cock pulsed with need. He put her hand back on him and forced her to rub it up and down.

He alternately sucked at the crest and flicked his tongue until she arched her back, offering. When she was in this state, he put his hand behind her head and pushed her against the grotto wall, pressing her hand between them.

"MacCarrick, what do you want of me?" she whispered wildly.

What did he want? Everything and nothing. With Annalía, he'd bloody well take whatever he could get. "I want to see you come tonight. One way or another." When she frowned in confusion, and removed her hand, his lips found hers, but she turned her face from him. "I can't *think*. My head's spinning."

He knew she couldn't think—or else she'd deny him. He hated that he was the type of man a fine lady like her shouldn't—wouldn't—consider for anything more. He pressed his hand against her skirt between her legs to palm her through the material.

"Wh-What are you doing?" Her eyes opened wide, meeting his own, and she let out a tremulous breath. He leaned down to press his lips to the top of her breast just as he stroked his fingers against her. *"Oh, my Lord,"* she moaned and relaxed into him.

"You like this."

"Yes," she cried.

"Do you want me tae keep touchin' you?"

When she nodded eagerly, he made some sound of amusement, then said, "No' so ladylike right now?"

Her whole body went rigid, and she pushed at his chest. She snatched up her blouse and swatted at his hand, though he resisted releasing her. When she peered down at his hand, shoved into her skirts, her face and chest colored, her eyes widening in horror. Too late, he remembered how she'd reacted the last time he'd made a comment like that.

Humiliated. She'd reacted as if she'd been hit.

He pulled his hand away. "Anna, I should no' have said that—"

"No, but it's true, isn't it?" She gave him a tight, false smile that didn't reach her eyes. And he knew the bloody choker would come back the next day like a collar. He hated the damn thing now.

He wanted to know who'd hurt her—besides himself. Who'd hurt her *originally.*

And he wouldn't mind knowing why he wanted to kill that person.

# Twenty-one

At odd times throughout the last two days, memories of the time in the grotto would surface, making Annalía blush uncontrollably. Actually, at most times. It was happening now, as she rocked along in the warm coach trapped with a man so intense she could *feel* him three feet away.

Worse, whenever she replayed the events of that night, she wanted to repeat them, no matter how sharp her shame was. What they'd done had only served to make her cravings for him a thousand times worse. She wanted to go back to that night and take what he had offered. She wanted to go back and give him what he seemed to need.

But even *he* must think that her actions were bad. *Not so ladylike,* he'd said when she answered that she wanted more—and she thought he'd . . . laughed. A barbaric Scot had teased free the fire in her blood, and then had ridiculed *her* reaction. Her behavior must have been wildly amiss. Why else would he continue to take the chair or the floor without a word of protest when they stopped for the night? Why else would he not even bother to try to seduce her again? Before, he'd always found excuses to touch her, was always staring at her, and now he'd stopped.

Each night she lay awake waiting, hoping he would take the bed again. Because then she could rebuff him! Yet nothing happened, nothing but mounting exhaustion and disappointment for her.

Last night, she'd realized, miserably, that she'd never planned to rebuff him.

She squeezed her eyes shut. Why should she be surprised? One *couldn't* escape one's fate. She'd tried so hard, been the opposite of what everyone expected of her. She'd tried, and all because of some rough Highlander's seduction, she'd failed. A seduction that vanished as if never there.

These thoughts made her head hurt, so she leaned against the coach side near the window and tried to sleep. She needed to make up for two nights without, and a breeze was blowing in the window. Sunlight teased her face through the tree leaves. Wonderful. . . .

When Annalía woke a short time later, she blinked her eyes to focus. Feeling heavy in her body, feverish, she glanced down, saw his huge hand slowly stroking her nipple through her blouse.

"Sleep well?" he said, his voice rumbling against her ear.

She scrambled away. More awake, she realized she'd been lying half on his lap, clutching his shirt. On the *opposite* seat.

While she marshaled her scattered wits, determining the most effective way to curse him for touching her while she *slept*, he said, "You talk in your sleep."

"I do not!"

"Aye. Just now and every night I've spent with you."

How humiliating! She smoothed her hair in place, checked her choker, then crossed her arms over her sensitive breasts.

"You shouldn't have . . . petted me while I was unaware!" she cried. "I know you are not a gentleman but this . . . this . . . It wasn't fair."

"Doona speak to me about what's no' fair. It's no' fair that I canna *stop.*"

He couldn't stop? Well, he had for the last fifty-nine hours. Or so. Oh, she was sorry off— Wait, he made it sound like it was *her* fault? How dare he turn it around? "I want you to apologize."

He curled his lips into a shadow of a grin, dismissing the idea so easily. "I'll never be sorry for that. Besides, you pressed against me, rubbing my chest and lower. Saying soft words in Catalan—"

"What did I say?" she asked, her voice shrill. Probably begging him to make love to her. She was so common!

"It's a wee bit dirty. Are you sure you want me to repeat it?"

"No!" she said, glad for a way out. "But I still don't accept that I did these things."

"Aye, you did them, as soon as I carried you onto my lap where you belonged, you started to."

Her jaw slackened. "You have no shame!"

"Annalía, we canna go on like this. I know why you're mad at me—"

"I'm not mad at you, I'm mad at myself," she lied, because actually she was furious with both of them.

"How's that? There's no way you can blame yourself."

"Of course, I can blame myself. It's just as you said. *I* wasn't behaving like a lady."

He glanced away and muttered, "If you knew how many times I've kicked myself . . ." Bringing his gaze to hers again, he said, "Anna, if anyone's to blame, it's me. That night I coaxed you into doing something you would no' normally do. Remember? I'm the ruthless bastard. I pushed you into it."

She shook her head insistently. He had no idea how much

she wanted him to touch her. How even now she craved it—

"Have you done what we did with another man?"

"No!"

"Then it was me. My doing." He sounded so confident.

"You've done this with a lot of women?"

He didn't answer, just continued to watch her face.

Other women. No doubt *many* other women. Like the women who stared at him on the street. Why did that make her furious? Scaldingly furious?

"Anna, I'm past thirty years of age. I have no' lived my life as a monk."

Bastard! She was just one of many. But she would never think of another man as she did him. In the grotto, before her humiliation, she'd felt wonder and awe. The feelings he'd given her were indescribable.

"I'm twenty-one, and apparently I have!" A thought occurred to her. If she was to be cursed with memories of him, he deserved no less. She wanted him to long for her above all the others—above all the shopkeepers and barmaids and farmers' daughters, the entire hateful legion she'd dreamed up—when they parted ways. She wanted to be better than all the rest.

Instinctively, she thought she could. . . .

When his voice grew husky and he said, "I want my next kiss," she met his gaze.

"Then take it," she heard herself murmur.

He appeared surprised, just before he cupped her neck with one hand and grabbed her waist with the other, pulling her to him. With an "Oh!" she realized he was drawing her directly back onto his lap. When he had her positioned on him, he put his hands on her shoulders to rub his thumbs over the sides of her neck.

"This is getting in the way, lass," he said as he began unfastening her choker.

"Oh, wait, you can't just—"

"I'll keep it safe for now." He carefully rolled it up and placed it in his trouser pocket.

She was about to say more, but he began massaging her up and down her back. Yet even when her lids grew heavy, he didn't kiss her. Again, she got the impression he was relishing that he was about to.

"*MacCarrick*," she said plaintively, shocking herself. It was all the prodding he needed. He leaned her back over his arm and settled her lips beneath his. His other arm brushed over her sensitive nipples, and she moaned against him. He stilled his body, as if deciding something, then brought his hand up to grasp her breast. Another moan. Soon his hand on her breast felt vital, as if she'd beg for it if he took it away.

As he kissed her deeply, stroking her tongue with his own, he palmed her, running his hands over the material of her blouse. When she writhed against him, she felt his manhood beneath her bottom, huge, jutting from his groin. But he drew back. Her thinking was so muddled, her craving for his lips back on hers intense, and beneath her . . . all heat and hardness. She remembered how good he'd felt in the grotto growing harder and larger directly in her hand.

She felt air on her chest, followed by his hot breath.

How had he bared her? Her blouse open, he tugged down the gauzy material of her chemise, uncovering her breasts. He stared, eyes intent.

Two nights ago, there'd been the music, wine, and *darkness*, but this was daylight. She could feel herself blushing from her chest up to her face and began to scramble up. "No, Anna, let me see you." He brushed the back of his hand over one breast, then the other, as if reverently. He grated some foreign word, but the *way* he said it . . .

"I-I don't know. MacCarrick—?" She watched his brows draw together as he bent his head to her. And cried out when he dragged his tongue over her nipple. An urgent groaning sound came from him as he set to her breasts, *licking* the peaks as he had in the grotto. Who had ever heard of this before?

He closed his mouth on one and drew. Her back arched from the pleasure, her bottom grinding against him. He raised his face and grated, *"Still, lass.* You canna know what you're doin' tae me."

She stiffened. "Am I hurting you?"

"Aye. Terribly." His face was solemn, deadly serious when he said, "You usually do."

When she didn't relax, he cupped her other breast and suckled.

"But I don't want to hurt you," she said between panting breaths. She meant it—she didn't like the idea of him hurting, and hated that she caused it.

Against her wet nipple, he rasped, "It will no' much longer."

Cool air on her legs. His palm rubbed its way up her thigh, well past her garters and higher. . . . She stiffened in his arms and pushed at his hand. He lowered it, but still caressed her thigh.

"I need tae touch you."

"No!"

He put his lips to her earlobe and flicked his tongue against her.

"Oh!"

His hand inched higher. "Let me touch you there."

"I can't. You'll be cruel to me."

*"Never,"* he bit out.

"You were before."

"Cruel? I was no' tryin' tae be. But you are now." His brogue was growing thicker.

"I am not!"

"If you knew how much I want my fingers against you . . .

You've got me at your mercy, Anna. I'd give anythin' right now." He pressed his face down against her breasts, nipped at the peaks, making her shoot up in his arms before he soothed her back down. "*Name anything.*"

He wanted this that badly? "Anything?"

"Right now I'd give my land, I'd sell my soul."

"Only touching? Nothing more?"

"I'll only do what you want me tae."

She was about to be embarrassed. He should be vulnerable as well. "Then I-I want to feel you, too—without your trousers—"

In an instant, and amid a fierce groan, he set her beside him. He looked to her and then nodded to his groin. When she stared helplessly at his erection straining against his trousers—how exactly did one begin this?—he twisted loose the waist fastening. He seemed to be preparing for something as he glanced around to snag a seat cushion. He placed it behind her, then eased her back, hooking the hems of her skirts with his thumbs and raising them to her waist. Again a palm against her thighs, massaging her resistance away.

Her chest was bare—his should be as well. She unbuttoned his shirt, and just when she'd finished, he guided her hand past the loosened waist of his trousers, inside them . . . until she fully touched his erection skin to skin. He closed his eyes and shuddered, and it pulsed in her hand just as all the muscles in his chest and torso contracted.

She was overwhelmed by how hot it was, how hard and big. He groaned deep, then roughly pushed her palm lower until she cupped him. Another foreign word hissed out like a curse.

Just as she flung her head to the side, looking away in embarrassment and amazement, she felt the most peculiar sensation. His fingers skimmed the slit in her pantalettes.

When he'd removed the locked grip on her hand, she

placed her palm around his erection and was squeezing him, nervous. Just when she thought he'd finally feel her, he took both sides of her pantalettes and ripped. She sputtered, outraged, until she felt his fingers brushing over her sex. She moaned and her head fell back. The pad of one finger traced her. He would feel how wet she'd grown. . . .

"Anna," he said with a growl. She tried to close her knees, but his hips had found their way between them. "Do you know what this does tae me? Tae feel you so wet? I've dreamed of this." His eyes caught hers, preventing her from looking away even when he said, "Tonight I'll taste you," just as his finger eased into her.

*Taste?* She moaned low in her throat, adoring the surprising feel of his finger, of the filling sensation, only comprehending she was still squeezing him when he bucked against her palm. With every push of his hips against her hand, his finger delved into her at the same time. When she realized he was doing this on purpose, as if he were imagining his hardness pressing inside her or forcing her to imagine it, she stroked him hectically to make him go faster.

He leaned down and put the tip of his tongue against her breast, flicking the crest, wetting one, then the other. She watched enthralled, never ceasing her hand on him. Then another, new feeling. Somehow he touched her inside and then rubbed and teased another part of her with his thumb. This made her breaths shallow, made her legs fall open.

"Yes, spread your legs wider for me."

She did, because he wanted it but also because the instinct was there. She needed to be open to him. She needed to say things to him, lurid things, thanking him for the wondrous acts he was doing to her, telling him how much he was pleasing her. She'd never felt such gratitude to another. . . .

"Anna, I lose my mind when I'm with you."

"Yes!" she said, completely understanding. She couldn't

call up a single reason why he shouldn't be resting between her legs, fondling her sex, with her skirts up to her ears.

"You want me tae," he said, as if he didn't quite believe it.

She nodded eagerly, not knowing what she was agreeing to. Just wanting to agree with anything he was saying since he was giving her so much.

His languid eyes widened, and in seconds he'd freed himself completely, looming above her, never slowing his fingers on her sex. He hung there, heavy and thick and magnificent, the muscles of his chest and stomach sharp as they tapered down, and all she comprehended was that she had to have her hand back on it.

She grasped him, and he threw his head back and yelled out. The strength of his reaction made the building tension inside her suddenly spike. *"Oh, Déu!"* she cried.

He faced her again and grated, *"Come for me. I want tae feel you."*

She moaned as her hips rolled against his clever fingers. Reason was lost. The tension exploded. As she arched her back, she heard his heavy breaths, felt them on her tight nipples, felt him drawing out her pleasure. Her body squeezed the finger inside her, needing it. She went wild, her hands on him everywhere.

When his touch became languorous, circling her, seeming to revel in the wetness, she opened her eyes, found herself still slowly stroking him.

"I wanted all of you, but I canna hold on. Will you help finish me for now?"

Whatever that meant. When she nodded, too content to do more, he raised her until she sat up against the side of the coach, then shrugged from his shirt to spread it over her dress at her lap. "Take me again." At once, she did.

He put one hand against the coach wall above her to lean over her, then fit his other hand around hers, his large fingers encircling hers and his manhood in a crushing grip below them. Tightly, shockingly so. It would bruise, possibly even break right there beneath her fingers. . . .

Then he moved his hand, and her hand, along the length just as his hips pumped forward. He swore in a deep, broken voice when his hips met their hands, his gaze never leaving her breasts, her neck, her face.

Annalía watched, bewildered, as their hands moved forward and then slammed back once more. The pressure increased.

His breaths were ragged. Low, tortured sounds broke from his throat. "Arch your back," he ordered and she did. He leaned down to suckle her, only freeing her to grate, *"Anna, I'm about tae come—"* His mouth returned, but this time his teeth pinched her nipple, and she cried out with pleasure.

The coach skidded to a stop.

He released her hand and nipple, though he rubbed his face over her breast desperately before he hissed a harsh curse and drew back. When he forced his huge, swollen member into his trousers, he looked in more pain than with any of his injuries before. He inhaled deeply, then exhaled in shudders several times as if he was getting himself under control. "We are no' finished with this," he rasped, his voice hoarse.

She quickly shook her head, but he studied her expression as if he didn't quite trust that she'd resume what they were doing.

Just after he shuddered again, he somehow remembered to smooth down her skirts for her as she pulled her blouse back in place. He opened the carriage door and bellowed, "Why the *bloody* hell have we stopped?" He sounded on the verge of violence.

The driver called down, "A tree's blocking the road. Probably from the storms earlier in the week."

MacCarrick slammed the door. "God damn it!" He reached for his bag and gave her a warning look. "I want you to stay down."

"Wh-What is it?"

"Rechazados. With bloody, *bloody* bad timing."

The rage Court felt that someone would seek to hurt her was nearly blinding. No, *kill* her. And he was the only thing preventing it. If he didn't get cold like he used to be, they'd both be dead.

So busy in her skirts that he wasn't aware of the danger they were in.

He snared his pistol and a bag of coin, retrieved his shirt with a bitter curse, then donned it and his jacket with more bullets in the pockets. *"Down, Anna,"* he ordered again, as he snatched his rifle from the overhanging net, then stormed out of the carriage, shirt still unbuttoned. He didn't bother to duck or cower, but strode to the front. Ducking wouldn't make a damn bit of difference with them, just would be the last thing you were doing when you got killed.

*"Turn the carriage around."*

The driver nodded, obviously shocked at Court's tone. Court stuffed the pistol into his pocket, then tossed the bag to him. "This is a quarter of what you'll get if you get her to safety until I return."

While he hefted the bag and said, "A *quarter?*" Court worked the lever on his rifle, laying it over his shoulder in readiness. He stalked up to the now skittish horses to snag a bridle, helping the driver work the coach around.

The first shot rang out, whizzing past his head. The horses shrieked but didn't bolt.

Court took aim at where the shot had originated and fired, then pumped the lever to fire three more times. With a second of time bought, he climbed the block as the driver prepared to flee, then in a low voice gave him new directions.

Court was just climbing down when two shots pitted the coach roof. Anna screamed, "MacCarrick, please come back!"

*Now.* Now he went cold.

The driver snapped his whip, and Court dropped down to return a shot of his own. He heard Anna scream again before they turned the corner.

# Twenty-two

*T*hat bastard!" What was he thinking, jumping off the coach like that? Who did he think he was? What had she ever done to indicate that this would be in any way acceptable?

She'd called for Coachy, ordered him to *stop,* but they sped recklessly on, road dust trickling in from the bullet holes.

It wasn't fair. Just as before—it was worse waiting, worse not knowing. Worse being sped away so fast she couldn't even jump from the bloody carriage.

Why not stay with her and run? No, MacCarrick had to make some grand, idiotic gesture. He hadn't even ducked! She crossed her arms in anger, but soon had to uncross them to hold on to the strap inside the rocking coach.

She didn't care. She'd find her brother and get back home eventually. She didn't need Courtland MacCarrick.

"Oh, *Mare de Déu,*" she said with a gasp. She didn't need him.

But she *wanted* him. Even though he was stubborn and aggressive and Scottish, she wanted him. And he would deny her to be some cursed hero?

Dismal hours passed before the coach finally slowed. She smelled the oddest scent and wrestled the working coach window down to find water stretching before her. The sea. They must have finally reached Calais, just across the channel from England.

She'd never seen the coast and had always longed to. For some reason kept mysterious to her, everyone who ever came back from the sea was happy.

Out of the corner of her eye, the sun was setting brilliantly, the waves meeting it ablaze with color.

And she felt none of the excitement she'd thought she would when she'd envisioned this day again and again.

The driver, inexplicably protective of her when he should be running away from a passenger who'd been ambushed and then abandoned, secured a room at a well-appointed inn directly on a cliff overlooking the sea. He even had a fine meal of fish brought up to her, but she could never eat when nervous. Instead, she stood on her balcony watching the lighthouse in England bandy with the French one on the next cliff up, their lights over the water like chalk on slate.

But where was he? She turned from the scene and paced until she thought she might drop. Why hadn't he arrived yet? She knew the most probable answer and refused it. Refused the deadening in her heart, realizing she'd never be the same if he died.

Annalía had hated her mother most of her life for her adultery, for throwing everything away for passion. Before MacCarrick, she hadn't understood how anyone could give up so much, but now she knew the feelings that could drive a person to risk it all. She'd give up everything she had to have him back, safe.

Her brows drew together in anguish. Though the night was slow to pass, the sun was rising. And he still was missing. What if he was hurt on the road somewhere? Oh God, what if he was lying in a ditch?

She'd go right back the way they came and retrace their steps. She'd browbeat Coachy if she had to, but she was going back.

Resolved, she yanked open the door. A dark figure stood just outside, and she nearly screamed in fright. "MacCarrick!" He looked more exhausted than she'd ever seen him.

He shoved her in, then slammed the door behind them. Without a word, he ran his hands forcefully over her, looking her up and down for injuries, then stumbled away. She knew he hadn't slept since he'd left her, and her heart constricted when she realized he'd returned to her as quickly as he was able.

*Still . . .* "You Highland bastard! Don't you ever, *ever* do that again. Don't you dare leave me!"

He stood his rifle against the wall. Before it had been shining and new. Now it was scratched all over, coated in mud, the handle dented. What had he gone through out there?

He sarcastically mumbled, "I'm alive and well." He lifted a ponderous chair like it was weightless, then wedged it against the door. "Doona worry yourself."

She watched in dismay as he lurched to the pitcher to guzzle water.

"I've been worried. I didn't know if you'd return."

Running his sleeve over his mouth, he turned. His expression revealed obvious irritation. "Have a feelin' you'd be fine without me."

"Likely! But that doesn't mean I don't want to be with you!"

He frowned as if her words had just stunned him, confused him. He stumbled again as he drew his pistol from his trouser waist and placed it on the table beside the bed. "Canna talk. Need tae sleep, woman. Doona leave this room or I'll make you regret it."

He fell to the bed, flat on his face, and passed out at once.

Her eyes widened, and she leapt forward to turn his head so he could breathe. Clearly he needed someone to care for *him* now. She discarded her shoes and sat, knees to her chest, beside him. The simple act of watching him sleep made the new feelings she'd experienced earlier return multiplied.

She reached toward him and smoothed his hair from his forehead. With a pang, she watched his brows draw together as if he was unused to the touch. Was he?

Of all the women he'd admitted to seducing, did none of them touch him tenderly afterward? She would when she made love to him.

Well! She hadn't realized part of her had had this discussion, much less that she'd decided. Even so, she believed it was a good decision, especially considering the three attacks on her life that would surely be followed by more. She refused to die with regrets. Now that she had a hint, a taste of what it would be like to make love to Courtland MacCarrick, she wanted it all.

After hours of trying to imagine making love to him, her eyes finally slid closed one too many times.

Near nightfall, she woke, still half asleep, remaining in position until she toppled to her side still in a ball. She could have sworn she heard him chuckle from across the room.

She cracked open her eyes and found him with his hair wet, drying off his very naked body beside a tub. He'd lit only one lamp, probably to let her sleep, but she could see his sculpted muscles tensing and flexing as he took the towel and ran it over his neck, chest, and privates. Continuing to feign sleep, she studied him through her eyelashes, until, to her great disappointment, he finally pulled on his trousers.

"I know you're awake," he said.

With an exasperated sigh, she sat up. "If you knew I was awake and watching, then why didn't you turn away instead of continuing directly in front of me?"

"I dinna hear any complaints."

The man didn't have a modest bone in his body! Yet she wouldn't argue with him because complaining had been the farthest thing from her mind. "So how long have you been up?"

"Not long."

She twined her hair, knotting it behind her.

"How many were there?"

"Three."

"You killed them?"

"Aye."

He didn't look proud of the fact. She'd learned after the second attack that MacCarrick wasn't bloodthirsty; he was blood weary. "Why didn't you even duck?"

"Would no' make a difference with them. But you would no' know I dinna duck unless you had no' been down as I told you."

"How could I not look? Please don't leave me like that again. I can help you." This amused him and she bristled. "I do believe I took out one of the two on the road to Toulouse. If you gave me a pistol—"

He froze. "I never want to see you with a gun in your hand, Anna."

"Why not?"

"You were no' meant to," he said simply.

"What is that supposed to mean?"

His gaze caught hers, and she saw his eyes were bleak. "It means people like me were put on the earth so people like you never have to do bad things and suffer from them."

After tense moments, she felt a confusing sadness seeping into her and turned away.

As he finished dressing, she asked, "How long will we stay here?"

"We have to wait till the morning tide to cross, then we'll take the train to London."

*A train.* She'd always dreamed of riding one, but they were rare in France, impossible in Andorra. Now she would, and she couldn't care less.

"I'll go downstairs and get food for you. And a fresh bath, if you'd like it."

She nodded absently, her mind on other things, such as how reluctant she was to see him go now, and how one might go about seducing a Scottish mercenary. Just like any other man, she supposed, which left her no better off.

# Twenty-three

*I* thought you'd be ready by now," Court said as he began forcing himself out of the doorway. The room was darkened but for one flickering lamp, and she was sitting at the headboard of the bed, clad in only her thin shift and a new bandage.

He'd given her plenty of time to bathe and dress, fearing he might see any part of her unclothed, and a glimpse of an ankle at this point would pain him. When he'd been assured she was safe, the memories from the coach began clawing at him. Even as he'd slept, he'd dreamed of a different ending entirely and woke heavy and aching for it. He'd even dreamed she'd said she wanted to be with him, though he'd realized on the ride back to her that she'd never meant to make love to him in the carriage. He'd pushed and had heard and seen what he wanted because he wanted her so badly.

And now to see her in nothing but a sheer piece of material, with her hair loose . . .

"Wait, MacCarrick. I need to speak with you."

He swallowed hard. "We can once you're dressed."

"Will you please come in?"

Why had he ever wanted her to learn to ask? Probably because he hadn't known it about himself that he couldn't deny her. He shut the door, then sat at the foot of the bed. "What do you need?"

"I've had a lot of time to think," she said softly.

He stared, dumbfounded, as she began crawling toward him.

When her breasts moved with each movement closer, he rubbed a hand over his mouth. "Uh-huh." If he'd known this was what he'd be returning to, he'd have been quicker about his tasks.

"This is a dangerous time for us."

She'd always had that accent that drove him mad, but when she purred the words . . . Her *voice* made him hard as hell.

"Aye, it is." Though the urge to pull her to him and get his hands on that body was overwhelming, he remained still, breaths shallow, curious to see what she'd do next.

"And I don't want to *wish* I'd experienced something. Not when I can. Now. With you."

"With me," he agreed mindlessly. She was in bed with *him*. She wanted him, a rough Highlander. This was no longer a dream.

Perhaps it should stay that way. . . .

"Anna, if you're doin' this because you were afraid when I was gone or because you feel beholden tae me . . . then . . ." *Court, what the bloody hell are you saying?* He shook his head hard. "As if I give a damn why. *Come tae me.*"

She did. When she sat up on her knees before him and her lips were close to his, she whispered, "I'm asking you to make love to me."

He'd been shot. Undoubtedly, they'd gotten him.

Yet he wasted no time rolling her shift up her body and working it off her, fearing she'd change her mind. She followed his rapt gaze, then quickly glanced up. At first she was bold, but as he was unable to stop gaping at her wholly naked body, she brushed her hair forward to spill over her breasts and tugged the cover before her.

He simply shook his head at her, slowly, in warning.

"B-But you're staring."

He pulled the material from her, then drew her down flat on the bed, running his fingers through her hair to skim the soft curls to the side. "I'm starin' because you're more beautiful than I could ever imagine and it gives me pleasure tae look at you, all of you. I'm starin' because I never thought I would." His voice was unrecognizable. He sounded like a beast. With her golden skin and plump breasts and tiny waist, she looked like an offering.

"I've never been unclothed this long outside of a bath."

"You canna be shy with me."

"Why not?"

"Because it's me." He swept another greedy glance down the length of her body and hissed a curse. "Woman, I doona even know where to begin."

She bit her bottom lip. "It'd be easier for me to be unclothed if you were as well."

He didn't say a word, just drew off his boots, then snagged his shirt over his head without unbuttoning it. He stood at the foot of the bed and unfastened his trousers, easing them over his erection before they could drop.

"Oh, my . . ." she murmured, her eyes bright. She sat up, as she might at a picnic, her legs bent and tucked to her bottom. Still the lady.

He put his knee on the bed, preparing to go to her, nervous that he was about to take this woman.

"Wait."

Of course, wait. He closed his eyes in frustration. What was he doing imagining that he was about to make love to her? He should have known she'd come to her senses. Had to have known his luck had *never* run this high—

"Will you stay there?"

He opened his eyes to see her coming to him.

"You are completely unclothed, and I want to . . ." When she was on her knees in front of him, her face still close to his because of the high bed, she leaned in to whisper, "May I just learn you first?"

He tried to keep the disbelief from his face and pulled his knee back to stand fully. "You can do whatever you want tae."

Biting her lip, she put her hands to his face, brushing her thumbs over it, gently tracing the scar at his temple. She ran her soft palms down to his neck and shoulders, then along his arms. She tilted her head at his hands as if she didn't quite know what to do with them, then placed them on her shoulders as if she were putting them away. "Let's keep them there for now."

She was very serious about this. With his arms up, she explored his torso, sometimes lightly scratching, making the muscles contract painfully, though he didn't let her know, and she'd never guess it by the way his cock was responding to her touches.

"Anna," he grated when he saw she'd begun panting her breaths, her breasts rising in time, her nipples hardening to tempt his mouth. With great satisfaction, he realized she'd become aroused by touching him.

Then with one hand, fingers pointing down, she rubbed along his belly. "Every inch of you is hard as rock."

As she was slowly following the trail of hair down from his navel, he could only grunt in answer. Every lingering, teasing inch closer was increased agony. Then a shock of pleasure hammered through him when she grasped his shaft with one hand. Astonishment when she cupped him with the other. He clutched her shoulders and hissed a curse.

"Except here." Her nails lightly scratched the base of his sack, and his eyes rolled back in his head.

He dropped his knee back to the bed, drawing her in by her shoulders. When he kissed her, she gasped and said, "I wasn't finished."

"I was just about tae be."

When she frowned, he took her mouth in a fierce, wet kiss, thrusting his tongue into her, delving it against hers, a kiss more aggressive than the one in the coach. His hands found her backside, squeezing her, kneading her, and he could feel that she rolled her hips toward him even as she grasped his face and met his tongue.

He brushed the curls over her sex, reverently, and rasped against her lips, "Spread your knees for me." When she did, he dipped a finger into her wetness, groaning, "Anna, you feel so damn good."

Her head fell back, and she held on to his shoulders for support as he continued to explore her. He'd felt in the coach that she was tight, but knowing this time he meant to be inside her made him realize she was *too* tight.

He laid her back on the bed, grasping her by the waist and moving her bodily to the headboard. He took her legs to each side of his and spread her, taking time to kiss her pale inner thigh as he'd wanted to do since he'd met her. The contact was grazing—she probably could feel the heat of his breaths more than his lips—and she shivered.

Once more, his finger inside her, stirring her. She moaned, back arching, and he ran his other hand from her chest down between her breasts as he tried to fit a second finger inside. She was slick, incredibly lush, but she was too small. He could *feel* how untouched she was, could feel that she was a virgin.

His hands were dark and scarred against her sex, against her thigh. They looked . . . wrong. He felt big and hulking, and he knew he was about to hurt her. *Isn't that the way of it?* a part of him asked. But he would hurt her and then he would ruin her. It seemed too much, too great a price.

It wasn't good enough for her.

He leaned forward, careful to keep his shaft from touching her below, and placed his forehead against hers. "I canna do this tae you."

She tensed; he felt it strongly. "You don't find me desirable."

He reared back, shocked that a woman like her could *ever* draw that conclusion. "That's no' it."

She turned her face away. "I'm waiting to make love to you, we both are unclothed in bed together, and you won't? I think it's because you've decided you don't want me."

He snatched her hand and shoved it against his cock. *"Can you no' feel how much I want you?"*

The minute she wrapped her fingers around him, her body went languid, and she looked up at him dreamily. "Now you're just trying to distract my thoughts. To pacify me, when we've learned how much I like this."

He struggled for words. *Pacify* her? His brows drew together. It was important that she realize something . . . What was it? . . . Ah! "I vow tae you that I want you—"

"No, I think I understand what you're trying to tell me," she murmured, never taking her eyes from her slow strokes. "You're a big man. You need a woman who is a match to you. Like with horses."

"That's no' the issue—" He couldn't bloody speak when she looked at his cock . . . longingly, with regret.

She sighed. "I must be like a runt compared to strong Scottish women."

He'd meant to be good. He'd meant to be noble to her.

"I will show you how desirable I find you. How perfect you are tae me . . ."

With flicks of his tongue, he kissed her neck, down to her breasts, stopping to lavish attention on her nipples. He loved how sensitive she was there, how much she craved that. Another night he would suckle her until she came. He'd fantasized about pressing his fingers into her only to savor her already squeezing.

He moved down her body, kissing her flat belly, forcing himself to pull his shaft out of her hand, though her fingers tightened on him to prevent him, and then her hand reached out, patting blindly for it, a reaction that pleased him mightily.

Finally, he rested his chest on the bed between her legs and cupped her bottom.

"MacCarrick?" she asked nervously.

With the first exquisite taste of her, his hands squeezed too hard. He was starving for her, but didn't want to frighten her. He forced himself to break away, to get control.

"What is this?" she cried. "You can't do this!"

She tried to wriggle out of his grip when he lowered his mouth to her once more. A long, leisurely run of his tongue, feeling her soft flesh. His eyes closed in pleasure.

She gasped, outraged. "You must stop at once."

"*Anna*"—her name came out like a growl—"*no force on earth could stop me.*"

"You," she began with a wavering breath, "you enjoy? . . ."

"Tasting you?"

She squirmed in embarrassment. "Yes!"

"I could lie between your legs and kiss you all night. But does this please you?" he asked before rubbing his tongue against her once more.

"No!"

He pulled back. "Liar."

"It's wrong."

"But does it please you?"

"It mustn't!"

"Let go. Let me bring you pleasure."

Her eyes were squeezed tightly shut. "I can't."

"Then all I ask is for you tae give me one last kiss and then I'll stop."

In a pained voice, she finally said, "Very well."

He bent down to her once more, licking gently, lulling her, before shocking her with the thrust of his tongue inside her. She arched off of the bed, moaning.

"Shall I stop?"

Her eyes still closed, Anna impatiently waved him on with the flick of her small hand.

He grinned smugly, then kissed her once more, sampling her, glancing up, loving her growing response.

It wasn't long before her taste was making him crazed and he was slowly grinding his hips against the bed. He spread her legs wide before him, forcing her to open to everything he wanted to do, and took her thoroughly, unable to get enough. Her head was thrashing, and she was lost now, needing to come.

He knew how much she wanted to, and it made him bear down on her madly, with little more thought than that of an animal. He removed his hands from her thighs and vaguely realized he was reaching for her breasts. With a groan, he put his arms to each side of her and clenched the sheets, head down, taking her with abandon.

She tried to pry them loose.

He broke away. "No. I'm no' . . . myself. I'll hurt you."

"Take. Please." She said the last as a moan, and placed his hands over her breasts.

Palming them, he groaned against her, tongue back to her soft, slick flesh, and she began to come under his lips, arching her back, pressing her breasts into his hands and grasping his head. Her cries had him bucking against the bed with need of her.

He moved to take her waist, to hold her steady, and watched, awed, as she skimmed her hands up her torso and brushed twice over her tight nipples before her arms fell over her head. She was completely lost to what he was doing to her, and nothing had ever affected him so. He kissed her with all the hunger he felt, wringing her, making her come longer, to a torturing degree, until her quivering finally eased and she went limp.

Reluctant to remove his lips from her skin, he lavished attention to her thighs and hips, then lay beside her so her breasts were just before him.

"Wait, MacCarrick," she said in sultry voice. "What about you? Did you? . . ."

"I'm fine," he grated before circling her nipple with his tongue. He would be. Because he was going to wait until she slept and then take care of himself. He would never ask her to finish him now, not after the thwarted time in the coach and then after his taking her this way tonight. He had no idea what would happen when he finally got to spend, having never ached for it so furiously—

"MacCarrick, I feel grateful to you, very grateful because of these things you've shown me—"

"You feel *grateful* tae me for this?" He'd take much more away—he'd replay this over and over in his mind for the rest of his life, starting as soon as she slept.

"Yes, and I will feel uncomfortable unless I can reciprocate." She placed herself under his arm, and rested her face against his chest. His body thrumming, he laid back and held her close, vowing he wouldn't ask her to make him come, even while feeling her breaths on him and shuddering. . . .

She began walking her fingers down his chest.

His nerves were screaming, his mind begging . . .

"Ah, God, yes!" His back arched, his whole body rigid, when she handled him.

She stroked him as they'd done in the coach, her grip hard, as he liked it. He couldn't make her stop—he was too far gone. Apologies in advance.

She moved so slowly. Tormenting him up and down. Hard, tight, but slow. Torture. Didn't matter. He'd still come. He'd be insane, but . . .

His voice low and wretched, he rasped, "Whatever you do—whatever I do—doona take your hand from me. . . ."

"I won't. But I thought," she began in a whisper before flicking her tongue against his chest, "I should lick and kiss *you* now?"

The thought of her licking his—

He erupted in her grasp, yelling out, heels digging into the bed and back arching, pumping his seed onto his torso. He reached around to seize her breast—clutching it, pawing it—and bent down to take her lips and tongue in a raw kiss. He ground against her hand, relentless, groaning between thrusts of his tongue, then tensing until there was nothing left of him.

It seemed hours before the world righted itself, and he finally stopped shuddering and released her breast and lips. "Did I hurt you? Did I hurt your arm?"

"No, not at all," she answered, her voice unsteady.

He put his fingers under her chin to bring her face up again, needing to know how she reacted to his total loss of control—and to her first sight of a man spending. Would she be disgusted? Upset?

No, her eyes were excited, her breathing rapid, as if she'd just witnessed a miracle. His brows drew together. He wasn't a modest man, but he didn't know how to feel about her expression of utter delight for him spilling in front of her.

Should've been a means to an end, *something that occurred* as it would've in the coach, but she looked as though it was a trick she'd want him to perform every night for her. Worse, she looked *at him . . .* differently.

He pulled his shaft from her hand and his arm from under her, then left the bed, swooping the top sheet with him.

And he certainly didn't like that he had to wipe himself off while her gaze followed his every movement, her eyes wide and curious. He threw the sheet in the corner, then returned to bed. Not close to her.

If she noticed, she didn't act like it. She crawled to him, putting her head back on his chest. "That was amazing," she whispered.

"It's no' exactly a feat."

"Why didn't you make love to me? Am I too small?"

"No," he said, in half truth. He'd never thought he would curse his size before he'd been between her spread legs, glaring down at himself.

"Then why didn't you? Were you afraid to get me with child?"

"That's no' the reason." He wished that was the reason.

"Then what?"

"You still have your virtue. Your future husband will demand that."

"Husband? I don't know if you realize this, but being kidnapped by a gang of mercenaries severely curtailed my husband hunt."

"You could go to America. Marry a rich man there."

"I don't want to go to America."

"I read your letters, Anna."

She stiffened. "Why are you telling me this?"

"I read the one from the railroader's daughter writing about her brother." The brother had planned to ask Llorente for Annalía's hand. "I've heard of their name before. They have more money than the queen. You could go there—"

"Aleix already turned down his suit."

"Did he, then?" he said, his voice deadened. Why should that surprise him? Court had obviously lost his mind during those moments when he'd thought, *What if I just keep her?* Lost his mind thinking she might come to want him for more. "Still, there are options, but only if you're . . . intact."

"Would you demand that of me?" She rolled over on her stomach and propped her chin on her hand. "If you were to be my husband?"

*I'd take you any way I could get you,* he thought again. "I doona consider those kinds of things."

"Why?"

"Because I never plan to marry."

"Did a woman hurt you?"

"No."

"I don't believe you. Why else wouldn't you want a woman to have all your own?"

"No woman's hurt me."

"So the issue is that you don't want *one* woman. You want your harem."

If she only knew. . . . After tonight, she'd *ruined* him. *Her hands brushing her nipples as he took her with his mouth.* Inward shake. "Why settle for one when you can have many?"

"It isn't as if men stop having other women after marriage."

*With you as his wife, this one would.*

"But it's been repeatedly explained to me that though a man might require others, he has the need to possess one woman to call his own, the need to protect her and any children they have. It must be so, because both marriages and affairs go on. If you ignore that need, you'll miss out on so much, MacCarrick," she said softly but with conviction. She curled up next to his side again and laid her arm over his chest. His eyes briefly closed with pleasure.

"Enough of this talk." Perhaps before he let her go, he would explain to her that not all men were like that. That she should expect better.

*Let her go.*

Let passionate, brave, beautiful Anna go. She'd come along as punishment, no doubt. For all his sins. She was his perfect torment.

"So after you reunite me with my brother, you will just leave me behind like all the others."

He didn't hesitate. "Aye."

"Then I thank you for not ruining me further. Because I *will* have a family and children."

Barely hiding his exasperation, he asked, "Then why had you no' married earlier?"

"I won't tell you—you'll think I'm silly."

"Tell me." When she didn't answer, he squeezed her to him.

She sighed. "I was waiting for someone . . . for someone I could love. I know you probably think it's a fanciful notion, but I've seen it."

Court had too. His parents had been mad for each other. "Then you could marry where you chose to?"

She nodded against his chest. "In the beginning, yes, but I couldn't find anyone, so the choice was taken from me. After Pascal, I understand how vulnerable I am as long as I'm unwed."

He'd avoided asking her about her future because he'd known he wouldn't like her answer, but now he said, "What will happen to you once your brother retrieves you?"

She yawned, then murmured in a drowsy voice, "He'll take me to Castile and get the family to find a husband for me who'll overlook the scandal. I suppose it won't be so bad." She ran her smooth thigh over his legs, relaxing against him, her body warming for sleep. "MacCarrick," she whispered, drifting, "if I'd known husbands touch like you do, I'd have been much more eager to wed."

Court, the blackheart, the mercenary who'd sell his sister for a pound, just took a direct hit to the chest.

# Twenty-four

When Court woke Anna early the next morning, she was slow to rouse, but when she did, she smiled shyly at him. He didn't even bother questioning why his chest reacted to the sight of it. "How do you feel?"

She sat up and gave him a surprised look, as if she'd woken in a foreign but more comfortable body. "I feel wonderful." She didn't seem embarrassed by her nudity, though the blanket bundled in her lap covered some, as did her hair falling over one breast. Which left one uncovered—

When she put her hands above her head to stretch, he ran his palm over the back of his neck, and grated, "Mind the arm, lass." If she were his, he'd always be there to see her stretch in the morning. And he'd make sure each night that she had no clothes on to conceal her.

"Oh, I'd forgotten about it completely."

He gave her a tight nod. "I'll leave you to dress. We'll go on the crossing soon."

Before he could escape, she asked in a small voice, "Why are you . . . different?"

Because he'd realized in the long hours of the night that she could never be his. Even if he didn't have a five-hundred-year-old curse shadowing him and even if he could somehow convince a fine woman like her to want to stay with him, Court could never have her. And now he cared about her enough that he refused to ruin her. "Because things will no' be the same between us once we reach England. We canna be together as we were last night."

"Then I want to stay here," she said, surprising him.

"No, you know we canna do that."

When she began to reply, he said, "Here. I almost forgot." He dug into his pocket. "I have your choker." He'd finally figured out the secret behind the choker, and held it with the length dropping down and swinging in front of her, hoping this would startle some sense into her about him.

He'd recognized it wasn't merely a piece of jewelry—it was a talisman that had been her mother's. Her mother wasn't buried with her father, but alone in Paris, away from Andorra and from her family in Castile. She'd somehow been disowned by both. By the way Annalía had acted after the grotto, he suspected he knew why.

She wore it so she wouldn't be like her mother.

To his bewilderment, her gaze flickered over it without interest, then returned, intent only on his face. "I don't want it. It doesn't fit any longer."

When she wouldn't accept it, he stuffed it into his pocket, then strode from the room. He shut the door and leaned back against it, thinking that once he got to London, his brothers would see that this woman had him twisted inside hey'd wonder how, if Court cared about her at all, he could let it get this far.

He wondered, too. How could he explain that as things developed between him and Anna, he hadn't felt that he was taking more than he ought?

He had felt that finally—finally—the pieces were falling into place.

Even the exciting steamer ferry trip across the channel did nothing to break up the tension between Annalía and Mac-Carrick.

He hadn't spoken to her in anything but one-word answers, except when he'd asked if she was seasick. She'd glanced around and seen that most everyone else was, but when she answered no, he appeared bothered, which hurt her feelings.

She scarcely cared that he was surly to her because she had much to think on. She wanted to memorize every instant of the night before because she never, never wanted to forget even the tiniest detail.

Before MacCarrick she'd gone about her life completely ignorant of the staggering pleasure a man can give a woman. She caught him scowling at her from the ship's railing and bit her lip. And the pleasure a woman could give a man. She'd seen it. . . .

He'd always been in control, yet she'd wrested it from him with naught but her fingers, and made him yell and thrash with pleasure with every muscle in that huge body going rigid.

Just remembering made her breasts grow fuller and more sensitive, and simply looking at his talented fingers gripping the railing . . . She frowned. They'd tightened so much around the wood they'd gone white. She glanced up, caught him studying her as she'd been staring at his hands. She parted her lips, and a breath shuddered out. He turned sharply away.

This wouldn't do. She couldn't keep thinking of the night before without longing . . . without lusting. There. She could admit it. Annalía Llorente *lusted* for a ruthless Highland mercenary.

Yet she felt tied to him, too, bound to him by what they shared. Last night, she'd acted blasé about his leaving her behind, but to tell the truth, she hated the thought. She'd actually entertained the idea of keeping the Highlander. Did that mean she loved him? She couldn't say, but she knew she couldn't stand the idea of being away from him.

She'd had moments where she anticipated a future of his lovemaking and cajoled half grins, but she didn't know how she'd accomplish this since she'd never be allowed to marry MacCarrick even if he'd "ruined" her.

Not that MacCarrick wished for marriage to her. He'd made what he wanted clear. "Why have one when you can have many?" he'd asked, which made her angry. She'd rather not have him than have to share him. Where had that thought come from? She felt like a jealous schoolgirl who wouldn't share her ribbon. She knew better than ever to be proprietary over a man.

Only one thing could keep a man by a woman's side—she'd seen it in rare couples—and that was love.

When the steamer began docking, and he took her arm, she asked him, "Do you want to know what I was thinking?"

"Anna, every man on board knew what you were thinking about."

"Oh." Annalía hated being obvious.

"Every one of them would have taken you up on it." He sounded furious as he steered her toward a railed gangway.

*He* was furious? She was the one who had reason to be. She looked back at the ship and in an innocent tone asked, "Were any of them husband material?"

He glowered at her so fiercely any other woman would

have quaked in her garters. After that, he said nothing, and his expression defied her to speak to him. Though she decided she wouldn't give him the pleasure, their next stop was proving unbearable.

He was taking her to London on a *train*. At the station, she had many questions, and she knew he could provide all the answers. It was like having a book in your hand with knowledge you wanted, but the pages were glued together. Sooner or later you'd want nothing more than to hurl it against the wall.

Then London was a chaotic snarl of noise and wares and food smells to be investigated, but he swiftly got them a hansom, and soon they were away from the city center riding into a charming residential area. Copious townhomes with late summer gardens queued along the brick-paved street. Trees abounded and lawns stretched in front of each with spotless perfection. "Fifteenth from the Throne" hadn't been lying when she'd said Brits had taste.

They stopped in front of a grand property with a stately red brick house. Large without being overblown, with every detail tasteful, the property bespoke the wealth of the owners. As was fitting.

"We're here."

She glanced at him, turned to observe the home once again, then frowned. "Did you give Aleix directions to this place?"

"Aye. He should find it easily enough."

"Do you know people who work here?"

He looked at her strangely as he opened his door. "Aye. I suppose I do." Then he was assisting her out and waltzing her up the freshly washed steps, directly to the double doors. The front doors.

"You can't just knock for entrance here, MacCarrick." If he had friends who worked here, he'd get them in trouble.

The skin around his eyes tightened as he rapped the huge ornate knocker. "I can."

Just as she was going to tell him to let her speak for them, one door opened to show a dour-looking butler, whose expression creased into a smile when he saw MacCarrick. "Master Courtland!"

"Erskine, it's good to see you."

As Erskine led them in, Annalía frowned at MacCarrick. "Is this your home?"

"It's my family's. My home's in Scotland."

"Oh." And precisely why would the mercenary's family home be beautiful and luxurious? "Is yours as nice as this one?"

He gave her an unreadable expression. "Do you like me better now that you know I come from money?"

She poked her chin up. The nerve. She wasn't exactly a pauper. "No, to like you better, I would have had to like you some." Though her answer was dripping disdain, her words seemed to please him.

"Then no, my home is no' near to being this nice."

In the next room hung a large portrait of a woman, clearly the focal point. Annalía inspected it, fascinated with the beautiful redhead. "Who is she?"

"Fiona MacCarrick." He said the words as though reluctant. "My mother."

"She's beautiful."

He nodded tightly, giving her the impression that he wasn't close to her. She lingered, noting the quality of the work. The woman was posed in front of a piano, making Annalía wonder if the family had musical talent. "Does she play?"

"Aye, even a Scottish woman can learn to play the piano."

"MacCarrick! Don't take meaning from innocent questions. Pianos are rare in Andorra and denote wealth. A family would be proud to have one and would pose in front of it whether they played or not."

"Then I apologize."

Still piqued, she muttered, "It's not as if I questioned her posing with a book in her hand," then continued her examination of the home. As he guided her into another spacious area, she recognized that something in the house was . . . amiss. "Are there any women here?"

"No sisters. I have two older brothers."

"Any wives?"

His expression tightened again. "No wives."

"Your brothers are older than you and still not married? What do you people have against marriage?"

"This subject's ended."

She hated when he said that. How dare he? *We are not kissing anymore. We are not touching. We are not talking about this subject.* She stopped and refused to follow him, weary of his orders and of his coldness today. "Fine, I shall try to determine answers to my own questions. They won't be as factual or flattering as yours would have been. For instance, I shall say that none of your brothers are married because they are like you—thick-skulled, ill-mannered barbarians. *Mal educat Escocès!* Rude Scots who couldn't hope to get a mate without a club—"

"Appears you've brought a guest, Court." A deep voice interrupted her.

She whirled around, then craned her neck up. And this would be one of the brothers she'd just been insulting. Yes, his brother was very like him, with the same black hair, the same dark watchful eyes.

"Aye, Hugh, this is Lady Annalía Llorente. She comes from Andorra and has no' yet been convinced of all my charms. Annalía, this is my thick-skulled brother, Hugh MacCarrick."

If he intended to embarrass her, he'd have to do better than that. She was a master at social situations, even uncomfortable ones. She glided over to his brother and held out her hand, smiling demurely. He took it and kissed it perfectly. "Delighted."

She turned to MacCarrick. "No, I would say he is nothing like you." When she smiled back at the brother, she saw the tight lines around the man's mouth relax for a moment and suspected that was the only indicator of amusement you'd see from him. She'd wager her Limoges collection that this one hadn't smiled in years. What an odd, solemn family.

She wondered if she'd imagined the subtle easing in his expression, because now he was all sternness. "We'll talk later?" the brother asked MacCarrick.

"Aye," he answered with a grim nod. "Later."

If she were fanciful, she'd swear there was some undercurrent between them, some unspoken . . . warning?

After their intense exchange, she and MacCarrick continued on. The rest of the house was just as lovely and spacious, the room she was to stay in stylish. MacCarrick had grown up amidst wealth. So what had driven him to become a mercenary? And why would his family tolerate such an occupation, even for the youngest son?

# Twenty-five

She'd eaten, she'd bathed, and now that she'd met him downstairs in the parlor, she was pacing, trudging back and forth across the plush carpets. Court sank back in a chair, knowing this wasn't a good sign.

"I need to go shopping," she informed him as she passed his chair. "For clothes."

"I just bought you clothing in the village."

"You know I can't go like that here."

He stared at her skirts swishing too high above her ankles and knew she was right. He also knew she wasn't leaving this house. "It's too crowded and too dangerous."

"Surely the assassins who want to murder me haven't caught up with us yet. And I'm not asking you to pay for them. I could *finally* sell a piece of jewelry."

"The hell you will." Did she think he fought her on this because of money? Did she believe she needed to sell her irreplaceable jewelry because he was *unable to clothe her?* "I'm no' letting you sell your things."

"Then I could go to my English friend's home and borrow from her."

He'd read some letters from that one, too. How many times could she drop that she was fifteenth from the throne? The idea of Anna asking for anything from that snob made his hackles rise—and his pride suffer.

While Anna was with him, it was his due to provide her with things she needed. He gave himself an inward shake when he realized that if she were his, he'd go into hock making her happy. "Forget it. I'm trying to protect you," he snapped. And hock it would be. He didn't have wealth like she saw here. This house was to be Ethan's. His eldest brother was laird and chief of the clan, and the title, the estates, and the family money were all his. On the opposite end of the spectrum, Court had returned to England with no income, no contracts, and no crew.

"Please let me send a note to her—"

"I said no."

She changed tactics. "I appreciate all you've done for me, MacCarrick, but I need to know that if I wanted to walk out that door and have my friends help me, I could."

"Damn it, Anna, no you could no'." He stood, catching her arm. "The only way you're leaving this house is when your brother comes for you. I estimate a week or two, so you'll just have to put up with me until then."

"Why? Our bargain doesn't seem to count anymore." She lowered her voice. "You said we can't be lovers. What exactly am I to you?"

What did she expect him to say? Did she want him to admit he desired more from her, when she only wanted to repeat the night before? "I made you a promise—"

"I'm a promise to keep?" she asked, giving him an expression as though she were disappointed in him.

"Aye. *No.*" He made some growling noise. "Christ, I doona know. Then what am I to you?"

"Honestly, I don't know either." She twined her fingers in front of her. "But you won't let me find out."

When she turned for the stairs, he sank back to his chair again, dumbstruck by their exchange. *Could* she want more from him? And what did it matter since he couldn't give it? . . .

"A word, Court?" Hugh intoned from the doorway. He turned for the study, expecting Court to follow.

How bloody much had Hugh heard? Court stood and pressed the heels of his palms to his eyes, walking without energy toward the study, but when he passed Erskine on the way, Court said, "Find a dressmaker or seamstress who will come here. A good one."

With a "Right away!" Erskine scuttled off.

Damn it, Court wasn't in the mood to explain Anna to his brother, but this appeared to be an opportune time to find out about his money. When he entered, Hugh was sitting at the desk, his face grave, his manner all business.

Court had barely gotten a glass of proper whisky and sat across from him when Hugh warned, "Watch yourself."

"It's good to see you, too." Court raised his glass. "Aye, that's right, brother. I managed to survive another campaign. Shall we discuss the investments made while I was away?"

"Later," Hugh said, plainly concerned with only one subject. "I've never seen you look at anything like you do her."

Court peered into his drink. "I can admit to some feeling for her."

"Want to tell me who she is?"

"It's a long story."

Hugh steepled his fingers. "She does no' look like she's going to be speaking to you this afternoon anyway."

True. So he detailed Pascal's treachery, Annalía's kidnapping and escape, and the danger she was in now. He related almost everything except what they'd done privately and how she had him so knotted inside he couldn't think when she was near.

When he finished, Hugh didn't have any questions, just said, "You're possessive about her. As if she's yours already."

"I will no' let those bastards get near her."

"It's more than that. I see it clearly." His voice went low. "I know because I've felt it clearly."

Yes, Hugh knew what he was going through. Hugh had wanted the same woman for years. Now that Court finally understood what his brother had been feeling all this time, he didn't know how he'd done it. Court had no doubt that years of this with Annalía would turn his mind to soup.

"So now that we know how you feel, what about the lass?" Hugh asked. "Does she care for you? It'll make it harder for you to let her go—"

"I doona think she'll have a problem once there's someone to take my place. Bring her a nice, wealthy gentleman and she'll be content."

Hugh grimaced as if in pain. "That bad?"

"She thinks I'm a brute. Lacking a Castilian's sophistication. You heard her—she's no' particularly keen on Scots in general."

His brows drew together. "She dinna seem averse to you like that."

Court drank deeply. "There were a couple of times with her when I was no' as strong as I should have been." *And she sees no reason for those times to end.*

"This woman obviously comes from a fine family."

Court muttered, "You have no idea."

"What do you mean?"

"Pascal wanted her because she has . . . well, she's a bit . . . royal."

Hugh tried to speak, then closed his mouth. On his second attempt, he grated, "Could you find any woman you were supposed to be with less? You ken you canna bed her without consequences."

"I have no' bedded her."

Hugh eyed him hard, then apparently decided he was telling the truth. "And you will no'?"

Court rubbed his hand over his face.

"You'd have to marry her."

"I know that," he snapped.

"Do you, Court? You and Ethan and I do a lot of questionable things among the three of us, but we've never gone about ruining young innocents. Consider the repercussions for a woman in her position."

"I would never ruin her."

"So you'd risk this woman's safety?"

"You think I doona go over again and again that she's in danger because of me? She was attacked three times and shot on my watch. She's been targeted for murder because of my actions. I know she would've been better off if she'd never met me."

"Then what are you going to do?"

"I'm going to fix her life. Then I'm going to get out of it."

"Why did you no' eat more?" MacCarrick asked as he escorted Annalía to her room that night. "You canna afford to miss many meals, lass."

Though she'd been put out with him earlier, his obvious concern for her over dinner mitigated her irritation. "I just have to get used to the different foods," she answered. "I've never had Saxon fare." Raised on a mountain, Annalía had never been overly fond of seafood. And the Brits seemed to eat little else.

"Be glad it was no' Celtic fare," he mumbled.

She glanced up at him. "Is Scottish food strange?"

He gave her a short laugh. "For you? Aye. It would be."

When he grasped her elbow and steered her up the stairs, she said, "The tension between you and your brother at dinner was thick. Did you fight with him?"

"I did," he finally admitted.

"Will you tell me why?"

He hesitated, but she suspected he wanted to tell her. At length, he said, "Hugh did something high-handed with my property. I dinna appreciate that he acted without my permission."

Though a vexing urge arose to point out that it must be extremely high-handed for *him* to think it so, she instead asked, "Did he have good intentions?"

"Oh, aye. But that's not the point. He thinks he knows what's better for me than I do for myself."

She couldn't help but grin at his surly tone and reached over to touch his hand at her elbow. "I thought that was a sibling's prerogative to think that way. Aleix is the same. When he makes a decision for me, I try to remind myself how fortunate I am just to *have* someone so concerned about my welfare—like you have your two brothers. I remind myself of this, then I set about thwarting him." Her look of amusement faded. "MacCarrick, are you sure Aleix will find me here?"

"I've no doubt. He'll travel to your school and receive the message and then it's only a matter of time until he arrives here."

She nodded slowly, lost in thought as they reached her room. He placed his palm at her lower back to guide her inside, but she paused in front of the bed, blushing from memories of the night before. She perceived his thumb faintly rubbing her back, and wondered if he realized he was doing it. When she turned to face him, his hand trailed along her waist before dropping abruptly.

"MacCarrick, will you think of me after I leave here?"

His face was impassive, concealing his emotions, but she sensed conflict within him.

"Anna," he began with an exhaled breath as if he were about to give some kind of an explanation. Yet after a long hesitation, he said simply, "Aye, I will."

Before she could respond, he said, "I'll be sitting right outside the door, so call me if you need anything."

"You're not staying?"

"No, I've made sure your room is safe—"

"But . . . But you've slept in the room with me every night." She hadn't anticipated this. They always stayed together. That was simply what they *did*.

He gave her a look as if riled with her—as if he wanted to stay but *she* prevented him. "No' any longer, lass," he snapped, turning for the door.

"Why?"

He didn't turn back when he answered, "Because I might try to . . . I might do something we'd both regret."

"Why do you think I'd regret that?"

She saw his shoulders stiffen, saw his hands clench. "You doona know me, Anna." As he shut the door behind him, she barely heard him mutter, *"If you did, you would no' waste your interest on me."*

Alone, she stared after the door. *"You would no' waste your interest . . ."* Too late—her interest was firmly engaged. With his words in her mind, she readied herself for bed and lay down.

Though she was exhausted, her skin was sensitive against the fine sheets when she remembered the details of last night. It felt like a lifetime ago that MacCarrick had kissed and touched her so passionately. It seemed a dozen lifetimes ago that she'd first found him by the river. She'd had no idea how much that man was going to change her life.

Part of her wanted to seduce MacCarrick just to make sure

she could. Another part was curious about that final step that he was denying her. Still another part of her was constantly aware that he wouldn't leave so easily afterward. She didn't understand why the thought of their never seeing each other again didn't affect him as it did her.

She'd been honest today when she'd said she didn't know what he was to her—the situation was so new to her—but one thing she was certain of was that each day her feelings for him grew. Where would that leave her by the time Aleix arrived?

She kicked off the covers, too warm to sleep. Wasn't it supposed to be damp and cold in England? *Must make the best of it.* She rose to crack open a window. When she pulled aside the heavy damask curtains and reached for the sash, she stilled.

She stared for long moments as if the site before her was utterly foreign and inexplicable. But it *was* foreign, and comprehension came slowly, and with it a sinking feeling in her belly.

He'd nailed her windows shut.

She tilted her head and contemplated the sight with detachment. The nail heads were matte against the glossy white painted wood. Around each nail the paint was unharmed. Of course, it would be. He had a steady hand.

With a ragged breath she released the cumbersome curtains. The understanding that she was a target had always been there weighing on her, but with the odd tableau she'd just seen, awareness seeped in until she thought she'd choke on it. She hurried to light a candle to chase away the darkness as she hadn't done since she was a little girl.

Even though the room was warm, she burrowed under the covers, hot, afraid, and lonely, and hours passed before she finally fell asleep in the unfamiliar room.

Instead of her usual dreams of riding across fields or, of

late, MacCarrick wrapping her hair around his fist as he tugged her close to kiss her, she dreamed of her death.

She bolted upright in bed, out of breath, shuddering. Her hand flew to her face and she felt wetness on her cheeks. Why would she have nightmares now when she was the safest she'd been?

Because before he'd always been with her—every night she'd felt his presence, felt him watching her as she drifted to sleep.

And because deep down she'd finally recognized a truth that she'd desperately fought. A fourth attack would be the last.

# Twenty-six

When MacCarrick approached her the next morning, she was standing by the breakfast sideboard, alternately staring at her steaming, laden plate and frowning at the disconcerted footman.

"I know you've explained this before," she said to the man, "but I want to clarify. These are *eggs?*"

"Yes, milady."

She mumbled in Catalan, "I know what eggs look like and these are not they."

MacCarrick peremptorily took the plate from her, and set it away so he could start her with a clean one. "Why are you so pale?" he asked, as he scanned the sideboard, unfailingly choosing things she would enjoy.

She heard Hugh at the end of the dining table turning the page of his newspaper, and suspected he was listening. Mac-Carrick must have as well because he leaned in closer when he asked, "Could you no' sleep?"

She shrugged. "I'm sure I just need to get used to the new bed."

He escorted her to the table, setting the plate in front of her, then selected an orange and an apple from the table center. He held each one up with a questioning look, and she nodded for the orange.

"Is something wrong with your room?" He began to peel.

"Besides the fact you felt you needed to nail the windows shut?"

His jaws bulged at the sides—a sure sign he was grinding his teeth. "To say you sleep heavily is an understatement. I'm trying to keep you safe."

"I know, I know," she said more gently as she took the section he offered her and chewed thoughtfully. MacCarrick took a roll from her plate, pulling a piece of it for himself and some apart for her. "It's just difficult to be reminded of how much danger there is."

Hugh approached, frowning at them. Only when she saw Hugh studying them did she realize how the scene looked. MacCarrick had been hand-feeding her, and they'd been eating from the same plate without even noticing. MacCarrick appeared uncomfortable, as if he'd been caught doing something he shouldn't.

"Court, if you need to catch up on some sleep, I'll be here all day," Hugh offered. "I'll check in on the two of you."

When he nodded in response and Hugh exited the room, MacCarrick turned to her. As his gaze flickered over her face, his irritated expression eased. "Lass, I think you're the one who could use a nap."

"I'm not tired in the least," she said, then betrayed her assertion by yawning. She thought she saw a hint of a grin as he took her hand to lead her into the library. He scanned the shelves and chose a book on Scottish history for her. "If you read this"—he held up the tome—"on that settee"—he pointed out a plush crimson settee—"you're guaranteed to be asleep within twenty minutes."

"Why is that?"

"The book is . . . detailed, to say the least, and that settee was the death of my studies often enough."

She took the heavy book from him with a pained smile—where was a good gothic novel when you needed one?—and sat where he directed, opening it without enthusiasm. . . .

She was startled when Hugh glanced inside—over an hour had passed.

Hugh's gaze fell on MacCarrick, who sat across from her on a sofa. With his eyes closed, his body motionless, and an arm stretched along the sofa back, MacCarrick looked as if he'd merely closed his eyes for a moment, but apparently he was sleeping, because Hugh looked satisfied and shut the door quietly.

As soon as Hugh was gone and with book in hand, Annalía crossed the room to kneel on the sofa beside MacCarrick. She studied his face and sighed, marveling that she'd ever considered him anything other than remarkably handsome. When the urge to feather her fingers over his lips grew overwhelming, she took up her book once more and sat under his outstretched arm, with her back nestled against his side. She briefly closed her eyes, luxuriating in his solid warmth, then turned to the last page she'd read. Her mood grew grave as she mused over what she'd learned so far.

Now that she understood more about what and who MacCarrick was, she felt ashamed of all the things she'd called him—ruthless Scot, brutish Highlander, ill-mannered barbarian . . . and she could write a page more. She'd insulted him again and again, and yet here she sat, enjoying his warmth and strength—alive only because he'd protected her.

Her face burned when she remembered her taunts and jibes. Andorrans lived in a state of constant peace—Pascal was the first threat since the thirteenth century—but the Scots had not. They would be different. MacCarrick was different from her, and she'd vilified him and his kinsmen for it. No wonder his men had given her amused expressions, as though she were just a silly girl. No wonder MacCarrick had looked as if he wanted to throttle her.

If he hadn't been a fierce Highlander and a trained mercenary, she'd be dead. How had she thanked him? With insults.

Annalía was just as he'd said, a small-minded Andorran shut off from the world.

She put her hand over her mouth in disgust and turned to curl up with her head against his chest.

She wanted him more than she ever had—had realized she wanted *all* with him—but she had to wonder if he didn't want the same from her because of her behavior. It was one thing to desire her physically but another entirely to like her, to respect her.

He was still protecting her, still keeping her safe, for nothing in return—she literally couldn't give away her virtue to that man—and maybe, maybe, he was doing it because he saw more depth in her than she'd given him reason to—

She heard his heart speed up and thought he'd awakened. He tensed, but after a moment, his body relaxed and his arm descended around her. As he slept once more, his heartbeat returned to slow and steady, lulling her.

Before she joined him, she decided that she never wanted to sleep without that sound again.

That night Court sat in his chair outside her room with his head against the wall, staring at the hallway ceiling, imagining her only a door away. She would welcome him into her bed the second he entered her room. She wanted him and made no secret of it, and he was humbled that she desired him. He was also amazed he'd stayed away this long. . . .

Waking this afternoon with her soft and trusting in his arms had nearly been his undoing—

"A lot on your mind?" Hugh asked, arriving then with coffee. A convenient break, as if he'd sensed how close Court was to crumbling.

"For certain," he answered as he took a cup.

"You stay outside?" he asked. "All night?" Hugh stared at the door, and Court knew Hugh was wondering what he himself would do if it were his Jane Weyland inside.

"Canna be near her."

Hugh slapped him on the shoulder. "You're a strong-willed man."

*No, Hugh. No, I'm really no'.*

When Hugh sat down against the wall with his own coffee, Court asked, "Do you ever think about defying it?"

"No. Da's death was warning enough for me." He looked lost in thought, no doubt remembering that day.

Leith MacCarrick, not yet forty years old and strong as an ox. The next morning dead and cold in bed with their inconsolable mother. And he'd *known* he was going to die. He'd believed. *"It's no' your fault, sons. The book will no' be denied. I'm just glad I got tae see the men you'd be."* Their mother, mad with grief, tearing at her hair and screaming, *"I told you no' to read it! How many times did I tell you? It always wins!"*

Yes, she'd forbidden her sons to read it, but she'd gone a step further to protect her husband after she'd failed to burn the book, or bury it, or escape it by casting it out to sea. She'd forbidden them to learn to read Gaelic. The clan cooperated, hoping their beloved chief wouldn't die before he was a glad old man. Everyone helped ensure that not one of them could read or write it.

Hugh and Ethan still couldn't. Court could but had only learned in the last few years, and mainly just for spite. Yet as their mother had said, *"It always wins!"*

Court had been twelve when it had happened, just old enough to answer her screams by bellowing back, *"Then why in the hell did you have three sons?"*

She'd answered that they'd tried not to. . . . At twelve years old, Court mightn't have been old enough to hear that.

"If that was no' enough," Hugh continued, "then Sarah's death convinced me."

No one knew how Ethan's fiancée had died, and since he wouldn't explain anything about her last night, many blamed him, which didn't seem to bother Ethan in the least.

Striving for a casual tone, Court asked, "Ethan's never gotten a child on any lass since I went away, has he?"

He shook his head. "Court, you ken he has no'. And no' from lack of opportunity."

Court exhaled. "Aye, I know." It was hard to believe that before Ethan received the scar on his face he'd been a favorite with the ladies—at least with those outside the clan who knew nothing of the book. Yet he'd not fathered a child. And though Court had worked tirelessly over the last decade and hadn't sown his path by way of skirts as Ethan had, there'd been ample opportunity. But nothing.

Court knew Hugh hadn't either—not that he expected him to since he'd partaken of women sparingly, which was understandable since he was always miserable afterward. Hugh didn't have an eye for the ladies—he had an eye for one lady, the English chit who used to torment him when he was just a young man. "Do you ever see Jane?"

"No' in years." He repeated Court's words, "Canna be near her."

Four summers spent with her and Hugh had never been right. He'd thought her too young for him, but from what Court had been able to discern, she definitely hadn't behaved like it.

After his days with that witch, Hugh would stumble home,

hands shaking, out of breath, looking like he'd been beaten dumb. Court remembered one time he'd asked Hugh what was wrong. Hugh had answered in a low, dazed tone, "Jane swimming. In a wet shift. Refused my shirt to cover herself. 'Hugh, darling,' she said, 'can you see through?'" He'd lurched off as though in pain, but Court had heard him grate, *"And, Christ Almighty, I could . . ."*

"I can take over here if you like," Hugh said.

"No. I'll stay."

"You look like hell. When was the last time you slept for more than a couple of hours?"

He shrugged.

"I'm going out of town tomorrow. Something I canna get out of. Be gone about a week or two."

"Weyland got a job for you?"

"Aye."

Court thought Hugh was an intelligent and brave man, but he must be one of those poor bastards who liked to be tortured. How else could he continue to work with Jane's father, continually hearing details about her life?

He rose and gave Court another slap on the shoulder. "I doona have anything to worry about here?"

"No' at all," Court lied, impressed by how convincing he sounded.

Yet it should be true—after all, he was supposed to be *strong-willed*. So much so that not ten minutes after Hugh left, Court opened her door. Just to check on her. . . .

The hinge creaked.

"MacCarrick?" she whispered.

"Aye, it's me."

He heard her breathe a sigh of relief and his brows drew together. "Did you fear it'd be someone else?"

"No."

"Did you need something?"

"You."

*"Besides me."*

"Then nothing."

He gritted his teeth.

"I had the most awful nightmare." She was shivering. She'd never had nightmares when he'd stayed with her in the past.

"It's over now," he said, as he retrieved another blanket. At the side of her bed, he shook it open to fall over her, then pulled it to her chin.

When he turned to go, she caught his hand. "Court-land . . ."

He said nothing. Just stood, tensed.

She used his hand to pull herself to her knees at the edge of the bed. "Don't leave yet. Even if you don't want to touch me, I still don't want you to leave."

He was stunned when she pressed her face to his callused palm, showing him tenderness. "Woman, do you think I doona want to touch you?" He lowered his voice and admitted, *"I crave it."*

"Then why?"

"Because it will no' only be touching the next time." He wanted her, wanted the pleasure they would have, but the urge to take her, to make her *his,* was overwhelming. "I'll be just outside." The door represented a barrier. Outside he couldn't hear her soft breaths.

"Or you could sit *there.*" She pointed to a chair that he could've sworn was closer to the bed than it had been before.

"I canna. I'm no' as strong as I'd like to be—"

"Yes, you are," she quickly interrupted, gazing up at him. "You are *very* strong. And brave."

Her comment made him frown. "I'm wantin' you all the time, and sooner or later I will no' be able to resist. Then there will be consequences."

"Yes, very well."

"Are you feelin' poorly?"

"No, I feel much better now. Ignore the chair, come to bed with me."

"Anna, do you no' ken what I'm saying? I'm no' the man for you. I doona have near the wealth you're used to." Nor the ability to afford his growing addiction to give her everything she wanted.

"I have my own fortune."

"Are you tryin' to insult me?"

She looked down, clearly embarrassed, and he regretted his tone. "I will no' ever be the Castilian gentleman you want. I will always be the rough Scot you think me."

"I want *you.*"

"Why do you continue to argue when you ken what will have to happen if I bed you?" he asked in a deadened tone, struggling to understand her behavior. Then realization came. "You think you can talk me from it. You think we can enjoy ourselves and then you'll be able to walk away. It might have been like that before, but it is no' anymore. You'd be forced to marry me."

"Why do you think I want you in the bed?" she said in exasperation.

His jaw went slack. "Are you sayin' *you* want tae marry *me?*"

She glanced down and nodded shyly. Marry *him?* His heart was hammering in his chest. "You would no' like being with me. You'd have to live in Scotland among strangers with strange ways." The gulf between their nationalities was daunting. His grandmother had been English and her ways had been infused in their family, but Annalía was far from English.

He loved the difference. He was charmed by her manners and captivated by the way she spoke, but he didn't know if she'd like how foreign Scotland would be for her. He didn't know how the Highlands would treat a vivid Castilian—who delighted in mocking a Scots accent—in return.

Why was he even considering this? As if this were the only obstacle? He was bloody *cursed*.

"I can learn. You said I learn quickly." Her voice was . . . hopeful? Couldn't be.

Best to end this. "And do you want bairn?"

"Children?" She smiled at him and breathed, "Yes."

Now it seemed like his heart stopped. "I canna give them to you."

She tilted her head at him, brows drawn.

"That's right, Anna—if you are tied to me, you will no' have them."

Her frown deepened. "Do you mean you can't have children or you can't father children?"

What was the bloody difference? "I canna father children."

"But you can *have* them. In Andorra it's very common to adopt."

He'd never expected this. It took a moment for him to work up an answer. "You're young yet. You'll come to want your own."

"What if *I* can't have any? The women in my family have never been fruitful. Did you not notice the age difference between my brother and me? Twelve years. My mother was an only child and her mother was before her." She added softly, "MacCarrick, would you not want me if the situation were reversed?"

"Christ, yes, I'd want you," he said in a rush, then wished he hadn't. But as usual the thought had returned: *Take you any way I could*. He was staggered. If he'd ever envisioned a scenario where she might come to want him, he'd always been so sure that upon learning he couldn't give her children, she would gasp, then demur, and then want him no more.

He forced himself to turn from her and strode outside,

knowing that that was why he'd been so hesitant to tell her now.

"What does it say?" Olivia asked for the third time in as many seconds.

"I could tell better if you'd stop blocking my light," Aleix answered with an impatient look over his shoulder.

They'd come to Annalía's old school on the off chance that her former headmistress might have some kind of information, and had been astonished when she produced a message for him from Annalía, written in Gaelic. Aleix felt constrained to tell the woman as little as possible, so she'd left them alone in the library with an ancient English-Gaelic dictionary and a worried glance.

Apparently weary of blocking his light, Olivia hopped up to sit on the table, tilting her head down this way and that at the message. He exhaled loudly, then returned to the words he'd managed to translate so far. Definitely directions. Concentrating, he could see patterns forming. "The Square Mile? Wait . . . London proper is known as that."

With more excitement than he'd ever seen in her, she said, "Then I believe we're going to England!" He shot to his feet, took her waist, and swung her around. She was smiling, genuinely, and it softened her whole face. A maddening urge surfaced. He wanted to know what it'd be like to kiss her.

As he was contemplating it, she leaned forward and pressed her lips to his. Surprised, he set her to her feet, but the hands clutching her waist soon moved to gripping her back to bring her closer so he could return the kiss. He did, harder and more intently, and when she moaned, desires he'd thought were dead came clawing back to life in an instant. She was slim and tall, and as he clasped her tightly, molding her to his body, she fit him well.

*Which couldn't be right since Mariette had been petite.*

He broke away, pushing her back, breathing hard. She appeared bemused, but she shouldn't be. This shouldn't have happened. He'd sworn to wed her, but he could never give her a true marriage.

With a wavering breath he sank back into his seat, fighting to ignore Olivia and how sweet her lips had been. Somehow he attempted to continue translating. It helped when she said, "I don't even like your ninny of a sister, but I can't wait to find her. It is so fitting that she be the mouse."

He clasped his head in consternation and returned to ordering the words he'd translated, then frowned. Annalía had copied MacCarrick's translation unaware she'd more or less written to her brother, "If you let them follow you to my bloody home, I will beat your arse."

The seamstress looked very aggrieved when she handed Court the bill.

He'd been prepared to be bowled over by the statement, and he was. Shocked because it was less than in the village. "What is this? Get her more."

"She said you'd say that and that I should disregard your orders."

He glowered and snapped, "Bring her more."

The woman appeared frightened, and as she darted away she assured him she would return with additional garments.

Court had brought the seamstress to Annalía and knew the consequences and could handle them. He wasn't destitute yet. Thanks to Hugh.

How ironic that Hugh's robbing his accounts would be saving Court's arse right now. Hugh had stumbled onto the new firearms company of Horace Smith and Daniel Wesson through his work, and had believed so strongly in it, he'd unilaterally invested for Court. Court had been prickly about his hard-earned money, but could only grumble now because this Wesson and Smith deal had begun providing income that would allow him to chip away at his debt. At least Hugh had the decency not to rub it in. . . .

Now Anna, with her obvious *forbearance,* was shaming him. He would *make* her accept more. His brows drew together.

Oh, she was *good.*

He found her as she was gathering more books from the library. "Why did you no' get more?"

"I'll only need a few dresses. Aleix will be here soon to collect me, don't you think? It will be silly to lug so much around and then all the way back home when we can return. Especially since I already have to use an entire bedroom for my dresses now."

"You can have whatever you want."

"I know. You are very gracious, but truly this is all I need." She leaned up to kiss him on his cheek before she turned for her room with books under her arm. Her face had been sad.

Surely she wasn't *this* good.

# Twenty-seven

*H*ow could Annalía show MacCarrick how different she'd become if he hardly spoke to her anymore? She'd thought that when Hugh left he would relax some, but if anything, he'd grown more on edge.

If he was denying her because he couldn't father children, then that was simply unacceptable. Whenever she thought about his admission, she wondered if he'd been ill as a child, and her heart hurt to think of him in pain.

If he was doing this because he saw her as spoiled and closed-minded, then she'd have to force him to see that she wanted to learn, that she wanted to be better.

Annalía knew the most pressing reason why he was distant with her. So clearly they needed to get this lovemaking completed so they could be together. Decided on her course of action, she began planning. Tonight she'd bathed with the scented soaps the seamstress had brought her—the peculiar woman had returned with more clothing and evidently everything else she could lay hands on. After her bath, Annalía had slipped on a new nightdress she'd chosen from the selection, chosen specifically for particular characteristics.

Now she was ready. She wasn't as nervous as she'd imagined she might be—after all, this would be a bold move—but she knew that this was the course she was meant to take. . . .

"MacCarrick!"

The door burst open a second later. "Anna, what is it—" He lost his voice when he saw her standing at the foot of the bed. "Go back to bed," he ordered in a harsh tone.

It didn't faze her. She stood determined before him and tugged the left string strap of her nightgown loose. The jet black silk slid down one side, just above her nipple.

His eyes widened as if in realization, then narrowed. "*Doona do this.*"

She reached back and unpinned her hair, shaking her head until it spilled down her back. Her fingers rested at the other tie strap of her nightgown, ready to pluck.

His hand was shaking as he ran it over his face. "You canna keep temptin' me."

She raised her eyebrows and tugged. The tie was on the verge of unraveling. She thought *he* was on the verge of unraveling. His body seemed to thrum with energy and tension throughout. She could hardly wait to touch it again.

His voice low, he said, "Anna, I am askin' you, please, doona—"

She pulled it loose.

The nightgown dipped, hesitating over her hard nipples before floating down past her waist and legs. "What were you saying?" she asked in a purring voice.

His jaw slackened. Taking down her hair had been merciless. The nightgown? Without the nightgown, the ground he'd managed to gain, or at least maintain, was now unrecoverable.

"If you keep pushing me, I will take you to bed, but it will no' be just to kiss you. It will no' be like last time." He struggled to keep his eyes on her face—away from her high breasts, away from her curving hips that he wanted to clench—yet even the look in her eyes was carnal. "There will be repercussions."

"I understand."

"I mean it, Anna," he said, his voice hoarse. "I will take you this night, I swear it." How could a man not be expected to make love to the woman he coveted above all things? When she presented herself like a newly unwrapped gift? He might as well be expected to voluntarily forgo breathing. Which was impossible. Denying himself the feel of her body?

Impossible.

Like a hit, things became very clear. She wanted him to make love to her, and he wanted her desperately. The reasons he'd come up with not to couldn't withstand this. Right now, he couldn't recall a single one anyway. He would take her so long and hard that she'd regret pushing. He kicked the door closed then strode to her, lifting her against his chest, forcing her to wrap her legs around his waist.

"Courtland," she said with a gasp as he carried her to the bed.

He sat on the edge, keeping her spread over his lap, his hands splayed against her bottom, squeezing. He scarcely believed she was naked on him, and had begun eagerly kissing his neck and face and removing his shirt as if she were hungry for him. He lowered his head to her chest, drawing her nipple into his mouth. When she cried out, he stopped, not quite kissing her, his lips just next to her skin. "*Mo cridhe,* are you tae be mine?"

She threaded her fingers into his hair. "*Yes.*"

He grasped her face and met her eyes. "In all the ways, Anna?" he asked, his voice a rasp.

"Yes," she answered without looking away. "I will be yours in all ways."

He wanted to revel in what she'd just promised, but when he shrugged out of his shirt, she pressed her breasts against him, moaning softly and shivering from the contact, and he could only clutch her tighter against him.

Her hands petting him, her sex resting on his . . . He grated, "You'll make me lose control."

"I want you to."

"I canna. I need to—" He hissed in a breath when she ground against his lap. "I need to make sure you're ready." He lifted her up until her breasts were before his lips and dragged his tongue across her nipple.

She moaned, "I am ready."

"Your body must be ready." When she shivered once more, he stood and placed her on the bed, then removed his boots and his trousers. Unclothed, he lay on his side, easing her to her back so he could trace his fingertips around her wet nipples and down her belly until her stomach twitched.

He said against her ear, "I need you wet." When she bent one leg and her hips rose, he captured that leg and put it over his side, locking her there, parting her to him. "I want you tae ache with need."

"I am," she assured him. "I do."

He closed his eyes at the feeling of her sex as he spread the wetness all around. "More than this. That means I'll need tae tease you again and again. . . ."

Slow, gentle strokes. Her flesh felt like heaven, and he groaned thinking he was going to be inside her tonight. When he slipped a finger into her, her back arched. As he continued to push in and out of her tight sex, she reached for his cock, but he drew his hips back.

"I . . . I want to put my hand on you."

"Canna do that." He could scarcely keep from bucking against her now. He knew she was about to ask why, so he cut off her question by working two fingers inside.

She gasped in surprise. "That's different than before."

He withdrew. "It is. But does it please you?" he asked with a slow push.

"I-I don't know," she said, beginning to sound nervous.

"There's no hurry," he lied. Already he wondered how he would get through this without losing his mind.

Luckily, after several more slow strokes, she grew accustomed and wetter. "It does please me," she whispered. "Very much." Her hands rubbed his chest as he did it again and again, learning her body, coaxing it to accept him.

"You like me touching you inside?" he grated at her neck where he'd been licking, though he knew she couldn't possibly like it better than he did.

"Yes!" She arched her back to come down hard on his fingers. She was so wet, so close even with his unhurried strokes. "I-I can't take much more."

He asked against her ear, "Do you need to come?"

"*Yes*," she whimpered, her body trembling, just on the verge.

That was his permission. He kissed her mouth hungrily as he released her, then rose over her to kneel between her legs. She was breathing fast, eyes heavy lidded, body supple. So desirable it hurt him. He returned two fingers to stir her. Just when she was on the verge, head thrashing, body tensing, he grasped himself to rub the tip against her wetness.

"*Si us plau*," she said on a moan. "Please," she'd said, sounding like she was in agony.

With care, he slowly worked just the head inside, though every part of him screamed to sink his hips into her. He didn't, even when she grew used to him. Even when she rolled her hips on the tip, the movement making her breasts quiver. *"Ah, God, Anna."* No greater torture.

Damn it, he had discipline. He knew what he wanted to happen, and now he just had to make sure it played out as he wanted. He put his hands against the wall and tried to focus on them—on the diametrical patterns of the paper, on anything but the exquisite woman writhing beneath him. *On* him. Focusing until he was not directly on the verge of ejaculating inside her.

The wall indented under his fingers, and the paper crumbled. Sweat dripped down his forehead. Every muscle in his body began to ache from strain.

He felt her putting her hands on his hips, trying to pull him inside. Somehow he resisted.

Finding no luck with his hips, she grasped the base of his rod. With her soft fingers wrapped around him, the head inside her . . . he could imagine . . .

He groaned, his head falling back. Without thought he pumped against her hand. He was losing control. "No, Anna—"

"Yes!" she whispered.

Control? He bucked against her hand again, pulled back to thrust harder.

Her hand was gone.

He surged in, ripping through the barrier, groaning from the tightness even as she cried out in pain. At once she tried to shake him loose from her. She shoved at him and struggled to close her legs.

"No, Anna. *No.*" He took her by the shoulders and held her. He didn't want her to stop now. She would only remember pain. He remained still, praying the hurt would fade. Praying he wouldn't give in to the screaming urge to pin her down into the mattress and pump into her as hard as he needed to. He shuddered at the thought.

She'd quit moving, but her eyes were still squeezed shut.

"You have tae let your body adjust tae me."

"This is what the girls at school talked about, isn't it? The pain."

"You will no' have it like this again."

She said without taking a breath, "It hurts."

He stroked her hair from her forehead and kissed her there. "*Mo cridhe,* I wish it dinna."

She opened her eyes. They were glittering. She was hurting, and he felt it a thousand times. He cursed himself. Too delicate, her skin too soft beneath his hands. He carefully began to withdraw—

"No, wait," she whispered, and he froze. "It isn't as bad as it was."

Maybe not for her. He hurt as he'd never known. His sack was heavy and ached, his body pained him. The throbbing pressure was unbearable when her body was squeezing him like a fist. He rubbed his face against her neck.

"You should finish."

He groaned, knowing it was over. No control. He took her legs and pinned them against his hips, then sank into her once. He pulled out and drove harder, gnashing his teeth from need.

He put his head down and licked at her damp breast, and on his third stroke he came. Like an explosion, shooting into her heat, unable to stop himself from grinding mindlessly against her as it went on and on. He yelled out from deep within his chest, lashed by a pleasure he'd never imagined.

# Twenty-eight

The way MacCarrick moved, the way his muscles rippled, and the abandon he must have felt did odd things to Annalía.

The idea that his reaction was so strong that he threw back his head, with his neck and chest straining and slick, and *yelled* like a beast made her breaths speed up.

Though on the whole she was *not* pleased with lovemaking. She found it exciting because it was a new experience, and she relished his response, yet it was vastly overrated in her mind because of the *stabbing pain* involved.

But then, after he'd finished, he remained full inside her. It wasn't . . . unpleasant.

His body was heavy on her, though. She moved to find a more comfortable position and was amazed at the feeling of his chest, slick with sweat, rubbing her breasts. His heart thundered against her, and the hair on his chest rasped her nipples. That felt . . . nice. His harried breaths on her damp neck made her tremble, which also was nice. And she loved the way his callused hand felt when he stroked her leg, the one still levered against his hip as if he were not ever letting go.

Everything added up until she was very aware that she had not reached *her* end, the bliss she'd been just one of his clever strokes away from enjoying. How would he know that she wanted his hands back on her? How did one go about asking a man to massage and kiss your breasts, with careful attention to the . . . She squeezed her eyes shut. She couldn't ask him. The next best thing was another wriggle beneath him. She sucked in a breath.

"Christ, I dinna want tae hurt you," he grated, as he rose up and began to withdraw.

"Please, stop." He did. "MacCarrick?"

"What do you want me tae do, Anna?" His eyes were so dark as he watched her face. She knew he was reading her expression, trying to uncover what she desired. She knew he would do whatever it was.

Yet she turned her face from him, unable to ask.

"Whisper what you want in my ear," he said, and leaned down.

"MacCarrick," she whispered hesitantly. "My breasts . . . ache. Please touch them."

He shuddered, every part of him tensing. Then, like a shot, his hands were on her, molding her flesh to his fingers before he put his palms behind her to arch her back and raise her to his mouth. He drew greedily on her nipples, even while groaning desperately against her.

She cried out and threaded her fingers through his hair, holding him to her until her head fell back. The feelings were so intense, and she was ever aware of this delicious fullness still embedded in her, making every pleasure sharper.

"*Mo cridhe,*" he rasped against her breast, "tell me what else you want me tae do."

She ran her hands down his arms in frustration. When she

didn't answer he kissed her neck, putting his ear close to her lips. "Tell me what you want, and I swear I will give it tae you." His voice was husky and deep.

"I want you," she said, panting, "to try me again."

He hissed between his teeth.

"Can we? Can you?"

"Anna, I never stopped being hard," he said, sounding surprised. "No difference." As if testing, he slowly pressed forward inside her.

A swift feeling of rapture swept through her, and she arched her back in shocked pleasure. *"Oh, Courtland,"* she said in awe. In that instant she understood why man and woman were made this way.

"You doona hurt any longer?" Court asked, as he withdrew and entered her again.

She shook her head but said nothing. He leaned down again, and she whispered, "I adore what you're doing to me."

*"Anna."* His hips bucked involuntarily.

If she adored this, then he wanted her to come with him inside her, to know that feeling. He leaned down and took her mouth hard, teasing her tongue, then making his way down to her neck and breasts. When he nipped at the peak, she cried out.

He raised his chest, then laid his hand low on her belly, resting it flat, and rubbed his thumb in time with his stroke. "Do you like it when I touch here?"

Her answer was an incomprehensible cry as she spread her legs wider and wildly scratched her nails up his chest, making the muscles tense in reflex.

With each pump of his hips, he fondled her. Her breasts bounced, her nipples were so hard and still wet from him, and he was on the verge again. Her hands flew to her sides, and she clutched the sheets, arching her back and undulating her hips harder against his cock. But he wouldn't end this until he felt her sex squeezing his shaft.

He stroked her flesh faster, and she cried, "Yes! Please don't stop!"

"I'll do this as long as you want me tae."

She moaned, her whole body tensing as she began to come. Her back arched, her hands flew to his shoulders, clutching, her nails biting into him. Inside, her body gripped his, and the pleasure from that was greater than before if even conceivable.

His head fell back, and he gave a brutal groan when he tensed to spend. Though the sensation was so intense he had to battle the urges to yell to the ceiling, to graze his teeth against her wet skin or clench her hips and wrench her down harder on him, he leaned forward and took her face in his hands.

With his last grinding thrusts, he caught her gaze, daring her to turn away from him. But she didn't. As his seed poured from him relentlessly, the words left his lips, *"Is leamsa thu. Naisgeam riut mi daonnan." You are mine. I bind you to me always.* He heard them as if someone else had spoken, then collapsed onto her.

Seconds later he pushed up, remembering he was too heavy for her. She looked at him with wonder, and, he hoped, something more that he didn't deserve. He put his arms underneath her and rolled onto his back with her. He was too big to lie on her, but even when she rested on his chest, he squeezed her to him hard and felt her heart beating fast. When her breaths calmed, she put her arms around him and squeezed back. His lips curled.

"Did I hurt you again?" He stroked her hair, loving how soft it was, loving her scent.

She shook her head against his chest. "Not the second time." In a voice so quiet he scarcely heard her, she said,

"Nothing could feel that heavenly." Her tone was marveling and he was proud. "But did I please you?" she asked.

When he chuckled, she rose up and looked at him with narrowed golden eyes. "What is so amusing?"

"Your question. You canna ken how much you did."

She bit her lip and put her face back to his chest. She was smiling against him. "I wasn't aware you possessed the ability to laugh."

"Aye. I've the ability." *Just not much opportunity before.*

"I want to hear it more," she said in a drowsy voice. Squeezing him one last time, she drifted to sleep. On this night, he knew more satisfaction than he had ever known, ever imagined a man *could* know. She was so warm on him, her hair spilling over his chest, her body fitting to him.

Before he grew even harder inside her again—even he wasn't enough of a beast to take her three times—he withdrew and set her beside him on the bed.

She protested in Catalan and her head fell to the side as she slept soundly as usual.

He rose to wash the sweat off him, soaking a cloth to run over his body, and saw blood. Turning to the bed, he spied it on the sheet like an accusation, and it twisted something inside him. He was a man, and no one had ever explained to him how to take care of his woman after he took her virginity. Not that conversations like that abounded, but Court was never supposed to *have* a woman of his own. Was never supposed to even entertain thoughts of a woman like her.

He wanted to lessen any hurt he had caused her. He knew she'd be embarrassed if anyone saw the blood on the sheet, and he thought that even though she'd be prepared for the sight of it on her thigh, it might startle her just the same. Brows drawn together, he soaked another cloth, then went to grasp her shoulder. "Anna, I'm goin' tae take care of you."

*"Of course,"* she murmured, making his chest swell.

He brought the cloth to her thighs and ran it over her skin, then over her sex. He could see her squeezing her eyes shut, but he didn't want her embarrassed in front of him. She was his now, and it was his due to get to care for her.

So instead of removing it, he held the cool cloth against her, thinking that it might soothe her. When he went to take it away, she softly grasped his wrist and held him there. Her breathing was deepening, and when her hand slipped to her side, he barely heard her whisper, *"Thank you."*

She trusted him.

She'd trusted him with her safety and her life and now her innocence.

He hoped she'd made a good decision.

With her asleep once more, he lifted her as he removed the bottom sheet, then placed her on the top one. He balled up the stained linen and tossed it in the corner, planning to wake before her and get rid of it. When he joined her, she curled into him, her body warm and soft. He brought her to his chest and probably held her too hard again.

Sleeping with her was a luxury he'd never thought to enjoy again. To be able to touch her and smell her hair *whenever he pleased* . . . To have her body wrap around him and to feel her breaths on his chest. *Could* his luck ever run this high? To have her accept his childless fate as her own. A short, amazed laugh. Not childless—just playing out a little differently than he'd expected.

*She was his.* And he was going to overcome any obstacle that might keep her from staying that way.

When Hugh returned, he would ask his advice on weaponry to kill the Rechazados to a man. Court had already sent word to his crew, ready to get this finished, and expected they would receive it soon.

Then he would have to take care of Anna's brother when he arrived. Llorente wouldn't have wanted a man like him marrying Anna—even before Court had fought him and delivered him to a despot. That would have to be worked out, which would be difficult because Court didn't have a lot of experience with working things out. But he would attempt it for her.

And then the task he dreaded—telling Anna that he hadn't been completely honest about her brother. He'd said he hadn't attacked Llorente, which was true, but they had fought. Would she believe that putting him in jail had saved his life?

Her hand trailed down his arm, and when she murmured his name, he pulled her closer to him with the inside of his elbow and kissed her forehead. Yes, she would believe him, and yes, Court would kill anyone who threatened her, and if Llorente didn't accept the situation, then yes, he'd bloody lose a sister.

Right now, even the curse felt beatable. The rest were mere . . . complications.

*She was his.*

# Twenty-nine

*A*nnalía slept through the entire night and woke to find Court's big warm body all along her back, an arm flung possessively around her waist. And she was sore in the most unique places. She turned to him, burrowing down closer to his chest, and slept again.

When she woke once more it was nearly noon, and he was gone. She sat up, rubbing her eyes groggily, then looked down at herself and scanned the sheet. No blood. Hadn't he made sure there wouldn't be? Her Scot was proving to be very considerate.

She called for a bath, and as she'd hoped, the warm water soothed her aches. But while she sat in the steaming water, she thought of the one dilemma she'd neglected to settle with MacCarrick. His answer would've been the only thing that could've kept her from proceeding.

They'd spoken about children and had settled that easily enough. He'd brought up the subject of wealth. It was probably good that he didn't want her fortune because Aleix would never approve the marriage and release the funds. Living in Scotland? She'd live on the moon with him.

There was only one thing she could never, ever tolerate. . . .

She took extra care with her dress and her hair, then descended, wondering if seeing him this morning would be awkward. When she saw him downstairs, he took one look at her and then glanced away.

Her lips parted and in that split second she had the urge to cry.

She only realized he was scanning the room for others when he stormed up to her. He cupped his hand behind her head and pressed her hard against the wall, kissing her neck with a groan. "You took too long to come down."

Better! "Why didn't you stay with me?"

"Because I woke up wantin' you more than I did before I bedded you. And even if I could have managed to let you leave the bed, I feared you'd be embarrassed."

"I was a little." She felt herself blushing. "When you . . . cared for me."

"I dinna know what to do." He raised his hand to the wall above her. "I only wanted to make you feel better."

She again thought she might cry. He took a curl of her hair in his other hand and coaxed it around his finger. Had it come loose? She hadn't even noticed.

He was acting as if he were seeing her for the first time. She understood. With him around her like this, she delighted in his size, loving his broad shoulders and deep chest. His shirt was white and crisp against his sun-darkened face and his expression was intent. She'd never seen a more handsome man. And he was hers.

She frowned. Was he hers?

"Anna, I'm as new at this as you are."

"You've never taken a girl's virtue before?"

"Christ, no, I have no' done that."

"Truly?" In a way she'd been his first as well. "Why did you start with me?"

"Because you tempt me till I canna think." He put his face to her neck. "You smell so damn good."

Her eyes slid closed. His lips on her neck . . . No! She had to know. "Is it something you would want to do again?" she asked, attempting a casual tone.

He reared back and shook his head emphatically. "No, even were it possible to go back."

"I meant with another woman."

He grew serious. "No. Never." His eyes narrowed. "Do you regret what we've done?"

She felt him tensing around her. This would be difficult for her to say, especially since he'd made his wants clear before.

"There will no' be another man for you." His voice was harsh, startling her. "You're *mine* now, Anna," he growled as he wrapped her hair around his fist. "*Look at me.*"

She did, shocked speechless by how quickly his anger had flared. Whatever he saw in her expression made the lines around his eyes whiten. "What exactly is it that you'd be wantin' for yourself?" His tone was seething.

She took a shaky breath and said, "Y-You said you wanted your harem, that you didn't want only one woman. I-I know this isn't the way of the world and it was ingrained in me never to expect it, but I . . . I want you to be *mine* too." How embarrassing. She felt unsophisticated, ignoring what she'd been instructed was normal and anticipated from the first day she'd ever heard of marriage.

She'd been told that a woman's misconception on this matter was what ruined marriages and made women bitter. But on the opposite side of the coin, she'd seen the devastation her mother's adultery had caused—why would Annalía think she would hold up better than her father had?

She could sense emotion roiling in him. "What do you mean?" At least his voice was no longer an angry rasp.

It occurred to her that she hadn't done any of this as she'd been taught, not making love, definitely not choosing a "suitable" mate. If she started now, the pattern would be interrupted and she rather liked where it'd taken her so far. She put her chin up. "I won't share you. If I'm to be loyal and faithful, I-I want the same!"

His jaw was slack. It was unreasonable, she knew, but the thought of him with another woman . . . She hadn't been able to tolerate it before she'd made him hers. "You distinctly warned me—"

"When?"

"The night on the coast."

He flashed a look of realization.

"Why have one when you can have many, you said, but the thought of you with another . . ." She trailed off.

"Finish what you were telling me."

She looked away again, her eyes watering. "I just couldn't bear it."

He put his fingers under her chin and turned her face. He wore some new expression, just as powerful, but unseen before. He kissed her fiercely.

But he was avoiding her question. She broke away and gazed up at him with all the hurt she felt.

"Anna, last night I made you mine because I want you above all others." He brushed the backs of his fingers along her cheek, then put his forehead to hers. "It will always be so. I dinna hope you would feel as strongly."

Over the next two weeks, when she was in the library or reading in the salon during the day, MacCarrick would come to her with his brows drawn and his body tense and hold out his hand to her.

No words and no need for them. The look in his dark eyes told her all. When she took his hand—she never failed to take his hand and would as long as it was offered to her—he would always mask a flash of surprise a second too late. Then as he led her to their bed, she sensed this masculine pride in him even as her heart sped up in anticipation.

Her Scot was attentive to her and thoughtful, sending out for her favorite foods and finding her books—though she was mortified at first when he'd secured several of the gothic novels she loved.

Each night, after or between the times they made love, they would share a book together in bed, sometimes with her reading the novels to him, her head in his lap as he caressed her hair. Though whenever she gripped the book, nervous as the heroine investigated a dark cellar, he never failed to startle and tickle her.

At other times, MacCarrick would read her bawdy poems, making his brogue thick and rolling, until her eyes watered and her stomach hurt, she laughed so hard. Of course, she'd had to learn a new set of vocabulary to be truly appreciative.

One day, he'd sensed something was weighing on her, and she'd finally confessed how much she missed riding. He'd given her a wicked grin and taught her a completely different meaning of bareback. That wasn't all he taught her. If she'd thought her fingers could work his flesh, she'd never imagined what her lips could do once she convinced him how badly she wanted to kiss him.

Then this morning in bed, she'd stretched, and as usual he'd said, "Mind the arm, lass."

But she'd replied, "I swear you care about it more than I do."

"I like to watch you stretch. Woman, I love to watch you stretch, but you have to be careful till it's completely healed."

"Will the scar make me less attractive in your eyes?"

"An impossibility, Anna," he'd said, nipping her neck. Then he'd turned serious. "Every time I look at it I'll remember how close I came to . . ." He'd coughed into his fist. "How close it was. *Mo cridhe,* we are fortunate."

They *were* fortunate to be together. Yet during this time he never mentioned marriage, and she followed his lead. There was no talk about the future. And each day that passed brought her closer to the day her brother would arrive. She'd had the brief hope that MacCarrick was waiting so he could ask Aleix for her hand. But that was an absurd idea.

He'd never *ask* for her. A man wouldn't ask for something that he'd already claimed.

So they went on in this state without a promise from him. She thought that once she had it, she might have the nerve to tell him she'd fallen in love with him so fiercely she felt like she'd fallen from a height.

# Thirty

When Hugh returned, Court had his arm around Annalía at the dining table, stroking the back of her neck and murmuring in her ear. His brother had barely been able to grate out an "invitation" for Court to join him for a drink after dinner. Court had wanted to go with Anna when she retired, but she said she was sleepy and wanted him to visit with his brother.

"Why, Court?" Hugh asked as he sank into the leather chair in the study. He pinched the bridge of his nose, appearing exhausted.

"I got to a point where I could no' resist any longer."

"That's no' why you took her virtue. Because you 'could no' resist.' You're one of the most disciplined men I've ever known. Which means you made a conscious decision." He exhaled a long breath. "You did it so you would be forced to marry her. And more important, so a woman like that would be forced to marry you."

His eyes narrowed. "No, she wants me, too."

"Do you think that someone like her is going to enjoy living in a drafty four-hundred-year-old keep? No' to mention that your propitious land grab just officially put your home in the middle of nowhere. A seamstress is no' going to ride through thousands of acres to get to your bonny wife out there."

"Where she lived before was no' exactly a metropolis."

"Does she even know who you are? Be realistic, Court."

"You mean a cursed, sterile mercenary living in a stone heap?"

Hugh raised his eyebrows and said simply, "Aye."

Strange how one word could feel like a punch he hadn't tensed for. Court didn't bother to hide his resentment before he strode from the room.

Afterward he walked the house, scowling at everything he saw. This was not how he lived. What she saw was gilded. Anna saw the wealth and the servants, and if she was comfortable here, she would not be at his home in the wilds of northern Scotland.

And what did she know about him? She had an idea of him as a gentle lover, but lately he'd been losing control, little by little.

Sometimes he wanted to take her much harder than he did. . . .

He entered her room, found her sleeping on her front, with the sheet kicked off and her hair spilling across the pillow just as it had when he'd gone to her room in Andorra. He'd stared at her that night, envisioning himself palming her thighs and sex until she rose to her knees. Court remembered how furiously he'd wanted her, remembered how he'd hated the fact that a fine lady like her would never have him.

Yet she would. She would right now.

He stripped down, then knelt between her legs, running

his hand up her thighs to her nightgown. She murmured but slept on as he rolled it higher to her waist.

He put his palm to her sex, his fingers higher, massaging. She woke with a gasp.

"*Spread your legs.*" She did without hesitation. "More." She did, trusting him.

He pressed his finger into her, closing his eyes at the lush feeling, the growing wetness that would soon be gloving him. When her breaths came faster he placed another finger in. She moaned, but he wouldn't push far within her—just enough to make her want more. He groaned when she tried to twist down to get him to take her deeper. Using small touches, he teased her to her knees.

"*Yes,*" he said, his voice hoarse. "On your knees. On your hands." When she was as he wanted her, he rolled her night-dress up her back and over her head, pulling her up against his chest so he could untangle the silk from her arms. He threw it to the side, then inhaled the addictive scent of her hair as it brushed his face. "I canna get enough of you, *mo cridhe,*" he rasped as he eased her back down.

Without his touch she must have grown embarrassed, because she started to lie down once more. He grabbed her hips before she could and steadied her. "No, I want you like this."

"Like what?" she whispered.

In answer, he spread her flesh and ran his thumb up and down. Her head fell forward and her back arched down. "But . . . it's how . . . it's how animals mate," she whispered wildly.

"Aye." He reached under her and cupped her breast, plucking her nipple, and she gasped.

"I can't . . . I don't know."

He pulled her up to his chest again, and brushed her thick hair over her shoulder so he could kiss her neck, then trailed his fingers down her belly all the way to her sex, plunging his fingers into her. She moaned and went limp. He captured her against his chest, with a tight arm wrapped over her breasts. Beneath them, he thrust his fingers into her again and again until she was close. Then he removed them, devoting both hands to her breasts, palming them wholly and lightly pinching her nipples.

She cried out, *"Please, Court."*

"What do you want?"

"You *know*."

"You need something filling you?"

She gasped but nodded.

He prodded her thigh with his now aching erection. "Put it inside you."

*"What?"* she whispered.

"Put me inside you. Now."

"How?"

"You know how."

When she hesitated, he circled her nipple with the tip of his finger as he ran his tongue against her earlobe. Her head fell back to rest on his shoulder and he grazed his teeth along her neck, saying against her damp skin, "Take my shaft in your hand."

He felt her hand closing over him, distinctly felt one soft finger at a time curling around him. He groaned with need, wanting inside her so badly. He wanted that fine woman from the bed, the one that he'd despaired of ever having, to desire him so strongly that she'd guide him into her own body.

She brought him to her wet flesh, and he thought he might come the moment the head pushed against her. He put his hands on the front of her thighs and pulled them farther apart, making her spread her knees wider. Then both his hands were back on her breasts, kneading, desperate, struggling not to buck into her.

He closed his eyes as she did it, as she worked his shaft

inside her tightness, loving that she moaned with each inch slowly sliding in. He hissed in a breath, but stilled halfway, letting her get used to him.

Because he was about to ride her harder than he ever had.

She put her hands back, grasping his thighs. He clenched her hips, plunging up into her, and she cried out.

"I need tae take you hard."

"Any way you wish—" she cried between hectic breaths, but the words broke on a moan when he rocked his hips into her again.

"You know what I want, Anna. Will you be givin' it tae me?"

Her fingernails dug into the backs of his thighs, and he heard her murmur, "*Yes.*"

He took her lobe between his teeth and growled in her ear, "Then go tae your hands."

She nodded, her hair brushing up and down over his arm. He placed a flat hand on her back to ease her down, then shoved her knees wider with his own. Clamping her shoulders, he pulled her along his cock.

He drew his hips back, then thrust again, going in harder than he'd meant to, but she cried, "*Ah, yes.*"

He bucked into her, his skin sounding against hers. "Arch your back down," he grated. She did, and in reward he reached around her to rub at her sex and place his flattened palm just beneath her breast so her nipple rasped against it with each of his thrusts.

When she moaned, he raised one knee up beside her hip and finally entered her as far as possible. She cried out again, but her growing wetness was all the permission he needed. He squeezed her lush curves, feeling frenzied, taking her harder and harder, driving into her bodily until she was forced to her elbows.

To his shock and pleasure, she tried to meet him, hastening

to her climax. He felt her tense, saw her hands clutch the pillow. He groaned, bit out a curse from the intensity as her body squeezed his, until she fell limp to the bed.

He turned her to her back, grabbing her leg and working it around so he could stay within her, still thrusting into her.

He took her hands and captured them over her head with one of his own as he pumped faster and faster. With the other he seized her breast and held it so he could put his mouth on her and graze his teeth over her nipple. At once, she began to come again, her knees falling open in surrender.

Just when he'd become too thick within her, he followed, never releasing her hands or her breast as he shot deep inside her, coming endlessly and forced to yell out from it, still driving until he collapsed.

MacCarrick's head lay on her chest, his arms wrapped solidly around her, still lying as he had been when she'd stroked his hair until he'd slept.

She believed that tonight he had been communicating something to her through his actions. She felt that the message could be one of two things. Either he wanted her to know he could be free with her, that he trusted her to understand the needs hidden within him, and to accept them.

Or tonight had been a blatant warning.

If the first, then she could accept him. She *wanted* his rough ways, craved that he made her feel so much like a woman just because he was so much a man. She thought of his teeth nipping her and shivered. She didn't want him to hold back or feel he had to hide anything from her.

If his actions had been a warning, he'd failed miserably. Because she desperately wanted everything he was warning her from.

Was there a message here that would reveal why he hadn't asked her to marry him? Were the Gaelic words he oftentimes rasped to her when they made love some type of promise? Once she had asked him what they meant, and he'd said only, "I will tell you soon." She wanted to demand answers, to force the issue, but these days with him were so precious to her that she feared jeopardizing them in any way.

She sighed. These thoughts plagued her because each day passing was a step closer to her ruin. Soon she would be given a choice, and if he hadn't made her his wife, if he wouldn't make her his wife, she would be forced to prove to all that she was just like her mother, that the Castilian blood ran far too hot in her veins. Because she would be choosing ruin to be with her Scottish lover.

He shifted positions, bringing her to him now, his head above hers. She knew he slept, but his hand unerringly went to her breast. His hand, so dark and scarred, stood out against her skin. Such a primal sign of possession. At once her nipple hardened beneath his hot palm.

What he couldn't know was how badly she wanted to possess him back.

# Thirty-one

Court drew Anna closer against him, her back to his front, her bottom tucked in his lap. He put his face to her hair and inhaled, recalling the night before and growing harder.

Then the doubts assailed him.

He'd taken a young woman, innocent and impressionable before she met him, and he'd bent her over and spread her and driven into her hard. And he knew he'd do it again—

"You're going to ask me if you hurt me," she said in a languid voice, reading his mind. He was just about to speak when she took his erection in her hand. "You're going to ask me if I was embarrassed." She stroked him. "You didn't hurt me." She guided him into her. "I'm not embarrassed." She wriggled her hips until she was better placed, then slowly moved down on him.

She was doing this? After last night? Though he was sure he was still dreaming, he met her and entered deep.

She gasped, then sighed contentedly. "See? None the worse for your wear."

"I dinna embarrass you at all?"

"Perhaps at first, but certainly not toward the end."

"Then maybe I'm no' wicked enough for you?" He nipped her ear and she laughed. He felt it. "I'm an old man with no more tricks in my bag?"

In an instant, he wrapped his arms tight around her, clasping her to him, and turned on his back. "Courtland?" she cried, when she lay atop him.

He spread his knees, locking her legs wide outside of them and set his hands all over her breasts and belly. She moaned when he dug his heels down to thrust up into her while his fingers flicked and played. He took her like this until she arched her back off his body, driving herself nearly down to the hilt, and when she melted on him, he spent hot within her.

Afterward he returned her to her front and reluctantly withdrew from the warmth of her body. He brushed her hair to the side and ran his thumbs along her slim shoulders until she slept again, then murmured in her ear, *"Anna, my heart is full."*

He rose and dragged on his trousers to return to his room. When he glanced back at her before shutting the door, she turned to her back, treating him to a view of her delectable breasts, and he groaned, knowing he wouldn't even make it till the afternoon before having her once more. He'd bring her breakfast and see if he could tempt her. He grinned. She was always as tempted as he.

In his room, he washed and dressed and found himself whistling. He wasn't a whistler. He shrugged, then stomped down the stairs, but when he was halfway down, his face fell.

Ethan was home.

His brother always looked furious, but this time markedly so, his scar whitening. *Bloody hell.* He gave Court one look and turned for the study. Court swore under his breath and followed.

"I have heard some of the situation," he began as soon as Court shut the door. "How long do you intend to stay like this?"

"Her brother will come soon," he hedged.

"And then you'll let her go with him? Even though you've slept with her?"

"Hugh told you?"

"He'd said nothing. Our mother is no' the only one getting reports from this house. I'd heard and then your face told me."

Of course Ethan knew. Ethan knew everything.

"Your Castilian has been asking the servants what a peculiar Gaelic phrase means." He skewered Court with a look. "Her pronunciation is extraordinary, I'm told. She couldn't have just heard it once in passing and then repeated the sounds so perfectly."

Actually, she could. She could mimic Ethan cold within five seconds of meeting him.

"You bound her to you?"

"Aye." The words had just seemed to flow from him. There was no stopping them. And yes, he'd told her that more than once.

"So she was innocent and of good family?"

"Aye," he said, putting his shoulders back. He refused to be ashamed of what he'd done.

An amused expression of disbelief. "You actually think you're going to marry the lass?"

"I will."

"Tell me, brother, do you hate her?"

Court narrowed his eyes.

From a leather satchel by the desk, Ethan withdrew a weighty tome and tossed it onto the desk.

*Leabhar nan Sùil-radharc.* The Book of Fates.

Court scrambled back, never taking his eyes from it as

every muscle in his body instantly went rigid with tension. The cover glimmered like the scales of a fish and showed none the worse for wear from all the times his forefathers had sought to destroy it. Court's stomach clenched, then roiled. The only marking the book had accepted was blood.

It was not as thick as it could have been—more pages could've been added. But they knew it ended where it did because there were to be no more direct descendants to have their fates foretold.

"You must hate her. You've put her in a situation where she can marry you or be ruined. Of course, she had better choose ruined. Much better than death and torment at worst, or at best a financially strapped mercenary who canna give her children."

"*Why did you bring that here?*" He looked around wildly, not believing Anna was in the same house as this cursed thing.

"I thought I might need to refresh your memory."

Court didn't bother to disguise his fury. He could kill Ethan for this. "As if I'd ever forget."

"But you have. And you've apparently forgotten what happened to the last woman engaged to one of us. Specifically me."

"It is no' like that, Ethan. I feel that this is different—"

"Of course you do." He exhaled and gave Court a rare look of pity. "You want it so badly you'll do anything to convince yourself it is, but all you're doing is hurting her."

Court was shaking his head, watching in misery as Ethan opened it to the last page. Their page.

"Good on you, Court. Why wait for 'death and torment' when you can meet it head-on? A career killing for money, seducing innocents . . . By the time you're my age, you'll have bypassed the deeds I've done."

That rocked him. Ethan was not a kind man. He'd always made the detestable things Court did seem petty.

"Strange," Ethan mused, "I feel no different than I did when I was still the most evil MacCarrick."

Court ignored his grim humor. "And what if her brother never comes? You have all the answers—what should I do then?"

"You know Hugh and I can find her a place of safety."

"I can keep her safe. I will go down there and destroy every Rechazado to protect her."

"But you still have to let her go. If you will no', you'll prove you doona care for her enough. If you truly did, you would never even *chance* her life. Look at Hugh—he refuses to be near Jane, but you think to marry yours." Ethan slammed the cover shut.

With a last revolted look at the book, Court stormed from the room, passing Hugh on the way out. "Watch Anna. And doona let him or that bloody book get near her." Outside he scarcely noticed the people on the street darting out of his way.

*"Out for a spell."* That was Hugh's cryptic answer when she'd asked where Court was. When she'd asked *two hours ago.* She didn't like it when he went out, could imagine far too many scenarios where he got ambushed, where he was outnumbered.

She paced the foyer, not caring that the servants gave her queer glances. They would anyway, since they all knew she was being bedded by MacCarrick daily, sometimes hourly.

Finally, he strode in the door from the drizzle outside, shaking his soaked hair like a wolf. He must have been walking outdoors the entire time.

"Where have you been? I was worried."

There was a bleakness in his eyes that wasn't there before. "What's happened?" he asked.

"Nothing. I just missed you and you didn't say good-bye."

He put his hands on her shoulders, absently rubbing her neck with his thumbs. She knew it was an unconscious gesture. "I was reminded of something today," he said, his words halting. He seemed to realize he touched her, because he looked surprised and cast his hands down.

"What is it?" she asked, becoming alarmed.

"I've realized things about us, about the way . . . about the way I feel, and I never want to hurt you. I am going back to—" He fell silent and tensed visibly, then turned back to the door, his body rigid and protective in front of her. His hand went behind him under his coat and rested on a pistol she hadn't known was there.

One of the front doors flew open, and MacCarrick relaxed the hand on his gun.

"Aleix?" He was well! He was here! She ran to hug him.

"Are you all right?" Aleix demanded as he took her shoulders to study her. "Are you unhurt?"

"Yes, I'm very well," she assured him. Seeming convinced of her well-being, his attention focused on MacCarrick. Aleix looked as though he'd kill him. "Now, Aleix, let me explain—" A figure drew Annalía's gaze. She turned back to the door, gaping. "*Olivia?*"

At that moment, Aleix charged MacCarrick, who met him, the two like animals after each other's throats as they fell into vases, pummeling each other. Oh, God, she didn't want either one hurt!

"You filthy Scot," her brother bellowed. "You put me in Pascal's prison, then you take my sister? You are about to *die.*"

Wait, Court put Aleix in prison? . . . He'd said he didn't. He'd said he never attacked them—"Oh!" She put her hand over her mouth. He never said he hadn't *fought* against Aleix.

*"Enough!"* Everyone froze. Annalía slowly peered over her shoulder to find a man—an older version of Court, but for the twisting scar running down his face. This must be Ethan. If possible he was more menacing than Courtland and Hugh.

Hugh strode in. Annalía heard Olivia mutter in Spanish, "Terrifying, petrifying, and horrifying."

"Court, I doona care who you're fighting or why," Ethan said. "Do it outside the house."

Court gave him a grim nod, then looked at Aleix. Aleix turned for the door.

When the sound of the fight ensued, she and Olivia started after them.

"Stop. Now," Ethan said to them, his voice low and threatening.

She stopped and noticed Olivia did as well as they both turned back.

"But we can't let this happen," Olivia said.

"They'll kill each other!" Annalía cried.

"No, they won't." When Ethan spoke she felt compelled to believe him. She relaxed marginally until he added, "Court will undoubtedly thrash him."

Both gasped. Annalía's hand went to her forehead. Olivia scanned the room, no doubt for a weapon, the little witch.

"Is no one pulling for my brother?"

Annalía could have sworn that this amused Ethan, not that you could tell by the granite expression on his face. Maybe the skin around his eyes wasn't as tight. His jaw not so clenched.

"No," she and Olivia said in unison, then glared at each other.

"I canna wait to have these dynamics explained to me. Shall I tear Court off your beloved . . . ?" He trailed off, expecting them to answer.

"Aleix! His name is Aleix, and he's *my* brother. And yes, you should."

"He's my fiancé and you should, but not because he needs you to," Olivia quickly added.

"No, indeed he doesn't," Annalía sniffed. A split second later: *"Fiancé?"*

While she restrained herself from clawing the witch's eyes out, the older MacCarrick walked outside, in a leisurely stride.

Minutes later, both men returned behind him, wet from the drizzle. Aleix's nose and lip bled, and both his eye and cheek were swelling. MacCarrick had no such marks, but then he was a professional killer. . . .

"Get in the carriage, Annalía," Aleix said between breaths. "I'm taking you away from here." To MacCarrick, he said, "When I get her safe, I'll come back to finish this. Make your peace."

When she didn't move, Aleix took her hand. She pulled it free to march in front of MacCarrick. "Please tell me you didn't put my brother in Pascal's jail."

His gaze was locked on hers. "I canna do that."

"Why did you never tell me? You said you didn't attack them. And I believed you."

After a long pause, he grated, "They—attacked—us," every word as though pulled from him.

"It doesn't matter," Aleix said from behind them. "You jailed us. You kept us from killing Pascal."

"Jailed, aye. No' killed," MacCarrick bit out. "You brought us farmers and ranchers. It would have been a slaughter." She knew he didn't often give explanations for his actions and was surprised that he would do it now.

"We were closing in on Pascal."

"You were closing in on the Rechazados protecting Pascal. Putting you in jail saved your lives. Ask Pascal's daughter."

With obvious reluctance, Olivia said, "It's true."

Aleix gave him a disgusted look. "I would rather have

risked it than have my people suffering." He offered Annalía his hand again. "Come with me before he decides to ransom you."

She waited for MacCarrick to interrupt him. To argue with him. He did nothing, just stood watching her. Her heart hammered so loud she wondered if everyone could hear it.

"Now, Annalía," Aleix told her in Catalan. "Leave your things and come with me."

MacCarrick had sworn he would get her to her brother. His task was complete. And though she'd thought they had made a commitment to each other, he'd never asked her to marry him and they'd never talked of the future. *You're mine,* he'd said like a vow.

Obviously, he'd done the same twisting of the truth that he'd done concerning the fight with her brother. *You're mine. For a time.*

Shoulders back, she walked to him. "You said you'd get me safely to my brother."

"So I did."

"Have you nothing else to say?" When he stood silent, she said, "Then thank you." *Don't cry, don't cry!* She offered her hand. "I appreciate your . . . help."

He didn't take her hand. He didn't take it and use it to draw her against his solid chest as he told everyone else to go to hell. Her heart hurt as though she'd been stabbed. His brothers stood near him with silent, icy demeanors. Their understood ruthlessness and will highlighted those same aspects in Courtland. She'd never had a chance with him. A man couldn't change his nature.

She'd worried about the decision she would have to make, but it had never been about *her* choice. He would let her go, and she was about to burst into tears.

"Very well," she murmured as she turned for her brother. "I'm ready."

# Thirty-two

*Anna's walking away from me.* Court couldn't think or reason beyond that.

He'd hurt her, then made reparations as best as he was able. He needed to get her away before he hurt her again. Next time he might not be able to fix the problem. *Death and torment* . . . The shining cover dared him to defy it.

She glanced over her shoulder, not pleadingly, but as if to memorize him. Then turned away. He tensed, hands clenching, barely preventing himself from acting on the command echoing inside him: *Get Anna.*

Behind him, Hugh must have noticed, because he said in a low voice, "You have to do this for her. Let her go with her family."

Her brother shepherded her away, already protecting her. Damn it, that was Court's responsibility. That was his *right.*

She was *his.*

Ethan put a hand on his shoulder. Coming from Ethan it

was a threatening gesture instead of comforting, and both of them knew it.

He turned to the two. Hugh frowned at Court's face as if confounded. Ethan took one look at him and scowled more, if possible. Court felt mad, crazed, and knew he looked it. "Only until I make sure she's safe," he said with difficulty.

"A woman like that doesn't belong with a man like you. Even if we weren't shadowed."

"You're killing her, Court," Hugh said. "Just like we killed Leith."

"*Wait.*"

She stopped in her tracks so fast her skirts surged forward.

At this she heard Hugh mutter, "Christ." Ethan hissed a startlingly vile curse, then said in warning, "*Courtland . . .*"

Aleix turned to her, his battered face showing his displeasure.

"How are you going to keep her safe?" Court asked of Aleix.

Annalía turned, tilting her head at him. She'd never seen this fierce expression, the wild look in his eyes.

"I'll protect my own."

MacCarrick nodded in the direction of the doorway, indicating the lone carriage waiting outside in the rain. "You doona have outriders. I'll wager you doona even have a weapon."

"You're begging me to prove that I do."

"She's been marked by the Rechazados."

Aleix's tone went low as though pained. "I know."

Olivia piped in, "We've been, too." Aleix gave her a harsh, warning glance, which seemed to delight her, then she sauntered over to inspect an expensive vase. Annalía suspected that vase would be found in their carriage momentarily.

"They've attacked three times already."

*"What?"* Aleix reached for her arm, but MacCarrick lunged forward and snatched Aleix's wrist.

"Doona touch her arm," he warned. She had nearly healed, but it would be tender if he'd grabbed it.

"What happened to it?" Aleix demanded with a withering glare at MacCarrick's grip.

"They shot her." MacCarrick released him. "And they'll do it again."

*"You let them shoot her?"* Aleix's tone sounded more frightening than Annalía had ever heard it. And MacCarrick? She couldn't make out his feelings at all, but sensed violence in him, sharp and ready. She had to cool this situation.

"Aleix, I ran from MacCarrick toward them. Like an imbecile, shouting for their help."

Aleix never took his eyes from MacCarrick. "You *let* her go?"

She put herself between them, standing on her toes to attempt to reach his line of vision. "I elbowed his throat. And he still ran right after me to throw us behind a boulder. That was only the first time he saved my life." Had Aleix relaxed the tiniest bit? "Two Rechazados attacked while we rode north. He took down one—"

"One?" Olivia surveyed Annalía with obvious newfound interest.

Annalía answered, "I got the other one. I had this rock hidden in my skirt meant for MacCarrick." Aleix appeared astonished, as if he didn't recognize her. "It had worked on him before."

MacCarrick gave his brothers a baleful expression as if anticipating their censure. "She told me she'd hurt her feet. When I went to look at them, she swung her dress around . . ." Hugh raised his eyebrows and MacCarrick grated, "She's *crafty.*"

Aleix took her elbow. "You can tell me about this later."

"You will no' take her from here," MacCarrick grated.

"You think to order me? You bloody, arrogant Scot—" And they were at it again.

Annalía flushed in embarrassment at Aleix's comment, wondering how Hugh and Ethan MacCarrick would respond. Annalía was learning that Ethan had one expression—malice just under the surface. Hugh shrugged. "Been called worse."

Court slammed into Aleix, hurtling him over a table, crashing it flat. Aleix clambered up from the wood to tackle MacCarrick, pushing them into the next room. "Will you help me?" she asked Hugh. Ethan was just too fearsome to ask.

Hugh swore, then strode between them throwing elbows. "You're behaving stupidly, Court. And much is on the line."

When they broke apart, both out of breath, Ethan spoke in a disgusted tone, "You have a common enemy. Excise the threat, then kill each other if you like." And then he was gone.

"They're right," MacCarrick said finally. "You want to kill me, which might even be fair, and I'm going to enjoy beating you down when you try, but we have other tasks at hand before then. I will no' allow you to distract me from them."

Aleix wiped his bleeding lip with his sleeve and labored to catch his breath. He gave MacCarrick one sharp nod.

Assured they'd stopped fighting, she hurried to shut the front door against the rain that had started to pour and splatter into the house. She could scarcely believe it when she spotted her horse tethered to their coach. "Iambe!" she cried, amazed that Aleix had thought to take her from Pascal.

"Anna, get away from the goddamned door," MacCarrick barked, striding toward her.

"How dare you speak to her that way," Aleix snapped as he followed. "Do you even know who she is?"

Olivia informed her, "Iambe is no longer my horse's name."

Annalía turned on her, ready to do violence, when she felt a hand clutch her neck and a cold barrel at her temple.

They'd come again.

She caught Court's eyes and saw the fury and rage firing in him, but this time she knew her luck had run out.

She really wished she'd told him she loved him.

# Thirty-three

*She believes she's going to die.* Her eyes met Court's, her expression telling him so. His hand eased back to his pistol, but the Rechazado shoved the barrel harder against her, a move that ripped the breath from Court's lungs.

He put his hands out in front of him. "Take me instead," he bit out.

Llorente said, "Me for her."

The man ran the barrel down her cheek. "We'll return for you both later."

*Think, God damn it, think!*

Where the hell was Ethan, where was Hugh? From where he stood, the gunman couldn't see Hugh in the next room. Hugh could take him out—he'd been trained to kill so quickly. . . . *"Hugh,"* he rasped in Gaelic, *"kill him. By Christ, please do this. Please . . ."*

He sensed his brother silently backing away.

The one with Anna opened the second door for another, who pointed his pistol at Olivia and indicated she should follow. She finally advanced toward him, but said over her shoulder, "It was still worth it, Llorente."

Both Rechazados backed down the steps, Anna stumbling in one's arms down the wet stairs, blinking from the rain but never taking her eyes from Court's. As if to gain courage.

"Doona fight him, Anna." He didn't know if she could understand the strangled words.

The fury was choking him, turning everything he saw black.

If the Rechazados got away, Court would find Annalía dead, discarded at the outskirts of the city.

"God damn it, Anna," he grated. "Just stay alive. Just hold on—"

A blast from the second floor. The man's head burst from one side. He tightened his arm in death around Anna as he collapsed.

The other whipped his pistol up at Hugh, but both Court and Hugh had already fired. He slumped to his knees, then onto what was left of his face.

Court knew he'd never forget what he saw for the rest of his life. Anna crawling from the body, eyes blank, lips parted. A bellow of rage roared from him as he ran for her, unable to get to her before her hands slipped from under her in the blood and carnage from both men and the cold rain pooling on the street. The low cries she made . . .

He slid down next to her, dropping the gun to snatch her into his arms, clutching her to him, his fingers tracing and retracing her temple, scarcely believing. *"Anna?"* He clasped her head to pull her to his chest.

She nodded faintly against him.

How long they stayed like this he didn't know, but Hugh had come from his vantage, and he and Ethan were outside, scanning for more.

Llorente was trying to take Anna from him. Court swung out blindly and connected hard with his face. Something broke beneath the blow.

Hugh took Court's shoulder. But he couldn't move.

"You doona want her to live through that, then die from chill," Hugh said.

The words made perfect sense.

"Come in, Court," Ethan ordered.

Only when she shuddered was he able to command his body to move. He drew her into him too hard and rose.

Once inside, in the bright light, when he saw the blood all over her, things became very clear. "Ethan?"

"They're taken care of, Court. Doona think on it."

Court swung his gaze to Hugh.

"Retribution?" Hugh asked.

"*A thousand times.*"

"I'll ride with you."

Court shook his head. "I already owe you more than my life."

"We leave at dawn," Hugh said, ignoring the last.

Erskine called down in a high, panicked voice that a bath was waiting.

Court vaguely heard Llorente speaking. *Not her husband. Must let her go. Can't care for her.*

He faced Llorente, felt his teeth bared, heard the other woman snap, "Don't be stupid, Llorente! He won't hurt her."

Court had started for the stairs when Anna finally spoke, "I'll be fine. I am usually stronger during these things." Her voice was faltering, her words sounding hollow.

*During these things.* If she'd died, he would have meted out death and torment as they'd never known.

"Why is everyone acting so strangely?" Anna asked.

Olivia said, "Everyone is acting strangely because your pupils are the size of tea saucers, you're covered in blood, and you have gun oil smeared on your temple. You're also deep in shock."

"Oh," she answered in a small voice. "Courtland, put me down, or I'll become embarrassed. You've never reacted like this before."

*Before.*

Llorente yelled something from below, apparently restrained by Hugh. *Monster, brutal, killer, blamed.* The last thing Court heard was Hugh telling him, "You're lucky Court didn't snap your neck out there." Llorente was. The impulse had been there.

In her room, he set her on the foot of the bed, helping her sit up as he undressed her. He'd done this a hundred times, yet he could scarcely get the first button undone. He ripped at her dress—surprising how easily the fabric parted—until he'd stripped her. Lifting her in his arms, he set her in the bath, then knelt beside her.

Cupping warm water over her shoulders, he asked, "Anna, are you all right?" He didn't recognize his own voice.

"Of course." She was looking straight ahead. Her eyes wouldn't adjust. So bright in this room, and her pupils wouldn't recede. When he determined she could sit up by herself, he rushed to the lamp to turn it down, then strode back beside her.

He took a cloth and brushed at the blood on her face and neck, scrubbed her wee hands. "There's a good lass," he bit out as he washed her hair. The oil at her temple didn't want to come clean, and he couldn't rub much harder.

She would already have a bruise from the barrel. He shuddered violently.

"Courtland? You must try to be patient with Aleix." Her voice sounded confused. "He is not like my fierce Scot. The fighting is new to him, and he thinks he'll lose me as he lost Mariette and the little baby girl. I am his last family."

"*Mo cridhe,* you know I will do anythin' you ask of me." He put his forehead against her shoulder.

"I do know that," she said softly.

He felt her relaxing, then tensing as she fought sleep, so he rinsed her hair and body, then placed her on her feet to dry her. A cursory glance around the room revealed a nightgown and some of Court's clothes laid out for them. He dressed her in the gown before bundling her in the bed under several blankets.

The sight of his clean clothes reminded him that he had blood on himself as well. Fearing she'd be alarmed later, he stripped and rinsed with the remaining buckets of water. He swiftly dressed then pulled a chair over so he could sit beside her.

"I don't know why I'm so sleepy." She reached out her hand for his. "I've been so tired lately." He took it, put his elbows on his knees, and leaned forward to press his face down against her palm. When she slept, he didn't let it go.

Llorente walked in shortly after. Court glanced up without interest, vaguely noticing he'd broken at least Llorente's nose.

"I want to see my sister." His voice was thick, from either emotion or injuries.

Hugh came striding in directly after him, most likely to protect Llorente.

"Hugh, relax, I will no' hurt him any longer," he said, but he eyed Llorente crossing to the other side of the bed to study her face.

Apparently assured, Hugh said, "We need to plan. Ethan wants to speak with you. I can stay with her."

"Tell him to come here. I'll no' leave her." Court noted his hand had tightened on hers.

"He's with Olivia."

"Bring her as well, then, but I'm no' leaving."

Hugh glanced at Anna. "We will no' disturb her?"

"No, she will no' wake."

When Hugh left the room, Llorente said, "And you would know that because you've been sleeping with her?"

"Aye." He defied Llorente to say something about it now. The look in his eyes must have dissuaded Llorente from that subject, becaused he asked, "Are you certain she wasn't injured?"

"She's bruised. She's in shock. No more."

Hugh and Ethan returned with a table and chairs, Olivia following. Erskine brought the coffee service and then exited without a word.

Court reluctantly relinquished Anna's hand and tucked it under the blanket. After he tugged the cover higher to her chin, he strode over to sit.

Llorente pulled a chair, uninvited, to the table, studying them. He would have to be wondering how Hugh could shoot like that, would have to be wondering about Ethan's lethal demeanor and how he'd received his twisting scar. Though Court knew Llorente was baffled by all this as well as Court and Anna's relationship, he wisely asked nothing.

Court began, "Ethan, I need you to stay here with her." He caught Ethan's eyes, showing him how much he was entrusting to him.

"Aye. I'll bring in some men as well," Ethan said.

"If we doona come back, you must take Anna to Carrickliffe among the clan. Make them swear to her."

"It's done."

"And what of Olivia?" Llorente asked. "She must stay with Annalía."

Court swung a glance at him. "You can take care of Olivia."

"If you're hunting the Rechazados, I'm going as well." He ran a sleeve over his still bleeding lip.

"You stay here," Court said.

"That's my land and my people. I need to be there if you're going in."

"He's right, Court," Hugh said. "He'll just follow us down anyway."

Court shrugged. "You'll get in the way of what I'm after only once."

Llorente narrowed his eyes at that, then said, "And Olivia?" He didn't understand what he was asking for.

Hugh said, "Ethan, just agree to it. They'll need to be together."

Ethan hesitated for several seconds, then inclined his head. And with that, a man considered wicked by so many—often rightly so—would now risk his life for both of them. "Court, what do you know about the order?"

Court leaned forward, struggling to become cold, to focus on what they had to do. "They prefer to stay as a unified corps, dispatching smaller groups. If we could get close enough to where they camp, we could take them out at one time."

"There will just be new ones enlisted," Llorente said.

Court shook his head. "If you take out all of them, who's to pass on their orders?"

Hugh added, "I've read about them as well"—read about them, no doubt, in a thick dossier with the instructions "engage at will." "Even if you canna take them all, if you eliminate their leader, it's like cutting the head off a snake."

"But it won't matter if Pascal lives," Llorente pointed out. "He'll keep sending men. He's got an army of deserters wanting to rise in the ranks."

"Then we have to kill them to a man," Court answered, obviously surprising Llorente. Court gave him a look of disgust. "Did you possibly conceive that I would leave a single man alive who would hurt her?"

"You're talking about the Rechazados, the deserters and Pascal. In one campaign?"

"Aye."

Llorente nodded slowly. "We'll need more men."

Hugh said, "No' for the Rechazados, if they camp together and if we have the right . . . gear." *Explosives.* "So we'd need men only for the deserters. Court, can you contact your crew?"

"I've tried and have no' heard back. They probably went east with Otto."

"I'm no' sure they did." Ethan said. "Weyland and I have been working to get the deserters out of Andorra for months. Which was how I'd known you'd chosen . . . unwisely to ally with Pascal. Weyland's pressured the British ambassador, who's pressured the Spanish to raise the bounties on the deserters. Exponentially. If I know our cousin, Niall would've determined how lucrative it could be. With Court's crew, it'd be like shooting fish in a barrel."

"You think his mercenaries are in Andorra?" Llorente asked. "That's good news."

"Aye. Good for us," Court said. "Bad for your house."

Llorente raised his eyebrows. "Should I ask?"

Hugh quickly said, "No' if you've any sense."

Llorente prudently returned to the matter at hand. "I've studied the deserters and you know the Rechazados, but I don't know Pascal and know you don't either."

"No," Court admitted. "He alters routines, moves domiciles. I could no' find a pattern."

"Neither me."

Olivia coughed delicately. They turned to her, saw her admiring her reflection in a silver spoon. "But I have."

When the others had retired, and Court took his chair beside Annalía again, Llorente remained.

"You care for her. Obviously a great deal," he said, taking a chair on the opposite side of the bed to face him. "Why didn't you marry her before I got here to tell you no?"

"Because I care for her a great deal."

"You kidnapped my sister and forced her into a different country. Apparently, you took over my home—while I was rotting in a cell that you had put me in. You stole from me.

You bloody broke my nose. It's hard to imagine that you could do much more."

"But I have."

"Yes, you have. She could be with child."

"She will no' be with child."

"How can you be sure?"

"Canna have bairn." Normally he would never have revealed this to someone like Llorente, but now it seemed so insignificant.

"I should believe that?"

"Aye, it's true, though I dearly wish it was no'." Odd that men always thought if they got a woman with child then they *had* to marry her. If Anna could be with child, Court would *get* to marry her.

Llorente hesitated, then said, "Is that why you wouldn't marry her? Not that I would let you anyway, but that's a plus in my mind."

Anna had said he'd lost his wife and daughter. Must've been childbirth. "No, that's no' the reason. Just leave it alone."

Llorente put his elbows on his knees and stared at the floor. "When we finish this I will have to go to Castile hat in hand and ask them to contract a sympathetic match for her. She will hate me for it, but it must be done."

Court gnashed his teeth at the thought. As if she sensed his anger, Anna turned in sleep. "Courtland?" she whispered. "*On és ell?*"

"She wants to know where you are."

Did Llorente not think Court could understand? Of course he didn't. Court was an ignorant Scot. "I can speak Catalan," he snapped under his breath. Then, dismissing Llorente, Court raised her hand to his lips to reassure her.

"*T'estimo*, Courtland," she sighed.

Llorente said in a dumbfounded tone, "Then you know that for some ungodly reason she just told you she loves you."

•    •    •

When he heard Ethan's men arriving near dawn, Court rose from his chair. Of course he hadn't slept—he'd taken every minute he could with her after Llorente hesitantly left them last night.

Court lightly touched her cheek, glad at least that her color was back and her skin was warm.

He wanted to kiss her and tell her how much he didn't want to leave, but if she woke and asked him what was happening, how could he answer?

I broke your brother's face last night; we're going to Andorra to stamp out anyone who would hurt you; and afterward, because I took your innocence, you'll be forced to Castile. We won't see each other again, though I'd intended to marry you.

If the Rechazados didn't kill him . . .

When he brushed her hair from her face, the bruise at her temple stood out starkly. He flinched and a coldness settled over him . . . enabling him to walk away. *"Is tu mo gràdh thar gach nì,"* he murmured to her before he clenched his hands and left. *I love you above all things.*

Downstairs, he found Ethan preparing for war—Court had expected no less—with Hugh directing the packing of supplies. Both left him with nothing to work on.

So to gain strength for what he was about to do—abandon Anna—he stole into the study and retrieved the book. He'd never voluntarily touched it before, and hated the feeling of it now, but he wanted to read it, and curse it to hell where it belonged. He'd just turned to their page when Llorente walked in.

*The timing.* Court was really beginning to hate him.

"Ethan told me I'd find you here."

"Did he, then?"

"MacCarrick, I've thought about this all night, and I want you to marry Annalía before we go."

This was unexpected, but still . . . "No."

"For some inexplicable reason, she loves you, and she won't want to go to Castile. As much as it grieves me to even consider you, I must."

"No."

"Do you think this is easy for me? I'm a proud man and I despise you—the very idea of being related to you pains me. Remembering the prestigious suits I smugly turned down only to be *asking* you now appalls me. But I will swallow my pride to see her happy."

Maybe he didn't hate Llorente. Had to admire the man's doggedness. Broke his nose last night and Llorente was asking him to marry his sister the next morning. For her. Must be difficult as hell.

"She has her own fortune."

Court's jaw clenched, and he gave him the look his comment deserved.

Llorente appeared surprised. "I apologize if I offended, but you *are* a mercenary."

The man wasn't going to give up until Court hit him again, which he could no longer do. He would give his explanation, and if Llorente scoffed, then he'd have tried.

"See this book? This is why I will no' marry her." He opened it to the last page and stabbed his finger against it.

Llorente advanced to the table, skimmed over the lines, then faced him with an expression of astonishment. "You believe you're cursed?"

Court sank back in his chair. "The things it says have all come to pass."

"Like what?" he asked, his tone almost amused.

"It says that none of us will have children and none of us ever have."

"Your brothers believe this, too?"

"Aye."

"Then it's a bloody good thing you can't have children,

because lunacy obviously runs in your family. My God, my Andorran grandmother wasn't this superstitious."

He looked disgusted and Court couldn't blame him. Court had looked the same way until they'd found their father dead.

"And your father? I suppose *his thread was cut?*"

"Within a day of our reading the lines."

But Llorente was hardly listening to him. "This is why you didn't marry her before we arrived?" He snatched up the book, as if to hurl it. He froze, slowly turning his face to his outstretched hand. He placed the book down as though it were as delicate as eggshell. Then crossed himself. "Return to the page."

When Court leaned forward and did, Llorente read again, his expression growing more furious. "There's blood there."

"A warring clan stole the book hoping to cripple us. There was a battle to get it back."

"You don't know what it says? Have you tried to wash it—?"

"The blood will no' be lifted."

Llorente shook his head. "But what it says could be heartening."

Court let out a breath. "Or it could be worse."

Llorente's eyes narrowed. "Yesterday. Do you think that was . . . ?"

"Do I believe Anna was crawling through an assassin's blood in the gutter last night because of my fate? Maybe, maybe no'. But I will no' risk the scarcest chance." Whenever that image of Anna arose in his mind, he struggled to replace it with an image of the future he *would* ensure she had. He saw her safe in warm Spain, among her own people, with golden-skinned children playing about her skirts. "She will be free of them and free of me."

Llorente glared at the book, read it again. His face was tight when he turned to him. "Then you must swear it."

Court hesitated, then finally nodded. "Aye, my word. Let me finish my tasks first, and I'll never have to see her again."

# Thirty-four

"These are eggs?" Olivia asked Annalía again as she poked at them on her plate. Eggs shouldn't move as these did. She leaned down to peer at them at eye level. "They don't look like eggs."

Olivia glanced up to see the chit put her hand over her mouth. Her face was turning green again. If Annalía didn't eat something soon and keep it down, Olivia might have to do something drastic.

She could just see herself confessing to Aleix that Annalía grew ill on her watch. For some reason before he'd gone, Aleix had taken Olivia aside—not Ethan, not Erskine, not a stranger from the street—and asked *her* to take care of Annalía. She'd stared at him for long moments, wondering what he really was asking her, wondering if he was jesting, then realized he actually expected her to protect his sister. "How have you been living off this stuff?" Olivia pushed her breakfast tray away. "I haven't tasted a single spice since we got to Britain."

Annalía sat at the headboard of her bed, still in her dressing gown, knees drawn to her chest. "MacCarrick often sent out for food for me. He always knew what I liked." And there went the bottom lip trembling.

Olivia smiled pleasantly. "After I marry your brother, I will have the kitchen stocked with spices. Expensive ones." She picked up a book from the stack she'd plundered from the library downstairs, licked her thumb, and flipped through with desultory flicks of her wrist. "And we'll get a Spanish chef who knows how to use them. And who will sing opera."

Annalía's eyes narrowed. "I know what you're doing. Even as my mind refuses to believe it. Every time I want to cry you say something to provoke me."

Yes, Olivia had been doing that among other things. For Aleix, she was keeping his little sister from going mad or getting sick. When Annalía had woken that first morning and run downstairs, searching frantically for MacCarrick and her brother, Olivia had patiently explained that they'd left early, ready to get this fight won.

"Did MacCarrick leave me a message?" Annalía asked.

"He told me to tell you that they would be through in a few weeks. And that Ethan would see us down when it is safe," Olivia had answered, veering from the truth. Llorente had told her that; MacCarrick had given no such assurance or message. When Olivia had asked MacCarrick if there was anything he'd like to relate—and yes, she'd asked—he'd only grated, "Olivia, if you are unkind to her in any way . . ."

So ever since they'd gone, Olivia had hedged the truth—and met every sign of tears with snide comments and crude observations. Yet she could only stem the tide for so long, and even now Annalía's eyes watered.

Olivia slammed the book flat on the table. "That is one thing I'm not looking forward to—a watering pot for a sister. The embarrassment of it!"

"How would you feel?" Annalía demanded. "The man I love was letting me go, though I thought we would be together. I'd just found out he'd given Aleix to Pascal. I was nearly murdered. Then MacCarrick left me without saying good-bye!"

"One more time—your brother would be dead right now if MacCarrick hadn't put him away, and MacCarrick never lied to you about that. He merely omitted, a tactic I know well and use whenever I feel that I'm getting just shy of hellbound. Say good-bye? He was with you the entire night before he left. I'm sure he said quite a few things"—she raised her eyebrows accusingly at Annalía—"yet it's *his* fault you weren't awake to hear them?"

"He could have left me a letter."

"Now you're just being silly. He's a *mercenary*—he's not going to go about penning love letters, and really, what would he write? 'Anna . . . love you . . . grrr?'"

Annalía ignored the last. "I just wish I could remember that night! It's all so confusing. And I feel awful—I *never* feel awful." She clasped her forehead. "How can you stand the bloody worry!"

Olivia slid her nail file across the tabletop to drop it in her palm, then leisurely filed. "Oh, I'm not worried about your brother."

"*What?*" Annalía swung her head around, her undone hair whipping to the side.

"MacCarrick will look out for him. To please you." Olivia wasn't fearful for Llorente in the least. MacCarrick? She gave him a one in two chance. "I'm confident he'll be safe."

"MacCarrick would do that, wouldn't he? . . ." She sniffed.

"Annalía, don't you dare—"

"You would cry in my position!"

"No, I emphatically would not. I'd scrounge something to eat in this blasted British house, and I'd take care of myself so that when I saw him again I wouldn't be skin and bones with

eyes red from crying. And if I had questions about Mac-
Carrick that couldn't wait, and I was stuck in a house rife with
answers, I'd find them."

"What do you mean?"

"The servants. Servants know *everything.*"

"I tried! Courtland often said a Gaelic phrase to me, and it
signified something important—I know it—but when I repeated it to Erskine and the cook and the maids *and* the foot-
men no one would translate it for me."

Olivia snorted. "*I* wouldn't have taken 'no' for an answer."

Annalía glared. "Should I have held them down and
poured boiling water over them until they talked? Really, I'd
like your expert advice."

Olivia rolled her eyes. "Of course not. You would use boiling *oil.*"

In a sighing voice, Annalía asked, "Why are you being so
nice to me?"

*Take it back,* Olivia almost sputtered. "I'm not *being* nice to
you, I'm *acting* nice to you. Your brother seems to think I can
*behave* appropriately to certain people." She began filing her
nails again. Annalía had told her that they'd be *more attractive*
if she didn't file them so sharply, and she'd cast her a long-
suffering look. A woman's nails had nothing to do with at-
traction. "I'm merely testing Llorente's theory."

Annalía pulled her legs in closer and rested her chin on her
knees. "You told me how the 'engagement' came about, but
you should know that Aleix had vowed never to wed again."

"I did know that." Olivia blew on her nails. "So it's a good
thing I came along to force his hand."

Annalía tilted her head at her and scrunched her lips. An
open book.

"I can see that you agree."

"If you are what makes Aleix happy, then I will have to tolerate you."

"Oh. Since I was awaiting your approval."

Annalía exhaled a long breath, her gaze settling blankly on the opposite wall. "MacCarrick never told me he loved me."

"What did he say when you told him?"

Annalía bit her lip.

"You never told him?"

"I wanted to. I was going to," she said as she stood to pace. Olivia wondered yet again if the trembling bottom lip or the pacing was worse. "I just wanted the perfect time and . . . and, very well, I lost my nerve."

"Would you have been able to tell him if you were pregnant? You could be, you know," Olivia said, wondering if Annalía would finally admit to her condition.

Annalía stilled. "That's impossible. We can't have children."

Olivia's lips parted in shock and she dropped her file. *Can't have children?* Oh, the devil's red boots, this was getting worse and worse. The chit had absolutely no clue she was pregnant. No wonder she didn't understand why she felt so poorly—or why her emotions were roiling.

Olivia had thought she was keeping it a secret, but no, Olivia was going to have to explain, and in terms more delicate than "In another month, I'll be the only one wearing your clothes." She repeatedly knocked her forehead against her hand on the table. Llorente *owed* her this marriage.

"I suppose it's a good thing," Annalía offered.

Olivia wearily raised her head.

"Since he was just going to let me go."

"You clearly want to be with him"—Olivia leaned forward as if imparting a secret—"so don't *let* him let you go."

"Don't let him—?" Annalía's brows drew together. "That's what you're doing with Aleix."

Olivia sat back and propped her half-boots on the table. "So far it's working. He has to return to me because I have his sister hostage." She briefly put her fingertips to her lips. "Did I just say that? I mean I'm protecting the baby sister and earning his trust."

After a few moments more of pacing, Annalía admitted, "I must say this is better than crying."

Olivia threw her hands up. "What have I been telling you? And you've got it even easier than I do. Llorente doesn't love me—yet—but MacCarrick loves you."

Annalía frowned, then said with increasing conviction, "He *did* love me. I might be inexperienced to a ridiculous degree, but I should be able to tell, right? A man couldn't simply pretend that."

He could with ease! But Olivia knew that wasn't the case here. "Right!" she declared with a firm nod. "Now you stew over your plan of attack while I go find some food in this place. If we have to subsist on tea and biscuits, then we'll start hoarding tins up here." At the door she turned back. "And, Annalía, if I come back and see that you've been crying"— Olivia made a clawing gesture with her "unattractive" nails— "I will give you something to cry over."

During Olivia's absence, Annalía had time to bathe, dress, and conclude two things. First of all, there was no way she was giving up MacCarrick without a fight. She quite liked this idea of simply not allowing him to throw away what they had. It gave her a feeling of some control over her life.

Second? Though she still had concerns about Olivia—Annalía couldn't determine if Olivia was intermittently evil or handily the strongest woman she'd ever met—Annalía knew she would've gone bloody mad in this tense, foreign household without her future sister-in-law to berate her. . . .

Olivia returned then, breezing in the doorway, her arms full of biscuit tins. Evidently, they were, in fact, hoarding. She stowed her loot inside the wardrobe, then drew out a smaller package from her skirt pocket, tossing it to her. "This came for you."

Annalía caught it. From a jeweler but addressed to Court?

"The guard dogs downstairs opened it, of course. Well, go on. I want to see jewelry."

Annalía pried open the velvet box and found her mother's stone inside, though without its ribbon choker. Instead, he'd had it set on a chain so delicate, so precious, it was like gossamer.

Olivia swiped it from her hand. She didn't cackle and abscond with it as Annalía expected, but whirled Annalía in front of the mirror, to fasten it around her neck. "I remember this stone. I considered owning this stone. The necklace makes it more valuable. Good for you," Olivia said, as if she'd earned it from MacCarrick.

Annalía stared in the mirror. He'd somehow figured out what it meant to her, what its significance was, and he'd turned something hurtful into something beautiful for her. The necklace was so exquisite it was like a caress over her neck and chest. God, she missed him!

Did he send this as a good-bye?

"You know that Gaelic phrase you were telling me about?" Olivia elbowed her from the mirror so she could try on the rings on the dressing table, modeling her wiggling fingers in the mirror. "What would you give me if I told you what it means? Would you give me an antique ring once worn by a queen?"

"Right now, the best I'll offer is that I won't slap you if you tell me."

Olivia raised her eyebrows, obviously impressed with the threat of violence. "Very well, I will tell you." She paused dramatically. "It means, 'You are mine. I bind you to me always.' According to my sources, if MacCarrick told you that, then you're a breath away from being married."

Annalía's eyes widened. "You lie! How do you know that?"

"I asked the Scottish woman downstairs. I *wouldn't* have asked for you, but I truly did expect you to give me one of—"

"What Scottish woman?"

"A new one."

"I don't believe you."

Olivia caught Annalía's eyes in the mirror. "I swear on all that is valuable that I own."

Annalía rocked on her heels. It was true! Her thoughts came hectic. He *had* planned for them to be together! Why hadn't he told her? He should have. She supposed he did repeatedly, but not in any language Annalía could discern. She'd learn Gaelic! She'd dreamed he'd come to her that last morning and tenderly brushed her hair from her face. Maybe not a dream? She took a deep breath, wondering why her stomach felt so unsettled. Last night she'd mindlessly eaten something kippered or coddled or some dish sounding equally as foreign and unsolid, and she must be paying for it now—

"So you are Courtland's," a voice said from behind them. "The servants wrote telling me as much. But I scarcely believed them."

Annalía whirled around, feeling dizzy. She'd stopped whirling, but her head seemed to delight in continuing. A tall, beautiful woman stood there. The woman in the portrait, Annalía realized with a gasp.

"I'm his mother, Lady Fiona." She was very genteel as she offered her hand to Annalía, but her eyes were lifeless and dark. And suspicious. "And you are Lady Annalía Llorente. I attempted to garner information about you from Olivia"— she cast Olivia a puzzled glance—"but after tea I realized I'd somehow divulged more than I'd learned."

When Olivia gave her a convincingly innocent expression, Lady Fiona returned her attention to Annalía. She tilted her head and examined her as if she were a stray—not cruelly but with detachment. "I never thought of Court falling for a tiny Castilian. Even one as pretty as you. But by all accounts—and even by his own words—he has." The woman's expression grew stern. "It matters naught. Lass, do you ken that you canna have him?"

Annalía, formerly the most gracious woman in social situations, the mistress of all decorum, promptly threw up all over the woman's skirts.

# Thirty-five

When Court, Hugh, and Llorente rode up the plateaus to Llorente's home, they had to dodge villagers camping out, weaving around the clothes hanging on their lines, their children playing, and their goats grazing.

They'd learned that most of the deserters had been scattered and that small parties raided the valleys, forcing the villagers to come to the one place they could be safe.

Oddly enough, the place where the Highlanders were.

Court noted that at the first sight of plaid, Llorente's hands clenched so tightly on the reins they should've disintegrated.

"And I believe Court's crew is in residence," Hugh muttered.

At the front door, Liam greeted them, graciously showing them into the home. He slapped the seething Llorente on the back and said, "Any friend of Court's is a friend of ours. You look familiar. Do you like wine? Whisky? Just tell me whatever you need."

Inside, Niall and still more men played cards, ate fruit, and snacked on river trout grilled on slate, delicacies that Vitale, of all people, ensured they had plenty of.

Court's men saw him and cheered, asking, "Where's *our* bonny Andorran?"

This made Llorente's look of fury turn murderous. He yanked Vitale along to the other side of the room, and Court heard him demand, "I understand about the villagers, but how could you let these Scots overrun us?"

Vitale appeared sorry but unbending, his only concern about Annalía.

Court jerked a chin at Niall, and he rose. "Doona worry about old man Vitale," Niall said as he joined them, slapping their backs. "Prickly sort till you save his arse from deserters enough times."

"We need to discuss some plans with you," Hugh said, all business.

"Well, there's a salon in the front we can go to." Niall pointed out the direction. "By the dismal look on our Court's face, I think he'll be wantin' to avoid the study and the desk."

Hugh raised his eyebrows, and Court scowled.

Niall again slapped Court hard on the back. This time in sympathy. "Lass steal your heart?"

Court surprised himself by answering, "I'll no' be gettin' it back."

Hugh called for Llorente, who reluctantly followed them to the salon, looking dazed with anger. He sat silently and stiffly, appearing uncomfortable in his own home. Court knew no man had ever hated him as much as Llorente. He shrugged.

Once they'd all taken seats, Niall outlined the situation. "Andorra was chaos with people fleeing to high peaks and the deserters battling to escape when the main route to Spain was blocked. We've cleaned the countryside of them, collecting the bounties, but there's a group of about two hundred huddled down around Pascal."

"How many Rechazados are left?" Court asked.

"We took out six in the shootout at the border." Niall looked up to the ceiling, remembering. "Poor MacMungan, the younger one, lost an ear. MacTiernay got shot through his hand. A hole only as big as a beer stein, so it was no' too terrible—"

Hugh interrupted, "Seven more down in addition to that. Niall, we're leaving today to assassinate Pascal and take out the remaining Rechazados for good."

Niall nodded in understanding. "And I suppose you rode here first because you want us to round up the remaining deserters? Make even more money?" He eyed him hard. "Only 'cause you're family." He glanced over at the silent Llorente, frowned, then turned back to Hugh and Court. "So what's brought down the wrath of the MacCarricks?"

Hugh answered, because Court could not. "One of the Rechazados shoved a gun to Annalía's temple and was seconds from killing her right before Court's eyes. Does things."

Niall's face went cold in an instant. "Why did you no' say so? The crew will be furious." He slapped his hands and rubbed them together. "It'll be a slaughter. . . ."

"Well, I've never been greeted quite that way."

Annalía's hand flew to her mouth. She ran for a towel by the basin to wipe the woman's skirts—the only thing she could think of in a situation like this—but heaved again once there.

Olivia chirped over her shoulder, "I told you there was a new Scottish woman."

Lady Fiona asked Olivia, "What is wrong with her?"

"Perhaps she's upset that Mr. MacCarrick has left her like this. She and Mr. MacCarrick, the Courtland one, traveled together—alone—for several weeks. Just the two of them. They became . . . very close."

What was she babbling about? Maybe Annalía had gotten sick because Courtland's mother just brought into relief something she'd been struggling with since they'd gone. *Do you ken that you canna have him. . . .* Why not? When he was all she wanted in the world? She gripped the side of the table, squeezing to get herself under control.

Lady Fiona's voice was halting when she asked, "Are you saying? . . ."

Annalía turned then and caught Olivia nodding slyly as the woman studied her.

"I'm going to change my skirts," Lady Fiona said, never taking her eyes from Annalía. "Olivia, dear?"

"Yes, Lady Fiona."

"Do not"—she raised her hand in a stopping gesture— "let her go anywhere."

As the strange woman bolted out of the doorway, Olivia called, "As you wish, milady." Her voice was so saccharine, Annalía nearly emptied her stomach once more.

When they were alone, Olivia said, "You need to clean up," then took her shoulder and ran a wet cloth over Annalía's startled face.

She did it hard enough that Annalía asked, "Have you never done this before?"

"Of course, everyone was so kind in Pascal's household, always caring for each other. What do you think?" She handed her a cup. "Rinse your mouth out."

Annalía quickly did.

The woman swept in directly after. "Now, Lady Annalía—"

Olivia interrupted to say, "Pardon me, but she likes to be called simply 'Anna,' since it sounds more Scottish that way. And of course that's what Mr. MacCarrick calls her."

Annalía swung a lowering glare on Olivia.

"Of course, Anna." Lady Fiona looked so pleased, so

touched, that Annalía didn't correct her. "So you and my son became close?"

Absurdly, Annalía looked to Olivia to answer. When Olivia nodded, she said, "Yes, Lady Fiona."

"You care for him?"

"Yes." Her eyes began watering. She loved him. So much her heart pained her all the time. She put her nails into her palms to stop herself from crying.

But Lady Fiona's sharp-eyed gaze flickered over her hands. "And it was only you and my son, together for all those weeks on the road?"

Olivia answered for her in a conspiratorial tone, "It's been just her and your son since then as well. He's exceedingly proprietary about her. He hit her brother when he tried to take her from him."

Annalía rubbed her clammy forehead. "What are we really discussing here?" she asked much too tartly.

"Lady Fiona is trying to determine if Courtland Mac-Carrick was your only lover."

She gasped in shock. "Of course he was!" she blurted, too late realizing what she'd just admitted. She was humiliated, her face flaming in front of Lady Fiona. She turned on Olivia, telling her with her eyes, *Rat. Weasel. All low animals* . . . Wait, why was the woman trying to determine that? It wasn't her business. "With respect to you, I must say this is a private matter that I will not discuss."

"But it's no' wholly private." Lady Fiona approached Annalía to stroke the damp hair from her forehead in a maternal gesture. "For this family your baby means so much."

"*Què?!*"

After swift preparations, the entire band rode out, arriving near Ordino late in the night. Niall's men were to remain outside the city waiting in ready while Court, Hugh, and Llorente slipped in.

The three found a vantage where they could assess the Rechazados' camp—an old stone manor high on a mountain cliff. "If I can find a fracture," Hugh said, scrutinizing it, "I can take the top of the mountain out."

"How are you going to get up there?" Court asked, scanning the mountain from the bottom to its sheer top.

"Scale it. I'd planned to anyway, to make sure only Rechazados were inside."

"Are you going to be able to scale down quickly enough?"

Hugh faced him with a shadow of a grin. "I'm bettin' on yes."

Llorente finally spoke to them to ask, "Do you need one of us to go with you?"

"I work better alone," Hugh said. He always said that.

Hugh slapped Court on the shoulder and said to Llorente, "You have the *privilege* of protecting them now. Doona hesitate tonight or you'll fail. And if you get my brother killed . . ." He leaned in toward him. "Just doona get my brother killed."

After slinging his ropes over his shoulder, Hugh carefully stowed his volatile explosives. With a nod, he casually said, "When you hear the bang, then."

Court and Llorente set out after he left and advanced to a smaller town house, not nearly as grand as he'd seen Pascal in last. "If Olivia has led us astray," Court began, "I'll return to England and kill her myself."

Llorente scowled. "She wouldn't lead us astray. See? Why would there be guards otherwise?"

Three guards did front it. "You goin' to be able to take down one?" Court asked.

Llorente pulled out his pistol. "I can do what I need to."

Court shook his head. "No' a chance. It's got to be quiet and quick. Ever slit a man's throat before?"

"Not exactly."

Court's brows drew together with realization. "Kill anybody before? A single deserter?"

He grated, *"No."*

"Oh, bloody hell, Llorente," Court muttered. "You might've mentioned this earlier."

Annalía paced, occasionally kicking the bed, sometimes affecting a Scottish brogue to mock MacCarrick. *"I canna get ye with bairn, Annha."* She didn't care that Lady Fiona stared on in bemusement.

"My dear, he truly believed it. And it *was* true before you."

He'd said he couldn't, and since her courses were irregular and often came late, Annalía had never even considered this possibility. Yet now it was an actuality. "I am no expert, but I know a man can't be . . . he can't be . . . fruitful with only one specific woman. Things like this cannot happen." This curse nonsense made her head hurt. If Fiona hadn't appeared so sad, so remorseful when she'd related it, Annalía would have laughed.

"But it has. There must be something among the last two lines about binding with the right woman, or finding her."

Annalía didn't believe in the supernatural. Her father had always told her in a derisive tone, "Why do people bring the supernatural into the equation when they can't even control the natural? Only a fool would."

"Please, I don't want to hear any more about the book." Annalía was already half delirious.

Fiona insisted, "If you'd just go downstairs and touch it, you'd feel there is something there, some power."

"Of course there'd be power," Annalía conceded. "Because

clearly the book was written by *elves*," she breathed with wide eyes.

Fiona chuckled, then appeared startled that she'd laughed. Annalía figured she'd laughed in the years before this as much as her sons had.

Olivia rolled her eyes at Annalía, then asked, "Lady Fiona, will you tell Ethan?"

Fiona said with obvious reluctance, "I will, but no' until Anna leaves. He's been most affected by the curse and, unfortunately, he'd think badly of her before he believed the babe was Court's. But Hugh I'll tell at the first opportunity."

"He should think badly of me regardless! I'm ruined. Courtland never asked me to marry him."

"Because he loves you and dinna want to see you hurt. After the attack he would have felt responsible. But he said words to you, words that you doona say to anyone but the one you want for the rest of your life."

"That's all well and good, Lady Fiona. And I appreciate the sentiment—it means much that he has said these things to me. But some Gaelic love words aren't going to give my— *Mare de Déu*—my baby a last name."

Fates *were* inescapable. *Look on the bright side,* she told herself, nearly laughing out loud. *At least I can no longer look down on my mother.*

"A little more efficiently, then," Court advised Llorente as the third guard dropped, though he wasn't completely unimpressed.

"Go to hell, MacCarrick," Llorente snapped.

"Give it time," Court mused. "Now move fast. We need to get there before Hugh sets up."

They entered the building, treading down the dimly lit halls that Olivia had mapped for them. Just as she'd predicted, they heard Pascal inside the manor's office.

At the end of the adjoining hall, they set up against opposite walls, Llorente with two pistols and Court with his rifle and pistol.

Court said in a low voice, "The men with him will believe the explosion is the arsenal blowing from an attack. When they run out, pick them off. Doona hesitate."

Soon after the manor quaked as the massive detonation sounded outside. Dust from the roof timbers and plaster ceiling rained on them, coating their shoulders and hair. "Andorran construction," Court said under his breath. Llorente cast him a black look.

At the explosion, the door flew open, and as predicted, four men ran outside. Court began shooting, Llorente followed, and the men dropped. But another four, this time Rechazados, had lined up, stealing glances at the doorway. Court exhaled. They were going to be here all night. This was what he'd always hated about the job. The bloody downtime—

*Wait* . . . "Llorente," he hissed in whisper, "shoot through the wall. *Now.*"

Taking out the Rechazados behind the walls required more bullets, but eventually they saw through a cloud of white dust and ricocheted stone that they'd fallen. "As I said, Andorran construction," Court mumbled as they advanced past the bodies. He swung his empty rifle to his back, then handed Llorente a handful of bullets. "Put one in each of their skulls to make sure they're dead."

He heard Llorente shooting behind him as he made his way to the doorway to the office. Inside, Court found the Rechazado leader armed with only a knife and scowled. Too easy.

He raised his pistol to fire, but his weight left the ground as he was wrenched from his feet. One of the fallen Rechazados had not been dispatched. Court scrambled up, swinging the gun around, and shot twice, killing the man, using two of his three remaining bullets. He spied Llorente grappling with another. He had the advantage, but Court couldn't risk it. "God damn it, Llorente."

"They won't *die!*" he responded wildly just before Court fired.

*That's why I told you to shoot them.*

Now Court faced the Rechazado leader with an empty pistol, knowing he'd never be able to reload in time. When the man tossed his knife back and forth, taunting him, Court understood what he had to do. "If you're goin' to play with it, let me know, but I'd thought you might get the urge to throw it." The man had no emotion on his face, even as he flipped up the blade to pinch the tip.

He flung it; Court dodged but caught it deep in his left shoulder. He'd known he'd catch it somewhere at this range. "My thanks," he hissed as he tore the knife from his shoulder.

Movement to his right. Court threw the knife blindly.

The last thing he saw before the Rechazado soundlessly plowed into him was Pascal levering the blade out from his collar area.

He and the Rechazado hurled toward the room's main window, crashing through the glass onto the street below. Court landed on his back, taking both their weights against his rifle, his pistol knocked from his hand. He scrabbled to his feet, struggling for breath. The man drew another knife from an arm sheath.

Court's lips curled into a sneer. He nodded at the Rechazado, then daubed at his neck, as though indicating to him that he missed a spot shaving or nicked himself. The man lifted his hand and felt the protrusion of glass jutting from where it was buried in his neck. Court would give him five minutes. Fewer if he removed it. Court doubtless had a similar wound that he'd been incapable of feeling and willed himself not to look down.

The man stumbled, but his knife stayed poised. Court

ventured a look in the window and saw Llorente and Pascal in a pistol-to-pistol standoff. Though blood had spread across his shirt, Pascal began speaking to Llorente, just as Court had known he would. The Rechazado lunged and Court skipped back, but all the while he could hear. . . .

"Surprising that my daughter chose a life with you over one with me," he said, his tone even and mild despite the injury. "And I'm not often surprised."

"I'm sure she had other reasons to leave you."

"Yes, I believe she found out that, sadly, the odds are against my being her father."

Court heard it all, but remarkably the Rechazado was still prowling. Court glanced up and saw Llorente's brows drawing together. *Don't get dragged in,* he wanted to yell, but knew if he distracted Llorente for a second he'd get him killed.

He began digging for a bullet, but the Rechazado flicked the blade up, readying to throw. Court put his hands up. They continued to circle.

"She didn't tell you?" Pascal made a tsking sound. "That's not very forthcoming of her, and I do apologize in the case that she actually is mine." He smiled a sheepish smile, looking so . . . sane, then added, "If you do happen to get out of this alive, please tell her that her dubious parentage is all her mother's fault."

The Rechazado lunged and Court dodged.

"I will never tell her that her mother was impure," Llorente grated.

"Did I say she was impure? It was her very purity that attracted us. Not only a devout widow, but beautiful as well. How could we not have her that night?"

At that Court had to glance up. Llorente's face was twisted with fury, his hand shaking just as Pascal intended. Court faced the Rechazado with an irritated look. "Be quick about this, man. I doona have all night."

Finally, he gurgled blood, and his knife hand drooped. Court strode up, knocked the knife down, and without slowing, he twisted the man's neck until it broke. Below the window, he collected the rifle, taking time only to load it with one bullet. He ratcheted his arms up, and set his shoulders.

Court drew a bead on Pascal and fired.

Pascal fired and fell.

Immediately sounding from inside: "God damn it, MacCarrick!" Then more weakly: "You got me shot. . . ."

# Thirty-six

"Stop your caterwauling," Court snapped. "Your sister's was as bad as this, and it dinna stop her from glaring at me with hatred for even a second. She never shed a single tear."

Truth was that Llorente's wound was a wee bit worse. The bullet had torn past his side leaving a sizable gash. Court himself had collected a good-sized shard of glass, and since it was wedged into his calf, sitting seemed much preferable to walking, even if he had to do it with Llorente. Hugh had found the two of them propped up against separate walls, drinking whisky and sniping at each other. He'd sent Liam to fetch a physician, then stood guard as they waited.

"She really dinna cry?" Hugh asked as he pressed his shirt to the ragged slashes on his face caused by the splintering rock. Though successful, Hugh had returned, shaking his head and mumbling, *"Slate. Who knew?"*

Court sounded proud when he said, "Bravest lass I've ever known." Of course he was proud, but he didn't get to be. She wasn't his any longer. His head fell back against the wall, and he stared at the ceiling.

"God damn it, Court"—Hugh kicked his good leg—"I'll no' tell you again to keep pressure on your shoulder."

"How could you do that?" Llorente bit out the question for the fifteenth time. "Make him shoot me?"

"I figured my aim was better than his. Looks about right to me."

"He bloody shot me!"

"If you had killed the others we would no' be in this situation."

"That one had a gaping hole in his stomach. How did he live through that?" Llorente set his bottle down as if he'd just comprehended something. "You've now done everything you bloody could to wreck my life."

Court swigged, then said, "I swear to you, man, Anna is no' the one who should wear skirts in this family."

Finally, Llorente appeared furious.

"Hugh, tell him what Pascal would've done if I had no' shot."

"He would've pulled the trigger soon. He was baiting you, and his aim would've been colder."

"Did you hear what he said about Olivia?" Llorente's words were a touch slurred.

"Aye," Court admitted.

"I'd wondered about her loyalties, could never quite see why she'd do this to her father." He added to himself, "She'd been loyal all along to her mother," then frowned. "Think I love her." He winced when he tried to move.

Court shook his head at Llorente's wound. That one truly needed to get sewn.

He could hear Niall and the others yelling and laughing in the distance as the shots became fewer and fewer. They were going to tear apart this place tonight looking for Pascal's stash of goods and coin.

Court figured they liked playing the heroes because they'd decided almost to a man to restore everything to its rightful owners before Andorra's typically harsh winter came to these people. Lucrative bounties made it easy to be a hero, he supposed.

"I'm going to contact Ethan now," Llorente said. "Ask him to send them home with escorts."

"What for?"

"Your brother said to leave it to him—not to you—when the time came. Now that we've won, is there any reason I shouldn't be bringing my sister and Olivia here?"

Both Llorente and Hugh waited for his answer. "No. No reason no' to. Ethan will make sure they're safe."

"You'll ride before then?"

Court felt a muscle in his cheek twitch.


Each hour that had passed on the way home was agony, but at least during the trip Annalía had stopped throwing up everything she ate. With every mile closer in that coach, she and Olivia had bickered, even after Olivia had said, "As far as spoiled heiresses go, you're not too bad," and Annalía had responded, "As far as conniving witches go, I've met worse." But truly, if they hadn't bickered, what else would there have been to do?

And though Olivia seemed unaffected by the news of her father's death, Annalía had kept her occupied in any event. "I keep replaying the scene we'll have when we ride into the courtyard," Annalía had told her. "I'll rush to MacCarrick. Aleix will push you into the lake. It will be *perfect*."

"Keep up your teasing. I don't care," Olivia had responded. "But after I tell Aleix how nasty you've been to me, what incentive will he have to be civil to *your* unsuitable mate?"

She'd had a point, but fortunately she suspected Olivia wouldn't tell Aleix anything.

And now, today, they were finally here. When the coach stopped and Ethan's guards deemed it safe to clear room, Annalía tumbled out and ran to the house. She tripped in breathless and hugged Aleix, who'd come to greet them.

He smiled down at her and then at Olivia when she entered. A peculiar smile for Olivia. A *loving* smile? She'd never really seen them together. Oh, Olivia did *not* just blush?

Annalía waved her hand in front of him. "Where's Mac-Carrick?"

He faced her, his expression turning grave. "Annalía, he's . . . , well, he's ridden from here. He went north, I believe."

A wheezing sound passed her lips as she sank down onto an ottoman. "I don't understand. Why would he do that? Didn't he know we were returning?"

Olivia walked up behind her. "Did he say anything?"

"He wished Annalía well."

"*Wished me well?*" Her voice was strident. She hadn't stopped throwing up. She believed she would right now.

"He's not exactly a man of many words, as you know. Annalía, he and I decided it was for the best. He wasn't the right man for you."

Her eyes narrowed. "You and he decided? The two of you decided my future? *Coach-and-six!*" she cried as she shot to her feet. "You . . . You coach-and-sixed me!"

He looked at her as though she'd lost her mind. She felt the blood leaving her face, and her legs buckled, forcing her right back down.

Aleix rushed to her and grabbed her shoulders. "What's wrong with you? *What did he do?*"

She dimly saw a hand snake from behind her to slap his sharply until he released her.

"Annalía, this is for the best. He's from a completely foreign culture and doesn't have wealth to keep you as you should live. And I don't know if he told you or not, but he can't father children."

She stared up at him, tears welling. "I beg to differ."

"Court, are you all right?" Hugh asked with a snap of his fingers.

"Huh? Why?"

"If your horse had no' sidestepped, that limb back there would've taken your head."

Court jerked around for a look. He'd never seen it. He'd been lost in thought wondering where she was right now, what she was doing, and knowing she was happier than he was. She *had* to be. He faced front again, surprised they'd already arrived at the drive for Groot's—though he shouldn't be surprised. They'd made good time since Hugh had led them off the main road to follow a shorter horse trail. Hugh hadn't taken any chances that Court might pass Annalía on her journey home.

"I was thinkin' about her," Court muttered. "Miss her."

"Aye, I know."

"I miss her so bad it's like . . ."

"Grief?" Hugh asked, as he swung from the saddle.

He nodded slowly.

"Court, I wish I could tell you it'll get better." Hugh gave him a weary look. "But it does no'."

If this wouldn't get better, if everything continued to remind him of her . . .

"Where's the pretty Andorran?" Groot asked the minute they entered the posting house.

"Safe at home," Hugh answered for him when Court could only scowl.

"Good to know," he said absently as his wife called him to help with guests. They had another full house. Court sank down on a bench because his leg was paining him, and thought to himself that the seat wasn't too uncomfortable. He'd sleep right here before he took the room he and Anna had shared before.

Hugh crossed to the bar and helped himself to pouring two whiskies.

"You know, Hugh, got a missive for you," Groot said, leaning in to add, "From Weyland himself."

Hugh's brows drew together and the bottle slammed to the bartop. "Now, Groot."

When Hugh ripped open and scanned the message, he went rigid and his face grew tight, the lines there deepening. The new jagged gashes on his forehead and the side of his face twisted.

"What the hell is it?" Court had witnessed Hugh once in a killing fury, and it was a memory he would never forget. The savage look on Hugh's face right now was so far beyond that—it was chilling. Court rose, then limped over to work the note from a hand clenched so hard it was white.

> *MacCarrick,*
> *Jane's life is in grave danger. Come quickly.*
> *Weyland*

"We ride now," Court said as he turned for the door.

"*No, Court.*" When he looked back, Hugh shook his head hard. "I go alone."

As if Court didn't understand what he was capable of. "I owe you a debt greater than I think you comprehend. And I'll be payin' it now."

"God damn it, Court, no. You're injured, and I'll need two horses, which means yours as well."

"Of course, but—"

Less than a minute later, Court stood outside with the

wind swirling around him as he watched Hugh ride off at a reckless clip. Court was confident he'd reach her in time, and could almost pity whatever force had jeopardized Hugh's Jane. In fact, his only concern was if Hugh would be strong enough to resist his feelings for her. For Hugh's sake he hoped the shameless chit had outgrown her teasing.

Court ran a hand over the back of his neck, considering his own situation. Damn it, Hugh had been all that had gotten him out of Andorra. If his brother hadn't been there to warn and rail and commiserate with him, Court doubted he could've left. Now the temptation to return and find her was nearly overwhelming.

He watched the setting sun through a veil of darting leaves, but everything was dead to him, the colors muted. He had no plans, had no idea what he would do. He could go east with the others and ride for Otto or head north for home. He could go south. . . .

Anna was better off without him. Established. But was she happy? Or was she as bloody miserable and bad off as he? Was she dreading her trip to Castile?

He'd given his oath to Llorente not to see her. Vowed not even to go near her.

And Llorente had proven himself a decent man. He'd presented Hugh with a fine steed for his help. To Court he'd offered a handshake, which was "much, much harder to part with."

In return Court again had given his word.

Hugh and Ethan had accepted their fates. But Court had dared to defy it for a time, and that was the only time in his life truly worth living.

He thought of the ten lines that had been seared into his mind the first day he'd seen the *Leabhar,* and narrowed his eyes. As the wind picked up again, rattling the trees, he turned to the south.

Court had a feeling he'd given Llorente his word as a gentleman.

Which was bloody convenient.

Autumn had arrived here on the mountain, and as regular as a clock, the meadow turned indigo with blooms. Annalía sank into the flowers to watch the sun go down —and to get away from Aleix and Olivia as they vainly tried to hide their feelings for each other. Annalía wanted to shout at them that she was enceinte, not stupid.

She plucked a bloom, then pulled the binding from her hair. Why not let it flow free? Would people talk? The way she was growing, in another month they'd have much more to talk about. . . .

In response to the news of her condition, Aleix had wanted to kill the Highlander or drag him back here and "force him" to marry her. Another dismaying option he'd talked about was going to the family in Castile. "Should I take her there?" he'd asked Olivia. Asked *Olivia!*

Annalía answered again and again, "I don't want to marry anyone you'd have to force to the altar or anyone sight unseen." Besides the fact that she was still miserably in love with MacCarrick, Annalía refused to go to Castile, the very image of her mother, carrying a bastard.

Olivia's solution? Do nothing until they found MacCarrick. "His mother will tell him soon enough that Annalía is pregnant. He'll know the book is wrong, and then he will find her wherever she may be. If she is wed, he will kill the unfortunate groom for touching her and collect her regard less."

"Yet it could be months before he returns to London or receives any message from us," Aleix had pointed out. "Years, even, if he rejoins his men to the east. Her child will be a bastard in seven months if we don't get her married!" But fortunately, he'd taken her advice. Olivia usually did give good advice.

Since they'd arrived home, Olivia had settled in here, which wasn't that difficult since the people at the ranch were grateful to her for freeing Aleix. Even Vitale liked her. Annalía could only guess that he sensed a hardness in her, a fellow survivor, and respected her. . . .

"It's getting chilly," Aleix said from behind her as he pulled a shawl over her shoulders.

Before long, the snow would come, sealing them in from the rest of the world as though in a cocoon. "I just want to watch the sun go down."

"The guards don't like you out after dark." Aleix had hired the men Ethan sent down, as they'd planned, until everything was settled in their country and around. She rarely saw them. Mostly they stayed at the foot of the mountain at the narrow passage to the plateaus. "How are you doing?" he asked.

She tried to answer lightly. "Besides being unmarried, with child, and abandoned, I'm *far* too splendid." She'd merely accomplished sullen, and sighed. "I believe I've topped even Mother's . . . peccadilloes."

"What do you mean by that?"

"Her affairs." She waved her hand as if she didn't care. "Everyone always said I looked just like her, that I *was* just like her."

"Affairs?" he choked out.

She faced him with a frown. "I've heard the rumors. I know she abandoned her family because of . . . passion."

"You think that's why Mother wasn't here?" he asked, his voice incredulous. "She had *an* affair with a man—a good man named Nicolás Beltrán—whom she'd been in love with her entire life." When she shook her head in confusion, he continued, "They were caught eloping, and the family sent her away. It would've been as if someone had forced Mariette away from me the night before our wedding to marry an older stranger in exile. Mariette would've wanted me to come for her and nothing would've stopped me."

"But what took him so long?" she asked, becoming completely lost in the story.

"When the family was through with him, he was penniless and in ill health. He had no idea where she'd been taken, and it took him years to find her."

She gave him a bitter smile. "Yes, but when he did, she left me, her own daughter, for him. It didn't affect you as it did me. You were grown, but I was devastated."

"Annalía, she didn't go voluntarily. When Llorente found them together, he disowned her, forbidding her to come near you. Beltrán took her to France, where she wrote daily to Llorente, begging him to let her see you. She journeyed here again and again, but he always intercepted her. She didn't stop trying until she died, a year later."

"B-But I always thought she'd left me for a man. I thought she chose him over her own family. That she'd never looked back and had crushed Father with her indifference."

"At Mother's funeral, I talked to Beltrán. She had been telling him she would never leave her children when Llorente found them together."

Annalía rose to pace. "That bastard! How could Father keep my mother from me? How could he let me think she had many lovers? Aleix, he warned me that I would be like that!"

"Though I make no excuses for him, I know he was devastated because he'd believed she'd grown to love him. Annalía, I never suspected Llorente would poison your thoughts like that or I'd have taken you away myself."

When she paced faster, he said, "We should discuss this later. Once you're feeling better."

"I've waited sixteen years for this! She'd told Beltrán no?" She was still shaking her head, disbelieving that everything she'd known was a lie. "She didn't leave me of her own will?" She took her necklace between her thumb and forefinger and felt the stone.

"I was well old enough then to see that no mother could love a daughter more. . . ."

She sank down and when the tears fell, she did nothing to stop them. "I wasn't at her funeral! I never put flowers on her grave." She leveled a watery glare at him. "Why didn't you tell me all this?"

"I never knew." He appeared dumbfounded. "You were so young when this happened, and since you never asked me about her, I thought you scarcely remembered her."

"I must go to her grave. I must give her the respect I never have."

"You know I can't leave until things settle here. But we'll see how you feel after the baby comes."

She wiped at her eyes. "I'd always thought about going, but I was so angry and so afraid that I would do something like she did. Or what I thought she did."

"Mother was a good woman with a kind heart. And you are just like her. I see it more every day. Tomorrow afternoon, when I get back from the council meeting in the village, I'll tell you everything I know about her, but you need to come in now. You're to be a mother now, too."

She exhaled a faltering breath. "Aleix, what am I going to do?"

"You're going to have a child that will be loved. We take care of our own."

"Then what? Will I grow old here on the mountain waiting for him?"

"Annalía, let's get through one thing at a time. All I know is that these choices are yours. And that I won't repeat history and try to marry you off to someone you don't love."

"Thank you for saying that," she murmured.

"Now you need to concentrate on being healthy. On caring for your new one."

He rose and offered her a hand, but she said, "Just a minute or two longer."

He patted her head, then turned for the house.

When she was alone, and the last light of the day was mirrored in the lake, she rubbed her barely rounding belly, frowning. "My new one," she said aloud. *Mine,* she thought. *And new.* She'd been so busy feeling sorry for herself and thinking of her *condition* as though she were ill, as though it were lamentable.

Now that she knew her mother had loved her, had never wanted to leave her, Annalía saw everything differently, as though she'd been looking through a filmy glass that had just been smashed away. She could be a good mother. She *would* be a good mother and would love as apparently Elisabet had. "I'm having a baby," she whispered as the full truth struck her for the first time.

If the Highlander couldn't take part in this because he was off warring for years, or if his mistaken beliefs were so strong that he ignored what was in his heart, then so be it.

He wouldn't be in their lives. And it would be his loss.

Because she and her baby were going to have a *glorious* time of it.

# Thirty-seven

$\mathcal{A}$s Annalía set out for her meadow, she passed Vitale with his friends playing dice and wished him snake eyes.

"You look different," he remarked as he squinted at her.

"Do I?" When she'd told Vitale she was carrying, he'd been delighted that another child would be running about the mountain, but he'd also confessed that he was pleased it didn't work out with MacCarrick. "I love you like a daughter," he'd said. "But following you to Andorra was one thing. There was no way I'd follow you to *Scotland*."

Now Vitale studied her. "You look . . . determined."

"I am." She patted her book on the Gaelic language. "Determined to learn Gaelic by next spring."

"*Ach, lassie,*" Vitale quipped, still sounding terribly French. His friends laughed uproariously. She even chuckled as she continued on.

When she'd found out she was pregnant, she'd asked Lady Fiona for an instruction book. The woman had given her tomes, so delighted that Annalía was interested in their culture and language, so proud that Court had found her. Even as Fiona regretted the past.

Annalía was starting slowly. Luckily, she'd only just been digging into Greek when MacCarrick came into her life. She believed her capacity for languages had a ceiling of five.

Although she'd been making steady progress, she couldn't seem to focus today. The flowers in her meadow smelled too wonderful, and the sun teased her face until she wanted to remove her hat.

And she kept returning to the book to trace her finger over the definition she'd found of *"Mo cridhe." My heart.* That's what he'd called her.

*"Neach-diolain."* That's what she would call him. *Bastard.*

She resolved to take off her hat, and was just shaking her hair loose when she saw something that could not be right. She leapt to her feet, heart thudding, her hat falling from her limp hand. She'd just gotten to where she wasn't crying herself to sleep each night!

MacCarrick spotted her and rode toward her. He looked tired and worn. And resolute?

Wait! She was furious with him. She didn't even know if he was here for her. He probably left a belt or his favorite pistol or a lucky machete he needed to retrieve before he went back to work.

She knew that must be why he was returning—any man who could *wish her well* after what they'd had . . . Yet she was still dizzy. She inhaled deeply and rocked on her heels. Her brows drew together, and as she saw the sun straight ahead, she muttered, *"Merda."*

She just collapsed? Court felt like he'd had his breath punched from him even as he spurred his horse. He didn't wait for it to stop before he swung off and rushed to her, scarcely noting the pain from his leg. She never got sick. She must be injured. He'd *kill* Llorente. What good were the bloody guards down there when she was outside and alone up here?

Fortunately, she'd fallen into thick flowers. He grabbed her shoulders and drew her up to him. "Anna!"

Cradling her head, he frowned. She didn't look injured or ill at all. He ran the backs of his fingers over her cheek. Warm, golden skin. "Anna?" When she blinked open her eyes they were clear and bright and focused on his.

"What's happened tae you, *mo cridhe?*" His voice was hoarse.

Now she rolled her eyes in irritation and stiffened in his arms. "I'm fine, thank you." She pulled away from him and sat up.

He reluctantly let her go. "Why'd you faint?"

She hesitated, then said, "My dress was laced too tightly."

He swept a glance over her dress and found it was snug across the bodice. Finally, she'd put on some of the weight she'd lost. His gaze flickered over her neck, and he saw with pride that she wore the necklace.

"Women faint all the time," she added.

They did. Yet he could name ten instances when she surely should have fainted and hadn't.

"Did you forget something?" she asked crisply.

His brows drew together. "No. I wanted tae check on you."

"I appreciate your *checking on me,* but I'm doing fine."

"Aye, you are." She looked amazing, more beautiful than he had ever seen her. Had he hoped to find her miserable? Bloody hell, yes, he'd hoped that. Because he was a selfish bastard, and he wanted her to miss him as fiercely as he did her. She never could eat when she was anxious or unhappy, and yet without him she'd put on flesh, making her body softer and rounder. She'd been content. Why was he still here, then? Why wasn't he turning away?

Out of the corner of his eye, he spotted her hand flitting in the flowers behind them. He peered over her at the book she was slipping under her skirts. "You're studying Gaelic?"

"Greek or Gaelic. Really, what's the difference?" she said airily, but at his look she added, "Very well. I have no personal connection whatsoever to Greece, but I've been treated shabbily by a Gael."

He flinched.

"You could've written. I would have responded that everything was well and saved you the trip."

"I wanted tae see you."

"*You* wanted to see me. You can't just go in and out of my life whenever you please because of what *you* want. You left without even a good-bye. After all we'd been through together, you *wished me well*."

"If I saw you, then I would no' be able tae leave you. I left you for you."

She tilted her head. "I don't understand."

"I need tae explain something."

"If this is about the curse, then your mother's already told me."

He lowered his voice to say, "She told you about . . . about the *Leabhar*?" When she nodded, he said, "It's no' something she has ever talked about since my da's death. Do you know what it says?"

"Yes, I read it."

He couldn't believe Fiona had allowed Anna near it. They would have words over this. "That's what I thought I would bring to you. The more I cared for you, the more I knew I had tae leave."

Her smile was cold. "Yet you're here now? What does that tell me?"

"Aye, I'm here. Because something that is in the lines has been proven false."

• • •

"What would that be?" Annalía asked, feigning nonchalance. She didn't want him to come only for the baby. He must've already gotten Aleix's missive to Groot's, but how so soon? Perhaps his mother had written before she and Olivia had even left. Annalía would always wonder in the back of her mind.

He was thrumming with some emotion, tense with it. "It says I will no' know love." He stood and ran a hand through his hair. "But damn it, I do."

Her lips parted.

His face was hard, intent, but his eyes . . . "Above all things I love you." His expression tightened. "I could be out of my mind. I want you so badly that I want tae believe the rest is false. I could be hurtin' you right now." His brogue was thick. "Maybe it means I'll no' know love from another." He winced, apprehension clear on his face. "I had no' thought of that."

He looked so guilty, she found herself easing to her feet and murmuring, "That's false, too."

He took her shoulders. "You told me once. But you were half asleep and hurting, and I dinna dare believe it. You could even after I left you?"

Her brows drew together. He was nervous. She laid her hand on his chest, curious. The simple touch made him close his eyes.

Nervous. Beneath her palm, his heart was thundering.

With that, the resistance she'd thought she could hold on to slipped from her fingers. The truth left her lips, "Your leaving hurt me. Badly. Even though I was so confused and afraid, I never stopped."

His eyes opened, and she saw they were full of pain. "I wish I had no' hurt you. I never wanted tae."

"I know," she said with a sigh. He'd always wanted her happiness, had always hated the idea of her hurt. How the attack must have seemed, the blame he would've placed on himself . . .

"I still feel that I canna risk your safety. I canna settle in with the idea," he said. "Though everything in me wants tae."

"MacCarrick, I really don't believe there's any risk."

He leaned in, putting an arm around her as though to shield her from being struck down. "We canna scoff at it," he warned in a low tone. "It is very real. And I've lived my life with that hangin' over me. It made me what I am."

She pushed him back to face him. "Then I thank it! But I must respectfully demand its exit from our lives. What we could have together is stronger than anything dire in that book."

He shook his head. "So much of it has come true. None of us with children because the book ends with our generation—"

"It ends with your generation because our children will make their own fate!"

His dark eyes revealed his regret. "Anna, you know that I will no' have—"

She took his hand and placed it on her belly.

Court grew very still. "What are you sayin'?" His hand on her began shaking. He'd kissed her there, caressed his fingers over her, and he knew that there to the touch was the slightest rounding

She pushed his hand away. "I'm saying the book seems to be getting everything wrong when it comes to you. And that you're getting more than you bargained for."

"You're . . ." He swallowed hard. "You are . . ."

She put her chin up. "I'm carrying your child."

*I bind you to me.* The first night—the first night he'd made love to her. He had bound her to him and claimed her. At the same time, he'd felt that everything he was became hers as well. They'd done this then.

She was carrying his child.

He stood, staggered. She was right. He was getting more than he'd bargained for. He'd only had a faint hope today of finding a way to be with her, and yet he'd discovered that she loved him. How the hell she did, he couldn't imagine, but he knew better than to question such fortune.

The babe would be his permission to keep her, and proved that the *Leabhar* had something else in store for him entirely. He felt the weight of that worry lifting for the first time since he'd read it. Suddenly, falling to the ground seemed like a bloody fine idea.

"Your mother says early spring."

"She knows?"

"Yes. She is very sorry about the past and wants to speak with you soon."

The only way he'd do it would be if Anna asked it of him, but he feared she might just. "How is she reconcilin' it, then?"

"Olivia came up with a theory." Impersonating Olivia's accent, she said, "'The ten lines begin with death and misery, loneliness and suffering, et-*cet*-era, et-*cet*-era, until the last two, which *obviously* say all of these unpleasant things will occur, until the *blockheaded Scot* comes to Andorra to pluck the *spoiled little ninny* from a mountain.'" She grinned. "Your mother believes it's something along those lines but nicer— perhaps about binding with the woman fate meant to be yours."

"And what about the man meant for you? Would you want tae be marryin' someone like me?" His voice was gruff.

"I can't say." She turned from him and said over her shoulder, "I need to know what type of life we would live. I won't have you going away all the time risking your life."

"Then I'm retired," he quickly said, striding in front of her.

She gave him a soft smile. "That's what I wanted to know."

But he continued on, "I've got a place in Scotland. Beinn a'Chaorainn, it's called. A long-neglected keep that needs work, but a lot of land. It's hilly, with mountains in the back, so you might like it. I vow I will make it so you do."

"Are you trying to *convince* me, Courtland?" She jabbed her finger at his chest. "Do you honestly think there is any way you will be leaving here without me?" He was stunned and didn't bother to hide it. At his expression, she grinned and ran that finger up and down his chest. "What does the Beiiiinnn-something mean?" She was touching him playfully as if she'd missed simply being with him, an idea more gratifying to him than she could know.

He felt the corners of his lips curl. *"Beinn a'Chaorainn* means . . . Land of Marsh and Pestilence."

"Oh." Her face fell, but then brightened. "You said it needs work." She asked hopefully, "Does that include draining swamps?"

He put his hands on her shoulders and stroked the sides of her neck. "I'm teasing you, *mo cridhe.* It means Hill of the Rowan Tree."

She cuffed him with the back of her hand, then returned it to his chest. "Hill of the Rowan Tree. *Pendant del Roure,*" she said, rolling the *r*'s in that voice he'd longed to hear, making his home's name her own. As she should.

"I do think you could like it there, but if you doona, then I'll take you wherever you can be happy."

She went to her toes to nuzzle her face against his neck, again stunning him. "I'm happy where you are."

His eyes closed from the tenderness in the gesture. *She wants to be with me,* he thought in amazement. *Damn, if she doesn't want to.*

She drew back and said, "But on the way there, we'll need to stop in Paris."

He swallowed and nodded. "Anna, I'll deny you nothing." If money was the only obstacle between them, he'd bloody well rob trains.

She tilted her head. "Oh, you think I want to go shopping."

He made his expression stoic.

But sadness flashed in her eyes. "Thank you for the offer, but I'll have to decline. This stop is of an entirely different nature." When his brows drew together, she said, "I'll tell you on the way. But if we're going to Scotland, then you have to get me over the mountain before I get too big to fit through the pass." She glanced around and added conspiratorially, "Trust me, you do not want to be stuck here for the winter with Aleix and Olivia mooning over each other."

He grinned and leaned down to put his forehead against hers. "Anna, I'll take you away whenever you please. I still canna believe that you . . . that we . . . I thought I'd lost you."

She twined her arms around his neck. "I don't suppose you can lose the woman fate decided was to be yours. You only needed to find her."

"I have found her. And I'll no' be lettin' her go." He laid his hands on her cheeks and gently kissed her.

"Actually," she murmured against his lips, "I found you."

# Epilogue

Not to marry, know love, or bind, their fate;
Your line to die for never seed shall take.
Death and torment to those caught in their wake,
*Unless each dark one finds his forechosen mate.*
*For his true lady alone his life and heart can save. . . .*

POCKET BOOKS
PROUDLY PRESENTS

# *IF YOU DESIRE*

## KRESLEY COLE

Available now in paperback
from Pocket Books

Turn the page for a preview of
*If You Desire. . . .*

Dedicated to the very real *sensation seekers*, a virtually unrecognized breed of Victorian, wild enough to imbibe, partake, and cavort with reckless abandon—and wily enough never to get caught by history.

*London, England*
*1856*

*A* hardened killer, denied his obsession for a decade.

That was what Edward Weyland was bringing back into his daughter's life with one cryptic message: *Jane is in grave danger.*

Since receiving Weyland's missive in France two days ago, Hugh had read and reread it with fingers gone white from clutching it in fury.

If anyone had dared to hurt her . . .

He'd dropped everything, including his task of seeing his younger brother Courtland back to England from the European country of Andorra. Court had suffered a battle wound there and hadn't been able to ride as fast as Hugh in his condition—so Court had been abandoned in a swirl of leaves as Hugh sped off for England.

Now after days, and nights, riding like hell was at his heels, Hugh finally reached the Weyland townhome. He slid down from his saddle and nearly toppled over, his legs gone boneless from so many hours in the saddle. His mount was as winded as Hugh was, its coat lathered and its barreled chest twitching.

As Hugh approached the side door, where he always entered, he encountered Weyland's nephew, Quinton Weyland—who also did *work* for Weyland—sprawled along the stairs.

"Where's Jane?" Hugh demanded without preamble.

"Upstairs," Quin said, seeming preoccupied and even a little dazed. "Getting ready for . . . for her night out."

"She's safe?" When Quin nodded absently, relief sailed through Hugh. Over the hours alone on the road, his mind had conjured too many ways she could be in *grave danger*. He'd prayed she hadn't been hurt, that he wasn't too late. Now that Hugh had been assured of her safety, the hunger and thirst he'd ignored for two days began to gnaw at him. "Who's watching her now?"

Quin answered, "Rolley's inside, and I'm trailing her tonight."

Rolley was Edward Weyland's butler. Most butlers in the exclusive enclave of Piccadilly were older with a hint of grandeur about them, denoting experience and the longevity of a family's fortunes. Rolley was mid-thirties, wiry, with his nose broken so many times it was shapeless. His fingers were scarred from his incessant use of steel knuckles.

"Is Weyland home?" Hugh asked.

Quin shook his head. "Not getting in till late. He said if you somehow managed to get here tonight, to tell you he wanted to see you in the morning to give you all the details."

"I'm going in—"

"Actually, I wouldn't do that," Quin said. "You might see Jane."

That was exactly what Hugh had been aiming for. He'd kept himself away from her for nearly ten years, yet now he found he burned to look at her and see for himself that she was safe. "Why would I no' want to see her?"

"For one thing, your clothes are covered with dirt and your face looks like hell."

Hugh ran a sleeve over his cheek, remembering the jagged cuts marking his skin too late.

"For another, Jane doesn't . . . well, she doesn't seem to like you much."

Hugh had ridden nonstop for days, and his body was a mass of knotted muscles and aching old injuries. His head was splitting. The idea of being near her again had been all that kept him going. "That does no' make sense. We were friends."

Quin gave him an odd expression. "Well, she's . . . different now. Completely different and completely out of control." He caught Hugh's eyes. "I don't know that I can take another night of it." He shook his head forcefully. "No longer. Not after what they did last night. . . ."

"Who? Did what?"

"The Eight. Or at least the three of them. Two of whom are my sisters!"

Society's notorious "Weyland Eight" consisted of Jane and her seven female first cousins. Remembering the brazen antics they'd encouraged Jane to take part in, Hugh felt his irritation building.

"But this is no' what I've been brought here for?" Hugh had abandoned his injured brother and nearly killed his new horse, a fine stallion that had been a gift for a service he'd rendered. "Because Weyland needs someone to rein her in?" Surely Weyland wouldn't be so foolish as to call Hugh back for this. Weyland knew what Hugh was, of course. He was Hugh's superior and dispatched him to deliver deaths in the name of the crown. But then Weyland had no idea how badly Hugh had coveted Jane. Nor for how long.

*An obsession. For ten bloody years . . .*

Hugh shook his head. Weyland would never have exaggerated the danger in his missive.

"Weyland didn't tell you what's happened?" Quin's brows drew together. "I thought he sent you a message."

"Aye, with little information," Hugh answered. "Tell me what—?"

"Bloody hell!" the butler Rolley suddenly hissed in whisper as he came barreling out of the doorway. "Bloody, bloody hell! Quin! Have you seen her?"

"Rolley?" Quin shot to his feet when the smaller man sped into view. "You're supposed to be watching her until she leaves."

Rolley flashed Quin a scowl. "I told you she knew we'd been following her. She must've gone out the window. And got that saucy maid of hers to walk about, tryin' on dresses in her room."

Seeing Rolley's alarm made Hugh certain there was, in fact, danger to Jane. He lunged for Rolley and fisted his hands in the man's shirt. "Where's she going and who's she with?"

"To a ball. . . ." Rolley glanced at Quin.

Hugh gave Rolley a shake, knowing he was risking Rolley's swift uppercut, usually accompanied by those steel knuckles.

"Go ahead," Quin said. "Weyland tells him everything anyway."

"She's goin' to a masquerade with Quin's sisters and one of their friends."

"What kind of masquerade?" Hugh asked, though he had a good idea.

"Libertines and courtesans," Rolley said. "In a warehouse on Haymarket Street."

With a grated curse, Hugh released Rolley, then forced his legs to cooperate while he crossed to his horse—who seemed to eye him with disbelief that their journey wasn't over yet. Gritting his teeth at his tightened muscles, Hugh mounted.

"You're goin' after her?" Rolley asked. "We're just supposed to follow her. The old man doesn't want her to know yet. Very sure on that."

"No, MacCarrick, rest," Quin said. "I'm sure they took a hansom, and the traffic will be mad. I've got time to saddle up and beat them there—"

"Then follow, but I'm going now." Hugh reined around. "Best tell me what I'm up against."

Quin's grave expression made Hugh's fists clench around his reins.

"Not what, but *who*. Weyland thinks Davis Grey's on his way to kill her."

A brick dropped into a purse was a necessary evil when touring the Haymarket district, Jane knew, but the drawstring strap was murder on her wrist.

As Jane and her companions—two intrepid cousins and their visiting friend—waited impatiently in queue for admission to the Haymarket warehouse, Jane shifted the bag to her other hand yet again, marveling at the sight that had greeted them. Tonight was by no means their first foray to *tickle* a bit at London's dark underbelly—their decadent haunts included the East End gaming dens, the racy stereoscopic pictorial shows, the annual Russian Circus Erotisk—but this lascivious scene gave even Jane pause.

A horde of courtesans fronted the Haymarket warehouse like a painted—and aggressive—army. Well-dressed male patrons, in clothing that screamed stock exchange funds or old money tweed and university, perused the wares, physically sampling before deciding which one, or ones, they would sponsor and escort inside.

"Janey, you've never told us what brought about this change of heart about attending," her cousin Claudia said in a light tone, no doubt trying to relax the others. "But I've a theory." She must dread that the others would back out. Raven-haired "Naughty Claudie"—with her scarlet mask—lived for thrills like this.

"Do tell," said her sister Belinda, a heads and tails opposite of Claudie. Belinda was brilliant and serious minded, here tonight for "research," and not euphemistically. She planned to expose "egregious social inequities," but wanted to write with authority on the subject of, well, the other side of inequity. Already, Jane could tell that behind her cream-colored mask, Belinda was eyeing the scene in terms of reform.

"Did we need a reason to come," asked the mysterious Madeleine Van Rowen, "other than the fact that this is a courtesan's ball?" Maddy was a childhood friend of Claudie's who was visiting for two weeks. She was an English girl by birth, but she now lived in Paris—a seedy Parisian garret, if rumors were to be believed.

Though Maddy didn't talk much and anything she said about her background was likely untrue anyway, Jane liked the girl, and she fit in with their set perfectly. Jane, Belinda, and Claudia were three of the Weyland Eight—eight female first cousins notorious for adventures, pranks, and general hijinks—and were the three born and bred in London. Like all young Londoners who had coin in their pockets, they spent their days and nights pursuing all the new modern pleasures to be had in this mad city, and all the old sins still available, within reason.

Jane and her cousins were moneyed, but not aristocratic. They were gently bred but savvy. Ladylike but jaded. Like Jane and her cousins, Maddy knew how to take care of herself and seemed perfectly at ease in the face of this risqué masquerade.

As if revealing a great secret, Claudie said, "Jane's finally going to accept that gorgeous Freddie Bidworth's proposal."

Guilt flared, and Jane adjusted her emerald green mask to disguise it. "You've got me all figured out, Claudie." She and Freddie were an item of sorts, and everyone assumed Jane would eventually marry Freddie—including Freddie. But Jane had yet to accept the rich, handsome aristocrat.

And she feared she never could.

At twenty-six, Jane *knew* prospects like Freddie would only become more and more scarce. And if she didn't marry Freddie, then who?

Jane *knew* the train was leaving the station, and yet she couldn't board.

She'd told her cousins she wavered because of his horrid mother and sister. In truth, she'd hesitated because, her upstanding father excepted, she didn't trust men.

Not after she'd been ruined by a black-haired Scot with a deep, husky voice and intense eyes—a man who had never even touched her, never even kissed her—no matter how hard she'd tried to seduce him. No, Jane had been ruined for other men.

Belinda frowned over at Jane. "You've gotten past Bidworth's family?"

"Yes, I believe so," Jane replied carefully. "I've just been moving slowly with something so important." Slowly? He'd asked her the first time nearly a year ago.

"Are these wild oats we're sowing, Jane?" Maddy asked, making Jane wonder how wild those oats would seem to a woman from the not-nice part of Paris.

"Did we need a reason to come," Jane said wryly, repeating Maddy, "other than the fact that this is a courtesan's ball?"

Luckily, they'd reached the bottleneck of the entrance, where a burly attendant with a shining pate accepted admission, so the subject was dropped. As the four labored to keep their skirts from being dirtied in the crush, Jane tendered a guinea apiece for everyone—mainly to pay for Maddy and not hurt her pride.

Though Maddy was attired in a lavish sapphire gown, Jane had seen the girl's trunks in Claudie's room and knew her hose and underthings had been mended and re-mended. Her jewels were paste. Maddy was broke, and sometimes the girl had a back-against-the-wall air about her.

Once the attendant waved them through, Jane blithely crossed the threshold, with the others close behind. Inside the warehouse, masses of perfumed bodies swarmed around a central dance floor, or danced to the jaunty music of a seven man band. Legally this place was termed an "unlicensed dance hall."

Those in the know called it "the Hive."

If the outside of the Hive had been rough and unassuming, the interior was lush. The walls were silk papered, and expensive-smelling incense burned, oozing a flat layer of smoke just over the heads of the crowd. Along the walls were massive murals, hanging from shiny brass chains and painted with nymphs and priapic satyrs in lurid poses. Beneath the murals were Persian rugs with pillows cast about. There, women kissed lechers and fondled them artfully through their breeches—or were fondled in return.

Anything more, Jane surmised, was taken to the rooms lining the back wall.

Happily-married Belinda murmured, "Just look at what these women are forced to do to earn their coin."

"Earn . . . *coin*?" Claudie breathed with feigned ignorance. "You mean you can . . . ? Ah! And to think I was doing it for free!"

Belinda glared, because twenty-eight-year-old Claudie was, in fact, carrying on a torrid affair. "Claudia, you might try doing it *while married*."

An exhibit, of sorts, silenced all of them—halting yet another sisterly row.

Men and women with shaven bodies covered in a layer of clay posed as statues, motionless even when admiring patrons cupped and weighed body parts.

"This was so worth attending," Maddy said with a quirked eyebrow, gaze riveted to the endowed and muscle-bound men. Maddy made no secret that she had an eye for beautiful males and would even turn to ogle attractive men on the street with a tilted head and a wondering cluck of her tongue.

Jane had to agree about coming tonight. Nothing like naked, real live statues to distract the mind from thoughts of rumbling-voiced Scotsmen who disappeared without a word.

Their group had little time to admire the scene because the crowd was like a current, circling the warehouse, and the press of people pushed them along. When they passed a table with punch dispensed from a crystal bowl, by a half-naked debauchee, they each eagerly swooped up a glass filled to the rim and made for a nearby wall to get out of the traffic.

Jane drank deeply. "Well. No one told us coverage from the waist up was optional—for both sexes," she observed when another half-clad woman sauntered by, breasts bouncing as she flirtatiously smiled up at her. Jane gave her a saucy wink back as she passed, as was polite. "Otherwise," Jane continued dryly, "I might have opted for a lower cut bodice and a bigger brick."

Maddy smelled her glass with a discerning expression, then took a hearty drink just as Claudie raised her own and said, "I'm just glad to be at a ball with punch *I* don't have to spike." Claudie had seen her older brother Quin doing that once, had noted the raucous results, and never failed to bring flasks to staid gatherings.

When a middle-aged roué exposed himself to the Persian-rug-women and they laughed, Belinda harrumphed. She shoved her glass at Jane so she could surreptitiously take notes, like a first-year plebeian might write up boys' school demerits. Jane shrugged, placing her own finished glass on a tray, and started on Belinda's.

She nearly choked on the last sips, because she spied a towering man in a long black domino pushing through the crowd, clearly searching for someone. His build, his stride, the aggressive set of his lips just beneath the fluttering, veil drop of his mask—everything about him reminded her of Hugh, though she knew it wasn't him.

But what if it had been? Sooner or later they would have to run into each other. It was possible she might see *him* on the carpets, with his knee falling open and eyelids growing heavy as a woman's skilled hand rubbed him. The thought made Jane drain Belinda's cup. "Going for more punch," she mumbled, suddenly longing to be away from the warm throng of bodies.

"Bring us back some more," Madeleine called absently. She was watching the tall man wending through the crowd as well.

As Jane scuffed to the punch service, she recognized that the antsy feeling in her belly that she continually battled had grown sharply worse. Ever since she could remember, she'd been plagued by an anxiety, as if she were missing something, as if she were in the wrong place with greener grass calling out for her. She felt an urgency about everything.

Now, after regarding the man who was so like Hugh, and imagining Hugh being serviced by another woman, she felt an *urgency* for fresh air. Else she'd lose her punch—

A shrill whistle rent through the din; Jane's head jerked up. The band whimpered to a lull.

"*Police!*" someone yelled just as more whistles sounded all over the warehouse. "*It's the bloody peelers!*"

No, that wasn't possible. These dance halls always paid off the police! *Who in the devil had forgotten the "payment for protection"? Who?*

All at once, a wave of screaming people assaulted the back entrance. The hive was suddenly a bottle turned upside down and the cork had just been pulled.

She spotted Claudie and Belinda across the current of fleeing bodies—Maddy . . . was nowhere to be seen. When Jane tried to reach them, only to get shoved back, Belinda pointed to the back door. Jane shook her head emphatically—that way out was choked with people. They would be crushed to death. She'd rather get nicked and have her name printed on the page of shame in *The Times*.

When Jane lost sight of her cousins completely, she backed to the wall. Being separated was to be avoided at all costs. Much less being separated . . . and alone. As the wave of people swelled until it engulfed Jane again, she felt the world spinning out of control.

Suddenly, two hands shoved against her back, sending her staggering. She whirled around and swung her purse, connecting, garnering a split second's worth of room, but the strap scraped down and off her wrist. Her purse was gone.

The next jostle she received didn't take her by surprise, but someone else stood on her dress hem. Jane flailed her arms, helpless to stop herself from being pitched to the ground.

At once, she scrambled up, but couldn't rise—her skirts had spread out over the floor like the wings of a framed butterfly—and just as pinned, by the stampede.

Over and over, she fought to rise, but always new boots trapped her skirts.

Jane darted her hands out between ankles, yanking at the material with desperate strength, struggling to collect her dress to her legs.

She couldn't catch her breath under the press of people. How had this night gone so wrong—?

A boot came straight for her head. She rolled to the side, dodging it, but then, even over the commotion, she clearly heard the eerie ping of metal breaking.

Looking up from the ground with dread, she saw the hanging mural directly above her, swaying wildly. The brass chain holding it had an opened link that was straightening under the massive weight.

The mural came crashing down.

When Davis Grey chased the dragon, he had no dreams.

In that hazy twilight of opium, his wasted body no longer pained him; no longer could he see the faces of the men, women, and children he'd killed.

*Chasing the dragon,* Grey thought with a weary exhalation, staring at the ceiling. What an appropriate saying to describe the habit—and his life.

In the past, the smoke had quelled the rage in his heart. But finally his need for revenge had overpowered even opium's sweet pull.

He rose in stages from his rented bed, then crossed to the basin to splash water over his face. In the basin mirror, he studied his naked, emaciated body.

Four crusting bullet wounds riddled his pale chest and torso. Though it had been six months ago that Edward Weyland, whom Grey had faithfully killed for, had sent him to his own death, the wounds still hadn't healed completely. Though half a year had passed, Grey could perfectly remember the order in which he'd taken each bullet from a trio of Weyland's hungry, younger killers.

Yet somehow Grey had survived.

Perhaps Weyland should have sent Hugh for the kill. But

then Weyland always spared MacCarrick the *altering* jobs, the ones that changed a man forever.

Those tasks should have been split between Grey and Hugh, but Weyland carefully meted out each one. Hugh was dispatched to kill people who were cut-and-dry evil, dangerous people who often fought for the lives Hugh sought to take. Grey executed the variables, the peripherals. Toward the end, he hadn't been very particular if children got in the way.

In dreams, Grey saw their glassy, sightless eyes.

*Weyland, that bloody bastard, hadn't even sent Hugh to kill me.*

That galled Grey more than anything, scalding him inside. . . .

Soon Grey would deliver his retribution. Weyland treasured only one thing in this world—his daughter Jane. MacCarrick had loved her from afar for years. Take away Jane, and two men would be destroyed, forever.

Grey had already let it be known that he was finally stirring. Weyland would send for his best gunman to protect his precious daughter.

Good. Hugh should be there to see Grey end her life. Both MacCarrick and Weyland should know the searing purity of grief.

There was power innate in having nothing left to lose.

Years ago, Weyland had said that Grey was suited for his occupation because he possessed no mercy, but he'd been wrong then. Years ago, Grey wouldn't have been able to happily slit Jane's pretty throat. Weyland wasn't wrong now.

With a shriek, Jane rolled out of the way just as a corner of the mural broke free, hammering into the floor just beside her. She didn't have time to gape at how close it had been because more charging people assaulted her. She couldn't breath.

With a cry, she was forced to duck down, raising an arm over her face.

Then . . . Jane lowered her arm, brows drawn in confusion.

The crowd had begun parting before her instead of treading over her.

She finally room to maneuver, a fighting chance. . . . She'd be damned if she'd be killed by the spectacle she'd come to leer at! She was able to gather her skirts. With another wobbling attempt to rise, she made it to her feet. Whirling around, she lunged forward. *Free!*

*No!* She dropped to her front with a thud. She crawled on her forearms, but realized she was crawling in place. Something anchored her down. More people coming in a rush—

Beside her, the middle-aged roué from before dropped bodily to the ground, holding his bleeding nose, staring up horrified at something behind them. Before she could even react, another man went flying over her, landing flat on his back.

Suddenly her skirts were tossed to the backs of her knees. A hot callused hand clamped onto her thigh. Her eyes went wide in shock. Another hand pawed at her clothing, and she heard ripping. Her head whipped around. With her mask askew and her hair tumbling into her face, she could barely see the man through the shadows of a jungle of legs all around them.

"Wh-what are you doing?" she screeched, flailing the leg he held firmly. "Unhand me this instant!"

With the back of her hand, she shoved her hair away and spied another flash of her attacker. Grim lips pulled back from white teeth as if in a snarl. Three gashes running down his cheek, his face dirty.

His eyes held a murderous rage.

Then the visage was gone when her attacker bolted to his

feet and felled another oncoming patron, before dropping down once more, fist shooting up in intervals. Then came another protracted rip. . . .

Before she had any idea what he intended, he'd swooped her up onto his shoulder.

"H-how dare you!" she cried, pummeling his broad back as he hauled her away. She vaguely noted that this was a bear of a man. The body she was looped over was massive, the arm over her, heavy and unyielding. His fingers were splayed, it seemed, over the entire width of her bottom.

"Don't go this way! Put me down!" she demanded. "How dare you paw at me, ripping at my undergarments!"

With his free arm, the man sent patrons careening with the ease of an afterthought. "Lass, it's nothing you have no' shown me before."

Her jaw dropped. *Hugh MacCarrick?* This murderous-looking fiend was her gentle giant of a Scot?

Returned after ten years.

"You doona remember me?"

Oh, yes, she did. And remembering how she'd fared the last time the Highlander had drifted into her life, she wondered if she mightn't have been better off trampled by a drunken horde.

*Lose yourself in the passion...*
*Lose yourself in the past...*
*Lose yourself in a Pocket Book!*

## The School for Heiresses ❧ Sabrina Jeffries

Experience unforgettable lessons in love for
daring young ladies in this anthology featuring
sizzling stories by Sabrina Jeffries, Liz Carlyle, Julia
London, and Renee Bernard.

## Emma and the Outlaw ❧ Linda Lael Miller

Loving a man with a mysterious past can force you
to risk your heart...and your future.

## His Boots Under Her Bed ❧ Ana Leigh

Will he be hers forever...or just for one night?